A HISTORICAL NOVEL

Truth Crushed to Earth

The Legacy of Will Parker, a Black American Revolutionary

"Civil War, First Blow Struck"
Lancaster Saturday Express
Sept. 13, 1851

HARRY W. KENDALL

Truth Crushed To Earth
The Legacy of Will Parker, a Black American Revolutionary
Copyright 1999 © Harry W. Kendall

ISBN: 0-7392-0294-4
Library of Congress Catalog Card Number: 99-95268

An EM-J Book

Printed in the USA by

MORRIS PUBLISHING

3212 East Highway 30   Kearney, NE 68847   1-800-650-7888

Author's Notes

Truth Crushed To Earth, is realism fiction of an event in Pennsylvania history that exposed the moral fiber of America when the institution of slavery made its strongest bid for survival. The insurrection and subsequent trial of the so-named Christiana Riot have already been examined by a host of historians and writers. A study of persons, prevailing attitudes, political intervention, the uncivilized enforcement of the fugitive slave law, and particularly the news media hysteria of that day, revealed a compelling potential for drama. After making my acquaintance with friendly and some not so friendly ghosts of yesteryear I was lured to study their mindsets, their peculiarities, and the area where the fugitive slave rebellion occurred in developing a plot.

Quite an experience, meditating with that legion of spirits, formulating an aesthetic quality from records at the Free Library of Philadelphia, Pratt Library in Baltimore, Moore Memorial Library in Christiana, libraries at Cheyney University and Swarthmore College. Historical societies of Pennsylvania in Philadelphia, and local societies of Lancaster, PA, and Norristown, PA, were supportive in helping me define or rather illustrate, the prevailing moral logic of that era. What compelled men and women, black and white, considered good or bad, to act as they did? Stories and celebrations abound on the commitment of particularly Pennsylvania and New Jersey Quakers to abolish slavery. We are familiar with the combined dedication of certain societies and individuals to crush it. Most of us are not aware, unfortunately, and so few understand how slaves and free persons' adoption of a forced-fed Christian ethic awakened the ancient Egyptian/African wisdom of appealing to a God of vengeance. The Spirituals, that infectious music of deliverance is one illustrative example. Will Parker is another. *Truth Crushed To Earth* is both deliverance and Will Parker.

The book's title was selected from a poem, *The Battlefield*, written in 1839 by William Cullen Bryant. I was struck by the force of its words, especially the phrase, *shall rise again*, which follows, *Truth crushed to earth*.

As realism fiction, my story is not an account—factual, accurate or otherwise—of any person living or dead. In developing likeable profiles, the personalities of many characters emerged as powerful as the historical force of slavery, driving the action from which the story was drawn. I used names that fit the personalities. For example, after studying Sam Williams, a member of the secret Philadelphia Anti-Slavery Society, and seeing a photo resembling him in the office of his Bolivar House Tavern, I could hardly name the character in my novel Bill Livingston or Peter Lambkin. The fate of each primary character is modeled after its historical persona. The role each of them played in my novel is similar, as far as I can tell, to its role in history.

I stumbled upon the story in a dream, an elusive dream in which I jogged from my home, some one hundred miles to the protagonist's birthplace in Anne Arundel County, Maryland. From there my dream weaver followed William Parker's trail along the byways, highways, and wooded terrain to Christiana, Pennsylvania. Yet, I knew nothing about him until months later. A friend with whom I worked, a white man who had lived in Chester County, suggested I read what history had said about Parker.

Sincere thanks to Ms. Mary Garrett of Atglen, PA.; Rev. Ambrose Hopkins of Quarryville; LaVerne (Bud) Rettew, manager of Christiana Borough; and Jonathan Katz, author of *Resistance At Christiana*. Ms. Garrett's lengthy conversations about Quaker mores during Will Parker's time answered questions history didn't. Rev. Hopkins, former pastor and member of Mt. Zion AME Church for ninety odd years, escorted me through the church's bygone days beginning in the late 1700's. I regret he and Ms. Garrett passed before I published the book. Bud Rettew has been an advisor-confidant throughout this entire project; thank you. A debt of gratitude I owe Jonathan Katz for copying his entire (out of print) book and authorizing me to use it. Katz's source collection is part of the Schomberg Center for Research in Black Culture of New York City.

Finally yet foremost, grateful commentary to Ms. Dale Dunn for proofing the entire manuscript.

Harry W. Kendall

Foreword

Harry Kendall has captured the essence of the black man's burden in America's past as well as present, certainly for us with the where-with-all to perceive it. Early on, one realizes the fiction, part of this epic tale that history can not claim, makes it indeed a sojourn that so conjures up personal experiences the reader easily identifies with Will Parker. The story was thoroughly researched and written, fact and fiction so intricately interwoven, both the casual and most astute reader easily sets aside any contradiction. History's term, *Christiana riot*, is a misnomer, really. The word, *riot*, is generally used by the press to describe a resistance of an oppressed group against their oppressors, particularly whenever the oppressed wins the confrontation.

More important, however, for the intelligentsia of our youth to extract the cultural value of the Christiana resistance, the story must be presented in a likeable literary form. Kendall has done that. He turned the Christiana resistance episode into an experience noble enough to lend itself to the credibility of black men and women of that era determined to live decently, despite the lowly dictates of their condition.

Will, a seventeen year old slave lad, left *Rocdown* expecting the Pennsylvania of 1839 to be some exotic place. Can that be imagined, even in this year, 1999? He arrived in the Chester-Lancaster County area with something more than the human credentials of a fugitive slave. His inner conviction had been pretty much set by Grandmom Roscy, Tawney, and encounters with prize-fighters, Master Mack, Mint-chewing Bob Wallace the black slave foreman, and Groit the overseer turned slave runner. They were teachers of lessons Will surely learned, and that is part of the intrigue in this novel.

Joseph Harrison, Ph.D. emeritus,
Lincoln University, Lincoln University, PA.

Prologue

Beside a lonesome road in the rolling hills of the Pennsylvania Dutch countryside a marker identifies the site on an Amish farm of a fugitive slave rebellion in a free state. A monument erected at the North end of a nearby southeastern Pennsylvania town in 1911, when it was the bustling hub of a farm community, solemnizes its pro and anti slavery sentiments of that bloody revolt. Banners dressed in American flag colors proclaim, *Freedom Began Here*, pinpoint this borough as a special place in American history.

Sept. 11, 1851, Dateline—Christiana—A gun-battle that claimed the life of a Maryland slave master awakened America to the stark reality of its impending crisis. News media questioning of moral principle in the fugitive slave law raised the Christiana insurrection to an issue of national concern. *That concern would penetrate the soul of the South*, declared the Maryland Governor. An editorial in the Boston Christian Register, *Resistance to the law was unlawful and impolitic. The defenders must be punished.*

United States President Millard Fillmore demanded the accused be charged with treason. Headlines in the Saturday Express of Lancaster, PA., *Civil War, First Blow Struck.*

A trial held in Independence Hall of Philadelphia drew international attention. The world awaited the court's verdict to see if and how the U.S. Government would enforce its fugitive slave law.

Inscribed on one surface of the granite monument are the names of thirty-eight black men charged with resisting and interfering with the capture of fugitive slaves. The names of two white men and reasons they were involved are etched in the monument's peak. Castner Hanway, grist mill owner-operator and abolitionist, befriended the black men. Edward Gorsuch, wealthy planter and Harvard graduate from Harford County, Maryland, died fighting to take back his human possessions.

Thirtieth on that list of freedom fighters is the name Will Parker. Parker, a fugitive slave, at the age of twenty organized the self-defense unit engaged in that rebellion. Parker stopped Gorsuch from dragging away his friends and relatives in chains. A brave leader indeed, damned by his oppressors, hailed by Frederick Douglass and John Brown. Indifferent to honor and gratitude, the young fugitive defied vengeance and retribution to rescue any person whose cry was within hearing distance.

From the beginning of slavery in America, Jamestown, Virginia in 1619, to the emancipation of that bondage by the thirteenth amendment in 1865, an unrecorded number of slaves—black men, women, and children—escaped from southern and border slave states to northern free states and Canada. Many were captured and returned to their masters. Others killed their children and committed suicide rather than endure certain tragedy. Free black people, legally exempt from slavery, were not excluded. Few state laws protected them from kidnappers, or from being dragged in chains to a magistrate by a slave master. Even if a person had credentials most free black people carried, a slaver's claim that said person belonged to him was an argument a white person speaking for the victimized person had to prove false.

Abolitionists, black and white, humble and affluent, formed secret societies to smuggle slaves by way of the underground railroad before the Revolutionary War. The Fugitive Slave Law of 1793 demanded the return of runaway slaves from anywhere. In 1850, Congress revised that law, a concession to slave states for continued union with free states, and a compromise for the admittance of California into the Union as a free state. It mandated the return of fugitives by government agents and required all persons to assist agents in the apprehension of slaves. Failure to respond constituted an act of treason, punishable by imprisonment, or possibly death.

Will Parker's story is the foundation for this historical novel.

Roedown, the plantation where Parker was born is still there in the rustic hills of Anne Arundel County south of Annapolis, along a ridge above the drying river bed of the Patuxent River. At the entrance to Roedown from Queen Anne Road, pines, tall hemlocks so thick the sun can't penetrate, and catalpa trees border a narrow lane that runs straight as an Indian trail to a circular driveway in front of the great house. It sits amid a cluster of trees in nostalgic silence like an old majestic actress longing for her time-stilled drama. The catalpas, bent into grotesque shapes, wind-whipped and graying with hitching rings imbedded in their trunks, lean and stare like old folks from the past with their memories of how it was back then in 1822 when Will Parker was born.

Few horses now romp the acres of green pastures surrounding the race track. Down in the valley one-hundred fifty head of black angus cattle graze in several cordoned south pastures. The cattle munch browning spikelets of grass and wander up a hillside to a wire fence that separates their meadow from recesses in the earth under an aged oak tree. The recesses are graves in a slave cemetery. In this shaded setting of thick green turf is interred the reality of life: our inevitable return to dust. Here, imagination intertwines history. In the meadows where cattle graze, visions of slave cabins and the old slave quarter slowly take form in the shimmer of June noonday sunlight.

Chapter One

In the near distance men and women, young and old, their faces black and sweaty, hoed long sloping rows of tender corn and tobacco sprouts. They floated like specters, the men wearing tow-linen pants and collarless shirts, the women wearing dresses made of the same course-towel material. An odd mix of old hats, caps and color-faded kerchiefs shield their heads.

Low wavering voices hummed woefully. Then a man's deep bass voice broke out in song and the group's answer resounded across hill and dale of this vast Brodgen horse-breeding spread. The call and response was a mixture of African dialects and Western-Shore Maryland colloquial English.

In the bottom land close by a grist mill and creek meandering past the tree line to the Patuxent River, Bob (Green Mint) Wallace, a trusty slave, was behind an old mule plowing. He pulled rein on the mule, jumped down the embankment, scooped up a hatful of sparkling water and poured it over his head. Atop the hillside behind the cemetery, Mr. Groit the overseer, sat ghost-like on a big gray swayback horse, fixed in the sun-baked landscape like the cemetery oak. He leered at Wallace, leered at the field hands, leered at excited children running from the quarters toward the lane.

David Brodgen, Master Mack they called him, and his wife, Mistress Margaret, alighted from a stagecoach at the entrance to Roedown. White Glove Charles the butler, placed their luggage in a surrey and coaxed a sleek Arabian horse into a smart trot. As they rode along the rolling hilltop above the slave quarters, a gut wrenching scream punctuated the haunting worksong. Mistress Margaret shuddered. Master Mack, a wealthy horse breeder, didn't even turn his head in the direction of the noise.

In the dell Aunt Katie snatched the door of a crude field worker's hut open and frantically waved to Grandmom Rosey. Grandmom, raw-boned, light-brown, smelling like blackberry pie and fried chicken, came running as good as an old woman could, stumbling down the slope.

"Rosey, Rosey, better hurry. Jesus God," Aunt Katie hollered.

Inside, Will Parker's head had already slid from his mother's womb. A slave woman yielded her position between Louise Sims' thighs to Grandmom Rosey for her to midwife the birth of her grandson.

"Ain't never seen a young'un hankerin' so for freedom," Aunt Katie said.

All the slave women gathered there laughed except Grandmom Rosey. Freedom? Better that he stayed in there, Grandmom Rosey thought. Ofeutey! Her soul screamed in the memory of her long lost husband while she separated Will from his mother. She watched the others clean him and tend to her daughter.

Old Major Brodgen, Master Mack's father, had made her daughter breed with a buck slave twice, punishment for Grandmom Rosey marrying her African chief without his consent. The buzzard couldn't break Ofeutey's will, killing him wasn't enough. Rosey had endured, praying and hoping God would send her a sign. But even at death's threshold, still hateful, shriveled and twisting in pain, Major slipped away before Grandmom Rosey could avenge her burden. Spitting on his rotten carcass did not ease her pain.

She stared at her grandson. His prominent forehead, the contour of his face, a shock of curly black hair and sparkling eyes so black he engendered in her one final ray of hope, after the many seasons had dwindled to only a few left to break the Brodgens' yoke on her family.

Grandmom Rosey swore Will knew everything he saw right from the beginning. When the slave mid-wife slapped life into him, Uncle Sammy heard him squeal like a suckling pig all the way down to the end of the slave quarter. Will came into the world in a way of speaking, like a seed in an apple or a rabbit in a pen. He was born in captivity. His mother didn't have fine linens or a comfortable bed in her crude field worker's hut. His father had been sold. Will was a slave for life.

A few days after Will's birth, his mother rose before daybreak and took her baby to the quarter. The quarter, a long, wood frame and flat roof building, stifling hot in summer and bitterly cold in winter, sat in a spot of narrow flatland between two rolling hills. There were windowless openings near the top, one each in its east and west ends and two on each side. In the huge open room orphaned children lived with slaves without families, the infirm, and older worn-out slaves. Gray ashes and pieces of charred wood lay scattered in two wide fireplaces at each end. The old men had rigged make-shift partitions of wood, cardboard, and rags for themselves and the older women near the fireplace in the warmer side. They claimed the early morning sun warmed the east wing first. Bigger children, usually the bullies, claimed space in front of the other fireplace. Smaller orphaned children lay on meager straw ticks shivering under thin blankets. In this hysterical place babies cried constantly, lonely little children whimpered, and old folks died in their sleep.

Aunt Katie, too old for the field, watched over Will while his mother, Sims they called her, Louise Sims, hoed corn and tobacco until the horn blew at day's end. After Will began walking, Sims often took him with her. He trudged along, asking all sorts of difficult questions especially about why he had to spend his days in the slave quarter under the suspicious eye and hateful tongue of Aunt Katie. She sat on a crate all day long, chewing nothing with her toothless gums, fanning herself, and humming the few times she wasn't fussing.

Will's early childhood years would have passed with as much significance as the same old sermon Master Mack's parson preached to him once a month except that he was a busy little boy driven by wanderlust to explore whatever his eyes could see. He watched Sims disappear each morning and soon after he'd sneak away after her. He never could find her, but the huge panorama challenged him so that with each day's exploration his longing for her changed to fascination with adventure. Didn't matter from whatever distance the wind or a strange sound beckoned, when he looked up, the great house, always in full view atop Roedown's highest undulated elevation, seemed so close yet so far away in a world far removed from his in the quarter.

All of Roedown sloped down in rolling hills around Master Mack's great house—the huge barn and stables, blacksmith shop, field after field of corn and tobacco, patches of vegetable and flower gardens, and broad meadows. In the valley behind it ducks swam in the pond, and honking geese often chased Will right up to the overseer's front door. Then a fat white lady with a voice that sounded like a mad peacock would run him away, throwing ugly words at his back. Deep spooky woods, full of boogey men and bears sure to eat little slaves, surrounded all of the plantation except the entrance from Queen Anne Road. Roedown Race Track with its covered grandstand, the finest among the genteel of Anne Arundel County, spread from the lane in front of the great house to Queen Anne Road. As Will grew older, on most sunny, warm days he would kneel on the ground against the white-washed fence at the far side of the track and watch the trainers work Master Mack's thoroughbreds and wild Mustangs brought to Roedown.

One humid July day after hours of imagining himself on a mighty stallion leaping the fence and dashing away past the line where the trees and sky met, Will eased himself under the bottom slat and curled against it. Mighty hoofs beating into the soft turf so close made his little heart pound until he could no longer sit still. Up and down he jumped in the quarter turn, waving at the jockeys. Without warning, one recently broken Mustang pulled from the pack. Galloping crazedly in the grassy strip, it bore down on Will. In the final second before his front legs would strike, the jockey forced him to jump in a clumsy vault over Will. Horse and rider crashed on the fence. Chunks of splintered wood flew. Master Mack's stallion flipped on a post and fell on his side. The jockey sailed forward and landed in a grassy spot between the fence and lane. The stallion neighed, tried to rise, groaned, then slumped in a pool of thickening red ooze. Will stood there, amazed at the entire episode until his master rode up, followed by his trusty slave, Bob Wallace. Master Mack jumped from his white Arabian. Wallace jumped from the brown swayback as if he were Master's shadow. Master Mack lifted his hat and wiped sweat from his face on his shirt sleeve. An aquiline nose and square face accentuated his rugged, somber profile. His dark brown hair, with a dusting of gray at the temples, was ruffled and wet. He towered over Will, breathing heavily.

"Who's little pickaninny are you?" Master Mack yelled.

Wallace shuddered. Master Mack seldom spoke to any slave, and mostly then when too angry to contain himself.

"This here Sims' boy," Wallace said. "Most like see him anywhere gittin' in all kind'a devilment and do." He didn't spit around Master Mack, but the pouch in his jaw sagged and his peculiar rank of chewed mint punctuated every word.

Will said nothing. His bottom lip spread wide in a pout that Wallace interpreted to mean that Will understood the old lowdown nigger's lie.

"Maybe the little bastard can't hear too good," Wallace said.

"Like hell!" Master Mack said, reacting to stubborn defiance, a will of iron behind a layer of frightened innocence in Will's bright eyes.

"Fetch my rifle and get to repairing this fence before I get so gawd-damn riled I can't hold my vengeance," he yelled. "Find this pickaninny's folks. Bring him and them to me in the barnyard!"

Master Mack didn't often give in to a shortness of temper, but when he did someone paid for it. When the shot that quieted the horse suddenly interrupted the routine sounds of the busy plantation, all of Roedown became still as the sawmill on Good Friday at noon. Workers at the track and in the stables busied themselves with whispering. The ringing from the anvil in the blacksmith's shop, and the woeful song of toiling voices in the fields ceased. The grist mill stopped turning. From field to barn to stable to great house, the word passed. At the same time the caw-caw of a huge black crow dipping and carrying on like it had been in Master Mack's sour mash caught Miz Sadie, the root lady's attention. Will zipped past her cabin in the direction of his mother's place. Sims' young'un done killed one of Master's brand new Mustangs.

Will hid under his mother's straw tick. But before long, Sims' gnarled arthritic fingers were grasping his ankles, tugging and pulling him from his secret domain. The bedstead fell on him and when she finally wrenched him free, a piece of the rough hewn bedstead was in each of his hands.

"Now, where we go'n sleep tonight? Naw, you don't know, 'course not."

Anger and despair welled in her heart for the only child she'd ever had with a man of her own choice. Maybe she just ought to take him to the Pautuxent and drown him. She'd at least know what happened to him.

She picked Will up by his neck and hurled him out the door.

"I didn't want Mr. Bob or the overseer to get me," he said, staggering backwards. "I weren't hiding from you."

Before he could regain his balance she clutched his wrist. "For God's sake, how in the world did you do it?" she said, half dragging him along the worn path up the slope and across the lane past the great house.

"What I do?"

She looked at him and knew like only a mother could know.

"You takin' me to Master so he can shoot me?"

How could she tell him no, when she had no idea what Master Mack had planned for the last child she'd ever have, a son who had only seen six planting seasons. "Master say you killed his horse," she said quietly.

"Naw, naw he didn't. Wallace say I always gettin' the devil his mint and Master, he started cussin'. Lemme go, momma, lemme run away." Will tugged and yanked Sims' arm.

She struggled against his powerful resistance. Only the reality of knowing that as surely as the day would pass into night he'd be devoured before she'd have a chance to pass away, made her hold fast.

Mr. Groit met them in the big circular barnyard where all lanes and trails of Roedown merged. "Wait right here," he said. "Don't move, you hear me now?"

Will looked over his shoulder. Closing in from all directions, slave parents with their children gathered. Aunt Katie came, herding all the orphans from the quarters. They were a noisy bunch. Big boys clung together, joshing each other. Girls stayed close to Aunt Katie. Sims' questioning look with blood-red and weak eyes at Mr. Groit drew an immediate answer.

"You'll know d'rectly." He laughed.

All the servants in the great house came from their entrance in the kitchen, marching single file down around Mistress Margaret's rock garden, and gathering across the barnyard from the field workers. They were an odd looking group, some more white than Master Mack, fairer with blue lines under their skin than Mistress Margaret. Some were yellow, and high-brown like Grandmom Rosey. A little girl whose face, arms and hair were as reddish-orange as the marigolds behind her, stood beside Grandmom. For a brief spell she was the attraction, all eyes on Will traced his to her. She wore a full length white ruffled apron over a print gingham dress and a white bonnet.

"Smooth down ya' apron, Tawney girl," Grandmom Rosey said. Tawney responded as if she were a wind-up toy and Grandmom had simply flipped the switch.

Silent Charles the butler, white-glove-wearing Silent Charles, cleared his throat and smirked as if he owned the whole plantation. Mr. Groit hawked and blew out a jaw full of tobacco juice. A gentle breeze blowing in from the Chesapeake Bay caught the fine spray. Silent Charles, Grandmom Rosey and some others among the house full of high class servants wiped their eyes and drew up their faces like they did when Shorty Glover, a field hand who could eat more collard greens than any three of them, would leave the door to the quarter-moon shanty open.

"Lordy no, Tawney girl," Grandmom said. "Miss Margaret be yellin' and throwin' things at you again. Here." She gave Tawney a kitchen rag she had in her hands.

5

Master Mack gazed down on his subjects from the veranda with the smug pomposity of a king ordained by divine providence. A fortune in slaves he owned, three hundred, give or take a few. They looked up, waiting and wondering, humble eyed ragamuffins. And he, kind master that he was, knew the only lasting way to control them was not by torture. Render them docile, reign supreme, keep their fear of God's wrath foremost on their minds. Gentlemen masters ruled with discipline wrought from fear of the unknown, not by whip lashing. He knew any one of his healthy prime bucks, the finest in all of Maryland and Virginia with nary a blemish or whip scar on him, would bring at least two thousand dollars.

Master Mack glanced at his wife and sighed at her staring down at Tawney, engrossed in every move of the nine year old chamber maid. He had bought the girl to satisfy the whims of a spoiled Southern woman. But Margaret couldn't stand the cute little pickaninny. Margaret couldn't stand genteel treatment, she was of poor peasant extraction.

Master Mack drummed his fingers on the banister and nodded to Mr. Groit.

"Whip his ass." Groit threw his belt on the ground at Sims' feet.

"Father in heaven," Sims said. "You mean beat my child for all the world to see?"

"Whip his ass," Groit said. "Now."

"Merciful God," she said loudly enough for Groit and all the slaves to hear, "take me on home to glory." She began trembling while wrapping the rawhide belt around her aching hand.

She grabbed Will's hand but he snatched it free. He stood there, his bare feet firmly planted in the dirt, dressed in nothing except a pair of short pants. A length of hemp held them to his narrow waist. His eyes swelled, his nostrils hardened and quivered, his stomach and chest rose and fell with every inhalation and exhalation of expected pain. Sims hit him once, twice. Will didn't even flinch. Then Sims' arm went limp and hung by her side, the belt dragged in the dirt.

"Gawd-dammit," Mr. Groit said, "you gonna beat his ass or Master Mack gonna beat yours."

"Just a damned minute," Grandmom Rosey said. "You wanna see his kin draw blood from him? He's my grandchild and I been here about long as you been in the world. Let me show you how old Major Brodgen would'a beat him."

Before Groit could answer she had taken the belt from Will's frail mother and held him fast. Each time the belt bit his behind he flinched and stared at the ground. Now that she had stretched Will's endurance to the breaking point, she began talking to him in a hushed manner through her teeth.

"Got to learn the ways of the woods 'n animals."

6

Whap! The licks really hurt but he wouldn't cry.

"Stay shed 'a the bear. Hear me, young'un? Don't mess with the fox."

Whap!

"Keep clear 'a the snake. Say Ofeutey."

Whap!

Groit nodded approval to Master Mack.

"Ofeutey. Say it, you mean rascal."

Whap!

Grandmom wasn't fooling Master Mack. He remembered back when he was a boy, the African prince his father couldn't break. He drew a line in his ledger beside Sims' name where he had written six years ago in 1822. *Her third pickaninny, named Will Parker, grandson of Ofeutey. Most valuable property, track him.*

"Dammit young'un, say Ofeutey," Grandmom said.

The belt reddened Will's burnt sienna skin wherever it licked his bare back and legs, but he didn't cry. He clenched his teeth together and made nary a mumbling sound. Grandmom Rosey's arm felt as if she had been toting an iron bound oaken bucket full of water. She let go of Will and stood there panting with fire in her eyes. Then Will began.

He looked up at Master Mack and screamed so loudly there was no doubt that the neighboring Dorsey plantation acres away heard him. Master Mack closed the ledger and watched Will jump up and down while rubbing his behind. Damned if he didn't sound like a wolf.

Grandmom tried stopping him. "Hush up, young'un," she said. "You go'n make more trouble for yourself than your narrow ass can stand."

His exhausted mother came and grabbed him by the nape of his neck, but little good that did.

"Oh dear. David, please shut that nigger's mouth," his wife said.

"What do you suggest, smother him, kill him? Hell no. He's got more heart than any fifty niggers down there running scared, wishing he'd stop. Besides, there ain't a nigger in the world that's ever owed me anything except him. He's got a half-wild Mustang to pay for, but his hide isn't worth a hay shilling at this point in his life."

"How in heaven's name could a slave pay a debt?" Miss Margaret asked.

"I'll think of something," Master Mack said. If he hadn't known any better he'd swear Will was telling him to go to hell.

Will howled at the great house and all the slaves he and his mother passed as she dragged him down the path toward their cabin. He didn't stop until she fed him his favorite corn pone and fried potatoes. After he had eaten, she poised a heavy skillet in her hands, daring him to do it again.

Sims, hurting and despairing, lay across the broken down bed and began snoring. It was the scariest sound Will had ever heard, reminded him of the throaty noise Uncle Sammy made that day Grandmom made him stop telling a story about the boogey man. Sims coughed and suddenly stopped snoring. Will got a crazy notion to shake her, he didn't know why especially since he'd been so angry with her for letting Grandmom whip him. She didn't mumble and brush her hand over the place where he touched her like she always did when he annoyed her. He shook her again.

"Momma, wake up." Her body rocked once to his hard pushing like a heavy log he'd tried to turn over.

He dashed from the cabin, past slaves mingling around the quarters in the twilight, in and out of hearing range of the strumming of a banjo, to the servants' entrance of the great house.

"Gra'mom, Gra'mom, Momma won't, Momma won't!"

"Whoa." She waved her hands in front of him. "Now what you trying to say?"

"Momma won't wake up."

Grandmom Rosey threw down the rag in her hand and ran behind Will to the cabin. She, being the only house servant that went to the slave cabins and quarter, drew immediate attention when she stumbled down the slope, hard on Will's heels. Miz Sadie the root lady, Aunt Katie and two other women Will didn't know, followed Grandmom. Seeing Sims, they escorted Grandmom and Will from the cabin.

"We'll fix her up right nice," Miz Sadie said.

Grandmom Rosey wrote in her Bible that his mother, her daughter, died in Will's sixth summer. The old woman could read and cipher enough to make notations, but she had no concept of years. A child was born, loved ones were sold or died at spring planting, in the summer, at harvest time, or in the winter.

Will didn't know of another person in the world to call family except Grandmom. She slept in a little cramped space behind the pantry. Even if there had been space, Will couldn't stay there. His burnt sienna complexion was too dark. Grandmom took him to the quarter and told Uncle Sammy to look after him. Uncle Sammy, a tall and frail chocolate man with large sad eyes and long wrinkled fingers, wasn't Will's real uncle, but he was sweet on Grandmom. For her he watched over Will. Watching over him meant making Will fend for himself and stay out of trouble with Mr. Groit. Uncle Sammy only talked to Will when Grandmom brought Will morsels of food from the great house kitchen every evening.

Will spent his time in the quarter usually alone, huddled in a corner dreaming and thinking about Master Mack living in his big house like King Solomon in the Bible. He owned the land farther than Will's eyes could behold—from the Chesapeake Bay to the woods, down to a place named Virginia and back again. He did nothing but ride around his fields all day on thoroughbred horses. In the evening Master Mack sat at his table drinking wine from fancy glasses while entertaining his gentlemen friends and their ladies, eating out of fancy dishes with silver forks and spoons. Will thought Master Mack owned the whole world, clean up to the sky.

Will would then think about himself with nowhere to live except an over-crowded dirty building not much cleaner than Master Mack's hog sty, without anyone to fend for him. Sometimes the ragged children rampaging through the quarters reminded him of wild animals. That was the way Master Mack raised them.

After he passed his twelfth summer, Grandmom stopped bringing him little pieces of sweet-bread and roast beef. Master Mack forbade it. Slaves ate slave rations only. The older boys would take it from him anyway if she didn't stay with him while he ate. Will was getting tough though. They were making him mean and he was stretching out. When Uncle Sammy told Grandmom that Will had begun fighting back, she sighed, prayed silently, and wondered how long it would take to make him understand his destiny.

One winter's day, snow began falling at dawn. The wind swirling the snow and slashing at the quarter sounded like a bullwhip cracking the air. By midday the storm hadn't relented. Blazing logs piled high in the fireplaces burned fiercely, but most of the heat rushed up the chimneys with the strong drafts inside. Shivering slaves huddled and jostled in front of the fire, blocking the little heat that radiated from it. Uncle Sammy ached so badly his moaning sounded as if he were chanting a dirge.

Will sat on his tick with his knees drawn up in his chest. His fingers were cold, but fire burned inside him. He brooded about his mother's dying and owning nothing, not even the hole in the ground where she lay buried. Where was his father, he wondered. Will's face and arm pits itched so that he scratched his taut skin until it bled. Had his father been sold before Will was born, as his mother had said? He had heard them whisper about how Master Mack's father, Major Brodgen, sold slaves he had bred to cotton plantations in the deep South. How could any man be so powerful and so cruel? The nerves in Will's wiry legs twitched. He thought of Master Mack living in his great house and fire blazed in his chest. A foot nudged him roughly in his side. The muscles in his back tightened.

"Get out of the way, little grunt. I'm taking this warm spot."

Will looked up into the face of a strapping boy named Burl. He was built like a wild boar with tight skin so black it shined. Will rested his forehead on his arms and stared at the floor.

"That ain't my name," he said.

"You trying to be bad, little nigger," Burl said. "Move, or I'll kick your frail rump clean out the door." He kicked Will on his thigh and reached to snatch him.

9

Will shot from his crouch and drove his fist into Burl's lips. A tooth jumped out of Burl's mouth, his knees caved in. Burl tried to shake the surprise blow from his rattled brain. Little children throughout the quarter gathered and began jumping and yelling, "Beat his ugly butt, Will. Pop him another good, hard one. Give him one for me too."

"You sneaked me with a lucky one, grunt," Burl said, "but I'm going to knock your tongue so far down your throat it'll lick your belly button."

Burl was bluffing. Will read that in his glassy eyes and, though he took a couple good licks, drove a hard right punch crosswise to Burl's chin. Will really hurt him that time. He knew it in his heart, but he hit Burl again and again until he sank to his knees.

"Don't hit me no more, don't hit me no more, Will." Burl's left eye was turning red and swelling.

Will stepped back, his right fist cocked and tense as a panther's paw. He wiped his bloody mouth and tears on the back of his fist and stood his ground. All the little children huddled around him.

None of the chaos in the quarter that Will generated was missed by the scrutinizing eyes of Mr. Groit, the overseer. But he didn't care. Watching Will fight was a warm and amusing relief from the winter's cold boredom. He certainly could hit hard. Master Mack would be happy to know how tough Will really was compared to the rough-house bullies.

Uncle Sammy later told Grandmom Rosey that Will's fists were getting him into a lot of trouble, that the old folks, especially Aunt Katie, were irritated with all the racket he was causing, that he was making a bad name for himself.

"Unh-hunh," Grandmom said, looking at the sky. Then she spoke too quietly for Sammy to hear, "Lord it sure seems like he's the one. Maybe he is like his grandfather. Sweet Jesus, you finally answered my prayers."

After the brutal days of winter had passed and the misery had taken its toll of worn, exhausted bodies, Grandmom Rosey went more often to the quarter. The days were longer and the warming sun was the spring's tonic for her and Uncle Sammy's aging bones. Not until after the coming harvest, providing the Lord was willing, would they need to drink Miz Sady's acrid brew to ease the misery of arthritis and wheezing coughs.

When the rainy spell passed and grass in the pastures began greening, Grandmom often walked with Will. All about them spring staged its resurrection; the turned up earth with its fecund odor ready for corn, sweet potato, and tobacco planting, Master Mack's prized stallions prancing impatiently in the pastures around Roedown track, mares with tender eyes watching their colts sniff and nudge the freshly white-washed corral.

Will and Grandmom Rosey walked beyond the bottomland through the woods along the creek bank for a spell, then took a path just below the ridge to Queen Anne Village, a riverport hamlet on the muddy Patuxent River. Will watched her pause at the landing beside the slave auction block, saying nothing, and looking across the water. She looked at the yellow sand in the bottomland that sloped upwards into wooded high ground. She studied how the runoff from the spring rain had cut a swath where it flowed down the ridge into the Patuxent. Downstream a short way she gazed at an old barge listing to starboard.

Lordy, Grandmom thought, how she hated coming here. She knew the time had come though, to test Will, to find out if indeed he was the promise from God to right the wrong that old Major, Master Mack's father, had done to her. She looked at the placid flow of the river and opened her mouth to tell him about the slave auction block. But her mind swept back to many years before.

She was a maid in the great house then, pretty as a rose in full bloom and had lived eighteen summers. That particular day she stood there watching old Major bring slaves up the river in a long boat. A tall sinewy Twi with a complexion the color of buckwheat honey was among then. His name was Ofeutey, and he didn't answer to anything else. Ofeutey was too proud for Major's chain to hold him. He ran off a few weeks after he had come. They caught him and old Major had Red Jack, the driver boss on his freight line, lay ten on his back and ten over the ten. Grandmom—everybody called her Rosey then—fainted when the first lick drew blood. That night she sneaked to him in the old meat house where he lay chained and put salve Miz Sady had concocted on his back. She held her hand over his mouth to muffle his screams when the black paste drew fire from his body. She knew that if old Major caught her with Ofeutey, feeding and lying with a rebellious, unbroken nigger, he would flog her nigh unto death. But she didn't care. She taught Ofeutey some words and before the season had time to change they were married. Both jumped over the broomstick one night with no one watching. Ofeutey ran away early the next morning, but she forgave him because she knew he could be no one's slave. Major whipped him again, but that didn't stop Ofeutey. They finally broke his body because Major's whip couldn't break his spirit.

Most likely the old folks called her a fool too, back then. She loved Ofeutey with a passion she knew they couldn't understand, and still, though how long ago that has been, she felt the anguish, the cruel hurt of loneliness welling inside her.

"Grandmom Rosey," Will said, "what you looking at so hard?"

She snapped at him. "How come you fight so much, young'un?"

Will hesitated. He thought she was angry with him. " 'Cause they pick on little kids and my friend Levi all the time."

Levi, a shy, slight boy two summers younger than Will, lived in a cabin with his mother. He hung around the quarter mostly while she toiled in the field.

"You gettin' in trouble, making a reputation for yourself on account of this Levi?"

Will hunched his shoulders. "He just cries and begs the big boys to stop hittin' em." Then Will blurted. "Grandmom, I'm big enough to run away."

Her eyes flicked wide and, turning her head surreptitiously, she scanned the ridge. "Hush, hush up, fool," Grandmom said. She raised her hand to smack him, but let it fall. It wasn't hurt or fear in his searching eyes that stopped her. She saw fire, the fire she knew so well from Ofeutey.

Grandmom began sweating. "You know how to run fast, young'un?"

"Yessum, real fast."

"Naw you don't." She must help him keep that freedom fire burning until his time would come without getting himself killed or sold down the river. "Maybe you can beat them little bitty boys you always whipping in the quarter, but you can't outrun the river. You can't run like the wind."

"Yes I can too," Will said and dashed away in the bottomland beside the river, only the balls of his feet touching down and kicking up yellow sand.

Grandmom began smiling. He is Ofeutey's grandson. Look at him go. Her heart beat faster as Will stretched his sinewy legs in stride with his pumping arms.

"Come back, Will," she called,

He disappeared around the bend, then made a wide arc without breaking stride. Approaching her, he wore a determined pout on his lips. His nostrils flared and tightened. There was nothing to doubt. Will was the one sent by God to break the chains of Brodgen bondage that had destroyed her will to love, that had killed her daughter, that had held her kin captive too many seasons.

"Faster, boy. Run faster than the Fullani. Faster than the Ibo too," she said in a quiet, husky voice.

Will ran past her and circled the auction block.

"Run fast like the Twi," she said and sent him off again.

Grandmom ran Will until she, not he, was exhausted. While they rested she looked down the river and told him how it fed into the South River and the Chesapeake, then into the wide Atlantic Ocean from where the great African warriors came. That made Will proud until she explained how some warriors had caved in under the whip, or died fighting it. He got angry all over again and Grandmom ran him some more, teaching him to check his anger, hoping he would understand that he was her only strand of hope. Before she died, Will must escape.

As spring turned into summer and the hot days wore on, she drove him and he ran faster. Sometimes she said mysterious things to him about animals.

"Remember a long time ago I talked to you about the woods, and snakes and stuff?"

"No'm."

"Well, that's all right. You couldn't listen then nohow, and I was just speaking a word in some words. But times' come when you must learn something about the fox, the bear, the rabbit, and the snake. Master Mack go'n be working you a right smart d'rectly, you go'n be on your own."

"If we were to go in the deep woods the rabbit and bear would show themselves right off. But all of'em would be watching. The rabbit, he'd scoot when you walk up on him, and think he's getting away when all he's go'n do is go a short ways and stop. He's a fool. The big ugly bear, he always wants to fight. Give'em his ground, stay out of his clumsy way. You won't see the fox unless he wants you to. He's smart that way and he knows everything. The snake, he's a natural born killer. Study his ways, know who he is aforehand. Don't, when you walk upon'em he sure go'n bite. Ain't no second chance. Figure out the folks acting like them critters and you'll be able to g'won about your business."

Will didn't understand her, but talking that way about critters made him proud of her. Wanting to be smart like his grandmom made him question himself about everything he encountered.

Master Mack rode up one clear and still October day at twilight, when Will and Grandmom were at the river's edge. She didn't act surprised, she had learned many years ago to live with hate and fear without revealing it.

Master Mack sat tall in the saddle astride a white stallion. Confidence rode high on his shoulders.

"I'm teaching my grandson to mind, teaching him to check himself, Master, before the strong wolf inside him takes over his mind," Grandmom said.

The slave owner smiled, but Grandmom recognized the deceit. In his blue eyes she saw the cold gaze of an eagle. She knew he didn't believe her.

Master Mack knew better than Grandmom realized, she was trying to teach Will purpose, trying to ground him in determination, trying to anchor him to his spiritual self.

Watching Will split logs, driving the axe into the wood with the might of a lumber jack, he suspected that a yearning for freedom had begun nicking him like a dull pocket knife scarring the back of his hand. He knew by the flurry Will made raking mounds of crimson, orange and brown leaves that fell from the catalpa trees. Grandmom was doing fine, making him stronger. He had big plans for Will.

When Mr. Groit told him that Will bounced three boys who jumped him out of the quarter into the cold November night, Master Mack thought about Grandmom and he thought about the wolf. When Mr. Groit told him that Aunt Katie was the only person that Will let coax him into letting them inside, Master Mack smiled. Will kept the quarter alive for quite a spell, Mr. Groit

13

said, and Master Mack told the overseer to let Grandmom, Uncle Sammy and especially Will see him more often, and with his whip.

Will began noticing things he had never given a minute's attention before. Mr. Groit blew the horn that sent the hands to the field and he growled at every slave on the plantation. His short body was about the girth of the cemetery oak. He had a tree-stump head with large ears, thinning blond hair, and a huge hairy chest. His mouth looked like a rake and he chewed brown mule tobacco. While driving the ox cart on a timber cutting expedition in the deep woods with Wallace's gang, Will saw a brown bear, and thought, there go Mr. Groit. But he didn't tell anyone, not even his friend Levi.

Sometimes Will would turn around and Master Mack would be watching him. He'd notice Master's sharp nose and the crafty shifting of his eyes, and he would think, Master reminds me of the fox. On Sundays after Wallace had taken him over to the Dorsey plantation to help butcher hogs, Will often hid in the woods watching critters and thinking about Master Mack owning him and Grandmom, and knowing everything. But did Master Mack really know everything? He couldn't. If Master knew what One-Ear Tom from over Dorsey's had told him about freedom and especially some other really bad things that scared Will, he'd whip him or maybe sell him. Master couldn't know that Tom had stirred freedom thinking in him so that it churned in Will's stomach like lye bubbling in water. No one could stop that freedom thing inside him if he kept his thoughts to himself.

Every morning for nigh two weeks when Grandmom looked up from kneading dough, through the kitchen window she saw the bear standing at the edge of the veranda slowly working his tongue over the plug of tobacco in his jaw. She'd get nervous. Throbbing pain would cut a path across her forehead. He stood there a long spell watching her. Grandmom knew this was the sign and if Will wasn't ready she'd soon know the sorrow. She and Uncle Sammy were too old, they wouldn't be of much use to Master Mack anymore.

Grandmom had been a faithful servant for the Brodgen clan for lo these many years. She remembered nursing Master Mack when he was a baby and serving a table to President George Washington. Him with his long, silky wig white as snow, sitting in the great house sipping old Major Brodgen's best brandy. Lord, spare her just a mite longer, long enough to see Will break that grip the Brodgen clan had on her family.

Some evenings, while Uncle Sammy pulled dried stems from fall's flowers on a slope beyond the veranda, the bear would spew Uncle Sammy's hands with a fine spray of tobacco juice. Uncle Sammy would keep right on pulling stems and leveling the ground, too afraid to scratch the nervous itch in his neck. He'd been a blacksmith and remembered way back when Old Major sold Master President Washington a white stallion. Uncle Sammy shod it tight. Mr. President said a laughing word and threw him a silver bit. Major let him keep

14

it. He hadn't been such a mean master then and gentlemen sometimes did that. But the bear with that whip was no gentleman.

Chapter Two

After the harvest season, a sadness came over Roedown. It hung like a pall over a coffin. Grandmom had lain awake listening to the hoot owls for the past three nights and her hip ached worse than any rotten tooth Master Mack ever had the horse doctor pull. Any day now the men in long buckboard wagons, pulled by teams of horses, would come and Master Mack would summon all his slaves to the barnyard. She sent word by Uncle Sammy for Will to meet her that night.

She measured him with an appraising look as they walked in the bottomland by the Patuxent River. Will's shoulders strained against the tow-linen fabric of his shirt. He smelled like hay, like horse manure, and his hair clung in tiny beads to his scalp. The sun was cooking him just right. His skin was tight and the color of chestnuts. His onyx-ivory eyes were hooded like a hawk's. He had Ofeutey's prominent forehead and walked as if he didn't give a damn if a team of mules were charging him.

As they waded among the fallen leaves, Grandmom began singing, "I'll fly away, oh glory, I'll fly away."

She sang quietly and didn't say one word to Will. Their feet made a crunching noise in the deep dry leaves. They walked to the auction block on the landing. Will couldn't keep the words inside him any longer.

"Grandmom Rosey, I got to be free."

Grandmom Rosey trembled. "Son, you just now passing through your thirteenth harvest, I don't want to know the sorrow."

"I want to go where I can ride my own horse fast and just keep riding and riding 'til I want to stop," Will said.

She looked into a clear just darkening blue sky. Star-pointed lights twinkled brightly. One billowy cloud hung suspended like a giant cotton ball directly over them. "When I die, hallelujah by and by," she sang.

Will looked at her and frowned. "How come you singing so much about dying and stuff?"

"It ain't about dying. It's about living free," she said. "It's about riding to glory on an iron horse that runs under the ground."

Will's eyebrows moved up suddenly. A wrinkle circled his forehead. "Aw Grandmom Rosey, you telling me a horse made of that stuff in Master Mack's blacksmith shop can run under dirt?"

She hit Will on his neck. It wasn't a hard lick, but enough to make him listen, really listen. "Pay attention to the words in the songs the old folks sing in the quarter tonight," she said. "Follow the words as they pass through the fields, on over behind them hemlocks way over yonder."

Grandmom sang with a raspy, wavering voice, barely louder than a whisper. "Swing low, sweet chariot."

"Maybe somebody will sing back," she said and sang again.

"Coming for to carry me home."

An inner calm reflected in her face. The sag in her thin lower jaw disappeared. Her lips were turned upwards.

"When you hear the words, Grandson, put your ear to the cornstalk. The first one might sing again. Swing low, sweet chariot."

Grandmom actually smiled. "Then a whole bunch of folks, they might be in a big circle around the lead one and will join in and sing back," she said.

"Coming for to carry me home," Grandmom sang.

"Pretty soon the whole field will be singing. Then it quiets to a hum. Sometimes it floats on away."

"Lord, Grandson." She balled her bony hand into a fist. The bitter look returned. "I don't wanna see no more sorrow."

Will's eyes searched hers. Grandmom Rosey saw the puzzled stare but he wouldn't understand. She knew what he needed more than anything, yet resisted an urge to tell him more about the Underground Railroad, to rub his head, to tell him he was a mighty fine and handsome boy, to tell him she loved him.

"You seen the bear and by now you ought to know the fox. Keep your mannish mouth shut and follow your spirit. Hear?"

"But Grandmom Rosey..."

Grandmom shook her head. "Do you hear me, Will? We best be gettin' on back."

"Yessum."

Exhaustion usually took over quickly after dark in the slave quarter. The fetid air was filled with hacking, fitful droning and contralto piping from the tired souls. That night though, after Will returned it buzzed with mysterious whispering long after the last coal-oil lantern in the old folks' end of the quarter had gone out.

Will lay on his tick mattress watching a crescent moon shine through the windowless opening. He labored with Grandmom's counseling between snatches of dream-weaving sleep. An iron horse with wings larger than an eagle's plowed through the earth beneath Roedown. When the horse reached the Patuxent River, it emerged and flew straight up, higher and higher northward on its way to freedom, bearing Will and some faceless slaves on its wings. Suddenly, from behind a cloud a boogey man jumped out and fired. They tumbled down, down, all the way down to the quarter.

Will's body jerked. He opened his eyes and in the dim light of the moon he saw Uncle Sammy stare at him and silently shuffle away. Then he heard a haunting voice riding on the wind as it blew through the trees.

"My Lord he calls me. He calls me by the thunder."

It was a woman's voice, husky, soothing, quiet. It seemed to beckon him.

"The trumpet sounds within my soul."

"I ain't got long to stay here."

She sang the last line over and over. Each time her voice seemed farther and farther away. It seemed to drift like an elusive ghost down towards the river. Will felt compelled to follow, but he didn't move.

Next morning the horn that sent the slaves to the fields at sunup didn't blow that brisk November day. The sun shone like splashing fire behind a bank of clouds beyond the ridge, as if something devious in the clouds was blocking it from Roedown.

Mr. Groit rode his swayback horse right up into the quarter and ordered everybody into the barnyard. He went to the cluster of field hand cabins and then to the great house, an opportunity he always relished before a slave sell. On this day, and only this one unless Miss Margaret needed him when Master Mack was away, he had control of the servants, that bunch of uppity nigras. At the front door he reached for the knob. But Silent Charles snatched it open from the inside and stood there in profile, looking down his thin nose with half-closed eyes. Groit wished he could choke him.

"You and the rest of ye," he pointed his finger in Silent Charles' face.

Charles blinked his eyes several times. Groit watched his nose quiver.

"In the barnyard and make haste," Groit said.

Charles held his hands high, buttoned his white gloves and strolled down the walk with the grace of a ballet dancer.

"Get along with you now, boys," Mr. Groit said as he ushered maid servants, man servants, cooks, dressmakers and house cleaners through the door.

"Master Mack's very busy. You over there, I say, Auntie, step it up."

But all of them, field hands, horse tenders and carpenters alike, shuffled along as if he hadn't spoken. In the distance a dust cloud rose off Queen Ann Road. They all watched twelve white men in six long buckboards turn into the lane. Each one hoped an angel of mercy would touch Master Mack so he would spare him or her one more time. They milled silently around the duck pond, on the slope between the yard and a peach orchard, and in front of the alcove between the horse stables and wagon shop. Mothers and fathers gathered and hugged their children in a rare moment of public affection. Uncle Sammy groped around alone until Grandmom Rosey took it upon herself to stand with the field nigger. They tried in a futile way to linger inconspicuously behind the younger slaves.

"They look like peddlers of death, don't they," Grandmom said.

"Lord knows they bringing a heap of trouble and I hear Master's losing right smart on his horses," Uncle Sammy said.

Will saw the men in long coats and wide brim hats that hid their faces. He heard iron balls and chains rattling on wagon floors. He saw whips coiled in their hands. Put your ear to the cornstalk, follow the voice in the circle as it weaves on over there to the trees, Grandmom's words rang in his ears. If only she had let him ask her, she could've explained in a way that he would've understood the mystery in One-Ear Tom's words. If only she had let him ask her, she could've told him if the fox knew everything. Then he would've known she expected him to steal away last night with the song. Now, where could he go? Run, he did, like an antelope one step ahead of a lion's jaws, past rows of barren blackberry vines, through a grape arbor and down in the dell behind the cabins.

He glimpsed his one true friend Levi walking up the winding path behind his mother as if he were an old man, his chin almost touching his chest. Will slackened his pace and cupped his hands to his mouth.

"Leeeevi", he called.

Levi turned around and squinted his eyes, even though the fall morning sun peeping now and then from behind the clouds was not bright. Will waved.

"The boogey men come," Will said, "a whole bunch of 'em too!"

"I know," Levi said, "but my mama say if I don't do what Master Mack want, he might sell her."

"How you going to stop him," Will said, "if he's a mind to do that?" Will stood between two cabins, mindful of the bear on horseback. "Better come on with me."

"I ain't a, a." Levi stuttered when excited or sad. "I ain't running away." He turned and watched his mother walking on.

Her long black hair was tied in a red scarf. She wore a faded calico dress and an apron made of burlap. But that didn't conceal her jutting breasts and tantalizing nubile curves of her tall, slim black body.

"I ain't running off," Will said. "I'm going to hide, that's it. I'm a hide in the woods until the boogey men leave."

Levi's mother looked back. "Levi," she said in simple despair.

"Okay," Will said. "Good-bye, 'cause I won't see you no more." Will set himself to run.

"Wait," Levi said. "But what if he sell my mama?"

"What if he sell my Grandmom?" Will said. "What if he sell you? What if he sell everybody? But he ain't selling me."

"Mama?"

"G'won, boy. Only God knows what's best and he ain't study'n 'bout no slave," she said, swallowing her pain of knowing loneliness.

They disappeared into the pear orchard.

The slave traders had come up the long lane past the Roedown grandstand and were circling the outer periphery of the barnyard. They moved behind the slaves, but they paid little attention to the traders or their braying horses. Everyone stared up at the veranda where Master Mack stood with one hand on the banister and the other in his vest pocket. He stood there observing all that his eyes could behold of his empire. The fields had been harvested. Pork from the hogs and beef from the cattle filled the smoke houses. The mares had been studded, their thoroughbred colts sold. Wine had been pressed, tobacco was curing. Now he'd weed and thin out his chattel as he had done to his corn.

Master Mack retrieved a gold watch from his vest, and with his right hand he pressed a little lever. The lid popped open and from the Roman numeral dial, he read the time—eight o'clock. He stepped from the veranda like a king descending his throne and strutted down a winding stone path through Mistress Margaret's flower garden. The wave of slaves fell back, cutting a swath through themselves as if an invisible shield were slicing through, forcing them to stumble out of his way. They bowed. A few said, "Morning, Master." On that day he didn't acknowledge any of them. He stopped in front of the alcove.

Mr. Groit came to the forefront and motioned to the slavers that the sale was about to commence.

Master Mack called Aida, Aunt Aida the field hands called her, and her two children. They weren't there, probably left last night on the Underground Railroad. Master Mack smacked the riding crop in his palm until his hand smarted. God, how he hated runaways. He was a good ruler, a kind master. Too kind for Aida to sneak off under the cloak of darkness with that goddamned Tubman wench. It had to be her. No other nigger in the entire Chesapeake-Tidewater area had that much nerve to sneak through the woods and rob plantation after plantation of its prime slaves better than a fox could raid a hen house. If the bounty hunters didn't hurry and find her she'd soon pick the Chesapeake clean. Aida even took her two children with her, his chattel property, his investment. That's gratitude, goddamned nervy gratitude and she'd pay dearly.

He walked among the slaves then stopped and pointed his crop at Burl. "He goes."

The slavers pounced on Burl, pried open his mouth, and with their fingers examined his teeth, eyes and ears. They formed a circle and made him drop his ragged pants. After the examination one asked, "What happened to his mouth, he's snaggle toothed?"

Master Mack chuckled. "It got in the way of a swift fist."

The slaver asked him whose fist, but Master Mack, ignoring him, continued his slow, methodical stroll until he saw Levi's mother, He pointed his crop, she yielded to the slavers as if her body didn't belong to her. The slaves around her shifted restlessly until Master Mack picked the next among them. He looked around and began smacking his hand with the crop again. Tawney should go. She had a lot of growing to do yet, but with her good looks and healthy body, she'd draw top dollar. But he wouldn't sell her, even if his wife couldn't handle her. Tawney had more of everything than Margaret except pride. Margaret couldn't accept that, forcing herself to believe she was taming her.

Grandmom figured he was looking for Levi. When he came and stood in front of her and Uncle Sammy for such a long time she knew their times had come. Hallelujuh though, he couldn't sell Will, the circle had been broken.

Master Mack turned suddenly and pointed his crop at Miz Sady, the root lady and Grandmom Rosey knew for certain, he was a-plenty hot. Miz Sady had come there way back then and provided the only doctoring his field hands would ever get. Many a poor white hired hand had drunk her winter misery potion and Master Mack had collected a right smart sum after he learned that Miz Sady was smuggling her honey-moon brew to white folks from as far away as All Hallows Church. Grandmom would always believe Bob Wallace, the dirty snake, told him about it.

She watched Miz Sady put up a fuss—something about a pot boiling right then—but Groit told her to shut up and Master Mack kept on walking and smacking his hand with that crop. He sold Josie and her two brothers, Dennis and Jacob, all in one fast swing and while the slavers yanked and snatched them this way and that, he called Groit away from the crowd. No doubt at all that Groit was catching hell. Grandmom knew from the way he made desperate gestures in the air with his hands, and the way Master Mack kept pointing his long fingers in Groit's face. Then Groit got on that big swayback horse of his and Grandmom couldn't see him riding off for the dust he kicked up. Master Mack argued some with the slavers and took their money. Then he climbed in a buckboard with two men who hadn't bought anybody and all of them left.

Miz Sady, Josie and the rest of them rode off in shackles, staring in space like they were sitting there dead except that dead folks could lie down and knew where they were going. No good-byes, no tears shed. The spared slaves walked off as if the unfortunate in the buggies weren't really there, there hadn't been a sell, just a break in the hard day's work routine.

Grandmom Rosey knew Master Mack would travel to Annapolis, pay his agent to hire more slave catchers and post rewards for the fugitives. Most likely, the slaver masters would raise the reward for Harriet Tubman too. Grandmom prayed.

"Lord, how bright will you make that one star tonight? How black will you make the dark night for the weary travelers? If mercy is in you like I want to believe it is, hide them who left last night in your shadow 'til they're safe in Canaan. Then give me a sign so I'll know my grandson done reached the promise land. After that you can carry me on to glory. My home ain't here nohow."

Will trudged through his familiar part of the woods fighting with himself. One-Ear Tom made him glow inside, made him feel better about himself than he'd ever felt before. But he scared Will too, especially when he compared Tom's words with Grandmom's about critters and folks. Much of what Tom said really didn't sound good and he knew better than to repeat it, except maybe to Grandmom. But she wouldn't listen and that made him irritable, especially raw towards Levi.

Overhead, a perfect triangle of Canadian geese barely cleared the tallest trees. "I wish me and my mama was one of them," Levi said. "We would fly away from here."

A sudden barrage of shotgun fire sent a tremor through the quiet air.

The blasting set the geese that had come to feed in the Chesapeake into honking hysterics and crash diving through the November woods to the ground.

"I'm glad I ain't a goose," Will said, with a startled voice.

He and Levi heard the hunters' jubilant voices not far from them. Levi's head twisted this way and that way like an excited rabbit. He began whimpering.

"Bunk that, Levi," Will said. "We got to hide."

He helped Levi grasp an overhead branch of a tall pine tree then grabbed a branch and muscled up past him. "My Grandmom move faster'n you," Will said.

Levi looked at the ground far beneath him, breathing deeply in jerks. "This is far enough for me, Will."

"Gitcha' ass peppered like you was one a'them ducks, you'll wish you'd listened." Will sat on a branch swinging his feet loosely above Levi's head.

"You just trying to scare me so's I'll run away with you." Levi hugged the tree tighter.

"If you stay here you're a real dummy. 'Course don't make much difference for you 'cause Master Mack going to sell you anyway. You cry and whine too much."

"Naw I don't."

"Not so loud, donkey mouth, them hunters will hear you."

"Yea," Levi said, "and if they take us back, Master Mack, he'll sell us for sure."

"I keep on telling you, ox-head," Will said, "he's going to do that anyway. If not today, then next time. So we got to hide in these here branches 'til night. Then we'll sneak back, get some apples and hoecake to eat 'cause we'll be running hard all night."

"You mean we wouldn't be able to sleep none?" Levi asked.

"Not 'til we get up North," Will said.

"I ain't going, Will," Levi said. "We too little."

"You too little," Will said, "too little in the head."

"Naw I ain't either. Anyway, you don't even know which way is up North."

"It's that way," Will said. He pointed in the direction from which the geese had come.

"Naw it ain't either," Levi said. "My mama say the Chesapeake Bay and Eastern Shore over there."

"The Chesapeake is that way." Will thrust his arm in a southernly direction and glared at Levi. "You don't think nothing for yourself no time, dummy," Will said.

"I do so," Levi said. "I know that North is too far and we might freeze in Canada. Who's going to feed us? You ever thought about that, mule-brains?"

An urge welled up inside Will to kick Levi on his head, but he really didn't want to knock him out of the tree. "Don't call me mule-brains, dummy."

"See," Levi said, "you get mad when I call you names." He stared at the ground, but looked up immediately and hugged the tree.

"Sure, 'cause you ain't smart one bit. Ever see the fox lookin' at you real hard? Ever hear the word in a word? The bear ever spit tobacco juice on your hand? Hell naw."

Will thought for a long minute. He climbed higher, determined to leave Levi with his stubborn self.

"You think you know everything in the whole wide world," Levi said, inching up the tree a little ways. "Will," he said.

"What the hell you want, runt?"

"Nothing, if I got to be a runt."

"Aw c'mon, Levi, what do you want?"

"I just thought that if we work harder for Master Mack he'll have to keep us."

"How in the hell?" Will stopped and thought for a long minute, mulling Grandmom's warning over and over—keep your mannish mouth shut—but One-Ear Tom's riddle was kicking up such a racket inside him, he couldn't hold it down any longer. "Master Mack is raising us to sell just like he sells his horses."

"Wonder why he do that. I ain't no horse," Levi said.

"May as well be one 'cause we something he and the horse-breeders call bucks."

"A what," Levi said. "What in the world is that?"

Levi sounded like the old folks back at the plantation. Will climbed down aways, closer to his timid friend.

"Ever see the size of that thing on his stallions?" Will said.

"Naw Will, I don't believe that, so don't even say it. How we going to ever be that big?"

"I don't know," Will said, "but when Master Mack go to sell you, you sure going to find out."

"And we be them buck things all the time?" Levi asked.

23

"When he sells you down the river to the cotton plantations, you be the buck all night and the slave all day. And cotton fields ain't half as bad as rice paddies."

"My mama say she know about the cotton fields, but she never talk about no rice paddies."

"They worse than cotton fields," Will said. He bent closer to Levi, making sure the hunters wouldn't hear him. "You have to work in cold, muddy water up to your neck digging weeds out of rice."

"I can't swim," said Levi. "What if I slip and fall?"

"You drown," Will said, "but that ain't worst of it."

Will stared as if he were seeing something far, far away, just as Uncle Sammy had stared when he threaded the warning yarn to Will. Will thought of the trouble it had caused him in mind until he asked Tom about it.

"Big water moccasins sneak through the water and bite you on the buck, and snake juice gets all in your eyes and knee caps and stuff. It makes you crazy," Will said.

"My mama say a mad dog's bite and snake poison run you crazy and then Master Mack will shoot you."

"He and Dorsey shoot crazy slaves, afraid they'll get all of us worked up into killing white folks and taking over the land. They calls 'em crazy niggers."

"Do? Where'd you hear about that, Will?"

Will hesitated. He really shouldn't tell Levi any more.

"Where'd you hear that, Will," Levi asked again.

"One-Ear Tom told me, but like he said, Master Mack and Dorsey 'n them don't like that kind of talk."

Levi squinted and rubbed his ear.

"He ain't from around here, Levi. Last time Master Mack sent me with Wallace to help Dorsey butcher hogs, old Tom, you ought to see him mess with a pig. One fast slice, zip."

Will ran his fore finger up his front from his groin to his throat. "Everything that stinks, chittlins, grunt and all tumble out in a bucket."

Levi frowned. "He only got one ear?"

Will pulled his right ear lobe. "This one's gone. They nailed it to a board and whacked it off."

"I don't believe that, Will."

"He ought to know about his own ear, dummy," Will said. "He killed some white folks with a guy named Prosser down in Virginia. That's why they cut off his ear. Tom said Virginia ain't far from here."

"I don't want to kill nobody. You, Will?"

"Nope, but I sure as hell going to be free."

Levi saw that wild look in Will's face when freedom rose up from deep inside him. The thought of it all—running and hiding, bloodhounds, patrols and whips—scared Levi again.

"I'm going back, Will. Right now. If Master Mack don't sell my mama this time, I'll tell him I ran away 'cause I don't want to be no crazy nigger."

Levi skinned down the tree, scratching his legs on the rough bark and protruding branch stubs.

"See what I mean, blabber mouth?" Will descended as fast as he could, but Levi had already crashed head-long into the brush. "I told you it was a secret."

"Don't tell me no more." Levi put his hands over his ears. "I'm going home."

"Home!" Will tripped over a fallen branch and cursed. Levi didn't look back. "You crazy, Levi. You got no home, you got nothing, not even yourself."

Levi turned around and yelled. "Don't call me crazy ever no more. You the one like them crazy niggers, and I'm going to tell."

"Yeah," Will said, getting up and mimicking Levi. "I'm go'n tell mama."

"No I ain't. I'm telling Master Mack. I'm telling him that..."

"You do and I'll bust your skinny face." Will's panicky shout frightened Levi. He backed away shrinking into himself as Will charged down on him with nostrils flared and rigid.

"I'm just going to tell him I ran away 'cause I was scared, that's all," Levi said.

"Naw, Levi, I don't believe you. After I take up your fights with Burl and all them big kids, this is pay back, huh?"

Will wrapped his big hand around Levi's forearm and squeezed. Levi struggled to free his arm but Will squeezed tighter.

"Master Mack probably knows just like my mama do when I ain't telling the truth," Levi said.

"Yeah, if you stand there looking at the ground and scratching your nappy head. You're a goner for sure if you tell him my secret. You get what I mean?"

Levi didn't answer. He hurried on in the autumn yellow Maryland woods with Will close behind him. When they reached the big road and turned towards Roedown, the afternoon sun cast long shadows of the two slave boys in the grassy lane. Will grabbed Levi's shoulder and stopped.

"Listen," he said.

Levi froze. They heard wailing among the slaves in the yard. Will and Levi started running. On their way through the pear orchard, Will heard a sad plea he recognized coming from Grandmom Rosey.

"Hush, child," she cried. "Don't bring no more punishment down on yourself."

"Sweet Jesus, only you can help her," Uncle Sammy said.

Groit drew back his whip. Its tip broke the air and lashed out as if it were a big snake attacking a frog. Tawney writhed on the ground in the same spot slaves had been sold earlier that day.

Will stared with his mouth hanging open. Tawney's head was capped with a mass of thick, disheveled reddish-orange hair. Her eyes were red and feline with lashes that swept almost to her temples. She contorted in the dirt, fighting back with such conviction of spirit.

All the slaves had come together again, begging Miss Margaret in their quiet way—pleading for Jesus—to stop the beating. Little children whimpered. Miss Margaret acted as if they weren't there.

Will watched her, a tall woman approaching her middle years and given to stoutness, standing on the veranda above the flower garden with skin so white it looked translucent. Her hair, hanging loose and straight, was pale yellow like a field of thirsty grain. She stood there looking down on her subjects with arms folded beneath her breasts in a faked pose of tranquility.

Groit looked at her. Will saw her nod yes. The mighty tenderer of discipline snapped the whip again. It cut across Tawney's up-tilted breasts, tearing from her body the flimsy covering she wore. A long dark mark like a knife cut turned scarlet and dripped red. Tawney put her hands across her face. The whip whined and bit.

"Aaah!" Tawney's body stiffened and then let go. She spoke with gritty huskiness, her voice barely audible. "You Eastern shore poor white trash."

Will winced. Anger rioted in his stomach as he watched the slave men with eyes down-cast. He saw Grandmom suddenly catch sight of him. She began trembling and moved towards him like a slinking black cat.

Will kept watching Tawney. He didn't know Grandmom was beside him until he flinched from the pain of her fingers, her bony, crooked fingers with brittle stub fingernails, pinching the nerves in his shoulders.

"Dumb nigger, you dirt dumb, dumber than duck shit. Got me praising God for delivering your worthless ass out from here and here you come sneaking back. After a sale too. Ain't nobody in all of Roedown that nimble-headed."

Will twisted free. He lowered his head then rolled his eyes up at her, big threatening onyx ivory eyes like Ofeutey's. But that Ofeutey look didn't melt her and she was too angry, too hurt, too disillusioned to be intimidated. Grandmom glared at Will so hatefully he wished he could've disappeared in the ground.

"Get the wind out of your jaw, and try growing up," she said to him.

Will heard her but he wasn't listening. She had broken the bond between them, and he couldn't trust Levi. All alone and on his own, he felt drawn to Tawney. It was more than feeling sorry for her. Watching her endure torture, she seemed ethereal.

Tawney's red eyes burned at Groit. She tried to rise, but stumbled and crawled toward him on her knees. Blood oozed from the raw welts across her breasts.

"You lower than a barnyard bitch," she said, spitting blood. Her hair was matted with dirt and sweat.

The overseer gritted his teeth and clenched the whip tighter.

"Nigger wench," he said with a thick tongue. "You ain't learned your place yet."

Miss Margaret nodded yes. The whip snarled and bit Tawney again. It cut across Tawney's back, wrapped around her narrow waist, and yanked her off her knees. She cried out, a blood curdling scream.

"Slut," she said, though she couldn't speak above a whisper. "Filthy slut."

She spit at Mr. Groit, but it landed on her naked body. He raised the whip again without looking for approval from Miss Margaret. But Tawney had escaped. She had slipped into unconsciousness. On her way out, she raised one weak fist at Mr. Groit and shook it.

The slaves looking at her naked body were not ashamed. They sensed a kinship with her soul, a feeling of unity that she had aroused in her sacrifice. Grandmom made a mental note to record the events of this day in her Bible. She would labor long after dark to write:

It happened at hog-killing time, after Will passed his fourteenth harvest. The mighty cut down Tawney in the flesh, but it made her rise over all Roedown in spirit.

"By the whiskers of Moses," the overseer said, "get her out of here."

Will watched Miss Margaret disappear into the great house. Grandmom rushed to Tawney and raised her head to prevent her from choking,

"By God, I'm a telling all of you. Get on back to your work. And I'm damn near tired a talking," said Groit.

The men shuffled away behind their wives and children, staring at the ground. Some wrung their hands, some hunched their shoulders.

Up to that day in Will's life, longing for freedom dominated his thoughts more than hatred. He hated his lowly life and separation from the abundance, but no person except Mr. Groit. Now watching his grandmother and two other slave women tending Tawney, he imagined Miss Margaret's neck in his hands, squeezing until her eyes bulged. He wished himself Satan, turning the bear on a spit in hell. He wondered if crazy niggers felt the way he did, with that madness coursing through him.

The stories of men that old One-Ear Tom had told him were foremost in his mind—Gabriel Prosser down Richmond way, Denmark Vesey from Charleston, Nat Turner in Southampton County. These places meant nothing to him, but the men stood out strongly. He imagined them standing before him as he wandered around aimlessly that evening, hearing Tawney's screams over and over again. He would go to her. At least tell her how she had made him feel inside. Tell her that if Groit was around when he got a little older, he would kill him.

Tawney had been taken to Miz Sady's cabin. Will rapped twice, three times, waited, then continued the racket until Grandmom answered the door. The odor of lye and hot tallow in brown soap and root medicine the old conjure lady had made hung close in the air. Will coughed.

Grandmom glared. "Get the hell away from here!"

She slammed the door in his face. But Will wouldn't be forced away. He sneaked around to the side of the cabin and peeped through a crack in the shutter. Through the eye of the pot-bellied stove he saw a crackling fire. On the stove a black kettle boiled and grunted. The lid popping up and releasing steam made Will think of a bullfrog croaking. Grandmom and her attendants ran around Tawney like bees in a hive. They turned Tawney on her back as tenderly as they would remove a cake from Master Mack's oven.

Tawney moaned. Grandmom opened the salve again, screwed-up her face and wiped the tears it drew from her eyes. She made a poultice of goose grease, pine-pitch and spider webs then applied it to Tawney's torn flesh with rags.

"Poor thing," Grandmom said, stirring hot water with a pinch of peppermint, feverwort and balm, "she's just a pretty slave girl in an old heifer's bedroom. Lift her head, easy now."

Grandmom forced the hot brew into Tawney's mouth. "Hold her a spell. She needs a little more."

Tawney's eyes were closed. Her face was empty and dark. Will breathed the cool damp air and exhaled warm vapors in jerking pants. Tawney opened her eyes. They smarted out of focus and then twinkled like water droplets on clear wet glass. Will's heart danced in his chest, a frenzied warrior.

Tawney closed her eyes and slipped into unconsciousness again. The warm feeling that had wrapped around Will like tender caressing arms left him. He felt lonely and cold, wearing nothing but his thin, tow-linen pants and collarless shirt.

"Tawney." He heard himself call her name. The feeling was strange. He had never called a girl's name before except in sneering. He longed for Tawney in his heart and stared, hoping to see just a faint stir from her.

"Tawney." He pulled the shutter open just wide enough for it to cradle his mouth. "Tawney, you wake?"

"What in the name of God? Fool," Grandmom said. She and the other women had finally sat down around the fire. She stuck her head through the patched quilt which when drawn together, separated Miz Sady's bed and mysteries from the inquisitive eyes of her callers.

"He's gone plumb crazy," Grandmom said. She grabbed a broom made of corn husks and dashed out the door with it poised overhead to where he crouched beneath the window. Will waited until he saw the flame in her eyes. Then with a sudden and irritated scowl, he eluded her wild swing and walked away, hearing the two women snicker.

"You're a fool, boy," Will heard Grandmom say. "Now your sap's rising. But woe be to God, you better stay away from this one."

I hate her, Will thought, hurrying on, feeling the cold air raise goose pimples on his bare arms and shoulders. Fussing all the time, really getting on his nerves. Feelings he had held for Grandmom, feelings that had made him remember his mother, were fading. He thought of his mother and immediately thought of Tawney. He wished the feeling would grow. It felt warm. Yet it puzzled him. He wished he could ask somebody about the strange thing that made him feel better than when he ran.

Will knew nothing about love, only once in his entire life had he heard the word. God loved him, Grandmom said when they were down by the Patuxent River. But what good would God's love do Will if he and Master Mack had the same God? Master Mack's preacher, the little man with the pear-shaped face and white beard like a billy-goat's, talked about nothing except Will and the young slaves burning in hell for stealing Master Mack's chickens. He'd rather burn in hell for being a crazy nigger than for stealing a chicken. Better than anything, he'd rather think about Tawney. The way she looked at him made him glow more than when he thought about One-Ear Tom and crazy niggers. He'd guard the secret with his life, tell no one except maybe her

"Especially not Levi," Will said aloud. "He's probably home right now blabbing to his mama."

Chapter Three

When Will and Levi returned from the woods, Levi wormed among Master Mack's slaves looking for his mother. He darted, stopped, jerked his head about like a rabbit in the briar and began calling her name, though not so loudly at first. Few people paid him any mind. Convinced she wasn't in the crowd, Levi ran down the lane to their cabin. Her belongings were setting outside, tied in a neat white bundle.

"Mama." He cried out with a high quaking voice, driving his frenzied self against the closed pine wood door. The sound of splintering wood startled him.

A woman lying on his mother's tick shrieked. She pulled her nipple from a nursing infant's mouth and wrapped her arms tightly around the child and her laden breasts.

"Where's my mama?" Levi yelled.

The baby cried furiously. It sounded like the bleating of a new-born lamb.

"Shsh," the woman said, talking to her child, while staring at Levi.

"Get out her bed," Levi ranted, going toward her.

She shrunk back into the corner, pulling a coarse blanket around her. "Boy," she said, "don't you hurt my baby none 'cause my man, he'll, he'll. He brought us here from the quarter."

Levi stopped and looked around as if to ask, where is he? The woman had frightened him.

"What's your mama's name, boy?"

"She named Josie."

The lady lowered her brown eyes from Levi. Her expression changed from fright to sorrow and he knew. He knew his mother had been sold.

"How many harvests you been here, little boy," she asked.

Levi acted as if he hadn't heard her, even though he didn't know. Without forethought, his mouth opened wide and let go a blood curdling cry from deep inside his chest. It sounded like the bark of a man riddled with consumption.

"Poor thing," she said, turning to her baby. "Hush now and sleep, it's all right."

But Levi standing there howling made it seem too real, her baby being snatched from her arms. "Go 'way from here. Go to your friends in the quarter. They'll understand. It happens to all of us sooner or later."

Levi burst from the cabin. The broken door banged against the outside wall and closed itself. He snatched his mother's bundle and wandered thoughtlessly up the lane toward the quarter. The sweet odor of her perspiration filled his nostrils. He squeezed the bundle to his chest as if to prevent the approaching chilly November night air from stealing it.

Go to your people, go to your friends, they'll understand. What people? Two uncles at Roedown who never gave him any attention? Will Parker his only friend who never talked about anything except running away and disobedience to Master Mack? That's what got him into this awful mess. Just like Master Mack's preacher said, disobedience to your master will curse you. If he had stayed with his mama, she'd be with him right now. Levi hated Will Parker more than he would hate living in the quarter.

Darkness came early and brought with it a dense fog. Moonlight on the eerie white mist intensified the heightened tension that had spread over Roedown. Armed sentries on horseback, poor white hired hands Groit had summoned on the advice of Miss Margaret, shuffled along between the inner circle and outer perimeter of the plantation. Groit imposed a twilight curfew, a long standing order that Master Mack seldom enforced, and warned all the slaves to stay in or risk being shot.

Glowing embers in the great house fireplace threw contorting shadows on the walls. The mansion looked spooky and mournful without Master Mack. Grandmom hastily prepared a supper for Miss Margaret that wasn't fit even for the lowest human. Just before serving it she drew a big mouthful of the soup and gagged. She spit it back into the pot.

Fires blazed inside the field hands' cabins. In the quarter, scrap kindling sputtered then blazed and flew up the chimneys like red pellets in the blue smoke. In front of the fireplace Uncle Sammy sat rubbing his feet.

"I declare," he said, "they so tender it hurts me to walk across a blade of grass." He wasn't joking, but he knew the old folks needed a good laugh.

Levi went to the back door of the great house. Too timid to knock, he stood in the cold darkness in his sad state of innocence. He smeared tears and snot across his face with the back of his hand, waiting to tell Master Mack he left the slave sell because he didn't want to be a crazy nigger. The longer he waited and shivered, the stronger it registered in his mind that a straw tick with the others on the floor of the quarter where Will Parker slept was the only relief for him from cold nights and lonely days ahead.

God, he was so cold. His teeth chattered. A knife dropped from the bundle. He stared as if it was a dark omen, something left by his mother for him to protect himself. He picked it up, stopped sobbing, examined it, and stopped shivering. Will had called him mean names, even dared Levi to call him the same. Will talked about nothing except running away, all the time running away. Levi walked toward the barn. He'd fix Will, fix him in a way that would make Master Mack sell him. Fix him so he'd look like a trouble maker. Fix him so he'd be no good for anything.

Will Parker sat on his straw mattress. He felt that at any moment the slave traders would storm the quarter and drag him away. Or else that when Master Mack returned, he would make Mr. Groit tie his arms and flog him. He draped his arm around his knees, leaned back against the wall, stared and stared at the rafters until he could see each one, though they were blackened with soot and covered with last summer's cobwebs. If Mr. Groit would beat a slave girl almost to death, what would he do to him? One thing was for certain, if Master Mack tried to sell him or if Mr. Groit tried to flog him, either one would have to do it running doggone fast. If Will slept at all that night, he did with his shoes on.

Will tried drawing an image of Tawney in the dark space above him, but so many thoughts rushed him. He had seen her about, but really hadn't known her. She lived in the great house, isolated from him. He was a field nigger. That's what he was all right, no more than a mangy soup hound pissing around with Levi, waiting for Master Mack to sell him. He had no more sense than Master's he-hawing mules. But Tawney was a servant and for that she had learned dignity. Dignity that Mr. Groit tried to strip from her. Dignity that Will would never have. That made her smart, smarter than he would ever be, maybe smart enough to help him run away. She touched something deep inside him earlier that night lying in the old conjure woman's cabin while the slave women pulled her away from death. She was brave too and didn't act dickty like Grandmom Rosey. Grandmom acted more and more like she was Master, ordering Will around like he was her nigger. But she was one too, a house nigger like old white-glove-wearing Silent Charles, the butler. And it made no difference how long either one had been at Roedown, Master Mack would sell them too as soon as he would get the mind to do it.

"Did you hear about it?"

Will's thoughts were interrupted by a long rusty man walking through the quarter talking loudly to his circle of friends. Rusty's reddish-brown curly hair lay in every direction. With small gray eyes, a raggedy mustache hanging over his lip and a gap where his left eye tooth had been, Rusty fitted Grandmom Rosey's description of a haunt. His back was swayed like a bay horse, his stomach hung like he had a ripe watermelon in it.

"Old Groit must be having a fit," Rusty said. "He knows better'n the rest of us that Bob Wallace is Master Mack's main nigger, but damned if he didn't hem him up against one of them Catalpa trees awhile ago."

Bob, a tall thin man with skin that shined like patent leather, spit green and growled at everyone except Master Mack. His eyes were big and white. The few times he laughed, he closed them as if laughing was a pain, a pain he knew his eyes couldn't hide. Bob smelled like the mint he chewed as if it were tobacco. Little slave children all over Roedown stayed away from him.

"Wallace stand up to'em?" Shorty Grover asked. Shorty sat on a broken wood crate smoking his own-grown tobacco and biting a pipe he had hewn from cedar wood. His brown eyes that had often sparkled and danced with Josie's were empty as a blank sheet of paper.

32

"Hell naw," Rusty said. "Wallace tried to tell him somebody beat the hell out of ole Jericho. But Groit called him, heh heh heh." Rusty rubbed his hands over his head and face while he laughed. "Woooee, he called him a loathy lump'a coal and said he'd stomp a mud-hole in Wallace's ass if he didn't git outta his face."

"I can see Wallace now," Shorty said. "He just kept on spittin' that shit and sayin' yessuh, yessuh. Then soon's Master come around he be bowing and grinning like nothin' happen and he's the best kept spook in heaven. But he ain't but a frog's leap from living in this here quarter with us. Master oughta' sold him instead of Josie."

"Bob may be Master's best nigger," Uncle Sammy said, "but he ain't crazy enough to jump on no white man. Now puff on that awhile, Shorty, and you Rusty, take that racket out of here. Some of us want to sleep."

Laughter at Uncle Sammy spread the length and breadth of the quarter, but Will didn't hear it repeated over and over again.

"I'm sneaking down there tomorrow," he said to himself.

Will tried to bring Tawney's image to himself again, but a sudden commotion along the wall close by startled him. A crouching shadow stumbled. Levi fell on a sleeping boy's head. Will rolled off his bed.

"Ouch! Help!" The startled lad, wrapped like a mummy from his head to his ankles, twisted and jerked in a thin blanket, trying to get up.

Levi regained his balance, but stumbled again. His knife slid across the bare wood floor.

"For real you'all, the boogey man's done got me." The boy's stocking feet rose from the floor and fell in a frantic motion.

"He sold my mama. Master Mack sold my mama and he the cause of it." Levi stood there crying and pointing his finger at the opened doorway through which Will had fled.

Will ran like only he could, past the field workers' huts in the dell, up the slope in the direction of the main entrance to Roedown.

"Always trying to get me to run away. Now see what he done."

"Gimme that knife, boy," Rusty said, picking it up. "Where you get somethin' all new and shiny like this?"

"He's Josie's boy," Shorty Glover said. "Leave him be."

All of them knew. They sighed together, even those seemingly half asleep, and bent their heads as if silently praying.

"Looks like Rosey's grandboy got two counts agin' him, don't matter what she done to keep him straight," Uncle Sammy mumbled.

"What's that you say, Sammy?" Rusty said.

"Oh." Uncle Sammy raised his head. "Nothing that 'mount to much. C'mon over here with me for tonight," he said to Levi.

"Something about two counts," Aunt Katie said. "And I know you talking about that fighting young'un 'cause he shot outta here like Satan's poured coal-oil on his behind and set it afire," Aunt Katie said.

"Rosey can treat that ugly rascal like he somebody's white boy all she want," Shorty Glover said. "But I can tell he go for bad, and now he preaching running away? Shit, he good as gone on down the river."

Well past ten o'clock, candles and oil lanterns burned as if it was the night before the Fourth of July celebration when Master Mack, exhausted from his long trip to Annapolis, stopped suddenly at the entrance from Queen Anne Road. Why were the goats he raised for milk and cheese out of their pen and wandering through his grape arbor? In a minute or so they would have been through the entrance and in the woods across Queen Anne Road. He turned them around and set the horse pulling his surrey to chasing them up the lane. Someone standing in the alcove beyond the barnyard waved a lamp. It wouldn't be Groit, Master Mack knew that. He called out to the man he expected would be there.

"Bob," Master Mack barked, "get ahold of those two goats there."

Bob Wallace chilled right down to the bone at the sound of his enraged master's voice. The quarter darkened as fast as it would if a windstorm had suddenly blown in from the Chesapeake right through the slave section.

"Yessuh Master, glad you back." Wallace held the light over his head.

It shone on the angry set of Master Mack's jaw. His cold blue eyes were dark as thunder clouds.

"You're not standing here just waiting for me?" Master Mack saw Wallace swallow hard, trying to manage an answer without revealing his fear.

"Why yessuh, Master, and I been out here seeing just what I could do for old Jericho."

"Well, c'mon. Out with it. What's ailing the mule?"

"I don't rightly know what happened," Wallace said. "One of his front legs broke. Somebody musta've done it after dark."

"I'll have your hide for this."

"Yessuh, Master."

"Just what in hell caused this?" He waved his hand as if to say he suddenly changed his mind. He didn't want the answer from a slave.

"A whole lot went on today," Wallace said.

Master Mack shook his head. "Never mind. Run tell Mr. Groit I want him. No, tell him I'm back. And be damn sure you tell him only that I'm back." Master Mack balled his fist and pointed his index finger at the spot between Wallace's eyes.

"He and the hired help been riding all over Roedown since before dark." Bob said. "There he go now."

They watched the overseer dismount and hurry into the great house.

Master Mack scowled. "You've been here a long time, Bob," he said. "I don't rightly know how long, Master." Wallace answered him in a soft, disquieting voice.

Master Mack rubbed his chin. It was a reflex action for breaking an iron rule. Never, for any reason, did he reveal his thoughts to a slave. If he spoke at all, it was a cold, simple directive. That's what he hired Groit to do, enforce his orders.

Wallace wondered why Master Mack asked him about his stay at Roedown. He knew he had been a trusty slave, one who didn't crave learning. He couldn't read or write.

"It's a right smart walk to the great house seeing how you been riding so long," Wallace said. His palm sweated. He wanted to scratch his arm pits. "You want that I ride you over there?"

"No," Master Mack said. "Unhitch the surrey and do what you can for old Jericho." Then he muttered, "Until I get to the bottom of all this." Master Mack disappeared into pitch darkness.

Bob began to worry. Master Mack knew he had been born at Roedown. As far as Bob could tell, he had seen between thirty-two and thirty-five harvests. But only Master Mack knew his correct age. His father recorded it in the big ledger. From the day Bob's mother told him he was a slave for life to that cold November night, he never thought much about it. Never cheated in his work, never dragged his feet. He just chewed his mint and growled inside himself while working from sunup to sunset, building fences, plowing, herding cattle, branding calves, pitching hay, picking tobacco, teaching little slaves the inevitable and doing everything else that needed attending. Why did Master Mack ask him? It could mean only one thing and Lilly's stomach had swollen about as far as it could swell.

Master hurried along the lane around the pond in the foggy darkness thinking. If it wasn't for that damned underground railroad and that wretched Harriet Tubman wench picking the Eastern and Western Chesapeake shores clean, he and other horse breeders wouldn't have much trouble finding runaways holed-up in the woods. He'd get tough like his brother, like his father Major Brodgen had been. Every morning at daybreak, a head count, and he'd check the ledger closely, keep track of the young ones. For every one that escaped, he'd sell two. Enforce the twilight curfew. Get rid of the infirmed and the no accounts. Stop feeling sorry for the old and feeble. Even make an example with the whip if it came to that. So engrossed in thought, he didn't notice the rhythmic stride of swift flat feet touching and lifting from the turf until the sound was almost upon him. Quickly, he drew his revolver, took a bead on the sound. But it moved away from him. He sensed it was a person, most likely a young slave on the run. He wouldn't shoot, too much money lost on a dead young buck, But he would get him, lay twenty hard lashes on his back and sell him down the river unless it was Will Parker. He was close to fifteen, big and headstrong. His body was a mass of muscle.

Will heard someone coming toward him. Too misty and dark for him to see but it was either Mr. Groit, or Master Mack returning. Grandmom's warning rang in his mind; the fox is watching you and if you see him, you better know that's what he planned. Probably wasn't the overseer. He was the bear and would've shown himself in one way or another.

"All right," Master Mack called out, "turn the dogs loose."

Jesus, Will thought, it was Master. His knees weakened. Any second he expected to hear a pistol shot, feel the deadly ball, or worse yet, hear the big, hungry dogs sniffing every step of Roedown until they found him. Oh God, what could he do? He really hadn't given much attention to the dim lantern shining near the alcove until Wallace swung it crosswise several times and blew it out. Steal a horse. No, Master Mack would hunt him to the end of the world. He'd kill him. Yet, a horse could run faster than dogs.

But somebody at the stable with a lantern had told Master Mack that Will was out there. His only chance, hurry to the stable from the back way, saddle up in the stall, and with a head-start on a fast pony, he could ride far away, that way, north to wherever Queen Anne Road would take him.

Will crossed the race track and climbed through the fence. There he crouched beside a fence post and waited. Who could that be near the alcove? Will sneaked closer, to the bottom of the slope down from the stable and lay still. The pungent odor of the stable lay heavily on the ground. Slowly, Will inched up the embankment. Then Wallace hawked. Will knew that sound and hearing it, he smelled the mint. It mattered little whether Wallace actually spit. How in the world could he know? But there he was, waiting to pounce on Will. The snake only needed one bite, Grandmom Rosey had warned him. Will slid backwards down the slope.

In the cold damp night Bob stood chewing and staring at darkness with the unlit lantern in his hand. Nobody except Master Mack handled the dogs. They would rip anything black into tiny pieces, Wallace too, and Master knew that. But the decision was not Wallace's to make. He would tend to the goats, then open wide the dog compound gate and pray.

Hearing Wallace leave, Will climbed the embankment and went inside the alcove. He walked by a few dark stables. Turning around to assure himself no one was creeping behind him, his gaze swept out across the high ground above the fog shrouding the valley, beyond the race track. Master Mack appeared in the circular driveway under the light of two lanterns atop ornamental poles at the oak door. Charles the butler opened the door and bowed. Master Mack entered, snatched the door free of Charles' gloved hands and slammed it so hard the shock tremor vibrated clear across the track.

The only lights burning were in the great house. Roedown was as silent as the graves in the slave burial lot. Every little sound startled Will; a flutter of wings in an almost barren tree, a chirping bird. An owl hooted, something rustled in the brush close to the quarter. He quickened his pace but didn't run, it wasn't the dogs. Will walked casually into the quarter, trying to conceal his fright, and fell upon his tick mattress panting and shaking. May as well face it, he didn't have the guts to run. He wasn't any tougher than the old broken down men who wanted to crawl into the ground when Mr. Groit whipped Tawney.

Late in the night, Wallace walked in the young slaves' end of the quarter as if he owned it. The lantern he had turned up so brightly cast an ugly, spooky hue across his face. Will eased the blanket over most of his face and peeped at Wallace, checking for empty beds. He examined the cot of every young boy and girl who lived there. Will faked sleep when Wallace found him on his tick mattress.

The bright light and Wallace's movement awakened much of the quarter. Many sat up, wondering and watching. Shorty Glover reached under his bed and gripped a piece of iron rod he had taken from the blacksmith shop. Wallace kept tracking until he found Levi wrapped in a coarse horse blanket asleep beside Uncle Sammy. Coming back to Will, Wallace stared, as if doubting that he was asleep, telling Will without speaking a word exactly what would happen to him. A voice deep within Will said as clearly as if it had been Grandmom Rosey, you are the rabbit.

After Wallace had left and darkness once again settled over the restless quarter, Will lay there scared, confused, and lonely, thinking of his first encounter with him.

They were on the ridge that day in the North pasture. Wallace was breaking Will in, teaching him how to slave. Will scuffled with the plow behind the mule, turning over new ground. His little arms couldn't steady the plow at an even level beneath the earth's surface, but Jericho kept on trudging along as if no one was behind him. Will pressed down on the handles as hard as he could. The blade dug deeper and deeper. Wallace walked along as if nothing was wrong until it went in so deep Jericho couldn't pull another step. Jericho made a mighty lunge. Will let go the handles. Wallace grabbed then and struggled. It took all the hee-hawing and jeering Wallace knew to keep the stubborn mule from tearing Master Mack's plow out of the ground and running off.

"Boy," Wallace said, "don't get the notion that you won't have to break the ground if you break the plow. You Master Mack's slave and if you want to grow up here in the best comfort of any place around, you better show Master you worth something to him."

Wallace placed his hand on little Will's shoulder, but Will twisted free and stared up at the trusty nigger. Wallace stared down at the defiant, scared slave boy.

That happened not long after Will moved into the quarter, long about the same time Grandmom began teaching him to run like the great African warriors and sometimes called him Ofeutey. He drifted off to sleep thinking about his grandfather.

Shortly before daybreak while jack frost was still doing his mischief, Grandmom Rosey sneaked into the sleeping quarter. She eased the door open enough to wiggle through and pulled back a pieced-together burlap sack partition around Aunt Katie's bed.

"C'mon in here child," Aunt Katie said. "I weren't sleeping much no way."

"Ain't got but a bite of time, just put my pot on. But girl, I'll bust if I don't tell you this," She lowered her voice to a softer whisper and giggled. "Sure glad my name ain't Margaret. Yes indeedy I am."

"Honey, hush," Aunt Katie said.

"Say what?" a female voice said from a dark place.

Grandmom tried but she could hardly whisper. "I couldn't hear everything. Master Mack took her upstairs to their bedroom, and he was raising cain in a way he don't do too regular. One hell of a mess you and that stupid redneck made, I heard him say."

"Master Mack said that?" A little wiry man with sad eyes and swollen sinuses sat up on a bed he had assembled on four tree stumps and two one-by-eight planks.

"She didn't talk back though until Master said she and Groit had ruined his investment. Told her that she had Tawney whipped only because she couldn't stand her looks."

Grandmom puckered her lips, switched her narrow hips and extended her finger in the manner of a dainty dame. " 'Damn you, dare compare me to that wretched nigger.' That's what Miss Margaret yelled at him."

The hushed roar of laughter sounded like old lions tickling each other.

"Then," Grandmom Rosey said, "Master woke up the whole house. That wretched nigger cost me a fortune to train so you'd have a maid personalized for your every whim. Now she's too refined for you."

"But Margaret wouldn't be outdone," Grandmom said. "You've lost ten times that much at the race track, she yelled and he yelled something, I don't remember what. Few minutes later the back door slammed and..."

"Well," Uncle Sammy said, "word's getting around that he's about lost his britches at the race track."

"Can't I talk to Katie without you, Mr. Nebbynose?" Grandmom said.

"Poor white folks, hired hands, everybody's talking about him like he's a dog," Uncle Sammy said.

"Sam, for God's sake."

"All right, go'n on, let the water out your trough. Can't get no sleep 'round here no way."

"I'm trying to tell you," Grandmom said, "the bear is dead. Master gave Groit two hours after sunup to clear out, whip, butt, and bucket."

"Say what?" Shorty Glover said. "Now who's going to hound the hell out of us?" A cloud of tobacco smoke enveloped him.

"Shut the hell up, Glover," Rusty said.

They waited in anxious silence, balancing between sudden joy and fear. Would the next overseer be as vicious as Groit?

"Ain't going to be no more overseer," Grandmom Rosey said.

Uncle Sammy sat up. "Wonder if he fixing to sell the plantation?" His voice cracked with emotion.

"He made Mint Wallace foreman," Grandmom said.

"Bob Wallace, that old weed-chewing nigger?" Shorty said.

"What the hell is a foreman?" Uncle Sammy said. He coughed. "Do Jesus, Shorty, ease up on that thing, will you?"

"I don't rightly know," Grandmom said. "But I know he's in charge of everybody in the field."

"Sure glad I'm through with the field," Aunt Katie said. "So long as he don't come in here messing around, me and that nigger'll be okay. I hope so, anyway," she said with a sigh.

"I guess this day had to come," Uncle Sammy said. "Black slave man overseer of another black slave man." He looked forlorn.

"She said foreman, Sammy, not overseer," Aunt Katie said.

"It's all the same. You don't understand what Master Mack's doing," he said.

"And I suppose you do?" she said. "Whatever he's doing, it's his business and there ain't nothing you can do about it."

Shorty took his pipe from his browning teeth. "If that nigger tries to flog me, I'll bury my knife so deep in his side, he'll think it's a broken rib."

"Uh-oh, you all getting too loud," Grandmom Rosey said. "I'm scooting out of here."

"Better give me your quiet ear just a mite 'fore you go," Aunt Katie said. Grandmom moved closer to here.

"Your grandboy and the young'un of that woman Shorty was running with. You know, Master sold her yestiddy."

"Josie," Grandmom asked.

"Yeah, that's her," Aunt Katie said. She whispered while Will slept and the old folks quibbled on about their dread, confirming their suspicions of Wallace.

"Young'un." Grandmom's biting voice shocked Will out of a reverie. She had circled the quarter and come in the young slaves' entrance. He sat up, rubbing sleep from his eyes, so sleepy he hurt all over.

"Yes'um," Will said. He didn't try to hide his gruff attitude.

"Lean over this way." She stood beside his bed.

Will just watched her, wondering if she would smack his face.

"Want me to snatch you, boy?" She knew better than he that strong discipline ran deep.

"No ma'am." He turned on his side, facing her.

"You ever hear that train song?"

Will turned his head to avoid her searching stare. Right then was a chance to tell her he simply didn't know who whispered the word in the songs that drifted across the fields, among the trees. But it was hard, she always seemed as if it was a task to keep from clawing his eyes out.

"One night, wasn't too long ago, I heard somebody singing like you used to sing. It was so pretty, I thought I was dreaming," he said.

"Whydn't you go look?"

"I can't say why 'cause I don't know, Grandmom."

Grandmom Rosey sighed. Her bony, dried fingers twitched. "Boy, you so hard-headed. How many times must I say it? You got to move fast with every chance 'cause you can't out-wit the fox. Running off before a sale, coming back with a snake..."

"Levi? Naw, Grandmom. I saw Mr. Wallace acting just like one."

"That boy tried to kill you, didn't he?"

"Levi? He wouldn't squash a gnat."

"His mama was sold today. He blamed it on you."

"Levi?"

"Everybody at Roedown knows that except you. He'll probably tell the bear you busted up Jericho and the bear will tell the fox," Grandmom said.

Will sat up. Scattered thoughts began connecting in his mind, Levi's shadow on the wall, his screams and yells at Will when he ran, a trap that almost snagged him.

"He got no more kin folks, Grandmom. He's scared."

"Fool." Her angry whispering sounded as if she were dragging her voice over gravel. "Can't you understand, a snake is a snake, it don't matter why. Stay away from him. Make yourself some plans. Be quick about it. Tomorrow may be your last day here. For sure it won't be much longer if Master Mack catches you hanging around Tawney's cabin."

Chapter Four

The rooster's crowing just before daybreak seemed to come only minutes after Grandmom left. Bob Wallace rang the bell in the nippy gray dawn that sent the gangs to the harvest fields. Then he mounted the big gray swayback horse that Groit had ridden, but word had already passed from the quarter to every corner of Roedown and just as Will suspected, Wallace singled him out, said he'd work the hell out of him.

Will knew Wallace didn't like him, hard work would be the price he'd pay. So what, all slaves worked hard and he was stronger than the best. Grandmom didn't like him either, and she suddenly didn't like Tawney. Only because he hadn't run away. If freedom was so easy and she knew so much, why was she still there, drying up and getting meaner every day? Mean like Aunt Katie, like Shorty Glover always threatening to kill somebody, or like Uncle Sammy always grumbling and gawking at Will sideways. Seemed like old niggers were naturally mean.

By the time red streaks of morning sun had reached across the sky and were burning off the late autumn fog, Will had split logs and cut a pile of fire-wood. He loaded an ox-cart, hauled the wood to kindling bins, went back to the woods and loaded the cart again. In the clearing he passed Master Mack astride his white stallion and felt a pounding in his temples. He passed Levi digging potatoes with an old slave. The pain extended across his forehead like an iron rod pressing against it. On the next trip he changed directions and hurried by Tawney's cabin. The pounding didn't relent, but a closeness to her, the image of her fighting back at least kept that freedom fire inside him from petering to ashes. He felt drawn to Tawney like moisture drawn from earth to the sky.

Sleep came easily. In the passing days, Wallace tried his best to work the defiant nature out of Will, tried to make him yield to the force of slavery. Each day though, passing by Tawney's place rekindled the fire of determination to withstand Wallace's demands. At night Will fell asleep with her on his mind.

One night while he plunged headlong in that narrow strip of time between stretches of sleep, his mother came to him. It seemed so real, her coming to him. Or was he going to her? She was in chains and crying. Was it her face? He couldn't really tell, she died so long ago. The face was lonely and cold as the dead of winter. An empty face, crying, chains—he had never seen these things in his mother. It must have been Tawney's face. His mother coming to him after she had been gone so long, with Tawney's suffering and pain. What did it mean? Who could he ask?

Will went by Tawney's cabin every day. He would stop and look around to see if Master Mack, Grandmom, Levi or Wallace were watching. Then he'd

41

walk away, telling himself again and again that Grandmom Rosey didn't know what she was talking about. Yet, he couldn't muster enough courage to ignore her warning. Weeks passed until anxiety overshadowed his timidity, overcame his reasoning. One cold winter's day he walked right up without looking around and knocked.

"Tawney, Tawney," he called, barely louder than a whisper. She certainly did take her time answering.

"Tawney!"

"Uh-hunh?"

"It's me."

"Who?"

"Sh," he said, "not so loud."

"Who is it, acting a fool?"

"Me, Will Parker,"

"I don't know no Will Parker. What you want?"

"I just come to er-ah. Think you might need a nice fresh drink'a water?"

"Sounds to me like you trying to ease your way in here," she said, "but I sure could use a cool drink."

"Thank you, Jesus," Will said quietly. First time in his life he had thanked Jesus for anything. He opened the door, looked at her face, and though it was twisted in agony, every single detail was just as he remembered. He felt the hurt he had felt before. Looking at her, not knowing what to say, he was suddenly embarrassed, standing there with his hair not combed, his shirt torn, his clothes dirty.

The furniture in her cabin was an odd configuration or another of packing crates. She sat on one, wrapped in old blankets made of many different things. The fire in the chilly room had dwindled to a single charcoal ember.

"Your water bucket is about empty," he said.

"Yes," she said, "and I thank you."

Will's heart jumped. "I'll be right back," he said, stumbling over his own feet in the doorway. The wooden bucket made a hollow clapping sound against the frame structure. Tawney watched him and smiled.

Will returned with the bucket half-full. His right leg was soaked from knee to foot.

"Ain't you cold?" Will said, while rinsing the cup and refilling it. With nervous hands, he gave it to her.

"It's cold in here most of the time," Tawney said, gulping the water, "but nobody much comes by now that I get around a bit." She drank another cupful.

She got up, struggling to stand, and walked stiffly to the wood box behind the stove. Will saw bruises and healing scabs where the tattered clothing exposed her arms and thighs.

"Ain't much kindling left and I have to make do so I'll have some left for tonight."

"I can bring you fresh water and kindling every day and I can sneak some food too," Will said.

"That's mighty nice, big boy." She looked at him with a bitter, painful expression. "But you musn't get yourself in trouble on account of me."

"I ain't afraid of trouble. I eat it and spit it out like tobacco juice."

"That's good, being brave, Will. But don't act crazy. Master's going to sell me. She'll make him do it."

Will raised an eyebrow. "If I help you that means I'm crazy? That means I got snake juice running through me too?"

Tawney looked at Will as if she had suddenly awakened from a deep sleep. "I don't know much about snakes," she said, "but if you sneak food from Master Mack and give it to somebody you know nothing about, yes, that's crazy."

"If I want to be free, that means I'm crazy?"

"You helping me because you want to be free? Lord boy, I just finished telling you..."

"If I bring you kindling and water, can we talk about running away together?"

"Run away?" She smiled a little to cover her uneasiness. "I can hardly walk."

"But you live in the great house and smart slaves live there. You could teach me things."

"You got no people here?" Tawney said.

"Grandmom Rosey, she's all."

Tawney chuckled. "She's a plenty, no doubt about that. Ask her to help you."

"She fusses all the time," he said. "Stay shed of the bear, don't cross the fox. And the snake, he only needs one bite. Then she gets mad 'cause I don't know what she's talking about."

Tawney's lip trembled slightly. "You've been here with me a good little spell. It won't look proper if you stay too long."

"I do like I promised tomorrow," Will said. "You'll see."

She looked away and nodded meekly.

Will went to her as winter dragged on into longer and colder days with the misery taking its toll on the old folks. Tawney accepted her good fortune of having Will to help her. They talked so much about the fox that when Will would see it, poised on one front leg, its keen nose tilted, he would turn in all directions looking for Master Mack. On occasion, Will indeed saw him.

The snake cared nothing about anyone, including Master Mack. Will questioned that until Tawney explained why it would never bite Master Mack. It hid inside certain slaves, was ugly, sneaky, and always mad. Master Mack knew that, Grandmom Rosey too. For that reason she talked in riddles—spoke the word in a word—sounding dumb at times. Master Mack manipulated the snake in certain folks, made them sneaky and say nasty things about each other. When the snake revealed itself, too late, it had already bitten.

Will sat on the floor, his knees drawn to his chest, the child-like look in his eyes, trusting and curious.

"And that's how snake juice gets inside you and runs you crazy, hunh Tawney?"

She laughed heartily. "Will, you only crazy if you act crazy. Old folks are afraid of crazy niggers because they make trouble for everybody. And now it's time for you to get back to the quarter."

One day he asked Tawney how many harvests she had seen at Roedown.

"Just two," she replied.

Will frowned. "Aww, Tawney, I don't believe that. You ain't no little baby."

She laughed. "I'm twenty," she said, and then explained to Will that fifteen harvests meant he was that many years of age.

"I was born in Virginia," she said. "Master Mack bought me when I was little and sent me to work in a mansion, a great big place with twenty rooms and plenty servants. I learned to cipher, to curtsy, to do whatever a rich mistress needed to keep her pretty. I lived there for a while, then Master Mack brought me here. After a spell, he'd take me back to learn more just for her, the poor, helpless critter."

"How can she be all that with so many niggers waiting on her hand and foot?"

"Trash," Tawney said. "If Master Mack owned all the world, she'd still be trash. It's in her blood, ain't nothing she can do about it."

"She make old Groit flog you?"

"Last time she smacked me, I threw her dirty bath water on her."

Will felt himself getting nervous. "Guess I be getting on up to the quarter." He didn't want to see it happening again in his mind. It made him feel so violent. Lately, he only wanted to feel warm around her.

Mid winter passed, the days grew longer. Will asked more questions. She gave him answers, answers that wrung out more questions, sometimes deep, sometimes more intimate. Then she would send him on his way.

The severe cold abated. A warming trend began. Will noticed tender blue, white, and orange crocus blossoms peeping from their winter hiding place under hardy branches of evergreen. He looked at them and saw Tawney's pretty face, his promise of hope. One early April day while he tarried there, Wallace came upon him.

"Boy, Master Mack say he's taking you to the fairgrounds today."

Will bolted, but Wallace grabbed his arms and bear hugged him.

Will struggled. "Master Mack ain't taking me nowhere."

"Aww chicken-shit, stop blowing hot air. Ain't nothing you can do about it except run away and run the rest of your life. Ain't many that don't get caught."

The nerves in Will's legs twitched. His heart pounded. "Lemme go." Wallace squeezed him tighter.

"That gal making you piss strong, making you think you a man. I keep telling you, young fool, you got your dreams mixed up. You picking them flowers, for what?"

Will twisted and turned, daring Wallace to release him. Wallace laughed and uttered in Will's ear.

"I heard Master bragging to some horse traders that you can really fight. Planting season's here. What little fighting you might can do beats working in the hot sun, don't it?"

Will couldn't force himself to believe Master Mack had said that. Though Wallace had earned a fairly decent reputation of trust among some slaves, he hadn't convinced Will that he wasn't a snake.

"Will." Master Mack startled him, descending the steps above the garden. He actually spoke Will's name, first time ever.

"Feeling good today?" Master Mack said.

Will didn't answer. He stood there, suddenly limp in Wallace's arms with his mouth agape, afraid to answer him.

Master Mack stood straight and expanded his chest. Will was almost as tall as he. He'd guess five-eleven or so and weighted about one hundred seventy. He still had a lot of growing to do.

"Let him go, Wallace. Did you eat good this morning?"

"Yes sir," Will lied.

Master Mack laughed. "Go on back to the kitchen. Grandmom Rosey's got a nice, hot breakfast for you. He can go by himself, Wallace."

Will felt Wallace's eyes boring a hole in the back of his head when he walked around the great house. Never in his entire life had anyone ever asked him if he'd had enough to eat. Eating was a matter of survival and he'd become proficient. Like wild animals and fowl, he ate what he could find or catch—apples, pears, raw vegetables, crawdads he caught in the creek and fried with a little stolen lard, a stolen chicken or two, anything to supplement the skimpy rations served in the quarter. He didn't know what to make of such good treatment. But he wouldn't worry about it now.

Grandmom Rosey stopped him at the door. "You ain't eating any of my food without washing your face and hands."

"I washed when I got up," Will said.

"Down there behind the quarter with the rest of them filthy young'uns? You half-washed, hit at yourself with the water, mostly missing."

Just the smell of it, hot biscuits and red eye gravy with grits and fried potatoes with a little chunk of smoked ham made his stomach jump.

"But Grandmom, Master Mack said..."

"Boy," Grandmom Rosey's feisty voice scaled to a high pitch, "I ain't studying about what Master told you. Don't ever tell me what Master Mack say when I tell you to do something."

Will noticed her hands shaking as if in any minute she might throw the hot skillet at him.

She suspected Master Mack was somewhere waiting and listening. But even if he wasn't, she was sick and tired of Will. All the effort she had put into making him reason things for himself, taking a chance on getting herself sold or punished, had resulted in nothing. He'd missed chance after chance to get away and now Master had captured his mind with one hot meal.

When he returned with a shiny new face and sparkling hands, Grandmom set his food on a crate outside beside a side door that was the slaves' entrance to the kitchen. They dared not use the main door that opened to the veranda where Master and Miss Margaret sometimes ate and entertained.

"Morning." Silent Charles the butler came into the kitchen singing the greeting for his early cup of coffee.

Grandmom chuckled. He would speak again for breakfast, but not anymore until tomorrow morning. Sipping the hot brew, Charles turned suddenly and stood there in his black suit and white tie glaring at Will, sitting on his reserved seat.

"How'd a field nigger come to get a breakfast like that and eat in my seat?" Charles had sat there every morning, weather permitting, for well now—as far back as he could remember.

"Get out my way," Grandmom Rosey said, frowning at him.

"Look at him hogging it down, eating better than you and I ever do. Damn disgusting, not one lick of class. Wonder where Master found him."

"Ask him," Grandmom Rosey said. "He's got a mouth. Now move."

"Tsh, tsh," Silent Charles said, going to the screen door.

Disgusting as it must have been to make Silent Charles talk, it was quite hurting for Grandmom, the immediate change reflected in her hungry young grandson's face, the worrying over Master Mack's aim for him. Will felt warm and mellow, like a pet pig, better than when Tawney had touched his inner self with words that made him sparkle.

Will's forearms and biceps strained against the fabric of his ragged shirt. A piece of rope around his slim, hard waist supported his pantaloons of which the ragged edges hung to his calves, revealing tight, bulging muscles. His stockings drooped over his shoe tops. Each curl of his dark brown close-cropped hair stood separate, tight and hard as bailed wire.

"My word, he's a mind to chew hisself up if you don't give him some more," Silent Charles said, talking loudly enough for Will to hear.

But Will wasted not one moment of thought on Silent Charles watching him. Nor did he notice Wallace watching until he spit a mouthful of that smelly mint.

"Master's waiting for you, boy."

Will looked away from the empty plate and sighed. There wasn't another person on the entire plantation who could say boy as nasty as Wallace. Sounded like he vomited the word.

"You ain't fool enough to run away is you, boy? If you do, Master's most likely to shoot you. Smart nigger knows he always totin' a gun,"

Wallace was probably right, Will thought, climbing onto the buckboard behind Master Mack. But if Master tried selling him, he'd have to gun him down or outrun him. When they turned onto the highway he wondered if he'd ever see Roedown again. Tawney? A voice inside him whispered yes. He guessed he'd miss Grandmom Rosey.

Chapter Five

Master Mack lit a cigar and set the black stallion to a lively gait in the high road along the ridge. He didn't say one word to Will, didn't even look around, as if he knew Will wasn't brave enough to run away.

Will sat there looking at the dense, quiet woods, visualizing it full of crafty foxes waiting to trap him and big ugly bears eager to eat him alive should he be fool enough to jump from the wagon.

They approached a fork in the road where a planter in a buckboard with four young burly slaves Will's age, waited beside a sign post. The left road led to Baltimore, the right one led to Annapolis. Master Mack took the one towards Annapolis and slowed the horse to a walk. The planter, robust with flabby jowls, put his swayback to trotting and rode up behind them. He wore a wide-brim hat and smoked a pipe that dipped to his chest.

"I see you brung your boy, aye Mack." The planter looked at Will. "You say he's powerful? Looks like he's hanging between death and a potato peel compared to my Nap."

"Money, Jonah," Master Mack said. "Idle talk pesters the hell out of me."

The two slavers rode along side by side while the young slaves stared at Will. He stared back.

"Don't reckon I'll be needing it, but I brought me some along just in case you're crazy enough to wager anything substantial on that little wiener boy of yourn."

Jonah slapped his knee and roared with laughter. So did the boys sitting with their legs hanging over the back of the buckboard. Will watched the planter slowly turn around. His jolly face and sparkling blue eyes molded into a scowl. His slaves guffawing ebbed. They stared at the ground.

"All right, Nap," Jonah whispered with a gritty voice. "Work him up."

"Hey," Nap said, "li'l ole burr head wienie nigger."

Nap was built like a pickle barrel with a cannonball head. Will acted as if he didn't hear him.

"Don't let him rile you," Master Mack said.

Rile me, Will thought, whatever that meant. He wouldn't fight that no-neck nigger just because he didn't like Will's hair. And anyway, he hadn't said anything nasty about Will's mother or Grandmom Rosey or Tawney.

"Hey wienie boy, you can't talk? You just get here from Africa and can't talk American like we talks it?"

Africa, Will thought and remembered Grandmom Rosey telling him about his granddaddy, Ofeutey, the African warrior.

"You're not afraid of him, are you Will?" Master Mack said.

"Will?" Master Mack turned around and caught Will glaring at him. "Say boy, I thought you had learned your manners."

"Naw sir," Will said. "I ain't afraid of nobody, but I can't fight unless I'm mad."

"This is different," Master Mack said. "This is prize-fighting and he's trying to get you all heated so you can't think. Makes it easy for him to kick your ass."

"Ain't nobody kicking me!" Will tried to snatch back his words, realizing to whom he spoke.

"Thatta boy, that's the fighting spirit," Master Mack said, though Will's impulsive outburst cautioned him to remember watching Will chop wood and sensing an urge for freedom cutting at the young slave. Smart master that he was, he would remedy that.

"Well listen there, Nap," Jonah said. "He can talk and he's got a little smoke in'em too. I don't expect much fire, though. Do you?"

"Just smoke, like a pile'a damp leaves, Master," Nap said.

"See what I mean?" Master Mack said.

"Yes sir," Will said sheepishly.

Some distance ahead in a clearing Will noticed a lot of excited white men in a circle yelling and jumping around like jack rabbits. He thought someone had started a fire until they were closer and he smelled their cigars. When Master Mack and Master Jonah stopped at the makeshift corral they each alighted from the drivers' seats, shook hands, and laughed at something they said out of Will's earshot.

In a circle Will saw two young slaves nose to nose trading punches with bare knuckles, bent on knocking out each other's brains. Their faces were puffed, raw, and unsightly as freshly butchered pork. Then Master Mack began talking loudly about Will's super strength and making bets. Master Jonah said he was a liar and told some jokes about Will. That actually made Will feel pretty good until over there under a clump of trees a sight and terrifying sound caught his attention.

A band of bedraggled men, all chained together, dragging by in single file near the clearing, made him stare still as if he had turned to stone. Behind them a two-wheel cart drawn by a mule moved slowly, with the lead woman of a solitary line of female slaves chained to it. The lot of them, tall and short, plump and lean, all shades of complexions, slow-dragged along, covered with layers of dust, tugging and twisting against the forward trudge of mule and men. Children and tots wrapped in filthy rags bounced around in the cart over the rutted trail. Their cries set the women to wailing, a wail that drew attention of the gamblers at the fight, set their nerves to quivering.

"Git that goddamn noise away from here. Stop spooking the fighters," one of the gamblers hollered. Others made the fighters continue hammering each other with threatening yells and gestures.

49

A red-necked little prune of a man waving a fistful of money yelled. "Gawd-dammit, feed'em, shoot'em, whatever. Only stop them niggers from conjuring up their demons."

Leader of the fugitive caravan, a short, stout man with puffy cheeks, a bald head and a sparse red mustache that lapped over his lip into his mouth, turned in the saddle and cracked his whip. The eerie wailing grew louder.

"Give'em some vittles and a cup full'a water," he said to several armed men surrounding the bone weary men, women, boys and girls. He climbed from the saddle and swaggered towards Will, gawking in Master Mack's wagon. His pupils were dilated, his mouth opened wide.

"He come for me or he come for you, li'l wienie boy," Nap said, "but I ain't goin' to nobody's Mississippi." He laughed. The other boys in the wagon stared woefully at nothing.

Will heard Nap but couldn't listen. He sat there startled at a woman breathing fitfully, her head hanging low. Their eyes met. Aunt Aida? Hers was a bland stare as if he was just another white man watching her pass. Master Mack turned away from the crowd and followed Will's gaze to the captives. If Will recognized the downtrodden woman, she was most likely one of his slaves.

"That's a healthy buck you got there," the slave hunter yelled.

He stood between Master Mack's wagon and Jonah's. Will watched his whiskey red eyes flicker from him to Nap and back again.

"Make you better'n a fair deal before that gorilla kills 'em." He nodded at Will.

The intensity of shouting at ringside made it increasingly difficult for Master Mack to play his bargaining game without yelling. He bit off the soggy end of his cigar and spit.

"Don't be so cocksure," he said. "Where did you get them? I won't ask how." He pointed to the captives.

"Grabbed a few on the run but mostly from Pennsylvania, up Lancaster County way. Damndest place you'd ever wanna go. That religious bunch'a Quakers got runaways living amongst 'em just like they was white. Protects 'em too. Place where I stop, they feed me, give me a warm place to sleep. But when I ask questions about certain slaves who favor the fugitives on my posters, well hell, they just up and run me off. But I sure as hell did trick 'em. Stayed in the woods and snatched me a few niggers each night until I got me a whole parcel. Most of 'em slaves." He grinned deviously.

They talked back and forth across Will sitting like a mute, wondering if the slaver's story was a tall tale, wondering if the captured woman came from Lancaster. She lifted her head and tilted it towards the sky as if praying, then let it slump between her knees. Yes, it was Aunt Aida, so hurt and frail.

"That one the boy's watching belongs to me," Master Mack said.

"He ain't breathed once since setting eyes on all twenty-nine 'a them," the slave runner said, "so I do believe you're lying. But if you got chattel papers tell ya what I'll do."

The ring announcer interrupted him. "You and Jonah, David. Get your boys up here."

"Her and a thousand for the buck," the slaver hunter said.

"You don't have enough for Will," Master Mack said, now concerned that the horror shown on Will's face would rule stronger than his masterful persuasion over him to win.

"Two thousand, five hundred. My final bid, not a damned dime more."

"Go to hell, you leeching blood sucker."

"Well now, Brodgen, you ain't so gawdamn pretty yourself. Your old man already done made a fortune breeding human cargo. Now you fixin' to git this buck hammered to hell so you can line your pocket with more."

"Get on over there about your rotten business," Master Mack said. He didn't like being reminded of his father's illicit past. He was of Quaker extraction and remembered the Quaker minister, John Wolman, coming to Roedown, begging his father to free the slaves. Though Master Mack was not like his father and he wouldn't tolerate cruelty, his manner of living demanded free labor. It was entrenched in the Maryland soil and, just as the vegetables, fruit and horses needed water and sun, he needed slaves. "Hang on a spell," he said in a quieted voice. "I'll think on three thousand, nothing less, but get the hell out of sight."

"Okay," Master Mack said to Will. "We've got better things to do." Before Will had time to think on what he had to do, or about Aunt Aida, or that hideous slaver, he was standing on an elevated wooden surface face to face with Nap.

"I'm go'n kill you," Nap said, "but first I'm going through you like a dose of black draught."

The roar of side-splitting laughter made Will so ashamed. "Unh-unh," he said, meaning he didn't want any part in killing, when all of a sudden. *Thud!*

He saw Nap's big fist coming, but didn't remember getting hit or falling. Yet, there he sat, flat on his behind.

"Get up nigger and fight, or I'll have your black hide for tallow," the red-necked little prune of a man said.

"Hey Mack," another one said, "What the hell is this you brought here?"

"He'll fight," Master Mack said. "He damn well better get up and knock the hell out of Nap for that."

"Come on nigger, gitcha ass-kicking," Nap said, " 'cause I ain't going to no Mississippi."

Now he understood. Beat the hell out of Nap or Master Mack would sell him to the cotton fields, or the rice paddies. If he refused or lost, goodbye Roedown. Will should have covered his head.

Wham! He saw a flash. Stars twinkled. His knees buckled. He felt a sting where Nap's fist drew blood from his cheek, then sharp pain. Damn Mississippi, damn Master Mack, damn Nap. Will ignited like a dry log in a fireplace. He bored in, head down, taking a left and then a right to his ribcage that felt like Nap had bricks in his hands.

"Kill the sonofabitch, Nap." They all sounded alike to Will, yelling, whistling, jumping up and down.

Pain from the ferocious blows knocked a yell from Will's throat, forced him out of the crouch. His head sprung up as if it were a jack-in-the-box, butting Nap's chin. Will heard Nap's teeth crunch, saw blood drip from Nap's mouth. He swung his left, bringing his fist all the way up from hanging at his side. The lick hit Nap's neck with enough force to move him sideways. Nap grunted. His eyes blazed. His lips were set in a menacing snarl. He bombarded Will with punches to his chest, his head, his ears. But luckily for Will, Nap's hammer-like strength had waned.

Will didn't fight with any sort of style. He stood there swinging like Master Mack had seen him chopping wood with that freedom urge driving him, and hit Nap flush on his chin. Nap's face twitched and sagged as if he had been seized by a stroke. Nap dropped his guard. Will hit him so hard on his right temple the shock locked his legs. Nap covered his face with his hands, uttered something Will didn't understand, and rocked back and forth. Will should have yelled timber.

He made a lot of money fighting that day and on the way back to Roedown, Master Mack threw him a silver coin. It bounced off his chest and fell to the ground. Will leaped out, but Master Mack didn't stop, didn't even lock back. Will scooped up his coin, ran a few steps, and leaped over the gate into the wagon. He was a champion. The coin and a grin from Master Mack made him forget the shame, even though he ached. Lumps on his head and body stung to the touch, they were constant reminders.

When he and Master Mack returned, folks in the quarter were surprised to see him. Will fell on his bed in a heap, forcing a spirited lad who had beaten two others for Will's bunk to jump out of his way. Will tried focusing his thoughts on that day's episode, especially the threat of Mississippi, but he couldn't even think without hurting. Every time he turned, his body ached in a different place. The misery would awaken him then he'd drift off again.

Two days later Wallace came for Will again. He whipped three rough-house boys in grueling bouts, but for his winning, Master Mack gave him not one single solitary coin, said nothing about his left eye being swollen and blood shot, or his puffed, bruised lips.

That night while Tawney tended to his bruises, Will offered her the silver piece.

"No," she said, "don't let anybody know you have this. If Master Mack asks you tell him you lost it."

"It's for you, I want you to have it. And me thinks I'll ask Master Mack about you moving in my cabin. We can throw Uncle Sammy out."

"You got a place?"

"Yestiddy," Will boasted.

Tawney felt strangely flattered. She had for some time felt an eager attraction working for him. Even while she tried to warn that innocent headstrong young boy, she felt her pulse skittering. She spoke quietly. He leaned ever so close to hear.

"No. My time's just about come to leave here. Master wants this cabin for his family field niggers, and I'm healed pretty well. These scars though, I'll carry to my grave."

Without giving it a thought, she bared much of her thighs. Quickly, she covered them, but radiated a vitality that drew Will to her as if she were a magnet. He was eager and erratic as a summer storm. Her body ached for his touch. She had little resistance left in her hungry body to reject his virile appeal. In him she stoked a glowing fire.

Prize fighting soon became routine. Most of his days began with a king's breakfast and often ended with Tawney in his arms. Each time he saw her the magnetic pull became stronger. One night while he lay wrapped around her like a blanket, he asked, "Tawney, you believe in heaven?"

"Why you ask a strange question like that?"

"Just tell me if you believe it is out yonder somewhere."

"Well, I ain't never been too keen on it, because us and white folks sure can't be going to the same place."

"I believe there's a place like that," Will said. "The boogey man who said it weren't talking to me, he was telling Master Mack about some place way up Pennsylvania way, 'cross some river. Reason I believe it, he was mad 'cause somebody named Quaker run him away from there."

Tawney eased away from him and sat up. "I want to whisper something. But promise, you'll never tell anybody as long as I'm around here."

"Course, sure. Why not?"

"Sit up and listen, Will. If you repeat this, it'll be the same as if you killed me." Tawney put her mouth next to his ear. "You ain't crazy, Will. You brave. Master Mack wants you to think that slaves who run away is crazy. But them who does soon learn they brave."

"Aunt Aida ran off long time ago," Will said. "I saw her chained to a long string of slaves the same day that snatcher tried to buy me. She looked most about dead."

"Shh," Tawney said, "talk real quiet. But she tried, Will. That makes her brave." She looked in Will's eyes and knew he didn't believe her. "Master

Mack is the fox because he thinks like one. Nothing is stopping you from thinking like the fox, long as you don't tell anybody."

"Me think like Master Mack?"

"No, Will, like the fox. You can't help acting like a crazy nigger, but think like a fox when you do."

"I'm going to find that place, Tawney and take you there with me."

She bit her lip in dismay. He raised a spark of hope, but it quickly extinguished. "I know it, Will."

Next morning as usual, Grandmom sat Will's food on Silent Charles' makeshift seat and acted as if he wasn't there.

"I scrubbed my face and hands good this time," he said, smiling.

"Eat with your feet," she said. "Makes no never mind to me what you do. You ain't nothing now but an ole crazy field nigger."

"No I ain't," Will yelled. "Don't call me no field nigger. I'm dickty, just like you and that white glove wearing, no talking butler."

"Just a minute, just one damned minute. 'Scuse me, Lord." Grandmom's voice cracked. "Snotty nose, piss smelling young'un, I'll knock the monkey shit out of you."

Her open palm against Will's face popped like a fly swatter squashing a greenhead. The nerves in his arms twitched, but he held them rigidly at his side. His angry scowl scared her, but she held her stare. Will's foot scraped in the dirt, a mad bull pawing the ground.

"Don't call me crazy no more," he said.

For the first time since he had begun fighting, she noticed bruised marks on his pouting lips. "Boy." Her voice broke again as she looked across the rolling hills to the slave cemetery under the oak tree. "My kin is scattered about this land like leaves in the wind. I saw the whip draw blood from your granddaddy's back until it broke. Thank God though, he died before he let it break his will."

Grandmom stared at Will so hard he felt as though she was talking beyond him to someone in space.

"Weren't I the one with your mammy when she labor on her tick and birth you, you low scoundrel? With her two other times she bring buck slaves into the world after old Colonel Brodgen made her mate-up. But she was Ofeutey's daughter, my child. You got a half-brother that's already been sold, and another one down there in the quarter. Before long, he'll be sold, then you. I'll soon be dead and it'll be just like Ofeutey was never here."

"Who, how come I just now got a brother?"

"Don't mind about who!"

"I will so mind 'bout who, and I know you mad 'cause I'm making too much big money for Master Mack to sell me," Will said boastfully. He saw the aged lines tighten in her face, lines of anger and strain.

"I thought I saw a sign when you were born. I thought I saw enough of Ofeutey in you to break Brodgen's grip on my family. But you ain't paid one bit of attention. Now you laying with that hussy and zooming in and out and upside down like a drunk horsefly."

"Why is she a hussy now? I heard you call her honey once before."

"Oh God," Grandmom said, "make him understand that I don't want my blood spilled on the evil plantation ever no more."

"Just tell me why," Will said.

Grandmom pounded the air with her bony fists.

"See there," Will said. "You can't."

"The fox's got you all wrapped up," she said. "You are his fool, his rabbit, his black bear all rolled into one. G'won, get outta my face."

Grandmom saw agony in his eyes, but she didn't care. She felt weak and useless, fearing she had lost Will to Master Mack. The vow she had made to Ofeutey long ago would not be fulfilled and the heavy weight of despair that dwelled in her lonely soul pulled her down, down, down. Watching them ride away on another trip to somewhere forced her to take a dose of that strong yellow dock root medicine Miz Sady had mixed to quiet the painful ache across her forehead. Jerking sobs racked her insides.

Will couldn't believe Grandmom would lie to him, yet he didn't believe her. Why did he suddenly have a brother after all the lonely times by himself? He couldn't do what she wanted so he was no longer her first of kin. She wouldn't know him anymore, would treat him like she did his brother, if he really had one. Lucky for Will that Tawney made him feel as tall as the cemetery oak, or Grandmom would have crushed him.

A hint of rain was ever present during their jaunts that June. One Saturday morning in Annapolis, as soon as Will and Baltimore's black bruiser climbed into the ring for the main bout, a cold, nuisance drizzle began falling.

"Damn, coon face," Will said. "Something sure's hell caught hold of you." He pranced around, looking at the bruiser's bloodied, battle-weary head and body.

"Another puny nigger," Bruiser said. "Better put a couple bricks in your hands and pour some sand in your britches."

"Break 'em up," a man wearing a pine shaped hat and looking as if he had been screwed into his topcoat, said with a hacking cough. "Wait until it stops raining. Too much money on these niggers to risk a freak accident."

"Break up nothing," Will shouted. "I'm a hit this nigger so hard it'll take a thunder storm to wake him up."

Howls of laughter revived the dampened spirits. Will did a little soft shoe and faked a punch to the Bruiser's head. Clumsily, he raised his guard. Will sunk a devastating right deep into his left side. Bruiser squawked like a choked rooster and collapsed. All the winners except Master Mack yelled and guffawed while collecting and counting their winnings. Master Mack stood off to himself, rolling the stogie's chewed end between his lips. Will had talked back to a white man.

He hustled Will into the wagon and hurried to the Chesapeake Bay waterfront, stopping at a cluster of little run-down shacks. The stench of it, so rank that Will almost puked, made him know it was a slave compound. He panicked at the sight of two burly slave breakers wearing gun belts around huge slouching bellies coming upon him. Then Master Mack gave him a pass, told him to show it and act dumb to any white person demanding it, and left. The breakers, simply indicating by a quick nod in direction of a path, ushered him in front of them. He felt their hateful eyes boring holes in his back, and knew they wished he would slip, spit, wobble, do anything suspicious so they could beat him half-nigh unto death. They locked him in a pen by himself.

What would happen to him? With trembling hands, he tried reading the pass, but didn't trust himself to recognize his own name, after all the nights he and Tawney had spent writing it with pieces of charred wood on fresh kindling. He retreated to a corner and squatted there, immersing himself in self-pity and self-hatred. Why had he been born in this world, black and ugly, a slave, a white man's nigger? Why had he been born?

How long the cooking lady, a short, haggard black woman with a rounded back had been hunched over a wagon watching him, he didn't know. She dished whatever it was from a pot in a wagon into a tin plate, then set it on the floor beneath the bars. With her eyes she beckoned to Will. They were icy and out of focus like a haunt's. He wished she'd take her pig slop and leave. But she slipped to her knees, quietly set the plate several inches inside, stared until she knew his attention was completely hers, then with her lips said "no," without making a sound. He frowned and gazed at her.

No? No what? What are you talking about?

She turned away and left him with his puzzling thoughts.

Think, Will. No, don't eat the food? No, he wouldn't be whipped? No, he wouldn't be sold? Think, Will, think like the fox. Act dumb, but think like the fox. She probably had heard the slave breakers talking.

Will sat with his head turned and resting on knees drawn close to him like a derelict in a stupor. He'd forgotten how much he hated Master Mack. All of Roedown knew he gambled and lost plenty at poker, and on the horses. Will was his only sure win, and for that Master had thrown him a few coins. Why would he sell him? Why would he pay the breakers to manhandle him? He was probably there so Master could gamble. Will's thoughts carried him on past evening and sunset, into the night while listening to the Chesapeake lapping the shore, fully aware of someone at certain times watching him. The fog horn of a ship in the dark distance snapped him out of a cat-nap.

Chapter Six

In the early dawn Will and Master Mack headed South, Master at the reins, Will in a back corner leaning against the side with a leg hanging over the tailgate. They rolled along at the horses' walking pace some twenty five miles in absolute silence and reached Roedown near late morning. A stable boy took the reins from Master Mack. Will jumped from the wagon and trotted down the slope. In the orchard where he felt certain Master Mack couldn't see him, he began running, but stopped suddenly. Wallace, riding hard on the big gray swayback and kicking up a cloud of yellow dust, approached the barnyard.

"Master, Master! You almost got me killed. That man put his gun right up in my face, just a cussing and yelling so," Wallace said, swallowing air in gulps. "Whydn't you tell me I was taking her to your agent!"

"Nigger, you dare question Me!"

"Naw sir."

Will could barely hear Wallace speaking above a whisper.

"I fought with 'im 'til he showed me the bill of sale. He said he'd blow my black brains out if it don't be for you needing me."

"He didn't, so get the hell out of my face."

Will didn't hear anymore, he ran blindly to Tawney's cabin. The door stood ajar. "Tawney!" A feeling of despair swept over him. He drew back and hit the door with a wallop that knocked it loose from its top hinge. Empty and lonely, Will squatted in a corner and curled himself into a ball, brooding for Tawney like he had done for himself the previous night. He tried telling himself that smart as Tawney was, she'd find that underground railroad, and he'd better find it before some prize fighter whipped him.

But who would tell him, especially since most things are better off not talked about except with close friends and he had none. He could run away by himself if the woods weren't so full of slave snatchers and agents. Maybe Uncle Sammy would tell him. Maybe he knew Will's brother.

Will ran to his cabin and charged through the door so fast he scared the wits out of Uncle Sammy. He asked a lot of questions, but Uncle Sammy simply hunched his shoulders. Then Will asked him if he liked living in the cabin and Uncle Sammy suddenly remembered. Yes, he saw them leave. Will listened in agony while Uncle Sammy dragged on, talking slower than oxen moved. Tawney climbed on the horse behind Wallace, but for some reason, things mostly do work better for good even when it is so hard to see the good. Will didn't know exactly what Uncle Sammy was hinting, but he didn't like what he understood it to mean, even when Uncle Sammy said he would probably understand it by and by. Levi had been sold too. He left by himself with his head bent low and a letter in his hand.

Yes, he knew Will's half-brother, Charles. Just Charles. Like Uncle Sammy, he didn't have a last name. He'd be in the quarter. Uncle Sammy even asked Will if he was hungry, but he couldn't eat.

When Will entered the chattering quarter and walked around the young folks section looking for the person Uncle Sammy had described, they stopped talking. After several minutes, pausing and staring with his face moody and eyes half-closed, the mumbling and snickering began. Shorty finally broke the cold exclusion of him from their midst.

"Damned if we ain't got company, the champeen nigger hisself, without ole Massa. You ain't got no business here, what the hell you want?"

Even when Will was a boy, he didn't like Shorty. Now that he could fill a man's shoes any day in any way, he would knock Shorty clean out of his flour-sack drawers, except for two damned good reasons. Shorty, mean like a hornet, was known to cut, and he had carried a knife sharp enough to whittle air as long as Will had known him.

"I'm looking for my brother," Will said quietly.

Shorty looked at him from up under then scratched his nose and sighed. "Ain't no brother of yourn looking for you."

"Uncle Sammy said he asked about me some."

"Sammy bigger liar than you," Shorty said.

Will wanted to hit him, just one good lick to lock up his mean, nasty mouth. Instead, he watched Shorty turning his head this way, and that way then focus his eyes on a lad near grown, sitting some distance away. Will, following a hunch, went to him.

"You Charles?"

The young man sucked his big, white teeth then slowly turned his eyes toward Will. "Whatcha want?"

Charles was slightly-built and two inches or so taller than Will, with skin so black and tight it cast a blueish hue around him. A prominent forehead, high cheek bones and stark white eyes with black pupils made him appear more African than anyone Will had ever seen. Will threw him a coin. Charles sucked his teeth in a most obnoxious way and rolled over on the silver piece in a manner of securing it. Will actually felt spit spray on his face.

"You and me some kin," he said.

"So's fat meat greasy. What the hell is you?"

"Man with guts enough to run the hell away from here."

"Sheet, you crazy. Ain't never said two words to me in your life, now you come for me to help you run off."

"Crazy like a fox. I know where we can work and get paid real money, like you got there." Will flipped a coin in the air, caught it, then rubbed it between his thumb and forefinger. "White folks' money."

"Yeah. Way off somewhere in the sky, like Canada," Charles said.

"Nope. about a week away, across state line in Pennsylvania."

"How's come you still here then?" Charles said.

"Been waiting my time, getting ready."

"Like hell. Been feeling too good about yourself 'til Master Mack sold your girl. That's what eating you," Charles said.

"Take the coin or give it back," Will said, turning and walking toward the door.

From his tone of voice Charles knew Will had reached the cutting edge of his patience. He followed Will outside, though at a safe distance. The first piece of money he'd ever squeezed felt good in his sweaty palm, but leaving what little home Roedown meant to him would take some doing. But money, freedom?

The night, perfectly still and laden with honeysuckle, bound Will in loneliness for Tawney. He couldn't think like the fox to himself, it didn't encourage him. Then Charles came and surprised him. He didn't give Will the coin. They talked through part of the night. Charles knew Will was his brother. Nothing big about that, he didn't know his daddy and probably had some other half brothers or half-sisters at Rocdown. Will though, had impressed Charles enough to befriend him. Yet, slaving at Roedown or running away, they amounted to about the same. Buckra would keep his big foot on you anywhere. Will never heard tell of Buckra. Charles felt good that he taught Will something. Then without giving it another thought, he asked Will when he wanted to leave. Will didn't know, he had to think on it some more, but he felt good knowing he had someone ready to make the break with him. Charles reminded Will that road agents with blood hounds were always looking for runaways. Once Charles made the break, though, he would never come back to Roedown alive. His tongue against his big white teeth made a loud slurping sound. Will believed him.

The rainy season curtailed a lot of prize fights. Then Will worked in the fields generally moping about up one row tending tobacco, or down another weeding corn. A few days after he had met his brother it rained again. Not hard, just a steady drenching spray, though hard enough for Will to ignore the bell that sent him and the other hands to the fields. So, in a way that even Will probably couldn't describe, he was waiting for Wallace when he rode right up to the door and kicked it open without getting out of the saddle.

"You know the rule, boy. Master say you ain't fighting today." He spewed the ground with a mouthful of mint-smelling saliva.

"I ain't going to nobody's field."

Wallace wondered for a minute if he had heard Will correctly. "Nigger," he said, "I been here all my life, twice as long as you. Listen to me close now, boy. You ain't going to be the cause of me going back to the fields. Seeing how you Master's precious parcel, I'm going to settle this right now."

"G'won the hell on and tell." Will waved his hands at him.

Wallace whirled his horse around and galloped off. Will watched him drive his heels repeatedly in the horse's side and suddenly began sweating. He felt the nerves in his neck twitch. He closed the door and sat on his bed, then jumped up and opened the door again. It seemed as if Tawney was talking: you can't help from acting crazy. He remembered Grandmom Rosey: the fox knows what you thinking before you do it. Tawney's words rang in his head: think like the fox. He dug into his personal things and found the pass. If Master ordered him whipped, Will wondered if Wallace would try it. He wondered if Master Mack would do it. He wondered if Master Mack could do it. Sweat ran down his back.

Master Mack rode up on his white stallion. His face was completely void of expression. "Where is the pass I gave you?"

Will handed it to him. Master Mack snatched it and inspected it carefully. "Who the gawddamned hell do you think you are?"

"I ain't no more field nigger. Two long years, ain't never lost one fight. That makes me dickty, more than them sissy niggers up yonder in the big house."

"Oh, you are now?" Master Mack said.

"Yup," Will said. "Put Silent Charles and the rest of them behind that ole farting mule." Will hadn't thought on saying that, it jumped out. " 'Fraid I'll catch my death of cold in the rain, been sweating so."

"Well now, we will keep you damned good and warm." Master Mack's hardened face was a glowering mask of rage. "Hitch up the oxen team," he said, pulling back his coat, revealing a pearl handled pistol in its holster.

No doubt in Will's mind at all about what that meant. In his seventeen years at Roedown, he knew of only two times Master Mack used his whip. Each time he sent the doomed slave to fetch the ox bow from the harness shop, in a breezeway across from the stables. Master Mack hid in the dark, waiting. One surprised lick from his whip spent half the doomed man's energy.

All of Roedown heard the terrifying news in the loud cackle of that ageless black bird dipping and carrying on above Will's head like it had been in Master's sour mash again. Slaves doing spring planting paused and followed the crow's flight over Will, then dropped their heads when he passed by. Shorty, puffing on his pipe as if sending smoke signals, almost dumped the wheelbarrow load of cow manure he was pushing along a slope between the high road and barnyard.

Will hesitated at the entrance to the breezeway and squinted in an effort to pinpoint the dark hiding places. His skin crawled. He heard nothing except the warning ringing in his ears and the slow crunching of his shoes in the sandy soil.

From an alcove Master Mack's whip uncoiled. Will instantly jumped back, hearing the soft whine of it slicing the air in its reach for him. It cracked and bit. Will felt the singeing white flame tear his shoulder. Blind fear seized him. With blazing speed, he grabbed the whip's hot tail and yanked. The force of his frenzied tug pulled Master Mack stumbling from his hiding place. Face to face they were. Master Mack's eyes were fierce like an eagle's, though he shook like a spooked slave.

Will didn't know that, he wouldn't look his master in the eye. Neither would he turn loose the whip. They tussled and fell, rolling, twisting and grunting. With a mighty heave, Will wrenched the whip from Master Mack's hands and straddled his chest. Their faces were so close he could smell Master's anger. His hands were locked around the grip on the whip. The hardened knuckles in Will's fist, protruding like pieces of broken stone, were eager to crush.

Tawney, writhing in the dirt, felled by the mighty sword that made Master Mack mightier than God. Aunt Aida, broken and longing for death. Grandmom Rosey, burning his hide with the overseer's strap. Ofeutey, the mighty sword severing his body from his soul.

Will couldn't strike, his arm locked. He felt Master Mack struggling for his gun.

"Help," Master Mack yelled, his voice loud and foreboding like the church bell in Queen Anne Village tolling its warning of impending danger.

Will jumped up and dashed away. Behind him the pistol shot sounded like an exploding thunder clap that would spew bits of him from there to hell. But he ran on, straight to the Patuxent River with nothing on his mind except flight. Some distance upstream after running in calf-deep water, he threw the whip away, entered the deep, wet woods and climbed his favorite tree way up top where the wind bent the pine in all directions, though he wasn't aware of the swaying. Time passed. No one came looking for him, but where could he sleep? With the oncoming darkness, every strange sound was a terror. Animals in the forest spoke a strange secrecy that only they and Master Mack understood. They were unfriendly and would tell Master where he hid. Baltimore was so far away. He would never get there by himself, even if he traveled the fields and kept sight of the road. Dangerous as he knew it would be, he was driven to get Charles.

From the edge of the clearing under the blanket of darkness, he watched lanterns burn and listened for the sound of a search party. He sneaked in as close as the oak tree on the slope that guarded the slave cemetery then dared get a little closer to his cabin. He threw a pebble against the door, waited a short spell and hit it again. Uncle Sammy didn't answer, so he threw a bigger one. A shaft of flickering light spread from a crack the opening door made. Uncle Sammy's eyes swelled and darted around at Will as if he were a ghost standing in the immediate darkness beside the dim light. "Ain't you got no kind of sense, boy?"

"Wrap my duds in a knapsack and tell Charles to meet me in the cedars, top of the hill beyond the graveyard. Please, Uncle Sammy?"

"If they ketch'a, you dead, Will. Word come from Wallace, anybody who much as speak your name will be whipped and sold. I'm too old, son."

"I'm so hungry. Ain't nothing in the woods in planting time."

"Grandmom can't help you either. She 'bout paralyzed, had a stroke today."

Will gasped. "Is she going to...?"

"It don't look good one bit. But you a man now, Will. So act like it. I'll see to Charles. If he's coming, he'll bring you a bite and your duds. Then get as far away from me and Grandmom Rosey as you can get." Uncle Sammy closed the door in his face.

Eating hoe-cake and fat-back on the run, Will pushed on through the night, fighting it. Charles followed him. They hardly talked, and even then, barely above a whisper. Freedom, once only on his mind, was now in his heart. But he had much to learn before knowing, freedom was more than one hard-fought thing.

Dawn broke when they had reached the fork. Will followed the left road, opposite the one he knew led to Annapolis. The sun brightening the countryside's sharp morning features made them suddenly tired and more afraid. He and Charles drank cold water from a nearby stream until their empty stomachs hurt. With their knapsacks under their heads, they slept like owls, too exhausted to worry much about the tree-top full of crows screaming directly overhead.

Will awakened in the late evening. "I smell molasses," he whispered to Charles, sitting up like a sentry, training his eyes on every stir, even the slightest movement of new leaves on the wild saplings.

"Moonshine still close by," Charles said. "Ain't nothing 'cept hog-slop smell rotten-sweet bad as that."

"Hungry?" Will asked.

"Could eat a mule," Charles said, "but not that white lightning stink."

"Ole Jericho ain't done yet," Will said, "and we better scat."

The oncoming night ended their first day of freedom. How many more before they would reach safety? Will didn't know where they were, but believed they were heading in the direction of Baltimore where they might find a place to hide. He relied on hope that Baltimore did indeed have a free black community about which he had heard while lingering with fighters at the fairgrounds.

He and Charles ventured out of the brush and walked along the high road. Only a few stars shone. Tall blossoming trees overhanging the wagon trail blocked the dull light of a quarter moon.

"You believe in haints?" Charles asked.

62

"I'm too hungry to play around with that," Will said.

"I ain't playing," Charles said.

Will's thick eye-brows drew together in a frown. "Go on," he said, "high-tail it back to Roedown if you scared. But if you start running, a haint'll run you until you drop, unless the road agents catch you first."

Will went into the brush and scraped around the forest floor. He found a stick about as long as he was tall and broke it in half. "Here," he said. "Can't nothing get you now."

"No stick can stop a haint. Everybody know that, Will."

"The hell mine can't." Will swung the stick over his head in a frenzy, reversed his swing, grabbed it with both hands, pumped his arms up and down in front of himself until he was winded. "Show me a haint what can get through that?"

Charles' face twisted into an amazed grin. It was hard to believe that Will was younger. He tightened his fist around the stick and bumped into Will every so often even though it wasn't so awfully dark that he couldn't see his brother.

"I'm so hungry now," Charles said, "I can taste my breath."

Will couldn't laugh. He knew that hunger would soon overtake him and Charles as they tramped on.

"We going to find something soon," he said, "real soon." He hiccupped. It tasted awful. "God," he said, frowning.

In the distance, Will heard a rushing sound, like water or a strong wind rustling leaves. Then the sky came in full view, the trees diminished in size and number. He and Charles were close enough to the sound to know it was a creek or river. Will saw the outline of a wall and stopped.

"See that over there?" He pointed westward, towards a clearing beyond the thicket in which they were walking.

"See what?"

"Damn," Will said. "You can't see that wall?"

"Too hungry to see anything," Charles said. "Can't drag myself no more."

"Two thumps on your watermelon head, a farm's close by."

"Hell no," Charles said, "nobody thumps this head."

"Better shut up," Will said. "A landing is probably thataway and that means somebody's close by. We go this way."

He prodded the ground before him with his stick and led the way along the creek bank. At the wall, about four feet high and meticulously built with all sizes of stones, he paused. Nothing visible except a circular tree line that extended several acres.

"Think we oughta go over?" Charles said.

"We got to." Will put his belongings at the base of the wall and jumped over.

"I don't know, Will. You hear any dogs barking?"

"You got a stick," Will said. "But if you don't want to come, plant your sausage ass right here on top and I'll bring you a mess of collards greens and a glass of buttermilk directly, suh."

Charles took more time getting over than it would have taken Uncle Sammy. Will watched him with mounting disgust.

"Yup," Charles said. "I can smell the horses."

"I see a barn," Will said. The blacker-than-night silhouette of the barn and a large oak tree were on the other side of the meadow. "We ought to find some apples and maybe some oats too," Will said.

"Lord knows I don't wanna get caught gnawing a mouthful of horse oats," Charles said.

Will grabbed Charles' forearm. "Ain't nothing funny. I know what runaway slaves look like after they caught." He thought of Aunt Aida and a pang for Tawney hit him. "I'll kill first." Sometimes he wished he could cry.

At the barn, Will noticed lamps burning in two upstairs windows of the farm house. "Stand right here." He spoke with a muffled voice. "If either of them lamps move, run over to the door and call me but don't yell. And for God sake, don't touch me. You liable to get your head knocked off. After I get inside, you come in."

Charles nodded his head indicating yes. Will raised a long wooden lever from its cradle and eased the door open. A hinge creaked. He stopped, waited for a signal from Charles, then eased his body through the opening and went through without touching. He smelled horses, cats and cows. Cows, he thought, and milk that is warm and rich. His heartbeat double-timed.

"We got us a meal," he said to Charles. "Soon's I find the cow."

"How'n hell you going to find it in here?"

"Smell, dammit. Don't you know nothing? Stand here by the door and scratch your stick on the ground if you hear something."

"Li, li, like hell I will." Charles stuttered, though he really wasn't a stuttering person. "We, we, we go together," he said, inching along behind Will.

Will heard the soft moo of the cow and after his eyes had adjusted to the interior, cracks between slats revealed the barn's interior.

"Here she is," he said. "Give you first feed."

"We sucking that cow's titty?"

"Touch of your hot, dry lips on her, and she'll kick you clean through that wall," Will said. "Lay down under her and I'll squirt milk in your mouth."

"Whew," Charles said, "smell like she just layed a big pie somewhere 'round here, but stop Will, gawdammit. You squirting it in my eye and it ain't funny."

Will couldn't help laughing. For a brief moment the terror of the dark unknown and tomorrow lifted from him as he took his turn and Charles squirt-

ed milk up his nose, and all over his face before finding his true aim. Then Charles stopped instantly.

"She gone dry already?" Will asked.

"Something hairy rubbed against my leg," Charles said. "It did it again." He swung backwards and walloped a cat. It tumbled over, hissing and fussing loudly.

"That's a tom," Will said. "He smelled the milk. We got to high-tail it out of here. Get your stick, let's go."

Will eased open the barn door and listened. They stepped out, hurried across the barnyard. He looked back. A lantern in one of the windows moved. A dog's bark broke the quietness of the night.

"I hope you can run," he said, stretching his legs in full stride.

"Think it's a blood-hound?" Charles asked, surprisingly close enough behind for Will to clearly hear him.

"Don't know," he said. "Sounds like something big enough to swallow us whole. Hurr'up, jump the wall."

They hurled themselves to the top, rolled over and fell to the ground. Up they scrambled, crashing into the thicket. Briars and vines scratched their bodies, slapped their faces.

Charles stopped. "We left our stuff."

"Them few raggedy duds? Leave'em for that hungry dog." Will hurried on until he came upon the swollen branch. At the water's edge he hesitated, watching it move swiftly and feeling its cold, yet soothing ripples on his stubbed feet.

"Work the stick in front of you like old blind Abe used to do. Remember?" Will said, moving slowly into the swift current. Up and up the water rose and closed around his neck. He clamped the stick in his teeth, and extending his arms at shoulder level, worked them like paddles, inching himself across.

Charles cautiously waded in to his knees, then his waist. The dog, barking furiously, didn't sound very far away. He went in up to his chest and suddenly disappeared then surfaced, sputtering and flailing. "I can't swim," Will."

Will looked back. Charles' eyes were two cotton balls stuffed with black olives. "You must be in a hole," Will said, reaching for him.

Charles lunged and thrust himself around Will's neck. After a futile struggle to pry Charles from him, Will submerged. Charles immediately let go, but when Will surfaced Charles reached for him again. Will grabbed Charles' neck in his strong hands and held him at arm's length. Charles though, fighting to stay afloat, was like a mad man clawing at his head.

"Don't rush me," Will yelled. "Come this way easy like. I'm standing."

Charles couldn't hear him. Fear contorted his face. Feeling Charles overpowering him, Will, his head bobbing in and out of the water, squeezed desperately. Charles' eyes stretched skyward.

"Can't breathe, Will," he managed to utter, coughing and struggling to pry Will's hands from his throat.

Will, pulling Charles to him, released the grip and hugged him. "Stand up, like I'm doing," he said. "You can touch bottom."

"My one leg's gone to sleep."

"I'll hafta carry you then," Will said, inching along, feeling with his feet for the creek bottom step by step with Charles butted against his right side.

Charles slumped from Will's arms to the sandy bank. "Ain't never hugged nobody before in my whole life," he said, kneading the numb leg.

Water ran from Will's nose, he felt pain in his rib cage. "Ain't never hugged a man, but brothers oughta' can do that," he said, pulling Charles to his feet. "I'd guess they found our things, we ain't got time to rest."

Night lay around them like a sleeping big black bear. In Will's mind, dizzy with fright, it seemed as if at any moment he might bump into the dark fur and the ornery terror would awaken. Black night, black night, darkness, still haunting darkness. Would the dawn ever come so he could slip into the deep woods, find a hiding place and sleep until night came again?

Charles trudged on behind Will, blacking out and stumbling, then waking again. He dreamed about Roedown, resting peacefully in the quarter with its tired souls snoring, talking and laughing in their sleep.

Will dream-walked too. Tawney encouraged him onward. The road widened. Will heard things scampering on the ground. "Heh, you hear that, Charles?"

"Hear what?"

Before Will could answer, sea gulls rising suddenly from bogs on the left side of the road startled them. Will watched them fly across a wide bay toward the gray mist of dawn filtering out the night. The tall black tree line fell behind them as if it were an ominous companion disappearing with the darkness, giving in to smaller trees, rocks, sand and brackish water. A light wind blew across the green water of Baltimore's harbor. A hedge of marsh grass whispered to the breeze. The damp air smelled like the sea. Soon the sky was a flight of gulls, the color of seashells. Will stared at them flying above the shore line in an extended loop and vanishing in the heavy mist. A ship there in the harbor with tall sails and rigging bigger than any he had ever seen on the Patuxent, reminded him of slave ships in the middle passage from Africa, about which Grandmom had told him so many horror stories. He and Charles had better hide.

Where? They were approaching a crossroads, a three-way intersection where their road ended and a larger one ran from the direction of the ship toward the sky. The bogs were on one side and the harbor was on the other.

They didn't have a choice, the only shelter from the day and its predators would be deep in the bosom of the cattails and marsh grass. A smell of dead fish made their noses run. Charles, numb from his toes to his fingertips, sat leaning against a rotted tree stump. He soon slumped over and stretched out like a cross.

Will slept in snatches. He dreamed Grandmom died there in the bogs beside him. He had lulled her to sleep in his arms as if she were a child, getting smaller and smaller until she completely vanished. He began crying, but Uncle Sammy, dressed like an African warrior, grabbed him by the nape of his neck and said, "You a man now, Will. Act like one."

He awakened with a shudder, actually feeling pain, and spent an instant with his eyes wide open seeing Uncle Sammy. Will sat for a spell, wondering how much of his dream was true.

Why none of the people passing above in the busy road gave any attention to the hissing and whining sleeping sounds in the brush was a mystery. Perhaps they thought it a bit strange, but two tom-cats could have been in the thick grass squaring off.

Heavy-eyed, groggy, too hungry to sleep anymore, Will shook his head and batted his eyes half a dozen times. The stench of stagnant water and rotting vegetation, the June heat and the fear of snakes were nearly unbearable. He looked at Charles' pantaloons hanging from his torso in shreds. He may as well have taken off the collar-less shirt. Will's clothes weren't much better. Two runaway slaves, so ragged they were just about naked.

He crawled to a spot where he could watch hucksters passing above and crouched like a frog. Some passed by pushing two-wheel carts laden with oranges, grapes, bananas, and vegetables. Others were in horse and mule drawn buckboards and wagons. He waited, poised to move, but each time Master Mack flashed in his imagination, and he receded back into hiding. While day dragged on and the travelers dwindled, the imminent danger of capture and lynching for beating his master was no longer foremost on his mind; hunger overwhelmed him.

Only one person left in the road, a whistling yellow man about Charles' size dressed in fancy boots, a straw hat with a black band around it, a bright yellow shirt and suspenders that held up red pants. He pushed a cart load of greens, apples, cured hams and grapes with a lively gait.

Will waited until the jolly fellow was ten or eleven steps past him. Inch by inch, he raised his head, his shoulders and his body like a haunt easing out of a grave. Then, springing like a lizard snatching a beetle, he wrapped one arm around the petrified man's neck and clamped his hand over the man's mouth.

"If you tell me one lie, yellow man," he said, "I'll conjure your tongue out. Where we catch that train that runs underground?" He snatched the man's head around and glared into a pair of eyes that told Will he knew. They looked like peeled onions.

Will smelled like a dead rat, an odor so penetrating it made yellow man's eyes water. With them he pointed in the direction of Baltimore.

"We's hungry," Will said. "Ate nothing since yestiddy."

With trembling hands he gave Will a bunch of grapes.

"If you yell when I let you go, you never yell again, boy." Will tried to sound as mean as Wallace. He released the huckster and began cramming grapes in his mouth.

"Where is we?" Will said. He swallowed in chunks.

The man wiped his mouth on the sleeve of his shirt and spat. "Straight down this road," he said, "you come to the colored section of Baltimore. But slave runner or bounty hunter'll be on your trail soon's the first white somebody see you, Rails. Anybody'd know you just left the big foot country."

"This here is Baltimore, hunh. If you lie, you'll sure see my three-legged monkey." Will reached for a bigger bunch of grapes.

"Damn Rails, you eat much more, I won't have none to sell." He gave Will the grapes.

"I need some pants, yellow man. Take'em off."

"Unh-unh, Rails. Hell naw. What chance a colored man got walking 'round 'thout his britches. I got me a right smart little business worked up over the years."

Will advanced on him.

"I don't mess with nobody," the man said, giving ground. "But you fixing to send me to Mississippi. Jesus, I got me a wife and children."

"I should give'em to my brother. He needs'em worse than me," Will said.

The man looked around frowning. "Hunger really mess with your mind, hunh? Both of you can't wear'em," he said. "If you can back-up off me and listen a minute, what I say'll probably save your life. I know you need some pants, and a bath, and a haircut, and a cut of mint for your breath too. So, with the shirt on you and the pants on him." He looked around for Charles. "Wherever he is, you still be runaway slaves.

"We got to find that railroad."

"Never make it, Rails. You on Belle Air. What you better do is follow it this way." He pointed in direction of the harbor. "Round the bend and in the brickyard there cover yourself with brick dust. Lay it on thick's you can. If any white somebody gets close and starts eyeballing, shake and dust to hell, like you going crazy."

"Yellow man, I'll put the moe-joe on you. You can't trick me."

"I'm saving your hide, Rails. Colored folks can't walk around like we damn well please. Don't be caught on the street after dark without Mr. Charlie."

"Who's he?"

"One guess, Rails. Yep, you guessed right, and you'd better be getting on."

"A parsel of fruit for my brother first," Will said. "He's hungry enough to eat you."

Something in the marsh stirred. "Lordy mercy. Here." He thrust several apples in Will's hand and looked past his shoulder. "Somebody's coming way back yonder."

Will didn't look around, he slid head first back into the deep recess. Charles was still in the crucifix.

Chapter Seven

Will wished he had pockets, he would have packed them with red dirt. He and Charles sneezed and coughed and twisted and brushed each other, watching all the white folks on their side of Belle Air Avenue hustle to the opposite.

"Whydn't you filthy niggers jump into the bay and wash a'fore you left the brick yard?" a merchant yelled while raising his awning. "Git off the sidewalk."

"We save some," Will said, stepping into the street. "One a'these hoojies might stop us and we got nothing, not even a pass."

"A hoojie?" Charles said.

"Mean white folks like that one. He'd turn us over to the patterrollers quick as he'd look at us if he knew we was running."

"How you come to know things like that, Will?"

"Traveling with Master Mack I learned a whole bunch."

They walked on, noticing Baltimore's changing street attire and complexion. In the distance Will saw black shingles and tar-paper on the roofs and sides of little houses all the same size and shape. From opened windows of some, curtains stirred in the June evening's warm breeze. Whitewashed picket fences made the houses appear smiling. Home folks sitting in yards chatting and tending gardens, stopped suddenly and hurried inside. They knew. Some other houses reminded Will of slave cabins at Roedown. The few people around them acted as if he and Charles weren't there. Chickens scratched in the dirt and at anything that stirred. A dog barked from under a house and charged. Will's foot sent him hurtling through the air and yapping then scrambling to right himself on spindly legs and fleeing down the street. Will and Charles followed the dog.

At Belle Air and East Lanvale Street they passed a white man riding a donkey, Saddlebags hanging behind and in front of him appeared full of pots, pans, brushes, and all sorts of weeds and things Will had never seen before. He and Charles began the furious dusting again. The man looked around and then smiled just enough for them to see it.

Charles looked at Will. "What we going to do?" he said,

"Let him make the first move. Remember, we together and we ain't going back. Say it Charles."

Charles stammered. "We, we..." His voice broke,

"Dammit," Will said. "Don't fill up on me now." He felt an urge of anger mixed with helplessness and responsibility for his brother.

Will watched the man. Auburn hair as long as Mistress Margaret's hung from under a stove-pipe hat. His face, long and tight. A pointed nose sat in the middle of a long brown beard. He winked and Will suspected he knew. If you see the fox he wanted you to see him. Grandmom's warning rang in his ear.

70

The strange man studied a paper then stared at Will and Charles. "Peace be with thee brethren," he said, nudging the donkey to a slow gait and singing out, "Pots aye, pans aye, herbs aye for your miseries. I got greens and things and sun-dried beans."

Townsfolk gathered around the peddler. Will and Charles felt the street closing in. Will's nostrils dilated and tightened. His heart pounded. Nerves in his shoulders twitched. A little boy came up behind him and tapped on his back. Will wheeled with his fist cocked.

"Mister," the boy said, "My daddy say come see Jocko?"

Will glowered. Charles looked all around them.

"See Jocko, that colored man in the yard?" The boy pointed with his head and ran toward the statuette.

Jocko? Why is that play slave dressed up like Silent Charles back at Roedown? Will stared at Jocko then at Charles in the manner that Grandmom had stared at him when she looked at something far away.

"What?" Charles said. He looked at himself and tugged at his ragged, red dust covered clothing.

"Not you," Will said. "Only Jocko is too dark to look like Silent Charles."

Charles studied the statuette. "That white-glove nigger over yonder holding a lantern put your mind on Silent Charles?"

"He wears white gloves, don't he? It means something, but what?"

"Means it is a trap, Will?"

"We can't stay here in the road," Will said. "What master would send a little colored boy fetchin' two runaways and expect them to come running. We go to him."

Charles studied Jocko as they crossed the street. "He do have a lot of Silent Charles in him, hunh Will?"

Will didn't answer. Times like these made him think so much of Tawney, making strange things Grandmom Rosey had said seem so simple. Tawney, he really missed her, but wouldn't dwell on wondering, it hurt. He rapped on the door. It opened immediately. "A, ah. I guess we come for Jocko," he said.

"Enter my weary sons. God has indeed spread his mercy about you." A stocky black man with drooping shoulders and a ring of thinning hair that reminded Will of salt and pepper, greeted them with a husky whisper. He bolted the door.

"I am Tighe Moore and this is my son, Jeremiah."

Jeremiah, the bright-eyed boy who had called them to the Jocko, grinned.

"My wife, Millie." Tighe extended his hand towards a woman about Grandmom Rosey's size, little with an oval face and a mouth that resembled a smiling flower,

"Young gentlemen," she said and curtseyed.

"I think they're just crossing over, Millie. Come fellows, we've not one minute to waste."

Tighe took a lit candle and moved towards the back of the small, cozy bungalow cramped with lanterns, chairs and tables. Will and Charles had not moved. They felt as self-conscious and conspicuous as two peeled cucumbers.

"We had to leave what few duds we had awhile back," Will said.

Lingering odors of supper made Will's stomach pang. "Lord knows we sure 'nough hungry," he said.

"Hurry," Tighe said. "No time for chatter. You'll eat directly."

In a back room beyond the kitchen, Tighe opened a pantry, unhooked the shelves from the back, took out the rough planks, and pushed on the back wall. It swung open. The candle spread an eerie light on a wall. When Tighe stepped through, Will saw steps leading into total blackness and smelled damp, cool dirt.

"You think we should?" Charles said.

They were passing through the pantry. Mrs. Moore closed and latched the food closet behind them.

"I guess we got to," Will said.

Will followed Tighe, descending to a tunnel barely wide enough for one person. Tighe inched along sideways. Will and Charles feared for their lives more now than ever, creeping behind him. Charles put one hand on Will's shoulder, digging his fingers into Will's flesh. Will didn't say anything, he sensed Charles near panic's end. The air was so close the candle flickered as if it would die. Will couldn't contain himself any longer.

"Hey, man, where you taking us? Hunh!"

"To a person," Tighe said, "Well, let's call him Quaker for now."

"I hear tell of him before," Will said, "but seems like we going to hell."

"Not hell," Tighe said. "the Underground Railroad. We're just about there,"

Tighe stopped. He held the candle higher and looked up. Will saw a ladder extending from the tunnel's end. Tighe ascended one step, stopped, listened then took another step.

"Dead folks sure don't need eyes," Charles said. "Do they, Will?"

"You must be quiet," Tighe whispered. He unlatched a trap door, blew out the candle, and eased it open ever so slowly. Watching Tighe reminded Will of the stories he and the boys at Roedown told smaller children about ghosts of slave overseers rising from the grave with fang-like teeth, dripping blood and snot. It wasn't funny now.

"Come up," Tighe whispered.

Will put Charles' hand on the ladder and motioned for him to go first. Charles shook his head and held steadfast. Will began climbing, but Charles looked back into the black hole and grabbed Will's leg. "I'm next," he said.

The trap door, part of a barn floor, locked from the underside. A light in the near distant night, dimming and brightening, caught Will's attention.

"That's him signaling for us." Tighe said.

They hurried across a sloping yard where all low branches had been cut from the trees. Will noticed Tighe following a line of trees with whitewashed trunks.

"Peace be with thee." A man standing in the doorway of a semi-dark log cabin beckoned them to enter.

He bolted the door, closed the window shutters, and turned up the wick in a lantern. He was the huckster, the pots and pans and beans and things man riding the jackass. The aroma of cooking food—onions and rutabagas, sidemeat, and hot bread brought tears to Will's and Charles' eyes.

They stood unmoving right where they had entered the cabin. Will stared as if his eyes were pasted on the peddler walking, taking long strides, to a little table on which were a stack of posters. He sat in a cane back chair, took his good old time hanging a pair of glasses almost to the tip of his nose. Tighe sat beside him. The peddler looked at the poster, brushed his hair behind his ear, extended his hand to Will.

"Will Parker," he said. "Thee certainly looks older than seventeen,"

"Go ahead," Tighe said to Will. "Shake hands. He's the best friend you'll find in these parts."

Really a task for Will, shaking hands with a strange-acting white man.

"Thee must be Charles, nineteen years old." He smiled and shook Charles' hand.

"That's right, Master," Charles said, even though he didn't know his age.

"I'm Ned," the peddler said, "the only master you have is God. Don't ever forget that."

"Yes, Mas, I mean ah."

"That's all right, Charles." Ned patted him on the shoulder. "It'll take some doing to wash that out of your brain. Let's begin right now." Ned said, looking at Tighe. "A bath, some decent clothes, and some hot food will probably do wonders for these weary travelers."

Will and Charles scrubbed themselves in a big wooden tub with soap made of tallow and lye until their skin burned. They sat at Ned's table, uncomfortable at being served by a white man.

"Which one of you will say grace?" Ned asked, heaping vegetables and pork onto their plates.

"What's that?"

"Food, Charles," Will said, looking condescendingly at his brother.

"Thanking God for our food," Ned said, as if he hadn't heard Will.

Charles returned Will's hateful stare.

73

"Old folks back at Roedown called it blessing," Will said, "but what we ate belonged to Master Mack and I just couldn't thank God for Master Mack's crop when we did all the raising."

"Could you believe you were blessed to have it to eat?"

"Hump," Charles said. "Master's green apples, his choke cherries, his crawdads from his creek, now and then one of his lost chickens, his everything even that slop Aunt Katie cooked up in the quarter? Will may owe him some grace, not me. He ate just as good as Master."

"Not master, not any man," Ned said, "give grace only to God."

"Master Mack and all that's behind you now, Charles," Tighe said. "Holding that grudge will make you hate your brother."

"Grudge?" Will said. "What's that?"

"Holding on to bad feelings for the sake of misery and making trouble," Tighe said, stepping between Will and Charles. While patting their shoulders and smiling at Ned, he said, "It's hard to understand the need for blessing when suffering from the mismeal colic is so painful. I'll say it."

Hungry as Will and Charles were, waiting while Tighe recited scripture and garnished it with their names, was a task. They ate for a long time, as if that would be their last meal.

"Will," Ned said. "The man who claims he owns you is offering $2,000 for your return alive. Charles, he's put $500 on your head."

"Master's put up a mighty heap to get me back."

"No," Ned said, "not Master. David Brogden is offering a mighty heap." He showed Will the poster. Will grinned at the picture of himself. Ned and Tighe frowned at each other.

"Brogden says you are dangerous, says you take fits. Have you been hit on your head, hit hard?"

"Not too hard, but I been hit a-plenty. I was Master's prize fighter."

"For how long?" Tighe said.

Will hunched his shoulders then burped and rubbed his stomach in the same manner Uncle Sammy had so often done.

"My word," Tighe said, shaking his head.

"I wouldn't let Master, er a Mr. Brogden flog me."

"So that's why thee run out of the lion's mouth," Ned said.

"Nothing run me out of nobody's mouth," Will said. "I run away by myself, me and my brother."

While Will recounted the story of his flight, Ned stroked his beard, knowing that every idle minute lost in conversation rendered Will closer to capture, or death if he fought back. And Ned believed he would fight.

"That was God testing thee," Ned said when told the story of crossing the rain-swollen creek. "The river was a mirror God sent to make Will Parker see himself."

"Why God need do anything 'cept help us to freedom?"

"He is forcing thee to know thyself. If thee had turned back, thee would have known thee didn't have the courage to undertake such a long, treacherous journey."

"I hear tell of a place in Pennsylvania," Will said, "where we can work and get paid just like white folks."

"There is such a place," Ned said. "Columbia, but you wouldn't be safe there. Every kidnapper, slave agent, federal marshal and scalawag with enough sense to study a poster is looking for thee. Thy only safety is in Canada."

"Is Canada close to Lancaster? Some time ago I heard a slaver talk about it."

"Thee will probably pass through Lancaster on the Underground Railroad, but dare not tarry there. Stay on the road with thy eyes open for Jocko." Ned held his pocket watch under the lamp. "How did you find him in the first place?"

"Jocko? First we ever hear tell him was when Tighe's boy told us to fetch up to that dummy in his yard," Will said.

"Small chance they would have to know that story, Ned," Tighe said. "Jocko standing in a yard or guarding a lane, boys, means that house is a station in the underground."

"Yea," said Will boastfully, now that he understood the connection. "He's the word in a word the old folks speak."

"What is thy meaning, this word in a word about Jocko?" Ned smiled with a bemused expression,

"He's some kind of conjure, like them things Miz Sady used to make out of mud with roots and chicken foots and stuff," Will said, suddenly feeling that he should have just listened.

"Gracious no," Tighe said, "Jocko is real. He was a twelve-year-old soldier in George Washington's army, the most courageous boy this country is apt to know in its lifetime. He was free, his daddy too. They fought with Mr. Washington in the Battle of Trenton."

"Thee could say he is a symbol," Ned said. "A strong symbol from God that binds the hearts of brave men and women who dare defy unjust laws."

"That's what he's come to be," Tighe said. "He froze to death, standing tall while he guarded Mr. Washington's horse the night he and his troops crossed the Delaware River and whipped the British. He made Jocko a hero and that little statue is an attraction at Mount Vernon."

"The story means very little to you now," Ned said. "But carry the tale of that brave lad in your hearts and trust him for safety wherever you see him."

Will nudged Charles whose head had drooped. His eyes looked as if they were full of muddy water. Ned held his pocket watch under the lamp.

"Gracious, young fellows," he said, "excuse Tighe and me for being so rude. Thee must sleep now, for when dawn breaks, you must be well on your way. So come, let's go to the loft in the barn."

Tired as Will was and content, being full of food, sleep still did not come easily. He couldn't open his heart to Ned despite the abundant generosity. Yet, he had quibbled with Charles, telling him Ned was genuine, while deep within he agreed with his brother. Couldn't trust him, his thee and thy funny talk didn't sound real, Charles had said. They were scared, Ned protected them. They were hungry, he fed them. Did they have a choice, Will argued. When he first heard about Quakers he hadn't thought about them being white, like Master Mack or Groit. How could he be so different than other white folks. Why was he so kind? He was though. Mr. Tighe had not tricked them. Then he heard Charles snoring like a bumble bee, zooming close, fading, and close again.

Suddenly, "Will!" Ned reached into the hay piled on Will and shook him violently. "Get up, quickly now."

Will sat up, dazed and breathing in the hazy morning air rife with honeysuckle and pine tree resin. He pushed aside the hay that covered him, sending dusk particles flying into the shaft of June sunlight that streamed directly in his face. His brown eyes, hooded like a hawk's, were wide and filled with sleepish resentment.

"Follow me! Oh, God," he said. "Spare them, spare these dear young brothers from the lynching mob."

"Charles!" Ned snatched his arm.

Charles turned over and grunted. He tried to bury himself deeper in the hay, but Ned grabbed his legs and pulled him to the ladder.

"Quickly, quickly! They're coming this way."

Will shot up like a coiled spring under him had been released. He plowed into Ned, sent him spinning into the hay.

"Wait," Ned said. "Thee must hide."

"Hide shit," Will said, rushing down the catwalk. "We git'n, Mr. Quaker."

"No, no." Ned scrambled down behind Charles. "Will, Charles, run from this barn and ye won't get a mile away. I know of what I speak. Come, or you'll soon be in chains or hanging from a tree."

Ned ran to the trap door in the barn floor. He stamped three times in quick succession and stepped back. The trap door cracked open.

Ned snatched it wide. "Get in there, latch the door, and don't open it for anyone."

Will and Charles climbed in. The trace of light dwindled to absolute blackness as Ned closed then in.

"Hey you, somebody down here that peeped, open this here door. You still here?" Charles said.

Not even an echo answered. Will had barely latched it before the thundering sound of shodden horses on the rough hewn floor planks clapped in their ears. It made his head vibrate. Charles forgot about the darkness. Voices, many of them talking all at once, fired angry questions at Ned.

"We know you tolled the bell that warned your loving niggers, and since we found..."

"I love ye too," Ned said, "all of ye, even in your tyrannical wickedness and though I know ye are not a favorite of heaven..."

"Cut in on me with your religion tomfoolery again, I'm apt to lose me patience."

"Get the magistrate out here, Groit," one of the gang said. "Teach this thee guy what obeying the law means."

Will's stomach seared as if a hot skewer had been thrust down his throat. Groit, grimy poor white trash. He saw Tawney writhing in the dirt with blood oozing from cuts on her body. He listened, remembering the promise he had made to avenge her beating.

"Smite me, brethren, if ye must in your moments of weakness, but ye cannot shatter the blessed rock on which I stand." Ned stood with his legs apart, arms folded across his chest.

"These here knapsacks," Groit said, "we found just over the county line belongs to them two." He showed Ned the posters of Will and Charles.

"I know both the niggers better'n old Brodgen do. Know 'em so well I know their smell, and I tell you they been here."

"If ye plan on staying here another minute, ye'd better find somebody mighty quick with a warrant," Ned said.

Ned knew the law demanded he surrender fugitives, knew it demanded he, as well as a free black person such as Tighe, assist in the capture of Will and Charles. In his heart though, it was unjust and contradicted God's natural law which declares all men brothers, linked spiritually to the one source.

"All right," Groit said, "by God, break the law, love your niggers, I'll do just that. It's high time you damned preachers learned some respect for the rules that bind men in power. Hey," he pointed to three of his motley crew, "stay here till we fetch a warrant to search this here place."

"Ye dare not stay on my land one minute longer, none of you." Ned fanned his muscular arm in the air as if spreading bird seed. "Clear out, I say." He glared at Groit.

Groit spurred his horse. "By the whiskers of Moses, you'll regret this." He and his crew galloped off. Clods of dirt from the horses' hoofs kicked back at Ned.

Ned knew Groit would return with a federal marshal and they would stay until every inch of ground and building had been searched. When Groit disappeared, he ran to the bell mounted on the barnside, and tolled it two rapid short strokes and one loud sustained gong. Old Barnaby would be leaving with his load of hay about now for his morning trip up Baltimore Pike to Susquehanna. Now that he had alerted the community, Tighe would get Will and Charles ready to travel.

Will stood in the black hole, angry with himself for not running and wondering why he hadn't. He shuddered at the thought of his and Groit's paths crossing again. Groit carried a gun, a whip and probably a dagger too. He would just as soon kill Will as look at him, Will knew that. But the old bear would rather whip him and Charles, and take them to Master Mack alive,

"Somebody's coming," Charles said.

"Yeah," Will said. "I hope it ain't ole Groit. He's tough 'n all that, but he'll have to kill me. I ain't going back." Will bit his bottom lip. For a brief moment he longed for Grandmom Rosey and thought about Uncle Sammy. "I wish Ned hadn't stopped me," he said.

"Will, Charles." The voice came from a lantern coming toward them from Tighe's kitchen, shining like a halo of blinding light.

"Mr. Tighe?" Will asked.

"You must leave right away," Tighe said.

"I'm scared, real scared, 'cause them slavers know we here. I heard Mr. Groit say so," Charles said.

"We're all scared," Tighe said. "Fear is a daily companion in our lives. My wife was a fugitive until I bought her freedom, but that's a long story. You, my young friend, must keep your soul's conviction alive. It wills you to be free."

"What you mean?" Will asked. "You say the kind of stuff the old slave preacher say back at Roedown. If I had a gun like that pig belly overseer, I'd show him how scared I am."

"A gun would only get you killed, son, and a lot of innocent black folks along with you. Why do I chance losing my life, my wife's or Jeremiah's for two downstate-horse-breeding plantation slaves I'll never see again?"

"You didn't have to. We don't ask nobody for nothing."

"You today, somebody else tonight, a dozen or so by next week," Tighe said. "Who doesn't matter. All of it is for the cause of abolition."

"Hunh," Will said. He and Charles followed Tighe up the stairs from the tunnel through the pantry.

"We're abolitionists. Our goal is to end all slavery in America, though it may seem unlikely. So whoever comes our way, we are obliged to help."

"Abolist, hunh?"

"Abolitionist," Tighe said slowly. He stared in Will's eyes and smiled a little.

"Someday Will, I pray you will say that what I'm about to tell you is no longer true. For now though, disbelieving is an invitation to doom. You listen too, Charles."

Tighe rubbed his hands together then jammed them in his pockets. "Every white person you see is a threat to your safe passage. Abolitionists are the only white people you can trust. How do you recognize them? It isn't easy. Look for signs, smiling eyes, a pleasant greeting. Do not be fooled by a grinning mouth. A smile on the lips can deceive, but not one in the eyes. Eyes are a mirror to the soul. If a man turns away or stares at the ground when you look him in the eye, do not trust him. Ask a person you can trust for Jocko. If you get lost or need a place to hide, look for Jocko."

"Now," Tighe said, "the hour is late. Someone else will see to your safe passage from Baltimore."

Tighe's wife, standing aside with an arm around Jeremiah, gave a packed lunch to Will. "Son," she said, "pray without ceasing for deliverance and it will come."

"Yes'm," Will said, sensing for the first time that he could remember a mother's love, and glancing away, not wanting her to read the fear in him.

She grasped Charles' shoulders. "Do not despair. Giving up for even a minute is an invite to defeat. God is on our side. We are with you."

Charles' eyes filled.

Tighe shook their hands. "I'm sending you to Barnaby. His stable is down the street. He won't say one word to you," Tighe said, "so when he stands beside the wagon and looks at you, crawl under and fit yourself in a pocket. Lay down and he'll fit the boards under you. He'll reach the Susquehanna River before dark. When he moves the boards, climb out and follow the river in the direction he points. God be with you, my sons."

"Bye," little Jeremiah said.

Will rubbed the back of his hands across his mouth and smiled warily as they ventured down the street. His dark eyes traveled over everything they passed. Charles' eyes were still filled with water.

"I wish we could stay with them," he said.

"Don't look back," Will said. "Walk steady and listen to every sound. That way, can't nobody sneak up behind us."

They passed a wooded lot, Will's ears immediately attuned so acutely that he even heard the soft murmur of the June breeze brushing tender new magnolia and oak tree leaves. Then, the sight of a wagon hitched to four mules and piled high with hay shot strength and spirit into him. A sudden image of freedom overpowered the fear of being captured or killed that had gripped him since Ned pulled him awake.

Barnaby's Freight Line and Livery, Will couldn't read the sign over the barn but he reasoned that a man, tall and skinny as a scarecrow, walking through a doorway from a lean-to attached to the barn, had been waiting. Will and Charles stopped abruptly.

"Hullo," Charles said.

The man didn't answer, didn't even look at him. The chin that jutted from his jawbone was flat as a plank. A ring of white hair around his otherwise bald head resembled a witch's broom. His eyes, blue and clear as a cloudless sky, twinkled and rolled in their sockets. His nose was painted with thin, blue, criss-crossing veins.

"Abe," a woman called to him.

Charles grabbed Will's arm in a manner of telling him to wait, observe before getting any closer. Will tensed. His nostrils dilated. The sinews in his arms swelled. The man stared at the doorway until the woman opened it and looked out.

"Oh," she said and disappeared.

"You Barnaby?" Will said from the roadway.

Abe rolled his tongue over a wad the size of a pullet's egg protruding from a pocket in his left jaw and spewed the ground with brown liquid. With his hand on the wagon side, he bent over and with his head motioned under the wagon. Will and Charles looked and saw that boards had been removed from an opening cut into the wagon's bottom. He nodded his head, then looked at Will and Charles. Again, as the situation had occurred so many times in the past four days, he and Charles either took the chance on blind faith, or lingered for certain capture. After quick inspection, they climbed in and lay flat side by side. Abe then shoved the missing boards into slots in each end. The boards would appear to any suspecting eye as a simple floor repair.

Never before in his life had Will heard anyone whistle to move his mules, but that's what Abe did. The high-pitched sound, almost as piercing as a scream, jolted the mules. After the wagon lunged forward, Will bumped his head time and time again, bouncing over rutted Baltimore Pike bound to the river. At least that's where he hoped they were going. He didn't know what turn of fate had brought them to Tighe's and Ned's places. He did understand that without the underground railroad, escape would be too big a task for two boys who had absolutely no knowledge of where they were, where they would stop next, or when they would eventually reach the end of their journey. He knew old Groit and his gang were lurking close by, but didn't understand why Master Mack, much smarter than the toothless poor-trash overseer, hadn't crossed their path. Will feared for his life. If he had known the grave consequence of escape when he took the whip and ran away, he certainly wouldn't have acted like the man Uncle Sammy said he was.

"Hold up, there."

Will knew that voice. He looked at Charles and indicated with his hands for him to be absolutely still.

"You seen these here two runaway niggers," Will heard Groit say to Abe. "I say there ole man, I ask you a question."

Abe didn't answer, he didn't stop. Groit snatched the harness near one of the mules' eyes and yanked. The mule reared and hee-hawed so loudly he stirred critters in the weeds just as a mother skunk and her brood were emerging from the low entanglement of brush, and Groit's gang began punching Abe's hay with pitch-forks.

Will heard the slight hissing of plunging prongs, but didn't know what they were doing. That strong, unmistakable acrid odor though. "Aww God, naw," he said.

The wagon shifted back and forth with the prancing of excited mules. Abe whistled and whistled.

"Sonofabitch," Charles said. "She got me. Holy cow, the lunch too."

"Back off," Groit yelled. "She's damned riled." He and his gang retreated to a safe distance beyond range of the mother skunk lifting her tail again at the edge of the wagon.

"Whydn't you gawddamned worthless sons of vultures get a job," Abe yelled at the slave runners. "By Jesus Christ, a God fearing man can't do an honest day's work no more without your kind pester'n shit, kicking up trouble."

"Go on the hell about your stinking business, old man," Groit said. "We split up," he yelled, "spread out, track them two bucks from every direction."

"I hate you worse'n I hate niggers," Abe yelled at Groit's back.

"First pair of real britches I ever had that don't belong to Master Mack all shot up with skunk mess," Charles said.

Shh!" Will cautioned. "Hear what Abe just said?"

"Twern't much. He said that to fool Groit," Charles said.

"He meant every screaming word, just like old Mack that day, mad as hell and making funny to keep me from knowing he was go'n strap me.

"But Tighe and Ned, they know Abe better'n you do, Will."

"That don't mean they know everything he thinks about," Will said.

"He could've let Groit take us," Charles said, "but he didn't".

"Ain't nobody with one lick of sense would trust Groit," Will said. "Abe could take us all the way back to Roedown, have all the money for hisself."

Abe bobbed along atop the wagon hearing incoherent snatches of the boys' excited conversation. He knew without a doubt that Groit and probably many others would be watching the river. Though Abe's word was his bond, Ned's only assurance that he would set fugitives on the northbound trail, Will—especially Will—challenged his moral conviction in a way it had never been challenged. A bundle of money few men would resist even killing each other to get.

At a crossroads that Abe knew would lead them to South Mountain, the barrier between Maryland and Pennsylvania, he drove into a grove of trees and pulled hard on the reins. The lead mule reared his head and bucked, forcing the other three to stop. Abe climbed down, made a cursory look about, bent under the wagon and pulled the boards that supported Will and Charles. They practically fell flat on the ground, much relieved however, that even though they did not know whether they were deeper in slave territory, they had not been delivered to their master.

"Which way to the river?" Will asked, crawling from under the wagon.

Abe pinched his nostrils shut with one hand and with the other, pointed up the road behind him. He replaced the boards, climbed atop his load as if they weren't standing there.

"Say," Charles said, "you can talk, we heard you. Where is we?"

Abe's eyes drilled a hole in Charles. "Hate niggers, hate slavery. I'll smuggle you to Canada, favor giving you your own free state, help send you back to Africa, do anything to stop God-fearing white folks from fighting each other for your wretched asses. I hope this evening will part me from you forever."

He left them standing in the trail.

Chapter Eight

"You think he sending us the right way, Will?"

"Hard to tell," Will said, walking with Charles in the woods adjacent to a dusty wagon trail leading to the hills of the Baltimore watershed. He could see mountains in the distance. "I been looking for that river with the long name," he said. "The Susque-something Tighe told us to always keep on our right side."

"How we know which way is North?" Charles said.

The evening sun. Yes, shining on the left side of his face. Will sighed, relieved that Charles' question sparked his memory that had become panicky and confused. So many warnings, so many new things to remember.

"We going the right way. Tighe said if we walk all day we should reach the mountains by night. Pennsylvania is on the other side."

He and Charles, both suddenly overcome with anxiousness, walked for a spell in fearful silence. Freedom so close, yet so far away over the mountains. So many dreadful hills and ridges full of road agents and slave hunters. Hide in the rocks if you must sleep, Tighe told them, but be careful of lying down in a snake pit. Travel in the morning with the sun to your right side. The higher and rugged mountain trails were safest, horses couldn't tread there so easily. Fugitives and free black men lived in the higher regions, but do not trust them. They survived on constant fear and would kill in an instant.

"Now what you thinking about so hard?" Charles asked Will.

Will smiled, "Kinda funny," he said, "I was about to ask you that."

"Wonder if that skunk," Charles said, "messed on Mis Emily's ham and cornbread?"

"I stink just like it, you too," Will said, tearing the wrapping off the package. "How bad can it smell?" The faint aroma of baked ham, the sight of yellow corn bread hastened his appetite. " 'N I'm hungry too, but we eat on the run, night is coming up fast."

"No fibbing, Will," Charles said, reaching for the package. "What you really think freedom's like?"

Will didn't speak for a minute or so. He gave Charles his portion of the lunch. After chewing and swallowing a mouthful, he said, "It's probably like being with a daddy, if I had one."

"Daddy? The funny things you say. We ain't got no daddy. Me thinks somebody may did bop you a mite too hard a time or two."

"Freedom could be something we go'n always be wishing for, Charles."

Will wouldn't tell Charles that he couldn't express to anyone exactly how he felt about freedom. He tried forming images of the good he had heard, as he had done years ago about his father. But they became distorted, fragmented images infused with fearful snarls already imbedded in his mind. Yet, those fragments were his only hope, the faith that led him, faith in the belief that maybe, just maybe he would find freedom. He had surrendered the belief that it lay like a big green pasture not too far away over the mountains and across a river, like the Jordan about which he remembered hearing the old slave preacher talk. He remembered Aunt Aida stealing away on the underground railroad, then seeing her in chains of captivity, headed for the dreaded cotton fields in the deep South.

"Think about her much, Will? Mama I mean?"

A vague image came to Will. He tried musing on some memory of her. "Grandmom Rosey wouldn't let me."

"Mama stopped raising me when you was born," Charles said. "Took me to the quarter, left me with that ole dried up cow, Aunt Kate.

"How's come you never said we's some kin, all them days I set in the corner," Will said, "crying 'n fighting to stay warm and stuff."

"You think you and me's the only somebody in the quarter that's kin and didn't act like it? Hell Will, Grandmom made you think you was somebody's God. I didn't like you, I didn't want you to know me."

"Why'd you run off with me from Roedown?"

"Cause you paid me to do it. Ain't nothing hard about that to see."

"Damn," Will said, "you too mean to think on freedom?"

"Look at us," Charles said. "Don't know where we going, most like go'n get caught, and you go'n hang. Maybe me too, but for sure, I'll be sold down the river. All because Master set you up so pretty and then took it all away." Charles sucked his teeth, but he had already infuriated Will.

"You a mule-face lie. I been thinking freedom ever since Mama died. If by now you can't see that running's only chance you go'n git for some kind of decent life to live, just give me back my money and haul ya ass on back to Roedown."

"How? I can't go back there and you know it."

"You can't go on neither, the way you acting, scared of the dark, scared of cats, scared of your own damned self..."

"You so damned tough, hunh," Charles said.

"Hell yeah. Don't," Will said, "you be dead by now, but I ain't carrying you no more."

"Didn't ask you in the first place," Charles said.

"You didn't have to, but I'm through talking about it. You and your spit-sucking self." Will walked faster, distancing himself from Charles in the oncoming darkness, challenging him to keep up while they trekked over the steadily rising and changing terrain.

In the dim after-glow of sunset shining through peaks of green hills towering high in front of them, South Mountain of the Appalachian Mountain range rose like dark clouds. The dark hills with their dense forest seemed to welcome him, yet they were forbidding. The night world spread its blanket earlier and much more thickly in the mountains. Trees blocked out the stars. Will stopped, rigid. He caught himself imagining the bent and twisted haunts of Master Mack, Groit, Wallace, slave agents. Will desperately wished he had a weapon of some sort to protect him.

"Oops." Charles bumped into him. "See something that ain't suppose to be here?"

Will noticed a quivering in Charles' quiet voice. He answered gruffly. "Hell no," he lied, staring into blackness.

Then surely, as if speaking made magic, his eyes began adjusting to the dark. A patch of clearing in the wooded hillside around them reminded Will of an abandoned Indian camp near Roedown. He could distinguish trees from boulders, from tree stumps and fallen trunks and broken branches, from clumps of underbrush. Before him and Charles a straight and narrow up-hill trail disappeared between two boulders wide enough perhaps for a person on horseback to pass through. One scary guess of what might lay beyond in that huge void of darkness convinced him, they shouldn't go in that direction.

"What we go'n do?" Charles said.

"What we go'n do," Will said, mocking Charles. "Over, there, thatta way. We go see."

Off to the right of him and Charles stood boulders with scrub trees growing from the cracks. Standing closer, at the base of huge rocks of varying sizes and shapes, and lying at odd angles, Will saw a narrow gully in the rugged ascending terrain probably worn there by streams flowing from mountain heights during spring rains.

"Think you man enough boost me up top?" Will said, backing Charles against the first boulder.

"Hell yeah," Charles said, "but ain't nothing to grab a hold of except them lil' ole twigs. I ain't no mountain goat."

"Let's just do it," Will said, waving his hands in disgust. He placed his right foot in Charles' interlocked fingers and put his hands on his shoulders. "It's a pretty good ways up," he said, surveying the boulder's height. "Keep your back straight, bend your knees some more, Some more yet, man. Christomighty, you got the rickets? That's good. Now, when you feel me moving up throw me high."

Will sprung and Charles heaved, but not enough. Will clawed at the granite a good foot below the top and fell, sprawled in front of Charles.

"Gawd-dammit," he said, rubbing his bruised elbows and slowly standing. "You ain't strong worth a hot damn."

"Who ain't? I could'a sent your narrow butt clean to kingdom-come," Charles boasted, "but I don't want to hurt you none."

"Don't worry about hurting me," Will said, preparing himself for the second try, "git me up top.".

Charles sent him up in good fashion, then turned around boastfully, looking in all directions as if a silent crowd had watched him. He suddenly felt uneasy as if doom itself, waiting for the right moment, was about to pounce on him. Will, scratching around in the dark for a strong enough branch or a hole in which to wedge his foot, kicked loose some dirt and gravel. A jagged rock the size of his fist fell on Charles' head.

"Oww," he yelled, rubbing the tender spot. "What the hell's wrong witcha, nig...uh ugly cullud boy!"

"Glad you changed that," Will said, lying flat on his stomach with his head and chest over the edge, and stammering to keep from laughing. "If you can see my hand?" he said, anchoring his feet, "Jump and grab a hold. I'll pull you up."

"Don't drop no more rocks on me, Will. I'm a telling you nice as I know how. Don't!"

"If you mad, gawd-dammit, come git me," Will said.

Charles jumped but missed his mark pitifully.

"Go'n have to do way better'n that," Will said, laughing hysterically. "Jump like the blacksmith back at Roedown just smacked you in the ass with a red-hot horseshoe."

"I'm a red-hot in the ass horseshoe you," Charles said, crouching then leaping so high that Will smelled the angry breath exuding from his lungs.

Will missed his hand, but Charles wrapped both of them around Will's extended wrist, nearly snatching him from the mooring. Charles' dangling body, the dead weight of it pulled and strained Will's hands and bruised arms. Yet, he held steadily, grasping Charles elbow, coaxing him to put his feet against the boulder, telling him to step up. When Charles was close enough to peer over the top, Will, unable to pull him another inch, let go one hand but grabbed a handful of shirt. It tore. Charles slipped. Will, grunting and mustering his last ounce of strength, grabbed him under an armpit. With his elbows for leverage, he helped Charles inch himself high enough for his chest to clear the edge. Charles let go the right hand and grabbed Will's head at the base of his skull. Will stiffened his neck and raised his head an inch or so, but Charles climbing over as if Will was a rigid log, ground his face into the granite like surface. Will grunted, felt the skin on his cheek smarting, but held fast until Charles rolled off beside him.

"Don't ever laugh at me, Will," Charles said. "I don't like it."

"Freedom damned sure make a man out of you," Will said, rubbing the bleeding spot on his face, and suddenly thinking of snakes.

He jumped up and began a slow ascension, one arduous step at a time over rocks, around boulders, wedging his foot wherever possible, silently praying he wouldn't put his foot on a snake. He grasped supple branches, pulling himself higher until the rocky hillside sloped at an angle that did not pose such a threat of a broken leg or a long fall. Charles followed, grunting and groaning. At the top the terrain spread into a broad, sloping plateau. On the far side mountains rose skyward again. They trudged on in that direction.

"I keep feeling some big eyes on me," Charles said, "so bad my skin's crawling."

Will stopped suddenly. "I smell smoke," he whispered.

Fifty yards yards or so from them behind a boulder, a fire crackled under a blackened pot. Its flickering made an erie circle of light in the black void. The aroma of coffee and cooking meat was strong in the humid June mountain night. Two men, Groit and a side-kick named Johnny Sledge, sat with their backs to a boulder eating roasted rabbit from sticks. In the shadow of the fire, a mongrel dog gnawed on bones and pieces of meat from the hot carcass. Two horses hitched to a low branch of tree, munched on tender sprouts of grass some fifteen yards from the men.

"Hell, Groit," Sledge said, "we catch this here Parker and his brother, we ain't never need track no more fugitives."

"And we gonna catch'em," Groit boasted, "since we found that secret trail through these hills. Ain't no other way for'em to go that ain't watched."

"That Parker's slick," Sledge said.

"Like hell," Groit said. "Nigger's just lucky, but don't tangle with'em. I seen him hit a nigger and rattle the bastard's brain so bad, Mack Brogden couldn't do nothing but hitch'em to a plow just like he was a mule."

Sledge bent over laughing, holding his stomach, coughing up phlegm.

"For crissakes," Groit said, "here." He thrust Sledge's coffee mug at him, then bent his whip into an upside down U and cracked it. The tip lashed out and tore a chunk of bark from a tree.

"Brodgen won't pay top dollar if they bruised up, Groit," Sledge said, leaning back against the rock.

"It don't make no never mind to me. I'd make more money making Parker fight for me than I'll ever get in rewards from Brodgen. Besides, the nervy sonofabitch's got more gall'n any man I know. Imagine him firing me and putting one of his niggers in my place."

"And the niggers still laughing," Sledge said. "So you planning on delivering these two and laughing in Brodgen's face when he pays you $2,500?"

Groit bristled. "Don't wanna talk about it."

"Maybe I'll get a spread and buy me a couple niggers," Sledge said. "About time I settle down. This nigger snatching business getting too gawddamn dangerous. Once a fugitive gets in a free state, can't bring'em back without a fight. So many dumb nigger-lovers. What in hell's the country coming to? Hey, didja' hear that Groit?"

Curt, a mangy underfed part German-shepherd and collie growled. "I heard something rustle, yea." Groit tore off a chunk of rabbit with his teeth.

"Rustle hell," Sledge said. "I heard a stick break. The mutt heard it too. You forget, these hills filled up with damn fool niggers."

"Why are you so itchy-twitchy, Sledge? Hell, Curt can smell'em a mile away."

"I ain't witchy one bit, but damn, we sitting here around the fire like two fat gooses in hunting season and ain't nothing around us but black night."

Curt gruffed and stood. His big ears moved. He raised a front paw.

"See what I mean?" Sledge said.

"Yeah, yeah, I do believe you're right," Groit said.

Groit reached under his saddle bag for a rifle. "Git yours, Sledge. Some mighty strange goings-on out there." He eased around to the dark side of the huge rock.

Not far away from the pass, Will and Charles also heard the rustling. They stopped.

"Something's out there," Will said, "betwixt us and whoever's around that fire."

They crouched.

"Sure hope I ain't squat'n over a rattler," Charles said,

"Shut up and keep your eyes on the back," Will said. "I'll watch the front."

Groit patted Curt's side a couple times. "Atta boy," he said softly. Then he put his mouth next to the dog's ear and said in a gruff tone, "Go, Curt, sic'em boy."

Curt disappeared in the darkness, barking loudly.

"Uh-oh," Will said. "Hell done broke loose."

"What we go'n do now?" Charles said. "He's sounds bigger'n a mule."

"I sure as hell ain't go'n let'em hem me up side a tree like I'm a coon," Will said, "and he ain't dragging me to that fire."

Between the two young fugitives and the bounty hunters Curt snarled and charged at a looming shadow darker than night. He yelped. Then all was quiet.

"Something shut'em up," Will said.

Charles began sweating. "And fast too."

"We got to get outta here," Will said. "Ain't but one way that I can see and it's thatta way."

"Right by that fire? Hell, we may as well give up, walk right in and tell'em we want to go back," Charles said.

"We can't stay here! We sneak past." Will began walking as if stalking a bear.

"What in hell's happened to Curt?" Groit said. "It's pitch black out there and so damned quiet you could hear a tombstone grin,"

Suddenly without warning, a hand with a grip stronger than a possum's trap wrapped around Will's ankle. "Oww." He yelled and fell.

Groit shifted from his fat behind to his knees. "Git outta the fire light," he said, cocking his rifle, aiming it at the darkness.

A black man as thick as an aged oak tree dragged Will to him and jammed his knee in Will's back.

"Don't move, lil' run away nigguh and you," he waved a knife at Charles. "Back up. Don't, I'm 'a cut his th'oat."

"Don't cut him in the throat, mister. He's my brother."

"Shut up and listen to me. Whooeee boy, you stink worse'n polecat. Both 'a ya." He pushed Will's face in the stony ground and leaned away from him as if struggling for air.

"Sit down, boy." He waved his knife at Charles. "Anybody that could climb up that rockside tells me they neck ain't long from the noose. But you cain't stay up heah in Darky mountain. This is Timbuh's world."

"We don't wanna stay," Charles said.

"Pleeeze, mister polecat, er ah Timbuh sir, my face," Will said. "You too heavy."

"We talk first," Timber said. "Y'all brung buckra up heah, so y'all go'n hep me run 'um out. Then I take you to the rivuh. Don't, I cut yo' th'oat and give him to buckra like I'm a give him his dog."

"We do it," Charles said. "You bending him near 'bout in two."

Will couldn't speak. He could though, nod his head a little.

"Seems like I got ya word on it," Timber said, releasing him.

Will sat up, gingerly touching his sore face and rubbing his ankles. He shook his head, disbelieving the height of Timber, head and shoulders taller than Charles standing near him.

"No white man evuh set foot up heah 'til now," Timber said. "Now, he done found a way up with his hoss, and I got to run him out in a way he ain't nevah comin' back."

"We ain't even got a good sized stick," Will said.

"What'n hell good is a stick upside a gun?" Timber said. "Buckra ain't scared 'a nothin' and whatevuh happens, he go'n suspect a trick. But in the lil' time it takes for'em to ketch on, y'all got to scoot, boy. He go'n start shootin' soon's his eyes pop back in his head."

Will watched, somewhat amused at Timber gumming his words. He had nary a tooth in his mouth.

"Sledge," Groit said, "I could'a swore I heard somebody yell a minute ago, and I just got a whiff of a polecat."

"Git your mutt back here, dammit," Sledge said. "Something's happened."

89

"I feel it in my bones, I tell ya. I smell him, I know the nigger's scent and Curt's probably treed him. Heh, heh." Groit laughed. "C'mon Curt," he yelled, and whistled.

At that instant the big dog's carcass hit the fire, covering hot, sizzling embers, plunging the pass into darkness.

"Holychrist! Indians! They done scalped Curt!" Sledge fired a shot in the air and drew himself into a ball.

Will and Charles, having already untied the horses, smacked them on their rumps and sent them running in the darkness.

"Stop it, ya crazy bastard! You just spooked the horses. I thought you knew how to trap niggers. Gawd-dammit, you couldn't sneak up on a dipper for a drink'a water."

Will and Charles followed Timber around the rock and were crawling along a path beneath a thick overhang of brush.

"Will Parker, you sonofabitch, hear me! I'll see your black ass in chains. I'll see you in Mississippi."

Will heard Groit and while he crawled on with his heart thumping, he knew deep within himself that he probably would have to kill Groit if he ever set eyes on him again.

They followed Timber for miles in the brush, winding, ascending and descending until they reached a clearing atop a hillside above the Susquehanna. At the edge, a chunk of hillside had broken off and slid into the river. Rising out of the black abyss the long branches of a leaning oak tree spread out over their heads. Timber grabbed a rope hanging from a branch and tugged at it.

"Y'all lookin' ovuh the rivuh into a free state, boys," he said.

"I don't see nothing but night down there," Charles said, "but if freedom's on the other side, hallelujah!"

"I done brung ya' across the state line," Timber said, "but you got to git along."

Will looked across the river below them to the dark mass of hills in Lancaster County. Then he asked Timber, "Why you pulling on that hemp?"

"Every trail from these hills is blocked. Soon's day come they be watching from the rivuh too. Ain't but one way they don't know."

Will looked at Timber. Timber saw the question in his eyes.

"Yup, you go'n hafta swing ovuh the hole to that big limb and climb down the tree." Timber moved back ten or twelve paces with the rope. "Git ya'self a big run like this and take off like a big-ass eagle." He laughed. "Back in Luzanna I'd grab me a vine hanging off a cypress tree and swing one handed ovuh alligators in the bayou."

He swung out a ways, disappeared in darkness and returned.

"You go'n hafta swing for real, boy. Still, you won't make it in one pass. When you swing out throw ya belly like this." He jutted out his big stomach. "When you swing back throw ya rump out like this."

Will and Charles snickered.

"Go ahead, laugh. But if you let go without wrapping ya legs 'round that branch, you go'n see Christ befo' you see freedom."

"Hell," Will said. "I been swinging from trees since I was a runt."

"It's black as Satan's britches down there," Charles said. "How we supposed to see?"

"Make yo' eyes see, boy, like you did scootin' out them hills while ago. Come day, buckra be settin' out theah in the watuh, watchin' 'n waitin'."

"C'mon Charles," Will said. "We got to do it."

"Ain't got much time either," Timber said. " 'N I got to clean them peckuhwoods outta Darky Mountain. Ain't had no problems 'til you, so don't lemme ketcha back up heah."

Will took the rope from Timber and began working it in his hands. He stretched it back as far as it would go, dashed to the edge and leaped. On his return Timber and Charles watched him jerk his body backwards and swing out over the hole again.

"My foot touched the branch," he said on his second return. He thrust his body forward and went out again. That time he wrapped his legs around the limb and hung there with the rope in his hands for several minutes. When the rope drifted back, Timber grabbed it.

"He waitin'." Timber looked at Charles.

"I'm a try it," Charles said. "But I might need a boost when I swing back. Hear, Mr. Timbuh?"

"Git the hell on out theah like he did and if you don't pump you go'n be left hanging right ovuh that hole."

He forced the rope into Charles' hands, pulled him as far back as he could and flung him so far out he almost slammed into Will. Charles' stretched eyes were wide and white as biscuit dough. Will knew Charles wouldn't pump so he readied himself.

When Charles returned Will grabbed his legs. "Hold on the rope," he said. "Stretch out so I can wrap your legs around the tree."

"Can you see the bottom, Will?"

"Damn the bottom! Wrap ya'self around this limb. I can't hold you forever." Will could feel Charles trembling.

Charles stretched his legs slowly.

"Dammit," Will said, "I'm a leave ya ass hanging here if you don't try to help yourself. Now, wrap one arm around the branch. Hold tight, let go the rope, wrap the other arm around the branch. Dammit, will you let go the rope before I knock the hell outcha?"

Charles wouldn't extend his arms from the rope or lock himself around the branch.

"All right then, piss on you." Will jerked him as if pushing Charles away from him."

"Wait, wait, Will. You and me is blood, now dammit. Just gimme a chance to get hold'a myself."

"Better hurry the hell up," Will said.

Charles got one arm around the limb. "Don't let go, Will. Please God, don't."

Will didn't answer. If he felt him slipping, he thought to himself, he'd let go. Damned if he'd fall in that hole. Charles sensed Will's thoughts. He released the rope and clung to the tree as if trying to squeeze life from it. After suspending himself there, trying to gain courage, he said, "Let's get the hell down from here, Will."

"Ease down real slow," Will said. Already, as he began inching himself down he felt the rough bark biting through his tattered clothes into his legs, arms, stomach and feet. He was moving away from Charles but he wouldn't wait.

After they had inched down the oak branch to where the Y grew out of the main trunk, Will stopped. The trunk was too wide for him to wrap himself around it, he'd have to jump. He could see the dark water beneath him and the growth of trees and scrub brush that had been pushed by the landslide to the water's mossy edge. In its place was a steep decline of bare stones and yellowish dirt. He looked up at Charles.

"We got to jump," he said, immediately releasing his legs and hanging by his arms.

He let go, lost his balance when his feet hit the dirt, fell backwards, slid on his back, sat up and slid on his rump, sprang to his feet and slid, ran, stumbled, then slipped to his knees, trying to regain his balance, Oh God, coming up fast, the river. He ran into it and fell. Charles dropped and fell, went head over heels, then rolled sideways over and over, down into the water.

Will moaning and Charles crying: two dejected, bleeding and aching figures silhouetted by the glow of moonlight on the water disturbed the peaceful sound of the Susquehanna lapping its western shore. The baptism of cool water on their stinging bodies, at first like angry hornets pricking them with fire, was their declaration of redemption. They had bridged an impossible divide into a free land. Yet, they were still to learn that freedom was more than one-hard fought thing.

Sleep would come so easily in the shallow, soothing water if they could lie still just a while longer, but Will heard a distant rooster crowing. They had better move on. Somewhere close to a bridge a free colored man ran a ferry.

Will should go there, call him by his first name. He would understand and provide safe passage across to Columbia,

"C'mon," Will said, "we got to cross the river."

"Can't move, Will," Charles said. "I hurt everywhere."

Will spun around and frowned so hard at Charles it seemed that his thick black eyebrows touched. "Git up."

"Aw shiiiiit," Charles said, staggering to his feet.

He never saw his brother's hands move. Will smacked him so quickly and hard the lick resounded and skipped across the river before Charles fully realized he had been hit. He lost his balance and stumbled backwards. Will wrapped both of his tough hands around Charles' neck, bent his head down to the water, and talked through clenched teeth.

"Gawd-dammit, if I'd waited for you we'd be back there hollering oooh at that rock, I'd still be up there hanging in that tree. I'm tired begging and fighting, so you go'n follow me. And if you think about acting crazy behind my back, don't. I can see from the back of my head and I'll throw you in the river."

Charles had never seen Will react violently so quickly, but his brother's gambit had been successful. The fear and awe Will implanted in Charles seemed obvious as they tramped along barefooted in the silt, Charles practically in Will's footsteps, among the driftwood and rocks that jutted from the water's edge.

Confident they were northbound, Will noticed the steep, wooded cliffs on both sides of the river gradually receding to sloping banks that had been cleared of many trees and thick brush. When they came upon a log cabin with a wharf and flat boat moored there, Will knew he should stop. But up ahead, in the deep purple of night fading to a violet misty dawn, a structure spanning the river was taking shape. His heart quickened. He called Charles' attention to it, the Wrightsville-Columbia Bridge, longest and widest span they would see. It curved over the river near the Columbia side, just as Tighe had said. By the time bright sunlight had cleared the sky they had climbed the wooden structure and were resting under the deck high above the river. Exhausted yes, but exuberant to the point that Will pondered making a hard run to the other side, even though Tighe's warning to rely on Looney the ferryman was foremost on his mind. He climbed out from the side, peered across the bridge toward Columbia, then down the road in Wrightsville, hesitated, and quickly ducked back under. The rumble of wagon wheels and hoof beats of trotting horses from Columbia grew louder, annoying Charles who had begun nodding off to sleep. Directly overhead the wagon stopped. While the driver paid toll, Will heard two men talking.

"I believe the magistrate was lying, even though he didn't appear so damned stupid that he'd defy federal law," Will heard a man say.

"That is the problem, Bentley. There is no way a young, simple nigger could have eluded our sentries without help. Absolutely no way, unless what we just paid to prevent has already happened."

Will nudged Charles. "Bentley, that's Master Mack's lawyer," he whispered.

Charles saw that far-away look in Will's eyes again, that flight look. But he didn't care. Throw him in the river, leave him, whatever. He was too tired to move his foot.

"You really do expect the magistrate will be true to his word, don't you? You're a poor judge of character, Earl. He doesn't have a patriotic bone in his body, yet you actually bought his dutiful commitment for one hundred dollars. One hundred dollars to find that prize-nigger Parker because we know the feds can't enforce the fugitive slave law. If a two thousand five hundred dollar reward didn't flush out him and the other renegade, what guarantee do you expect from a measly hundred?"

"Earl is Master Mack's brother." Will said, rubbing the palm of his hand across his perspiring forehead.

Earl spoke again. "The hundred dollars is only a guarantee that he'll put Parker in jail and notify us before any other slaver claims him or the other young buck."

"Well, it's David's money," Bentley said. "Get smart, buy land here in Lancaster County like some of the big planters around Baltimore are doing. Warren Kipp brags that when he comes for his runaways, he gets them. Buy land, he says, sway local opinion in your favor, control the good old boys in Harrisburg."

"That is not the answer," Earl said. "We need a slave law with sharper teeth. Helping runaway slaves is a crime gainst the government. It should be an act of high treason too, punishable by hanging."

"Personally," Bentley the lawyer said, "I don't think David wants the nigger to surface, probably hoping he's dead, or in an Alabama cotton field, a thousand miles from civilization."

"He's definitely licking his wounds," Earl said. "I've often warned David, he's too easy with his niggers."

The two men rode on.

"What we go'n do, Will?" Charles said.

"You stay right here out of sight."

"But what if..."

Will glared at Charles. "What if what," he said, climbing from the structure and pitching a stone the size of his fist to Charles. "Coldcock the first somebody that comes up on you and run for that cabin. That's where I'm going."

Will climbed down to the river's edge and sneaked to within a stone's throw of the cabin by the ferry landing. He threw a pebble against the door and ducked behind a clump of low bushes. A tall wiry black man with one strap of his suspenders over his shoulder opened it and peered out. Will threw another pebble that landed in the weeds. The man looked in the direction from which the pebble had come. Will waved frantically.

"You Looney?" Will called out to him.

"That be's me, young'un. Who'n hell's chucking stones at my house?"

"Me and my brother done come a long ways."

"God a-mighty, I kin see that," Looney said. "Hurry on over here, boy."

Will's thick, nappy black hair was full of briars and twigs. Looney detected fright in his indigo black eyes and recognized Will from posters, the pear-shaped face that looked as if it had been carved from mahogany.

"I wanna cross the river, find a man name Whipper," Will said, approaching the ferry captain.

"Gitt'n too close to daybreak. White folks'll be coming soon for the ferry. Mr. Whipper ain't much for runaways coming around in the daylight. He's a rich man. Got a good business, made it off white folks."

"But they laying for me on the other side. I just heard my old master's brother and his lawyer up yonder on the bridge. They been talkin' to the magis—something."

"Yep. Agents and bounty men all over the county looking for you, boy. I hear'em say you killed your master."

"Ain't killed nobody. Quaker man told us you'd take us across the river on the underground railroad."

Looney studied Will for a minute or two. "Son, cain't much blame you for being scared." He sighed. "Where you hiding?"

"Under the bridge."

"Go back and wait for me. I be along d'rectly."

Looney watched Will disappear then studied the position of the sun rising in the East over Columbia. He walked up the river bank and from a hiding place he took a shiny tray and focused it on a fixed metal object across the river in Whipper's lumber yard. Three times he bounced the sun's reflection off the object that flashed in Whipper's kitchen. Within minutes a hired worker hoisted the American flag. Looney flashed signals that meant urgent, come for the cargo. When he saw four men pushing off in a canoe, he disappeared into the woods behind him and soon thereafter came upon Will and Charles.

Will and Charles stretched out on a plank between two uprights close to each other, sounded like two laboring steam locomotives hauling freight—hissing, blowing and whistling. Looney poked Will in his side with a long piece of driftwood. Will's body jerked, he made a startled sound, and on his sudden rise he swung so hard that if Looney had been close the lick would have driven him to his knees.

Hot damned if he ain't a tough one, Looney thought. "They coming to fetch you over yonder," he said, "better wake him too."

Will and Charles crouched with Loony in the rushes and watched two black men jump from the canoe in shallow water, sling sacks over their shoulders and disappear in the woods.

"A change of clothes in them sacks. In a minute, crawl over there and put on what on they taking off," Looney said. "Then wade out to the boat and jump in. For God sake, don't put on that you don't know what you doing."

After hastily dressing, Will and Charles waded to the canoe. "G'won get in," Will said, I'll hold it steady."

"How y'all doing?" Charles said, but neither man spoke.

One of them stood and shifted his weight on the opposite side while Will climbed in. They rowed away in silence.

Chapter Nine

William Whipper was an extraordinary man. Not that he was the son of a rich white Wrightsville merchant and a black maid servant, but that he was a wealthy black lumber dealer, an abolitionist, and an underground railroad agent. William's father had raised him in the main house with a step-brother and endowed William equally to his son by a deceased white wife. Whipper's house sat next to the long bridge, on the Columbia or east side of the Susquehanna River. Jocko stood in the yard, testimony by day, like the candle that glowed in a window by night, that a weary traveler leaving the slave empire behind, could find a safe haven there. The candle glowed from twilight to early dawn like a beacon from a light-house.

Columbia, the riverport at which Will and Charles arrived in June, 1839, a month after leaving Roedown, was a prosperous town, but one in turmoil. It had a fairly sizeable black community of freed men, women, and children and a growing population of fugitive slaves. Many fugitives were coerced to stay by merchants, farmers and industrialists to satisfy an immediate need for laborers. These businessmen offered destitute black men all sorts of wage-paying jobs. Black women, particularly single ones, found safety and employment as servants, maids and nannies in homes—opportunities they could not refuse.

Providing Columbia with an abundance of labor earned free persons and fugitives organized protection by the benevolent sector of the white community, but it created problems for Whipper. An increasingly agitated borough council, yielding to the anger of its white laboring class and immigrants, slave owners and bounty hunters, had recently ruled the hiring of fugitives illegal. Some businessmen resisted. They said blacks worked for cheaper wages and worked harder. Torment from scalawags after them, or from immigrants after their jobs were the only problems that affected their work. Whipper's fortune, amassed primarily from the white community, was threatened by the hostility.

In Whipper's house, Will and Charles hid for five days. They had scrubbed themselves until their skin shone like the leather on Whipper's saddle. Whipper outfitted them in new clothing. A colored barber styled their hair and shaved the fuzzy stubble from their chins, thus removing all physical signs of self loathing that easily identified slaves. Now, time had come for them to travel. That evening, they were sitting at a small round table in the cellar.

"After dark," Whipper said, "a man is coming for you. He'll take you to Lancaster in his wagon and tomorrow you will be on your way to Pottstown. From there someone else will escort you to New York state."

'That's what we been doing all the time since we left Roedown," Will said. "Riding the underground railroad—that ain't nothing but walking all night, sleeping in the woods and hiding from crackers."

Charles watched his brother shift his position. "I'm about tired of it," he said. "Seem like we been walking all planting season."

Whipper, a powerfully built man, tweaked his nose and began patting his foot rapidly on the floor. He suddenly stood. Will watched him, thinking that Whipper surely must eat too much. Distended sinuses extended like stretched tubes from the sides of his nose down puffy cheeks and flattened out below his jaw bone. His rotund stomach, accentuated by a tight vest, hid his belt. Suspenders, buttoned to his trousers, stretched below his vest and puckered his shirt the full girth of his waistline.

"That's all behind you," Whipper said, retrieving a watch from his vest pocket, and checking the time. He rubbed his fingers across the cover and put it back into his pocket.

"We ride trains here like anybody else if we can pay the fare. The Society has paid yours, so all you have to do is keep your eyes wide for slave agents. They ride trains too."

"I hear tell long time ago that Lancaster was nice like Canada, but not so cold," Will said. "We might get a job there and pay our own way later if we don't want to stay."

"Why do such a fool thing? Lancaster's only twelve miles away. You won't be any safer there than you are here."

"I remember a slaver trying his best to buy me from Master Mack talking about how mad it made him that black folks and whites got along so good around Lancaster. I thought how nice it must be, and here..."

"You're too young to understand how the law works for them, and that you got no rights whatsoever." Mr. Whipper talked rapidly, shaking his fist in front of him. "You must get away as fast as you can!"

A single sharp rap on the door checked his outburst. The caller rapped out a code. Whipper ushered Will and Charles into a wall behind the cider press. Will heard the man call.

"Mr. Whipper." Whipper opened a thick oak door to Big T Jackson, a fugitive from Richmond who had lived in Columbia twelve years. Big T's eyes were stretched wide, his face damp and flushed from running.

"That preacher, Dorsey 'n his gang come for Jack Diamond, but he ain't running. He go'n stand and battle if it comes to that and we go'n stand beside'em."

"God Almighty," Whipper said. His fist tightened on the door knob. "Who, man? You're not telling me black men here are getting ready to shoot it out...God have mercy!"

Will came from his hiding place and watched Whipper's face twitch, while he coaxed Big T into the house. Will, hearing Dorsey's name, immediately thought of the neighboring farmer to Roedown where he had met One-Ear Tom.

"Ain't getting ready," Big T said. "We already agreed and you can't stop us."

He stopped talking and frowned at Will crossing the room toward him with Charles following. T and Will faced each other in a steady gaze. T suspected they were fugitives, Will read that in his eyes.

"Where is this crazy meeting?" Whipper said.

"At Diamond's place, but they ain't go'n let you in."

"Then why did you come?"

"You done saved a heap of us and we all mighty beholding, but they don't want you in it, seeing how you the only black man around these parts with a whole lot worth sacrificing and..."

"What kind of poppycock is that? Don't take me for a fool, T."

Big T rubbed his head. "Awh, Mr. Whipper, you got roots here, you got a rightly good trucking business with the white folks. Your daddy was rich 'n white. We understand how you can't see things the way we do."

"That's not the point," Whipper said. "All of you..." He breathed heavily and turned to Will and Charles. "I've taken more chances than any black or white man in this community on losing my business, my life, every dime I own. Diamond better make a good point if he plans to keep me out."

"Point's already been made, Mr. Whipper. Everybody brung a gun. We ain't asking no white folks to help us."

"Diamond is making a mistake that will get him killed and probably a lot of other people too." Whipper again looked directly at Will. "So you think there's a good life here, You don't believe slave runners will haul you off to Georgia or Mississippi? You don't believe that shiftless white trash kidnap wives and children who never been slaves and sell them, hunh?"

He turned around to face Big T, but T had gone. Whipper inhaled deeply and sighed.

"Come along with me," he said to the two young fugitives.

There had been other times like this one in Will's seventeen year old life when his heart lay like a stone in his breast. Again he felt overwhelmed with longing for freedom. Was he really better off now? In an attempt to stifle self-pity while he and Charles easily kept pace with Whipper, Will actually tried to count his blessings. He had a full belly, good shoes on his feet, warm, clean clothes, his and Charles' fare to Canada. They wouldn't have to walk. But Canada was cold even in the summer and so far away. He had heard bad stories about slaves freezing or starving there, or being thrown overboard in Lake Erie.

He sighed while observing the pale, ghostly moonlight following them and touching the fronts of rows of stores and houses. Soft yellow lantern beams spread from windows across Main Street. Just as they turned the corner toward the colored section of town, a team of mules pulling a load of freshly cut logs rounded the bend trodding along dusty High Road.

Will froze. Charles rubbed against Whipper. Whipper acted as if he was alone, and waved to the driver who stopped the team in front of the Quaker Dowel Company.

"Long working days, Walt?" Whipper asked him.

"Aw yes, my good man," the driver, Walter Inman said wearily. "Certainly need workers. It's hard making customers' orders on time. My colored lumberjacks aren't much for working in the forests these days. I understand and rightly so. I'd be afraid too." He smiled at Will and Charles. "I could use two good young men starting right now in the shop."

"Well, it will make me short handed," Whipper said. "But perhaps I can send two of my laborers over tomorrow morning. Of course, I'll ask around, see if we can't find you some permanent workers."

Walter Inman smiled at the ground and shook his head. "Of course, William," he said. "I respect your reasoning."

Will turned away from Whipper rather than glower at him, and caught sight of a picture in the window of a small printing shop a few doors past the dowel company. A huge, smiling white man with an expanded chest and biceps twice the size of Will's, balanced a bottle of Indian medicine on his right flexed muscle. The more he stared to keep from exploding at Whipper, the more he thought about the gritty, bitter juice Miz Sady, the root lady, made at Roedown. It smelled worse than the bog he and Charles had slept in on the road to Baltimore. The taste, God Almighty, drew his jaws in against his teeth the moment it touched his tongue and set his stomach to growling. When Grandmom Rosey made him drink it she said enough of it would right everything inside him that was wrong. Enough of it would completely rid him of the misery.

If he would survive, made no difference whether in Lancaster or Canada, he must, beginning at that moment, right everything that seemed wrong. Whipper didn't like him or Charles, they were fugitives. Two paying jobs offered by a kind man desperate for help, but not for them. Whipper was not a man to be crossed. Not even by a white man. Maybe he could run them out of Columbia, but he couldn't make them go to Canada. Tired of running, tired of owning nothing, tired of being cursed, Will would stand with Diamond and fight.

A lantern that had spread light on the poster suddenly diminished. As the door opened, a tall gaunt man with a high starched collar came out of the dark doorway. His eyes searched out Will. Even to his own amazement, Will stared back, rather than at the ground or with a half-glance as he had done so many times in the past. The man backed against the door as if, in the dim light of the moon, Will exemplified the personification of Satan. Whipper smiled and spoke.

"A fine evening, Mr. Swenson," he said.

"Be on about your business," Swenson said. "Or I'll have the lot of you run in."

In the dark shadows, Will saw fear glittering in his eyes.

"A fine evening I said, Mr. Swenson."

Jon Swenson, editor of the Columbia Sentinel, stared and stared at Will. "Still up to your old tricks, eh Whipper? Won't be satisfied will you, until every runaway in the country is here and the blood of decent hard-working white folks turn the dirt to mud just like it is in the western territories."

Whipper faced him squarely. "It is no fault of mine or either of these boys, Jon."

"I have not one ounce of sympathy left, Whipper. I screamed louder than anyone in these parts when the Legislature revoked you free colored people's right to vote. Since then I've relayed too many messages over the telegraph wires about white folks murdering their own kind out there in Kansas and Nebraska to save these fugitives from labor."

"Swenson, you've never seen these two fellows before in your entire life. You know absolutely nothing about them."

"I know you," Swenson said. "I know they wouldn't be here if it wasn't for you. Really Whipper, I have a hard time believing you are the intelligent man we think you are. Borough Council boycotts every business that hires run-aways. Yet, you, a Negro, probably the only colored man in all United States and its territories who's called mister by just about all the white folks who know you, hustles fugitives as though you had a special permit from Washington."

Whipper waved his hands in front of him while shaking his head from side to side. "I don't need sympathetic hate, Jon."

"You better count your blessings, Mr. Whipper."

"Pity yourself, Mr. Swenson." Whipper waved to Will and Charles. "First lesson," he said. "Let us be gone from his presence."

Will didn't move. He continued frowning and staring at the publisher and editor until suddenly it dawned on him that he was not afraid. Will, a black fugitive slave on the run for his life was no longer afraid of the white man with hate bubbling from his eyes standing before him. He didn't know what he was feeling, but it certainly was not fear.

Perspiration wet Charles' face. "C'mon brother," he said, walking side-ways, watching Whipper hurrying on.

Then, watching Swenson still plastered to the door, Will knew. He had never even thought it possible that a white man would be afraid of him.

Swenson had never seen him before, was taller than Will, had the law on his side, but was deathly afraid. Why?

During a short, brisk walk to where High Street became High Road, Will, Charles, and Whipper passed black men at different locations, standing behind trees whose branches were full with spring's growth of new leaves. The houses looked vacant and boarded-up. No shafts of yellow lantern-light danced in the street. The early night's silence was broken only by the loud yapping of yard dogs and the occasional baying at the moon by a lonely hound. Whipper called each sentry by his first name.

At Jack Diamond's house Whipper rapped twice in quick succession. The door opened only wide enough for one stretched eye-ball to scan.

"Mr. Diamond?" William Whipper asked in a pompous manner.

"Diamond who?" The voice dripped with sarcasm.

Whipper pushed against the door in an agitated manner, only to feel a rigid foot jammed behind it. "Jack," he called out.

Will heard noisy scuffling and angry voices, then nothing. Whipper jumped away from the door, waving Will and Charles behind him.

"Diamond," he yelled, "have you gone mad?"

"Might say I'm crazy, Mr. Whipper. But I'm a long way from losing my mind. Let'em in, y'all." The timbre of Diamond's baritone voice made it sound as if he was speaking from the bottom of a well.

"This is suicide," Whipper said, rushing through the opening door into the kitchen. "I won't let you do... Hey, wait!"

"How'n hell you aim to stop us," Diamond said.

Will flinched in the doorway and retreated a step. The flickering from a lantern cast dim light on Diamond, a wiry man of medium height with a keen, elongated face, standing in front of an oak table turned on its side. His double-barreled rifle and the long gun of a man crouched behind the table were trained on Will, Whipper, and Charles. Diamond's angry eyes were bloodshot. A sentry at a blanket covered window near the door resumed his watch through a pair of peep holes. Two others armed with long rifles gaped through slits in a covering over a side window.

"Ain't much need of being here without a gun," Diamond said. "Who's them two jokers?"

"They're hurrying on to the next underground depot," Whipper said, grasping his one slim chance to convince Jack the danger in fighting was far greater than in his leaving. "Like you were eight years ago."

"Then," Diamond said, "I was nothing, had nothing or nobody, not even myself."

"You did good for yourself, Jack," Whipper said, "but you're still a fugitive in the eyes of the law. Think about the burden on your family if they capture or kill you." He looked all around.

All the knickknacks, dishes, kitchenware, furniture, bed clothing and window decorations had been taken from the frame bungalow. Diamond's chocolate nostrils dilated and quivered. "Won't be no capture, we fighting to the finish. Y'all better keep them eyes peeled to the outside," he said to the men in the other rooms who began voicing their support.

"A dozen or so armed men," Whipper asked, "against a whole countryside of white men lusting for a reason to run all of us out of here? Decent white men will stand up for us in court, but they won't get involved in a knock-down, shoot-out fight."

"Damn all of'em, Whipper," Diamond said. "I guarantee you Dorsey won't take me twice. That Jack-leg hypocrite and his white trash Gap gang of horse thieves roped me once before. Made no difference that I told him I wasn't his nigger. They all jumped me. When I come to my senses, they had propped me up behind a mule and a plow in Dorsey's cornfield. Let him come again with that batch of low-life suckers."

"Be sensible, Diamond. Leave. Go to Canada or Massachusetts. How much money you need?"

"Whipper, gawd-dammit, you can't come in here riding your high horse priming me."

"I ask you humbly, Diamond. How much?" Whipper said. After the shooting began, it would be too late, especially for him. Who'd believe Whipper was there only for peace's sake. He'd be ruined, the business he had inherited from his father, his life's work, his personal worth rendered useless as rubble.

"Damn your money, we go'n make a stand."

"Who said that?" Whipper wheeled around and stared in the direction of a dark corner.

"I did, me. Josephus Washington, mister half-white big shit."

Will chuckled to himself. A husky man with a gentle face and comical eyes that danced while he spoke with fire in his voice like Grandmom Rosey, leaned away from his peep hole at a window in an adjoining room.

"One hundred dollars in gold, Diamond," Whipper said.

"Don't insult me Whipper. I got me a right niceable stake here. That ain't enough even if I was to leave."

"If that preacher, Dorsey, convinces the squire you are his runaway, you won't own anything. Will two hundred convince you leaving now is best?"

"Whipper, I be gawdamned if I'm going to run from a sonofabitch just because he's white and his word means more than mine, 'spite the fact that he's lying through his teeth. 'Sides, my wife and kids need seeing about."

"I'll take care of your family while you get settled. You have my word."

"Would you run off and leave your property? Hell no, and I ain't either. I own this house, another one cross the creek, and a stretch of land that's worth four hundred seventy-five dollars, cash money,"

"Give me the power of attorney," Whipper said. "I'll sell them and give the money to your wife."

Will watched Diamond's mouth suddenly drop open.

"Give you hell, I can't trust you with all that I own, Whipper."

"Why? Because I'm not white and don't have a big desk in the bank?" Whipper spit out the rush of words. "Doesn't matter that I've got more money than any man in this town. Doesn't matter that I'm offering you and your family a new hold on life."

"You ain't doing shit, except making me more hopping-John mad."

"The power of attorney, man. God," Whipper said, "listen to reason. We free black folks don't have anywhere to go. I can't run to Canada. I'll send your family wherever you are if you'll go and take these two with you." He pointed to Will and Charles."

"We ain't running," Will said.

"Now see here, boy, stay out of this," Whipper said with surly crispness. "There's a price tag on you and him," he said, pointing to Charles, "that could turn this town into a river of blood. A few days out of slavery, what could you know about fighting for freedom?"

"Didn't take long to know," Will said, "that freedom ain't what it's cracked up to be, so what's the use of running and keeping on running?"

"Parker, you're just a growing boy, a simple minded field hand," Whipper said, "who's stuck his nose in men's business. You'll start a riot, Jack."

"He's talking pure stuff," one of the armed men said. "Let him have his say."

"Speak your piece, boy," Diamond said.

Every pair of eyes in the room, even the ones that had been glued to the peep-holes in the blankets, were trained on Will. He stared at the bare wood floor and felt his breath coming and going. "I run away before I'd be a field nigger," he said. "I was master's prize fighter. Went everywhere busting heads, just him and me, Baltimore, fair grounds in Annapolis, across the bay to Eastern shore."

"Kicking black butts, eh, boy? So I don't wanna hear no testifying." Another man Will didn't know, expressed an opinion of him.

"Kicked master's butt too," Charles chimed in, "damned if he didn't. That's why we run off."

"I used to hear a guy," Will said, "ole One-ear Tom, back at Roedown talk about crazy niggers killing up white folks, and white folks cutting crazy niggers' ears off, and burning them at the stakes. Scared me so bad, I used to see it in my sleep. Then one day when the overseer beat Tawney damned near to death, I felt like Tom said crazy niggers felt, just like I'm feeling now."

"Tawney was Miss Margaret's maid," Charles said, "best kept thing at Roedown."

Will noticed Diamond rubbing his index finger across his lips and though his eyes narrowed questioningly at Will, they did hint of a sparkle. "And you still alive, ain't you boy?" He grinned at Will.

"I did it with these," Will said, balling his fists tight and holding them chest high.

One of the sentries at a side window in a back room, called out to Will. "Ooowee, gawd a-mighty boy, whipped your master?"

"Young braggard, they'll lynch you," Whipper said. "Soon's that Gap gang gets wind that you're in these parts, every black person here will be in that much more danger of being smuggled."

"I ain't running no more," Will said.

"Young, still-wet-behind the cars runaway fool," Whipper said, "you don't have enough sense to care about anybody."

Will flinched, His thick eyebrows almost touched, accentuating the sudden and fierce hostility in his face.

A warning voice whispered in Whipper's head. "Jack," he said, moving to the other side of Diamond, putting him between Will and himself. "Maybe you've forgotten that it's illegal to hire runaways. Borough council doesn't enforce the rule, the county lets it slide too. But if you start a riot every cracker in Lancaster County'll be down here...

"We ain't starting shit, Whipper."

"Hold up," an excited sentry yelled. "One somebody by hisself, riding to beat the band. Seems like he's coming Lancaster Pike way."

"What the hell you mean, seem like?" Diamond bellowed.

Will watched him turn the lantern down to a point where everybody looked like shadows.

The sentry didn't answer. He dropped to his knees, raised the shade a few inches, pointed his rifle through the opened window and looked down the gun's sight. Will watched the others position themselves by the windows. He, Charles and Whipper were the only ones not armed. Diamond sat in a straight back chair, aiming his long, double-barreled rifle at the door.

"Trust me for the next six months," Whipper said. "You have my word. Give me the power of attorney. I'll sell your property, give the money to your wife."

The horse stopped suddenly. "He ain't tot'n no rifle," the sentry whispered, and I don't 'spect he saw our boys hiding outside.

"They're coming," the rider cried. "Dorsey and must be twenty or twenty-five of'em coming for you, Jack. Left the Gap Inn sometime ago."

Will heard the rider spur his horse into a gallop. They all knew he was a white man.

"Jack," Whipper said, "where's Gretchen and the children?" He squinted at the dial in his pocket watch.

"In a safe place," Diamond snarled.

"Please, man," Whipper said, "for their sake, come home with me. You Will, Charles come along too."

"Sounds to me like the tough one, Will here, is his own man, Whipper. You heard him say he's through running."

Whipper turned away from Jack Diamond and looked directly at Will. "Of course I can't make you go and I probably spoke too harshly, Mr. Parker, trying to convince you that I'm scared too. Have you any idea how many people will be stole back to slavery and beat-up while every white scoundrel too lazy to work ransacks every black home in this county hunting you?"

Mr. Parker? The gentleman's title caught Will off guard. Him, a runaway with nary a coin in his pockets, owned by a white master, being called mister. Maybe he and Charles do owe that much to all the good people who have helped them. Especially now that he and Charles won't have to walk to Canada.

Whipper waved his arm in a semi-circle. "G'won home, all of you. Jack, you, Will and Charles come with me while there is still time."

"Unh-unh," Diamond said. "The first somebody who tries to leave is a dead man. We fight to the finish soon's they start it. Burn down the whole town, if they kindle one home."

"Burn?" Whipper yelled. "Burn down Columbia, my lumber yard, Main Street? This is home, Jack. Never!" He seized the lantern, snatched off the globe, turned up the wick burning in coal oil and held it at arm's length. "Shoot me, or clear out. Send them home, Diamond, or I'll set this place afire. Better tell them outside."

"Whipper," Jack said, quite astonished. "You'd burn me out?"

"You'd torch me! My word is my bond. I'll take care of your family. Now clear out, don't make me anymore anxious."

Diamond sighed. "He got us to rights, fellas," he said to the grumbling, slow shuffling men. "Go home. Hopefully, they won't mess with any-o-y'all. All right, Whipper."

With the lighted wick in his hand, Whipper opened the door, stepped out into the moonlit night and didn't look back at Will, Charles or Jack Diamond following him.

Chapter Ten

To the cloppedy-cloppedy gait of two gray sway back horses, Will and Charles bounced atop sacks of hog and cattle feed in a Conestoga wagon jogging along Lancaster Pike. The driver, Caleb Judd, a rawboned husky man with rounded shoulders and whiskers as long as a lynx's, squinted and pulled a narrow brim straw over clear and observant eyes, shielding them from a bright morning sun in the eastern sky. Jack Diamond rode on the high seat beside him.

Will stared at the undulating waves of orange, yellow and red wildflowers in the meadows, but he saw none of them. Nor did he hear the horde of insects singing to the first day of summer. He sat there as if reeling with shock in the aftermath of a fierce battle. Why hadn't black men living in a free state stood tall and protected themselves? Was freedom so lopsided that it granted only some of them the right to work for pay and none of them the right to live free from fear? Snatchers stole black folks under the cloak of midnight, or trapped and hog-tied anyone so foolish to travel alone, Will knew that. Yet he felt, though he could not explain it, that even bullies, the most vicious were apt to leave alone men who stood their ground. He suspected there was something weak and spineless a man saw in another who wouldn't fight, particularly when attacked.

What Will felt, though he couldn't name it, was valor, the virtuous soul substance stronger than any man's power to deny him. Without knowledge of such a strong spiritual force, this seventeen year-old fugitive slave could only relegate such discomfiting feeling to the attitude of a crazy nigger.

Now that Will's dreams, his visions, his hopes of freedom had been scattered, what obsessed him was fear. He feared scalawags, and bounty hunters or slave runners jumping him in the night, and banding immigrants denying him work. He and Charles were in graver danger than they had been at Roedown. Back there, at least until the very end, he hadn't lived with fear of capture or mayhem every waking or sleeping minute. He stole a glance at his brother sitting there expressionless. Guilt gnawed at Will's conscience; with a coin he had actually bought Charles and dragged him along.

Compared to Columbia, Charles himself would prefer Roedown any day. The only redeeming thought, one that he and Will equally shared, they would be with Jack Diamond, surely a sturdy and courageous man. Even though a fugitive who surrendered all to save Whipper, he was a small measure of security. With him they felt less like small children alone in the dark.

They were passing the Lancaster stockyards where wagon trails from all directions converged in a circle at the edge of town. Noise! Penned livestock shuffled and stamped, braying, grunting, and squealing. Cursing drivers jockeyed their wagons and carriages in the thick dust. Wagons loaded with farm machinery, produce, hay and tobacco manned by drivers anxious to get into the city or away from it were unbelievable sights to Will and Charles. Caleb turned right three-quarters of his way around the circle onto Queen Street. At that hour of the morning the street was active with people—white and black—coming and going from the shops and markets, most of them stepping along quickly. Some folks were dressed quite differently than what Will and Charles were accustomed. Mennonites, Caleb called them, strict religious folks like the Quakers, Women dressed in black—bonnets, dresses, stockings and shoes—walked behind men with long black beards, black derbys and black suits. Everything black—clothing, horses, carriages—except their faces.

A cloud of dirty thick smoke suddenly billowed into the sky a short distance ahead of them. Diamond shifted on the seat and brushed his hands over the lapels of his blue Sunday suit. He cocked a black dress hat he had been holding in his hands, on the side of his head over his right ear. A long, shrill whistle pierced the air. Will and Charles jumped straight up, their eyeballs stretching and rolling at the sight of a big iron monster coming into full view, inching across North Queen Street towards a wooden platform. It snorted and hissed, steam rushing out from its sides and bottom like a leaking, giant black kettle.

"What in hell?" Charles said. "Can't nothing in the world be that ugly."

"That is the steam engine, me lads." Caleb laughed heartily and directed the horses to a hitching rail. When the engine released one last belch, the wagon lunged as if the force of escaping steam had driven the horses backwards. 'Whoa, boys," he said, pulling up the reins.

"Seems like he been out-running buckra a long time," Charles said.

"If it was alive, she'd be one mean critter," Caleb said. His gaunt and leathery face broadened into a wide laugh.

"Look a there, them things around her middle," Will said, "them things what look like saddlebags hanging over a mule's rump. And look up there?"

He pointed to the coal tender on top of the engine aligning a pipe that extended from the side of a huge barrel over the engine water jackets. The sudden roar of water gushing from the barrel into the jackets when the attendant pulled a rope agitated the horses again. The wagon heaved.

"Whoa, up there," Caleb said, tightening the reins.

"Ooooh wee," Will said, grabbing a stave to keep from falling. "Damned if it ain't thirsty." He stared at the engine, suddenly thinking of Grandmom Rosey, clearly remembering her singing about riding to glory on an iron horse that ran under the ground. He understood they wouldn't be riding underground. They would get on board and ride away from there to a safe haven. Grandmom

Rosey's word in a word again rang true to him—railroad station, underground railroad; iron horse, steam engine. It fed his dejected mood.

"Watch your step." Caleb pivoted in his seat and looked at Will and Charles. "Boogey men hang around railroad depots. It's dangerous, youngsters."

Folks lingering in front of the Glove Tavern ticket office hurried to the station platform, Charles studied every movement of the railroad agent dragging a mail sack on board and pulling one off. Across the street from the ticket office, men, some of them wearing guns, gathered in front of the North American Hotel.

Diamond cleared his throat, calling Caleb's attention to a man approaching. Will had already seen him, a tall, lean gentleman with pale blue eyes and a coal-black beard extending from his ears and under his nose to the middle of his chest. He wore a long black coat and a stove-pipe hat, yet seemed cool and relaxed in the warm morning with both hands in his slanted coat pockets. He looked up and smiled at Will and Charles.

"You're traveling early, neighbor," Caleb said. "Was it a dark night?"

"No bother," the man said. "The North Star was very bright."

"Have you ever traveled the railroad?" the stranger said to Diamond.

"Some little distance," Diamond said with a slow secretive smile.

Caleb's face widened into a satisfying grin. He looked at Will and then the stranger. "I have one bale of dark wood," he said.

"And one large parcel that I'll take when I return," the stranger said, turning and walking away.

Will and Charles looked at each other.

"They talking about us, hunh, Will?" Charles said.

"Wood and parcel?" Will shook his head disgustedly. "I guess so."

Jack Diamond quickly turned around, the wrinkles across his prominent forehead furrowing into creases. "I 'spect another agent coming for you two."

Will stuck out his bottom lip. "This'n suppose to take us too?"

"Too hard for one agent to protect all three, laddy," Caleb said.

"Looks to me like Mr. Whipper done tricked me and Charles."

"He wouldn't do that, boy," Diamond said, looking at Will like a harsh school master facing an unruly student. "Respectable man never bends his word."

"He would'a burned down your house if..."

"Shut up!"

Diamond and Will gawked at each other.

"It ain't easy, Gawd-dammit!" Diamond turned away and alighted from the wagon. His voice drifted into the breeze. "I don't need you reminding me."

"The Whipper I've known for nigh forty years," Caleb said, "wouldn't sacrifice his reputation, laddy. This isn't his decision, anyway. I'm responsible for your safety until another agent takes you."

"You know this man that's taking Mr. Jack?" Charles said.

"Never saw him before in my life," Caleb said, "but the chance of trusting him is mine to take and I'll do that only if he shows certain qualities about himself."

What happens if the other'n don't come?" Will said. "What if he changes his mind after he sees us?"

"Boys, for God's sake," Diamond said, "be on the lookout for trouble, but don't talk it up. That high, mighty fellow over there in front of the North American looking this way and talking to the old man is doing his damndest to hear everything we say."

Caleb looked abroad for a second. "I'm afraid we've made a scene, laddies, but we daresn't stare."

The tall abolitionist who had come for Diamond walked up behind without their noticing. "We're riding the Pioneer Line this time," he said.

Caleb whirled around. "Just hold on," he said, jumping from the wagon.

"Another agent will be along any minute," the stranger said.

"Tipping up behind folks makes them question your sincerity," Caleb said, standing so close to the stranger their noses almost touched.

"True nature of a man is revealed when he's not aware of anyone watching him, brethren," the abolitionist said, not yielding an inch.

With a broad smile, Caleb handed him a coin with a tiny hole drilled in the imprint of a star. The stranger took a coin from an inside pocket, stepped back and compared the two, then smiled and traded with Caleb.

"Thanks brethren," he said tipping his hat. "Let's be off, my good fellow," he said to Diamond.

Watching him and Jack Diamond walk away, Will felt a part of himself leave with then. Charles sighed and wondered wearily about himself and Will.

Caleb cast a wary eye at Will. "That fellow dressed like a Mississippi gambler's been watching you like a fox that's singled out a prize rooster. He's apt to follow, maybe even stop you. Don't stare too hard, but do you recognize him?"

"He looks like the devil," Charles said. "I mostly keeps a field or two twixt and between him and me."

"What'll we do if nobody comes for us?" Will said,

"Don't think that way," Caleb said, though quite concerned himself about Will's and Charles' safe departure and getting back to his dear family in Columbia before day's end. Sensing alarm in Will and Charles caused him to worry more about his own, especially his oldest son fighting so often these days for no explainable reason. Caleb wasn't so naive to believe the secret society of abolitionists to which he belonged was so secretive its membership had never been revealed.

Though Caleb still had grain and animal feed to deliver, they waited, but nobody came. The high, mighty chap wearing a wide Stetson hat, high riding boots, bow tie with a stiff white shirt, and a big gun strapped to his leg, now by himself at the nearly abandoned depot, kept watching. Then he made a few long easy strides across the street and stopped in front of the ticket office.

"No question about it, he is big trouble," Caleb said, releasing the brake and reining his horses to turn the wagon around.

"Where you taking us?" Will said. "We got no place to go."

"And you just told that to the gun slinger," Caleb said, lifting his hat and scratching his head nervously.

"What'll we do, Will," Charles said, "if he comes up on us?"

"We got one chance," Will said. "Act like you scared, roll your eyes big and wide, all around at the ground, upside a tree and the sky, but don't look him in the face. When I spit, we jump'em at the same time, tackle'em good, hug both his legs. I'll bust him in the face. We'll take his gun."

"His gun! Heavens no," Caleb said, "Oh my God."

"He's got one!" Will glared at the abolitionist, clenching his teeth.

Caleb shuddered, then sighed heavily to conceal a sudden stab of guilt he felt in his chest. Jesus help us white folks, he thought, if armed fugitive slaves, their patience worn beyond the point of reasoning for compassion, began rampaging the lush and peaceful Pennsylvania Dutch farmland of Lancaster County. He tried driving it from his mind as he set his horses to loping eastward along Lancaster Pike.

"The one person I know in this neck of the woods who could find a place for you two is Doc Dingee, over London Grove way in Chester County. He'd know what to do."

"The high dressed man mounted up," Charles said, "he's coming this way moving slow, like creeping death."

"Let's pray," Caleb said.

"For what!"

"Son, for God's sake, don't yell at me. I've a son about your age. If he'd talk to me so dad-gummed raw, why I'd..." Caleb's voice trailed off to a whisper. "We pray for the divine light within to protect and guide us to a safe haven. We pray for courage and stillness in our hearts so we can hear God's quiet voice."

"I ain't your white son," Will said. "Slave owner, soul snatcher, overseer, poor white trash can carry guns," Will volleyed at Caleb, "but you carry me everywhere I go, protecting me from them so I won't need a gun. Whatever me and Charles pray for couldn't amount to much more than thanking you."

Deep within the heart of himself, Caleb reckoned that Will's irritating belligerence was not without due cause. Fear did make men act like fools, young men more so than older.

"I daresn't tamper with the reasoning against you being armed, son," he said, "but I'm against guns. I'm against killing, no matter who."

"What'd you do if he tried to shackle your neck and fasten irons around your legs?"

"My conviction to love thy brother strictly forbids me from physically attacking anyone. It demands that I lend a helping hand to the downtrodden, protect the underprivileged."

"Do it," Will said." Pray that he leaves us alone. If he tries to take me and Charles, we go'n take our one chance on him. We'd even fight him for you."

"Lot of good that would do to kill slavery," Caleb said, "though I appreciate it. Most of us in these parts have sworn to do all we can to make slave holders and the government understand the destructive wrath of God's law that is sure to rain down on the wicked. Slavery will be destroyed. Unfortunately, a lot of good people will be destroyed with it."

"Your chance to tell him is coming on fast," Charles said. "He's tramping along behind us."

"Let's sing," Caleb said, "that'll keep him away."

"Should auld acquaintance be forgot," he bellowed, "and never brought to mind?

"Should auld acquaintance be forgot, and days of o' lang syne?

"For auld lang syne, my dear, for auld lang syne.

"We'll take a cup of kindness yet, for auld lang syne."

"Never liked singing too much," Will said. "And even if I did, I don't know them words."

"Sounds pretty good " Charles said, "would sound better if it'd keep that high, mighty somebody back there."

"It will, Charles," Caleb said, jubilantly "act happy, make up some words. You'll see."

At the crest of a long sloping hill Caleb turned south off Lancaster Pike in a cluster of shading oak trees and traveled in a southerly direction until he crossed Baltimore Pike. On the other side after passing through a covered bridge, he turned sharp right and followed the wagon trail along a hillside. Down in the valley on the other side of the creek the soul snatcher appeared again, riding abreast at just about the same pace as they. He sat astride a sleek chestnut-brown stallion. Charles stopped singing and nudged Will. Caleb turned and saw him.

"Doc Dingee's place is just beyond the top of the hill," he said.

Two little children, a tow-headed boy about Will's age when Grandmom Rosey had first told him about his grandfather Ofeutey, and a smaller girl with golden hair were skipping stones across a shallow brook. When the wagon rumbled over a narrow bridge spanning the sparkling water, Will thought it strange to see the children running up the bank to the wagon smiling and waving. The boy didn't pull his mouth into the sour scowl which Will and Charles had come to accept as normal. His sister didn't cower as if she would be swallowed in one gulp should Will or Charles so much as open their huge black mouths.

Caleb returned the greeting then turned to Charles and Will. "They want you to wave back," he said.

"We don't much mess with little white kids, especially girls," Will said.

"For jiminee sake," Caleb said, smiling down at the children hurrying along toward the house beside the horses. "Are they throwing stones or calling you names?"

Will's nostrils quivered. He set his dark face in an angry expression. "White man, you don't even try to understand."

"That was cold, Will, totally uncalled for, not an inch of truth in it."

"But do you ever think we got good reasons for doing things? "Will said.

"What an odd question, Will. But if I must beg pardon for what seems my ignorance, so be it. However, for you to refuse the friendship of two sweet and mannerable children is beyond my reasoning."

"There's two of the best reasons you ever need, over there in the flowers watching."

"Them? Doc and Mrs. Dingee? There isn't a more humble and sensitive man dedicated to freedom for black people in these parts. And she's dedicated to him." Caleb waved his arms in a big half-circle and called out "Hallooooo!" He pulled rein and jumped down, leaving Will and Charles in the wagon.

"Ellen," Mrs. Dingee called to the girl. "Come over here out of the way."

The boy walked around the wagon and stared up at Will. "Hello," he said with a smile.

Will looked at him then quickly stared off into space with a strained expression on his drawn face. Much of the Dingee nursery reminded him of Roedown, the gazebo at the edge of the yard near the babbling creek, the cherry, apple and pear trees, but without slaves pruning the branches, and roses on both sides of the pike to the distant tree line. A two-story brick house sat amid a sea of red, yellow, white and pink fragrant roses. They reminded him of Miss Margaret. He would hate her—the trashy, stringy-haired, pale, bottomland-Chesapeake bitch—as long as he lived. She had made the overseer beat Tawney.

"Man, Will," Charles said, "what you thinking about so hard?"

"I wish these gawdamned people knew how tired I am of them talking about me like I was the size of this boy here, or some old stray cat they oughta' run off but need for the barnyard. Yea, he's ugly and smells like he been rolling in donkey dew, and sure needs cleaning, but who's going to do it for him this time. It just keeps on all the time, Charles. I just want a job so I can work and be left alone to take care of myself."

113

"Maybe we shoulda' gone on to Canada," Charles said.

"I can't believe it's any different," Will said.

"Naw, Will, Tighe say once you cross over it's a great big change."

"He did, hunh? That's what we believed about here." Will's dark face was hard as a stone mask. "For all we know, they take them niggers out in the deep water and make'em jump in. Wouldn't surprise me one bit."

"Will, Charles," Caleb called to them.

"That little boy gets on my nerves," Charles said. "We going over there, Will?"

"Ain't much else we can do," Will said, alighting from the wagon. "Don't mind him none, act dumb."

Caleb hurried to meet them. "I think you may get your wish."

Will didn't respond one way or the other. He had already made eye contact with Doc Dingee, strong unrelenting contact, watching the nurseryman raking his eyes over him.

Doc Dingee noticed the young fugitive's loping gait, his taut body dipping slightly with each step, his long, muscular arms swinging loosely from wide shoulders. Will held his head erect on a dark mahogany neck, strong and sinewy like the trunk of a fir tree. In Will's dark hooded eyes, Doc Dingee saw the strain of fear, the certainty of rage not very well concealed within. He suspected that Will's insights about white folks, the good and the bad, went far beyond those of the usual seventeen-year-old illiterate black slave. Though he wondered if Will were worthy of his trust, he admired him.

Charles walked a step or two behind. His eyes revealed despair, and the doctor wondered what Charles had been subjected to that Will had not. What was in Will's head that was not in Charles'? For Charles he felt pity.

Caleb, Mrs. Dingee and Doc formed a semicircle with Mrs. Dingee in the middle. Caleb extended his hand across the front of her to Doc.

"Boys," he said, "This is Charles Dingee, doctor of flowers and, more often, of ailing folks too in these parts." He laughed.

Mrs. Dingee nodded her head in a playful manner. Doc Dingee thrust a long arm to Will and nodded while waiting for Will to shake his hand.

Will's jaw moved as if he were chewing. He wiped his hands on his trousers. Doc kept his hand in front of Will, though he didn't smile when Will finally shook it. In Doc's icy-cold, sky-blue eyes, Will saw a hint of kindness. He was a tall wiry man, taller than Will, with a powerful grip that drew an immediate challenge from Will.

The harder Doc squeezed Charles' hand the more limp it became. Even when Doc winked and offered him a wide smile, Charles only half-glanced and looked past him.

"This is Mrs. Grace Dingee," Caleb said.

114

Her eyes, set in a small, round face and green as lily pods that grew in the creek, had irises like dewdrops in their centers and sparkled when she smiled. Will could see that she was a little on the stout side. He heard Doc Dingee clearing his throat.

"Mr. Parker and Mr. Charles, is it?" she said with a nod of her head and a little curtsy. "My granddaughter, Ellen," she said. The little girl holding her hand looked up with sparkling eyes, and curtsied.

Will and Charles looked at each other as if suddenly beset with splitting headaches. Will wished he could run and hide. Sweat popped all over his bottom lip. Charles rubbed his arms against his sides, trying to ease the itch in his arm pits. Doc cleared his throat again.

"Come, Ellen," Mrs. Dingee said. "It's time to prepare dinner."

"And the little fellow here who's trying to make friends with you," Caleb said, "is Jay, Doc's grandson."

"Jay is short for Japheth," Doc Dingee said, looking at his grandson with a certain sternness. His voice, though deep and commanding, carried a gentle ring of compassion.

"Uh-oh, Doc," Caleb said, "you got company."

"It's that snatcher," Charles whispered to Will. "What we going to do?" he said with a trembling voice."

Will grabbed Charles' arm and dug his fingers in so hard that Charles winced but said nothing.

"You have encountered him before?" Doc said to Caleb, all the while watching Will and Charles.

"He followed us all the way from Lancaster."

The man with the wide Stetson and the gun strapped to his thigh rode up as if he had more time than anything else and dismounted. His wood-smoke-colored eyes, narrow and hard, seemed to have been chiseled into a square face. His keen nose dipped over a thin mustache and thin-lipped mouth. He cocked his head a little to the side and walked upon Charles.

"Who is your master, boy!" He spoke with a loud, gruff voice.

Charles stared wild-eyed at his brother. Will stepped between them.

"God," Charles said, surprised at his boldness standing there eye to eye with the snatcher. "Same as yours."

The snatcher's right eyebrow arched in stark amazement. He twisted his head to the right and cupped his hand behind his left ear. "What's that you said, boy?"

Charles didn't answer.

"Your name, boy! What the hell is it?"

"Ain't none of your business." Will stood there wide-legged, concealing his fright.

"Well now," he said pointing his finger in Will's face, "I have no doubt at all about you. This here poster says it all."

"Touch my brother, I knock you out!"

Caleb wavered. His eyes rolled as if he had been jarred out of a deep sleep. Doc Dingee acted as if he heard nothing.

"I be gawdamned," the snatcher said, turning beet red and wondering if he had heard correctly. "You folks realize you've got a dangerous nigger on your hands?" His top lip curled up on one end. "Lookit here." He read from a handful of bills. "Poster is right, says he takes fits, but I'll whittle him down a couple notches so's he'll know how not to talk to a white man, in particular, a man of the law."

Will didn't flinch, didn't bat an eye. He stood there with what appeared to Doc, as a strangely humorous, yet defiant expression—a demeanor of courage that Doc Dingee had seen in very few fugitives he had smuggled, and free men he had befriended in court.

The snatcher stroked his chin, regarding Will carefully. "I deputize you two," he said to Doc and Caleb.

"Deputize us!" Doc said. "By what authority and for what?"

"Authority granted me by the United States Government to enforce the fugitive slave law. These two fugitive darkies are worth two thousand five hundred dollars, that's what the hell for."

"Lord God, Almighty, what did they do?" Doc said, pulling the poster from the snatcher's hand and reading it. "What's the charge? Where's your warrant?"

"Word is, Will Parker killed his master."

"So you're a marshal, a bounty hunter without a warrant. Pennsylvania Liberty Laws protect no one, fugitives, free men, black or white, from justice. You should know that. Any court, any JP, would issue a bench warrant on a murder charge, mister... Who are you, anyway?"

"Know me, Alonzo Snoot, constable from the Quaker City and United States Marshal. I seldom flash my badge. Decent, honest, law abiding white folks, even free darkies who pay their rent and behave themselves, shouldn't feel threatened by me. I'm hunting fugitives, and this here scum..." Snoot's voice rang out as he pointed his finger menacingly at Will.

Doc Dingee walked slowly toward Will as if testing the challenge of a wild animal, his long arms swinging loosely and rhythmically with each stride. "If I take wings of the morning, and dwell in the uttermost parts of the sea," he said chant-like, urging a power within him and stronger than he to probe through layers of Will's ironbound fear, anger, and distrust. He looked at the sky, then at Will and placed his hand on Will's and Charles' shoulders.

Will held that same demeanor, he and Doc, eyeball to eyeball. "Even there shall thy hand lead me," Doc said. "They work for me," he said, turning to Marshal Snoot.

Snoot's eyes darkened. "You some kind of darky-loving preacher man?" He stood wide-legged, making sure Doc Dingee noticed the gun.

"I'm Doc Dingee, not a preacher. I spoke to Will in a way you'd never understand. For your information, they are fugitives from nothing, they are not slaves. We have work to do. Get off my land."

"Dingee, Dingee, aw yes. I should'a known, the man from London Grove who grows all kinds of fruit and fancy roses. I can't understand what kinda devil's got into you people out here, protecting niggers, making then think they good as us white folks. What kind'a man are you anyway, letting them sleep in your house, hang around your women-folk?"

Only Doc Dingee's eyes spoke. In them Snoot saw storm clouds gathering, dark and full. "If they ain't free darkies I'll be back," he said, climbing into his saddle. "You can count on it."

"Dare trespass without a warrant, you may not have time to repent."

"I'll have one, just to keep you out of trouble." Snoot coaxed his horse to cantering.

"There blows an ill wind," Caleb said, walking to his wagon and climbing into the high seat. "I'm a long ways from Columbia and the day is getting long."

"Heathen, barbaric swine," Doc said. Then he looked at Will and Charles. "Boys, would you unload these sacks and give me a minute with Caleb? Then we'll talk."

"Oops," Caleb said, "plumb forgot."

"Stay in your seat, I know which ones are mine. But I need the bill of lading," he said, while busying Will and Charles with the unloading.

Caleb opened a metal box that was under his seat, and removed a ledger. "I suppose you don't believe," he said, tearing out a sheet and handing it to Doc, "that one named Will is capable of murder."

"There isn't a slave alive who isn't capable of murder, Caleb, but that heathen has no concern for justice. I do believe there's more to Will than is revealed on that fugitive bill. But tracking a black man, actually a boy, accused of murder without the warrant that would be so easy to get? There couldn't be a slave runner so stupid. Not even Snoot," Doc said with amused contempt.

Caleb laughed. "This day has really been one for tribulation. Take good care of yourself and yours, Doc."

"Godspeed, Caleb, until next time," Doc said, waving him off.

After Caleb crossed the sparkling branch and disappeared over the hill, Doc turned and observed Will and Charles where they had loaded the sacks onto a two-wheeled nursery buggy, talking between themselves.

"Boys," he said, "my stomach tells me its well past lunchtime. Let's eat first, then we'll discuss your plans, and my needs, and take it from there."

They went with Doc to a well near the bottomland and between the folds of two overlapping slopes. After pumping water for each other, lathering their faces and hands with a strong lye soap, rinsing and drying with the same towel, they gathered in the gazebo at a table laden with blueberry pancakes, maple syrup, coffee, and fresh fruit. Mrs. Dingee, Jay and little Ellen joined them. It took some cajoling for Mrs. Dingee to get Will and Charles to really satisfy their enormous appetites. When Doc sensed that at least the food had cut through their defenses, he pushed himself away from the table and stretched.

"Will and Charles," he said, "You happened along at precisely the right time. Unfortunately though, I can't afford both of you. But," he said with a deliberate smile, "a friend of mine, a fine man with a wonderful family in Bart Township needs a good man, too. He reasons much like I do, doesn't want any somebody to simply work. I'm looking for a young man who's willing to learn the business and treat it as if he owned it, someone I can rely on with total trust. If you two can stand to be parted, decide who goes over there and who stays here."

"We're strangers everywhere we go," Will said. "How far away is it?"

"No more than half a day's walk."

"Not a far piece. Yeah, Will's all I got in this world," Charles said. "What kinda' business is it?"

"He grows all kinds of grapes, Charles. His vineyard stretches for miles. I think you'd like him."

Charles felt a heaviness in his chest, but was glad Will and Doc couldn't see it. He was a man, he was older than Will and really didn't want him always fending for him. Yet, parting would be hard.

Will noticed Charles' eyes and wondered if parting would be safe. Without Charles he couldn't have crossed those mountains to Pennsylvania. He probably wouldn't have run from Roedown.

Doc noticed it too and was irritated with himself that he hadn't been more careful in revealing his thought. He believed that Will, more aggressive than Charles, would be the harder worker, and he could not in good conscience, pass on Will to his trusted friend with any suspicion of murder hanging over him. There could be some truth to the matter, something deeper than a bounty hunter's motive for tracking him. The thought of jeopardizing his own family weighed heavily on Doc. Yet, two illiterate slave boys with a bounty on them that so-called literate men would sacrifice their families to get, were running from their captors on borrowed time. Will and Charles needed grounding, they needed someone with whom they could identify. And he, Doc himself, if indeed harboring a criminal... That would damage the entire abolitionist movement. He must know the truth before the marshal returned with the sheriff or a posse of unscrupulous rascals from the notorious Gap Gang.

"Well, boys," Doc said, "who stays, who goes?"

Will puffed his cheeks and exhaled, as if blowing out a candle. Charles looked at Will and rubbed his hands across his lips.

"All right," Doc said, "here's a lesson to learn about making decisions. If you don't make the decision, the situation will make it for you. Tomorrow, first thing, Will and I will take Charles over to Jeremiah Moore."

Doc lay awake for several hours, disturbed by his thoughts and every creaking sound in the night. He hoped Jeremiah would need Charles immediately so he could hurry on to Squire Mapp. He greeted the dawn later than usual.

Across the creek from Doc's place the trail to Jeremiah's homestead led through a lush virgin wilderness that Will hadn't noticed yesterday. Whoever made wild flowers smell as good as Doc's roses, made robins and insects serenade each other, he reasoned, couldn't be the same person that made the woods down Roedown way. All that was pretty and nice in that country, slaves made. While the three of them sat quietly that morning each absorbed in his own thoughts, Will realized that no human hand worked what had caught him up in its splendor.

Charles was still mystified by the newly acquired belief in himself, a result of telling the snatcher without thinking it, that God was his only master. He broke the silence. "If by chance this man won't take me, I'll hoof it on to Canada."

"Without me?" Will asked, quite surprised by what he felt was a sudden change in Charles' attitude.

"Alone," Charles said, in a stern, convincing manner. "I'm older'n you, seen more of life than you have, and know how to deal with it better'n you."

"Since when?" Will said with a rough, boastful voice.

"Since I made up my mind last night, listening to you calling hogs in your sleep."

"So," Will said in a belligerent manner. "Ain't no need of acting like it's you without me against the whole world."

"Yeah it is, Will. You won't listen no other way. I left Roedown 'cause you pushed and pulled me so. You left 'cause Master Mack sold Tawney. Sure, some times I might'a went back, but you couldn't."

"You wanted freedom," Will said. "That's what you told me."

"Where'n hell is it, Will? Don't ask Joe Diamond, don't ask his friends back there ready to make one last stand. Look back at us sliding down outta the sky, clawed and chewed up by a mountain. Look at you, scared enough to drown me if I hadn't kept up. I hadn't thought it then, but now I know. Stay with the Doc, Will. I got a better chance of moving on without you."

"Fellows," Doc said in a commanding, but apologetic voice. "In the first place, Canada is too far for anyone to walk, and..." He breathed a long sigh. "Perhaps I was too hasty yesterday in forcing you to decide so soon."

119

"Nope," Charles said, "It was a quick learning, made me see myself without Will."

"Maybe we should hang together a while longer," Will said.

"Got to stand by yourself sooner or later, boy," Charles said. "Ain't nobody ever give a damn if I live or die until you come along needing help."

"I dared that snatcher to mess with you yesterday," Will said, "or don't that count." He set his lips in an ugly sneer.

"Don't us fight each other, Will. You my baby brother."

Will stared at the floor-boards and began digging at his fingernails.

"We're just about there," Doc said.

He turned sharp right onto a trail under a row of black walnut trees. The resin and roasting-nut scent of the forest relented to that of fermented grapes. On both sides of the lane, Will noticed a rich black mound of compost around the base of every grapevine. He didn't look up to see the slender stems with little green balls the size of sweet peas on them stretching a distance ahead to a bend beside a stream of brackish water. Near the bend, a tall, round shouldered man in bib overalls and a wide straw hat straightened himself from bending low. He squinted at the wagon approaching.

"Well, I do declare," he called out. "Doc."

"Howdee this fine morning, Jeremiah," Doc said.

Jeremiah Moore placed his hands inside the overalls and rubbed his lower back. "Mulching roots, whew. I wish I knew an easier way."

"Certainly is," Doc said, "a helper with a yielding back."

Jeremiah walked gingerly to them. Each step was a pain. "I need a hired hand who won't follow the allure of fermenting grapes into my wine cellar."

"I understand," Doc said with a chuckle, "how the temptation could be overwhelming."

"I take it they are interested," Jeremiah said, nodding to Will and Charles.

"Charles is," Doc said, placing his hand on Charles' shoulder. "Let's chat for a minute or so. Not long. Morning is a precious time for me too."

First Doc then Charles alighted from the wagon. Will didn't move. Charles turned and looked at the somber expression on his brother's downcast face.

"One of these days, Will," he said, "I'll be big enough to say I love you."

Charles completely befuddled Will. Love between two black brothers? Talking about that in front of white men?

Jeremiah frowned. Something in these youngsters' lives had caused an acute misunderstanding. They were fugitives no doubt, in need of shelter. He extended his tough, purple-blue hand which Charles readily accepted with equal vigor. While he, Doc, and Charles talked in quiet tones, Will sat there trying to block their separation from mind.

"Back at Roedown," Charles said, "the old folks made squeezings from most everything that growed, but I met the sun every day with my hoe digging out weeds."

"Very well stated, young fellow." Jeremiah said. "Thee will find a comfortable bed, hot biscuits, rich buttermilk and decent God-fearing folks."

"Thanks, Jeremiah," Doc said, climbing into the wagon. "We'll be in touch."

While Doc coaxed the horses into a canter, Charles combed Will with probing eyes that demanded a response.

"I'll be over soon's I find my way," he said.

Charles waved and nodded his head in the affirmative.

A strange, moody youngster indeed, with a strong personality. Doc suspected that Charles had struck a deep emotional string in Will that made him withdraw. With the situation unclear and likely dangerous, Doc was compelled to probe. Will talked openly about his scuffle with Master Mack, and prize fighting.

"Why didn't you hit him?" Doc said, making note of Will's cool demeanor.

"Don't know, never thought much about it. I thanked him for taking care of me all them many years."

"You don't hate him enough to kill him?"

"I reckon I do, but I had no need to do that."

"What did you do? I'll bet you were afraid."

"Can't say that I weren't," Will said matter-of-factly.

"I imagine you and Charles have been through a lot together," Doc said.

Will set his mouth in a defiant pout. "This ain't got nothing to do with Charles. Mack had a notion to sell me after my last fight, even after I won him a whole pocketful of money."

"How could you know his plans?"

"He had me locked up in a slave-breaking pen somewhere close by Annapolis. I was scared near-mind to death. If it weren't for a little hunch back woman, he might'a made me more of a teenie-weenie rat than he made Levi. She made me look hard enough at everything about myself to believe I wouldn't be sold."

"Was she Tawney?" Doc said.

Will stared at him with utter disdain.

"I'm simply confused," Doc said. "Never would I insult you."

"I don't know a better way to tell you that I slept a little after that. When Mack came for me at daybreak I knew I wouldn't melt like a splat of lard in a hot pan whenever he belched or frowned at me."

"I suppose he knew it too," Doc said.

"I guess so," Will said, smiling slightly at the thought.

Then Will talked openly about most aspects of his life at Roedown. Doc listened attentively to the fascinating story of Grandmom Rosey infusing him with determination. He couldn't think of another question that would reveal an overwhelming hatred in Will to murder without planting the seed of mistrust between them, and reasoned that Master Mack lost control when Will defied his whip. The truth, at least that part of it not iterated by this young fugitive, would forever remain concealed. An embarrassed Master Mack's obligation to the slavery system dictated the accusation of murder and high bounty. Will, a fugitive in a free border state, represented a dangerous threat to the system.

Chapter Eleven

At home again, Doc introduced Will as an apprentice to his daily workers, and instructed his most trusted employee to keep Will very busy close by the house, not out of his eyesight or hearing range. Then he hurried to London Grove Village. After a promise of strict confidentiality from Squire Mapp, he repeated Will's unbelievable tale, and began an inquiry through the secret abolitionist society that would track Will as far south as possible to Roedown.

Several days later, while Will pruned the self-perpetuating June climbers that overflowed the east fence, a fat, scrubby man came riding up on an old unkempt horse and glowered at him. He stayed a spell then slowly trotted away. Every day for a week he watched Will from the woods beyond the nursery just out of Will's eyesight, but not out of Little Jay's.

Jay came often and made it his business to occupy himself close by wherever Will would be working. Will noticed him, but not enough to know how closely Doc's grandson observed the green boughs of giant elm trees, already showing a faint tint of coppery red and shooting their broad arches across the Philadelphia-Baltimore Pike. A horse braying or the sudden snap of dead branches carried some distance in the summer air to Jay's keen ears.

Will was preoccupied, fusing his steadily increasing predicament with a strange and new imaginary world. At times when leaning against the white-washed gazebo looking across the clear brook that prattled under the bridge and disappeared in an underwood of fern and bramble, he would see a wildcat. It crouched on the outlying branch of an oak tree, staring with yellow, dubious eyes. The wildcat's constant presence reminded him of a conjurer working the bad eye on him, reminded him of soul snatchers. He felt cooped up like a doomed rooster, or a fattening pig. Quite often he was tempted to venture close enough to see if the eyes were indeed real, but Doc's warning not to venture beyond the fence on either side of the nursery or beyond the creek in the back burned in his mind.

One afternoon the scrubby chap dropped in on Will again from out of the woods. His face was unshaven and swollen, his eyes protruding and watery. He came right up to the fence. "You look like my slave, nigger,"

"Then come take me, gawd-dammit!" Will threw a rake so hard it hit the fence and broke. A jagged piece of the handle flew into the air over the abductor's head. He turned and scampered into the brush. With a bound, Will went over the railing without touching, hesitated for a moment then started after him. Little Jay saw all of it and ran, calling his grandfather. Doc came running and calling. They both called but Will didn't answer. They went to the woods, to the spot where Jay had seen Will so often staring and found him probing the edge of a dense forest on a hillside above the valley, looking for the scalawag or the bobcat, Will wasn't sure which.

"He's daring you to enter his domain, Will, and of course, you know better," Doc said.

"You can say that. He ain't looking you in the eyeball every day."

"You're not afraid of him. Will..."

"I ain't afraid of nobody."

"We know that, Will, but jumping over the fence after that half-a-cent ale sap, you didn't use common sense."

"What I supposed to do, let him come on over and drag me away?"

"He baited you, Will. He made you angry enough to disregard common sense just to prove how tough you are."

"Common sense, common sense! Did it ever bring back anybody who been snatched away? What's it mean to folks afraid to leave their children more'n a few feet away from them, or theyselves any distance from a white somebody like you? What's it mean to a man needing to take him a wo...? It's enough to run a body crazy."

"Go over the fence again, they'll drag you back to slavery. There's too many of them for that kind of nonsense. I will not be responsible if you don't heed my warnings or take my advice."

"Nonsense hunh, I don't want you feeling thataway about me. I broke the rake, take it outt'a my wages and that be's that. I'll get my few rags and be on my way."

"Few rags! Do you mean your duds, and be on your way to where? First you want to fight. Now you're ready to run only because you won't or can't discipline yourself. If you must fight, for goodness sake, fight with a purpose. By yourself, you can't end slavery, but you could be a link in the mighty chain that will eventually crush it. But first you have got grow up, make yourself useful to the cause for freedom."

Will thrust his hands in his pants pockets and moved them around while looking past Doc. His angry expression melted into bewilderment. Though he could not understand the perplexities of compassion that kidnapping instigated in the hearts of God-inspired intelligent, caring folks, Doc touched something deep within him. Will had not actually tasted the terror wrought by abduction, but Doc's insistence of a concern for himself caused greater anxiety. He worried about Charles, in silent moments he agonized for imagined victims of road agents. Doc could not see the anguish Will suppressed for being constantly at another man's mercy, the tormenting state of helplessness that occupied his thoughts while digging, planting, pruning and weeding every day.

Yet, with Doc's subtle prodding, the forces of change, like a cooling night breeze after those hot summer days, blew gently on Will. Drinking water from the same well, having his own bedroom in a lean-to attached to the big house, sharing the same facility with the crescent moon door, and going to church or to Quaker Meting took some adjusting. But similarities of the Dingee Nursery to the sprawling Roedown plantation began fading from his young memory. He ate breakfast, dinner and supper with his boss' family except on the Saturdays and Sundays that he visited Charles in Bart Township. Charles was always more at ease than he and often chided Will for "worrying-up" trouble.

Then Doc one evening hurried home from London Grove Village and, after an excited minute with Mrs. Dingee, called Will into the kitchen for a whopping piece of apple cobbler.

"There is no record of you beating your master or taking his whip, which ever way it happened," Doc said. "Those genteel gambling men of Baltimore added $1,500 to Brodgen's $1,000 when they heard you had escaped."

"Who they?" Will asked.

"Your fans, Brodgen's chums, who made big money when you fought. Now," Doc's laugh-filled voice changed to one of deep resonance and cool authority. "I need to know if you'd rather be a prize fighter than a nursery man."

"Never gave fighting for money much thought," Will said, "after me and Charles made off."

"Very good," Doc said. "You may see your picture on a new poster that claims you are a fugitive prize fighter who whipped forty-five Goliaths, then got lazy and run away. But don't be alarmed. This is a new beginning. Leave that old life behind you. Tomorrow we'll go wild turkey and pheasant hunting."

"With what," Will asked, "a sling shot?"

They both laughed.

"I know you're not Little David," Doc said, his resonant voice ringing beyond the kitchen.

Mrs. Dingee cut him a stern, but gentle stare.

Doc began paying Will five dollars a month, making good his promise to pay more as Will progressed in both his apprenticeship and elementary levels of reading and writing. On the hunting trips Will quickly developed an eye for wild game that flew fast. The first time Doc saddled Dempsey, his thorough-bred, and asked Will to run him, he saw a natural affinity and was surprised that Will had never ridden before. While rubbing Dempsey down, Will told Doc what he remembered of a childhood dream to gallop away faster than time could leap. He suddenly put his brush down and looked far away.

"Leap to where?" Doc asked.

"Wherever mighty men go," Will said. "Back then I probably thought maybe I'd find me a daddy."

Will took to Dempsey and soon the steed took to him. Doc observed in the grim and determined Will astride the steed what he imagined Grandmom Rosey had seen, running him along the Patuxent River—a mighty warrior for the cause of freedom.

Will befriended the men who worked for Doc, hobnobbing with them during lunch or after work. Chewing the rag they called it, about sowing wild oats, and jobs and mad white folks. They teased Will about his lack of interest in girlfriends and tried coaching him in the fine art of noting the best and spotting the worst in a young woman. Inevitably though, their conversations drifted back to the terror of soul snatching. Will's aroused attention would turn to a wounded resignation.

Often in quiet evenings, Doc would use the Liberator—William Lloyd Garrison's newspaper—in the course of tutoring Will. They discussed Garrison's writings, Doc explaining how Congress made laws and why it had passed the Fugitive Slave Act.

After work one day during Will's second summer, Doc sat down on a stump beside him. "A freedom fighter is speaking in Hamorton Saturday," he said. "Have you ever heard of Frederick Douglass?"

Will hunched his shoulders and shook his head, avoiding the nurseryman's stern gaze.

"He and Garrison, the abolitionist from Boston, will be at Lyceum Hall. Mr. Douglass will be good for you," Doc said. "Both of them will be good for a lot of people. You, I and Mrs. Dingee, we'll go hear them speak."

A freedom fighter? That was easy enough for Will to understand. But standing on the side of justice, not being an ostrich with his head stuck in the sand, what did it mean? Already he'd been forced to understand more than he'd ever believed he could learn. That night while lying on the bed with his long legs crossed in a clean, comfortable resting place that he had already taken for granted, he could hear Doc over and over again. *Learn to read, Will. Knowledge is the key to liberation of your people. But not without understanding. So pray every day for understanding to reason out why men act the way they do. Time is not on your side.*

He had to learn so much. He wondered if he had remained the dumb nigger at Roedown would Master Mack have sold him by now. The thought disturbed him and in turning away from it, shadows of his body a flickering oil lamp cast on the wall caught his attention. He wiggled his fingers and made circles in the air with his feet, kicked his legs straight up, opened them into the widest V he could make, jumped up and swung his fist harder than he had ever swung it before. How strange it seemed to him that never had he made his shadow do what he wanted it to do. When a little boy, he hid from it. While growing larger, he simply turned over so he wouldn't see it. Now he felt strange. He couldn't express what he felt in earning his rights of passage into manhood, developing into a new kind of person, extending himself into the personage of an intelligent Will Parker.

Will felt proud of himself pulling up on the carriage reins, forcing trotting Dempsey to a walk. No, he felt darn proud with his hair slicked back and parted. Not once during the ride from London Grove to the Lyceum had he hiccupped or sweated under his armpits with Mrs. Dingee sitting content and smiling in the surrey between him and stone-faced Doc. But as they approached the outside band shell of the town meeting hall, Will grew awkward and apprehensive.

So many strangers—some walking, some riding mules, others in carriages and on horseback. Never had Will seen so many black and white people coming together, rallying for one cause; to outlaw slavery. Families—mothers and fathers in clean, pressed clothes, children's faces smooth and sparkling as if they had been polished with emery cloth. No identifiable fugitives stood among the crowd in tattered clothing, with fright in their eyes, or anxiousness written on their faces. Yet, Will knew soul snatchers and thieving poor white trash lurked in the evening shadows of the trees, looking for an opportune second to whisk away an unsuspecting man, woman or child. Despite Doc's warning that he was quite foolish to wish they would pick on him, Will felt he'd still sacrifice himself. He had a far better chance of fighting them off than a little boy, his sister, or his mother. So strongly was being snatched on his mind that he actually visualized it happening and began worrying about Charles.

"Watch yourself, Will," Doc said.

Will didn't see the deep rut in the roadway. "Uh, oh yes sir."

"Simply yes, Will," Mrs. Dingee said.

Will didn't answer, though her gentle correcting made him feel good. He drew back on the reins at a tethering post in front of a long water trough, and rubbed his sweating nose.

Sweet honeysuckle and ripening blackberry flavored the humid air laden with the pungent odor of many thirsty, relieving horses. Before they alighted from the surrey Doc began greeting men and tipping his hat to ladies. Soon they were pressed in with the throng moving slowly across Baltimore Pike toward the covered band shell in Hamorton Village Square. Off to the side a group of black people assembled. Others eased out of the tide and joined them. Will readily accepted the segregated practice; he would join them.

Mrs. Dingee though, had read his mind. "You'll sit with us, Will?" Then she lowered her head and cleared her throat into a dainty handkerchief. "Unless, of course, you mind my asking."

"Matter of fact, ma'am, I really don't." Will's answer, the tone and directness in which he had spoken like the Doc himself, surprised him. Even Doc cut an amused side glance without surrendering one bit of the stone in his face.

The lyceum consisted of a stage with a covering shaped like the top of an eggshell cut in half, and two covered sections of rough hewn oak benches the length and breadth of a colonial church. The Longwood Meeting of Progressive Friends stood close by to the west, quietly aloof like a fortress protecting the spirits of the deceased interred in the cemetery behind it. Doc, Mrs. Dingee and Will sat in the third row. Five cane-weaved chairs were arranged around a podium at center stage.

Soon the benches filled, people clustered along the sides and back. Then three white men, a white woman, and two black men walked a short set of stairs and strolled to center stage. All of them sat except the lady, she stood at the podium,

"Doctor Ann Preston," Doc said, leaning across his wife and speaking to Will in a hushed tone. She lived in the homestead adjoining Doc Dingee's.

"Yea," Will said. "I seen, er ah, I saw her more'n a couple times."

"But you don't know she is a conductor on the underground railroad."

"Yea I do," Will said. "Jocko is in her yard."

"They are about to begin," Mrs. Dingee said.

Doc smiled approvingly at Will and straightened himself in his chair.

Dr. Preston reminded Will of Miss Millie back in Baltimore; her smallness, the quiet yet assuming manner in which she moved about, the way she combed her black hair straight back into a bun, her dark eyes set in a small, tapered face. She wore a flowing ankle-length blue dress with large white rose imprints.

"Greetings, and thank ye, Friends, for responding to make this meeting the most aggressive abolitionist declaration ever in our appeal to abolish human bondage in these United States of America. We are quite fortunate to have with us two of the strongest proponents in America to date for the cause of decency, and brotherhood: William Lloyd Garrison, publisher of the Liberator and founder of the American Anti-Slavery Society, and Frederick Douglass, a former slave but now the most eloquent voice the world has heard speak of that incredible experience."

She turned around and extended her right hand to Garrison, the left one to Douglass as the audience applauded. They stood.

"Friends," Dr. Preston said, facing the audience, "this is Mr. Garrison's first visit to Chester County. He has not long returned from the International Anti-Slavery Convention in London, England, but refused his seat in protest of discrimination against women. We ascribe to your principles of moral decency, Mr. Garrison. Your cause is ours." She stepped away from the podium.

Garrison, slightly built, rather tall and bespectacled, moved slowly toward it. He was completely bald on top. Will noticed the sudden gust of hot August wind tousling long, brown, hair that ringed the speaker's ears and the back of his head. Garrison nodded at Dr. Preston. She curtsied.

"The seven weeks I languished in a Baltimore prison some years ago, not far from here, forced me to recognize just to what degree these Pharisees will wrench and twist the meaning expressed by our founding fathers in our Constitution. These serpents are forcing their way of life on us, and demand the right to punish when we rebuke it. At this very moment, slave state planters are buying land right here, and in your neighboring county of Lancaster. Wealthy men they are, collaborating with your state legislators, buying their way into your system of government. The vicious trick is to undermine your moral conviction, but you'll not let them do that. These blind guides cry slavery is justifiable for harnessing the wild of our land and shaping it into a nation. But they'll need a stronger case to justify the barbaric treatment of black folks, and murders of homesteading white families in the Kansas-Nebraska territory. Their vicious plans are obvious."

Will didn't understand why they were applauding. He wondered why he had come. He had no reason to ever care about white men killing each other. A vivid image of the editor of Columbia's newspaper appeared in his mind's eye. He remembered the editor wanting to kill him only because he was black and a fugitive slave. His rising anger was fueled by self-pity, but he forced himself to listen.

"God-fearing brethren, they are the cause of blood letting. That's not surprising. Anyone savage enough to treat slaves in the manner of which the underground railroad has made us Northerners see it certainly has no respect for mankind."

The applause resounded again. Garrison held up his hand and waited for the clapping to subside. "I have added another quill to the Liberator. It is the voice of an abolitionist, a self-styled scholar, a former slave with firsthand experiences of its dehumanizing atrocities. Ladies and gentlemen, Mr. Frederick Douglass."

A man with wrath imbedded in his barrel-like body approached the podium. So strong was his resentment, the aura of it spread like a mist over the lyceum, setting it in a mood like his. Will, caught-up in this somber trance, returned the angry stare. Mr. Douglass stood just under six feet, an inch or two shorter than Will. He reminded Will of a blacksmith. A round, leathery face etched with deep lines and puffed sinuses bespoke of his slave existence. Steel gray eyes told Will he trusted no one, and watched haunts from the corners of them.

"Many thanks for a warm greeting," Douglass said, "Your fervent piety makes it impossible to see you without saying, there's a Christian. There's no sorrow for which you do not shed a tear, no innocent joy for which you do not smile. You give bread to the hungry, cloth to the naked, comfort every mourner who comes within your reach."

His resonant and articulate bass voice began working its charismatic effect on the gathering.

"But heed my warning, though it be shrouded in plea. Conscience cannot stand much violence. Slavery has proven its ability to divest Christians. Once broken down, who is he that can repair the damage? It may be broken toward the slave on Sunday, toward the master on Monday, and toward the abolitionist or the innocent non-concerned on Tuesday. This is happening in every free state and in every territory."

Will watched Douglass, becoming more and more irritated. Mrs. Dingee watched Will from the corner of her eyes.

"Slavery can not endure such shocks," Mr. Douglass said. "It causes the worst kind of violence that demands the Christian try to justify himself to himself. One needs little knowledge of moral philosophy to know that Christianity and slavery cannot stand together. One undermines the other."

When he stepped away from the podium, resounding applause spilled out of the lyceum across the green to the village square.

"Goodness," Mrs. Dingee said, "he is such an articulate speaker."

"I believe he came from your neck of the woods, Will, somewhere along the Chesapeake," Doc said. "Care to meet him?"

"Naw."

"I understand," Doc said. "That was in your other life and you'd rather forget it."

"He got his big words," Will said, "I got my fists."

"But, Will, he's such an inspiration," Mrs. Dingee said, "and Dr. Preston would be thrilled to introduce you, all of us."

"Nope," Will said, feeling tight in his chest. Douglass' speech, most of which he didn't understand, had elicited a respect that Will would have never dreamed possible for a black man from white folks. But he didn't want to talk about it, not with her, not with Doc, not with Dr. Preston. They pitied him, Will knew that now, because he couldn't tell his story like Douglass. He wanted to run fast as he could and block everything out of mind, the way he had done along the Patuxent with Grandmom Rosey driving him until he had expelled all the pent-up anger for being a dumb nigger.

"Will Parker! Anybody seen him? Parker." A panting black man rushed into the milling crowd. He caught immediate attention and startled Will out of his huffing attitude. But Will didn't reveal himself to the unknown, frightened man, even though quick, disturbing thoughts about his fugitive brother lumped in his chest. Will sat with his head bowed, watching the sweating intruder until he was almost in front of him, then jumped directly in his path. They collided. Will seized him and squeezed until he went limp in Will's vice-like grip.

"Who wants to know Will Parker?"

He looked up at Will with fear-glittered eyes. A shortness of breath and sudden contempt tempered his voice. "Better let go and listen, man mountain. Snatchers 'bout to haul Charles down the river."

Will released the man and for an instant stood as rigid and emotionless as a wooden post supporting the lyceum's cover. He opened his mouth several times and pointed in the direction from where he thought the man had come, but no words came out.

Pity spread over Doc's face. "Where is Charles now" he asked.

"In Squire Jacobs' office," the man said, "I 'spect the hearing's on right now."

"He's only a few miles from here in Kennett Square," Doc said. "Why'd they not have the hearing in Bart Township? How did you know Will would be here?"

"Grab me a buggy and follow them," the man said. "Charles tell me some time ago his brother work for a Doc Din, Dungee, somebody like that. Folks over Dungee's way see Will pass, believe he be here."

"Dingee, my name is Doc Dingee. I think it's a trap to catch Will too."

"Go'n save my brother. Ain't worried 'bout no trap," Will said. "He's all I got in this world. How you traveling, man?"

"Percy, that be's me," the stranger said. "Over yonder." He pointed to a freight wagon drawn by two quarter horses, and began running to it with Will.

"Make'em git up," Will yelled.

"Yah, yah. Giddap." Percy set the horses to galloping down the winding hill from Hamorton to Kennett Square Village.

"If it's Groit that's got'em," Will said, shaking his head from side to side and hanging on tightly, "I'm a kill'em, I'm a kill'em."

Doc and Mrs. Dingee watched Will hurry off. The abolitionists and sympathizers who had heard the alarm and had observed Will's reaction, many of them the Dingees' friends who knew Will, gathered around.

"Dear husband," she said, wringing her hands, "We must do something."

"Charles is a goner for sure if he interferes," Doc said.

"Go with him," she said.

Doc thought about it. "I really should, but I'm afraid that if I'm forced to argue before Jacobs with a slave runner or Will's and Charles' owner, you know who will win. That would be a very unwise and compromising position for me."

"I'll go with you," she said.

"To do what?" Doc said, looking around for someone with whom she might ride home. "I could be charged with perjury and arrested."

"My conscience is in accord with yours. As you, so I. We'll serve time together," she said, and began walking from the lyceum. The throng moved with her as if she had suddenly become a charismatic figure, not aware of her powers. Doc was reluctantly swept along with the wave of human tide that climbed into their wagons and followed them to Kennett Square.

"Up there," Percy said, hurrying through the village toward the Square. "See that long buckboard hitched to them two black horses?"

How well did Will recognize the buckboard, the slavers' wagon that he had learned to dread from his Roedown days at slave selling time. Their horses were tied to a hitching rail in front of a two story white frame building on the south side of the village green. The first floor housed a court room, squire's office, small jail, and constable's office. The words TAX OFFICE were printed across two front windows of the second story.

"Charles still there," Percy said.

Will leaped from the wagon and raced across the village green to Squire Jacobs' office. Inside, he sped headlong down a narrow hall toward the voices he heard to yank and tug the knob on the courtroom door. Then, a slide bolt from inside the door banged against its metal stop. What emerged from the court room stopped Will just as if an iron gate had suddenly dropped from the sky right in front of him.

Groit came out first. Seeing Will, he tightened his hold on the chains that bound Charles and grinned his tobacco-stained, snaggle toothed, menacing looking smile. Charles' sad, spiritless eyes combed over Will as though he were a stranger, a nobody, a mound of dirt in his path. A metal collar harnessed his neck, from which a heavy chain extended to his ironbound hands and to a heavy ball chained to his ankles.

All the warnings that had been hammered into Will's head about slave agents and slave masters from Grandmom Rosey, from Tighe and Quaker man down Baltimore way, took flight from his consciousness. He heard a roaring in his ears like the Chesapeake in a rain storm. Over the din of that, a deep commanding voice made sounds he couldn't discern. Ofeutey, his African grandfather, whose spirit the slavers couldn't break, Will felt erupting inside, tearing at his guts to get out.

Groit had a whip in his other hand. "I knowed I'd git'cha sooner or later," he said. A pistol hung from a gun belt slouched around his huge waist.

"Ain't taking me or my brother, lessen you take me feet first stretched out on a plank before I break your neck," Will said, and grimaced at five motley-looking men filing out with the squire behind Groit and surrounding Charles.

"Hear that?" Groit said. "That's what happens when these lowly lumps of coal get so damned uppiddy. Grab the bastard, Sledge."

Before Sledge or the others could move, Will rammed his fist into Groit's face. He hit him, God Almighty, didn't he though. Pain shot up his arm, through his armpit, and lodged behind his shoulder blade. Groit rocked back and forth like a tree struck by lightning, swaying precariously to right its balance. His eyes searched for stars momentarily then glared unfocused at Will. A curse dribbled from his mouth.

"Death is on you, nigger," he said, with a weak, trembling voice, still holding the chains that bound Charles. "I'm a sell you to Brodgen, then snatch your soul from its worthless hide, hang your carcass from your master's catalpa tree."

Will, not believing the old man took the pounding that had driven young rugged brawlers into the ground, set to hammer him again. But Sledge hit Will full force on the side of his head, driving him back against the opposite wall.

Squire Jacobs, at the sight of Percy running toward him with two other black men he had summoned, yelled for the constable. Groit's gang shifted nervously, ready to battle. Jacobs ducked back into his court chambers.

Percy slammed an iron piece across Sledge's head, knocking him to the floor. Will bounced off the wall and began battling his way through a frenzy of fists, grunts, and groans to Groit and Charles. Doc, with friends and passersby drawn to the ruckus, began wedging themselves between Will and the slave runner. Sledge, lying on his back dazed, bleeding, and getting stepped on, pulled his pistol.

"Git back, gawd-dammit," he yelled, "the whole lot of ya, back up."

"Bloomin' idiot!" Groit said. "Kill up these white folks and hang you will, but by your damned fool self!"

"Pull away from him, Charles," a white man in the crowd yelled.

"Not a chance," Groit said, backing out of reach with Charles in tow. "He's mine. Papers signed and sealed by the justice here."

"Don't give up so easy," Will said. "Make him carry you."

A loud blast of shot from a musket cut the ruckus abruptly. Through a broken window Will saw the constable pointing his smoking rifle to the sky. Percy and his pals hastily retreated out the front door. Squire Jacobs came into the hall flanked by deputies, their loaded guns trained on the battlers.

"Who is responsible for this?" He looked at Groit. "You've got your prisoner, now clear out. The rest of you better have a good explanation."

"No," Will said, pushing and shoving his way through the log-jam of people. "He ain't no prisoner, he's my brother."

"Stop, I say!" Justice Jacobs said. "Who in tarnation are you?"

"Another fugitive," Groit said, "that's been hiding here in the protection of you God-fearing, good, law-abiding white folks for well nigh three years."

Squire Jacobs pointed a warning finger at Groit. "Shut up." He waved his hands in a circle. "Why are you people here?" he said, looking at each face in the crowd until he he recognized Doc. "Mr. Dingee, surely you are not meddling in the court's business?"

"We are not doing what it appears we are," Doc said. "I beseech you, spare us a few minutes before you release Charles to that scoundrel."

"My patience is worn thin, and before I consent to anything, tell me, are you responsible for him, that brawler and his bunch for being here?" He pointed a warning finger at Will.

"No," Doc said, "but I am responsible for Will's grave concern for his brother."

"Dingee! Dare you confuse me anymore, the whole lot of you may need bail and lots of it to enjoy supper at home this evening. Once more, is there any difference in what I asked you and what you're telling me? A simple yes or no before my patience completely evaporates."

"Yes, of course. Will is his own man. That's why he's my apprentice and knows more about planting roses and tending fruit trees than any worker I've ever had. Obviously, sudden word of his brother shackled in chains unnerved him."

"He's a fugitive, a half-crazy dog killer," Groit said, "with a two thousand dollar reward on his head for attacking his master." He put his whip on the floor and pulled from his pocket a wrinkled, faded poster with Will's profile and vital statistics.

"Well now," Squire Jacobs retorted sarcastically, "an apprentice, a mad dog killer, a fugitive, all that inside one black body. Lord, give me strength."

"It ain't no fake," Groit said. "Read it for yourself." He attempted to give it to Jacobs, but the constable snatched it and handed it to the squire.

Will's attention was drawn from Jacobs reading the bulletin to Mrs. Dingee, with several women from the lyceum, hurrying to the squire's office. Groit stealthily summoned a strapping, portly member of his gang and wrapped an end of the chain that bound Charles around his hand.

"This could justify a hearing," Jacobs said. "However... For what ridiculous reason would these women be here? I'll not permit this intrusion to become anymore of a spectacle that it already is."

Mrs. Dingee and the women with her retreated to a bench on the green under a tree.

"Justice," Doc said, "please stop shocking the consciences of us who strive to live the Christian ideal. How many black persons in our midst are not fugitives in one way or another? Round them up, every last one, babies too, and send them across the Mason Dixon with that blood-curdler." He pointed to Groit.

"I enforce the law to maintain peace, Mr. Dingee, not to satisfy myself. Your abolitionist conscience makes that difficult. Yet, I tolerate you strictly from the goodness of my heart, not that I'm duty bound by any law. I warn you, don't make that indignant mistake again. Mr. Groit presented enough evidence to substantiate a warrant for the arrest of a fugitive slave named Charles."

"However," he said, turning to the slave runner, "this poster, even if it is bonafide, is more than two years old. I'll not issue a warrant. Without that, Will

Parker is protected by state law to personal freedom. Otherwise, Doctor Dingee, I'd be taking a sworn statement from you to keep this apprentice of yours out of shackles. Now, Mr. Groit, get out of my sight."

"No", Will blurted, "he ain't stealing my brother."

"Silence," Squire Jacobs yelled. "Another utterance regarding this matter from any of you will be considered a contempt of court."

The man who had urged Charles to pull away from Groit stepped from the circle around Will and approached Jacobs. "You'd better cite me, Justice. That young man you call a fugitive, and God only knows what else, has rights too. He is gainfully employed, having worked a long time for Jeremiah Moore."

"Hrump, meaning what?" Jacobs said, wiping his hands across his thin lips.

"This better be good, mister..."

"Joseph Scarlett, sir. Who may I ask, testified in Charles' behalf?"

"How dare you question the validity of my court. Why the hell weren't you here to speak for the nigger, Mr. Scarlett, sir?"

"His name is Charles," Doc Dingee said. "I introduced him to Mr. Moore some years ago."

"I do declare," Squire Jacobs said, "that's bloody unfortunate because without a responsible person speaking for him, I had no choice. I thought..." Squire Jacobs pointed at Groit. "You said this fellow," he looked for Charles, "the prisoner killed your dog and you tracked him here. Where is he?"

"My men you deputized," Groit said, "took him away to avoid..."

"You let him," Will screamed at Jacobs, flailing his arms all about. "You let him sneak my brother. You in cahoots with that raggedy mouth boogey man." He pointed at Groit. "I better get'em back, 'cause if I don't, hell go'n see you too."

Doc and the others surrounding Will, backed away.

"Arrest him," Jacobs yelled to his deputies.

Will bowled right over the two who came towards him and dashed out the front entrance.

"Arrest him for what?" Doc and Scarlett spoke as if singing a duet.

"I'll think of something."

Jacobs' deputies didn't follow Will, they watched him from the squire's office window.

Chapter Twelve

The buckboard had disappeared. Will zigzagged across the square, demanding an answer from anyone who dared listen if they had seen slave agents riding off with his brother. Mrs. Dingee and the women with her told him Charles hadn't come out front. Will circled the building, banging and yanking at the locked rear doors. A man he didn't ask, simply pointed south down Wilmington Pike.

"Here, Will." Joseph Scarlett called him. "Take my horse."

Will ran to him. "Wouldn't be totin' a gun that I might take a loan of, would you?" he said, swinging himself over Scarlett's white stallion.

Scarlett shrugged his shoulders and looked at the ground. Will drove his heels into the horse's side, galloping hard, bending his head over the mane, riding into the wind, blaming himself, and punishing the beast. In so great a hurry, he didn't think to ask the passing wayfarers if they had seen a black man chained to a buckboard with five white men until he had run through a crossroads. He didn't slow down. Random thoughts came to him as fast as the clods of dirt the horse kicked up.

If Charles hadn't been so frozen with fear, he could have done more to help himself. Quaker man in Baltimore a long time ago asked Will how it felt coming out the lion's mouth. He had laughed, though he didn't really know what Quaker meant. Now he did. Will hit Groit hard enough to coldcock a bull. Yet he, certainly an old man now, only rocked a few times and spit out a mouthful of rotten teeth. What in hell made him so tough? Frightening. What if next time he ran upon Groit without Doc? It probably would be without Doc. It must be without Doc. He'd be all right with a gun, with comrades, men who would get down mean and dirty like, damn the worse and fight back.

Mindless of the grave danger in which he had put himself, Will spurred Scarlett's horse right up to the lion's mouth, the Mason-Dixon line, the clearly marked boundary of demarcation that divided North from South, slave state from free state, Delaware from Pennsylvania.

I know you want me to jump in. I know you want to swallow me up, you ugly sonofabitch.

He stopped there, wondering, though not conscious of waiting for the thought that bound him to that imaginary king of beasts to materialize, to manifest itself. Overhead, an eagle appeared out of the oblivion of space. He watched it grow larger and suddenly nose dive. Then he heard the squawk of a smaller bird, the eagle flying away with its talons imbedded in the pitiful creature's body, its head hanging loosely on its broken neck. The realization sunk in, he would not see his brother again.

"I'm a fix you," he mumbled to the lion. "I'm a make you feel the hurt, make you taste the ugly."

He turned, letting the horse set its own pace in a trot toward Kennett Square. Beside a brook where he rested while Scarlett's stallion drank and grazed, Will sat in silence: Tawney, Levi and his mother, Aunt Aida and her children, now Charles. He proclaimed in his heart, anybody within hearing distance of him, anybody his eye caught sight of in danger, he would save or die in the trying.

When he finally reached Kennett, the sun could barely peep over the horizon. Scarlett greeted him with a sigh of relief.

"That was a mistake, Will. I've asked myself a thousand times over why I acted so stupid. You could've been captured or killed."

"If you feeling sorry for me," Will said, dismounting, "stop."

Scarlett took the reins and cleared his throat. Will's face was set in grim repose. The anxiety, the fright, the helplessness that had tendered Scarlett to help Will earlier was no longer obvious.

"Mighty fine horse you got here. Thanks," Will said. "I aim to get me one soon."

"If you're ever over Christiana way," Scarlett said, swinging himself into the saddle, "stop by. Could use a good hired hand anytime."

Will nodded good-bye without answering him and turned to Doc, Mrs. Dingee and the others who had been holding vigil in the Square for his safe return. They gathered around and consoled him as if Charles had died and Will had just returned from the graveyard. Some held his hand, others simply grasped his shoulder while their faces offered sympathetic expressions. A little lady with rounded shoulders and her hands clutched in front of her spoke softly.

"Will, Mr. Parker, we can only ask for thy forgiveness and pray that somehow my telling this will lighten the burden in thy heart. Thy brother worked for us. I am Sarah, Mr. Moore's daughter." She nodded her head towards tall, austere Jeremiah standing behind her.

"Dad knew all about Charles' slave life."

Jeremiah sighed when Will's somber eyes swept over him. "Decent God-fearing people can't even be about the business of their work without agitating, vicious neighbors and worthless, thieving scoundrels," he said.

"We found Charles withdrawn," Sarah said, "and of a suspicious nature. For a time we were fearful, but as he shared his slave life at Roedown with us, he simply melted into a conscientious and faithful young man. That faithfulness cost him his freedom. Judge for thyself when I tell thee. Toward the last of his living with us, bounty hunters came for him several times but failed on each attempt. We were afraid they would come again when Charles and I were alone, so before my parents left to spend several weeks in Bucks County, Dad begged Charles to visit thee, but he wouldn't. 'No,' he said, 'I promised Jerry I would tend the stock and things.' He stayed. Few white men would have done that under similar circumstances."

Will turned away from her without uttering a word, and climbed aboard Doc Dingee's surrey. The good-byes were hushed and solemn when he, Doc and Mrs. Dingee began their trek homeward. Doc held the reins. Will bobbled along with every movement of the surrey in absolute silence until Mrs. Dingee, with her soft motherly voice, spoke quietly.

"Sometimes a good cry, Will, removes enough of the pain so you can at least hear God speaking."

Will looked afar, his hawk-hooded eyes still burning with a fierce energy. "Ain't never cried in my life," he said.

"Well," she said, fidgeting and smoothing her waist, "I didn't mean..."

"But that don't mean I ain't seen pain," Will said.

Doc noticed the gruffness, the smoldering anger, the determination in Will's voice. It wasn't so much a matter of what Will said to Mrs. Dingee that made it profound, it was the manner in which he spoke.

"Doc," Will said, "I been working for you more'n two years now. You pay me good and only God could count how much you taught me, ciphering, reading, the Bible and so much more. Mrs. Dingee treats me mostly like a son." He almost laughed. "And I thought I was a man back then."

"It's been a fair exchange," Doc said.

"But now, I think it best I be getting on up the road."

"Oh," Doc said, acting surprised.

"We'd like for you to stay on," Mrs. Dingee said. "The roses you tend are so pretty."

"Naw, what I got to do now won't be good for your business. I don't want to see things grow pretty no more."

"That is not good," Doc said. "I hope you trust me enough to tell me why."

"Somebody's got to stop slave runners from stealing us. Somebody's got to bear up when they come breaking down doors and running off with kids' daddies, killing them if they try to protect theyselves."

Doc sighed long and deeply. "I can't disagree," he said, "but who?"

"I aim to do it."

"You?" Mrs. Dingee said, "why, why if you try taking the law..."

"Law! Law that gives white men the right to hunt me down like a coon?"

"They'll kill you!" She huddled close to Doc as if Will had suddenly become a menacing stranger.

"Sorry I yelled. But your laws don't protect me," Will said. "How in the world can I respect them?"

Doc put his arm around his wife. "I knew this day would come, I knew it the first time I saw him. I could see it in his face, and he's right."

"At least try to reason with him. What is it that he's going to do?"

"I'm going to save my people." Will looked straight through the dimming sunset.

"Oh, Doc," she cried. "There's going to be killing. I can feel it."

"Don't get yourself all worked up," Doc said. "We're safe and sound at home now." He inhaled the humid London Grove evening air and exhaled slowly as if the exhalation was a preview of the turmoil he and the abolitionists worked so hard to prevent.

That night Will and Doc talked until almost midnight. Mrs. Dingee, having gone to bed, had begun praying before she reached the top step.

"A revolution, dear God, don't let it come to that." She thought about massacres she had heard happened in Virginia, the panic that gripped the countryside as far away as they were in Pennsylvania. She prayed for a deeper understanding of the cause for which Will had been driven to act, and fell asleep.

"Will, are you sure?" Doc sighed and closed his eyes. "Will." He opened them and looked directly at Will. "You realize I hope, that you'll probably go to the gallows for this."

"I'm a take Groit and his satans with me."

"My dear friend with that attitude you will hang for sure. There is possibly a humbler way to go about your rescue mission that won't..."

"Slave runners got to see the ugly, they got to taste the hurt."

"You're bent on killing," Doc said, "that is a big mistake."

"Won't let you talk me out of it, Doc. If it comes to killing, I won't lie down and let it happen, but I ain't afraid to die."

Doc rubbed his hand across his chin nervously. "Uh-that's not exactly what I meant. Tell you what," he stood. "I don't think Mrs. Dingee would mind if I cut her rhubarb pie. You make some tea."

"Don't feel much like drinking," Will said.

Doc set the pie on the oak table, acting as though he hadn't heard Will.

"A taste of hot spice probably would go along nice, I guess," Will said.

They hustled quietly about the kitchen, not talking or facing each other until seated and enjoying the dessert. Hopefully, Doc thought, Will might listen to reasoning.

"I know you'd like to, ah well, I guess you could probably slaughter all of them and not even bat an eye. But remember, when your dagger has drawn blood from a slaver's or his agent's throat, beneath his facade of greed and hate is a human being, a child of God just like you."

Will began twisting in the chair and frowning. "Don't ask me to believe that, Doc. How come God don't treat us the same?"

"I don't really know," Doc said. "Punishing is the Creator's business. You can liberate only with God's grace. Rescue, take measures to prevent stealing if you must, but I warn you, do not seek revenge."

Doc began breathing heavily and slowly pacing the floor. Will saw his face actually glowing in the lantern light, and knew that Doc was opening the channel deep within himself to that inner light. Doc spoke in a chant-like monotone.

"The down-trodden can be held in captivity by their brethren only so long as they don't know that all men are endowed with the same gifts of the spirit—peace, love, and the pursuit of happiness. Truth crushed to earth shall rise again. Sooner or later the down-trodden will rise and take what is rightfully theirs."

"Seems like I hear you saying it's bound to happen," Will said, "but telling me don't do it."

"Certainly not double-talk, Will. Sounds like it, well, because I'm wrestling with a confession I owe you. Mrs. Dingee and I... Well, I'll get right to the point. Your leaving will shatter my personal commitment to show that tendering a young slave with family kindness, letting him see the fruits of his labor would somehow render the bitterness and ugliness of bondage ineffective. I was banking on you to prove that it will save all of us from untold suffering which is sure to come. Men, especially evil men, must see us abolitionists striving not only to end this scourge of slavery, but to mend the country. But I'm on the side of justice. That presents demands that can't be overlooked, Will. If you become a threat, there won't be much I can do to protect you."

Suddenly, Mrs. Dingee screamed. Doc knocked the chair over on its side and ran upstairs two steps at a time. She was sitting up, wide-eyed and wet with perspiration.

"I'm sorry," she cried. "I'm sorry."

She told Doc of her dream that Nat Turner was downstairs plotting with him to wage war against the slavers, plotting with him to kill everybody in the Pennsylvania countryside sympathetic to the Southerners' cause.

Doc called down to Will from atop the stairs. "The hour is quite late," he said with a crisp voice. "No, on second thought, I'll be down in a few minutes."

Doc finally came back to the kitchen with an envelope in his hand. "You haven't said where you are going, Will. But wherever, you will need money. A little extra is in here with your wages."

"Don't want nothing that ain't mine for working."

"It's yours. We've been saving it for you, hoping that... Consider it a bonus. We'd better get some sleep."

How could Will sleep with his mind charged full of loathing and despair? Even though a new feeling of self worth surged within him—he owned more money than he could have imagined—haunting loneliness, the longing for woman that generally invaded his senses in the wee hours after midnight, came again. A pain seared through his groin, desperate wanting, but with a mounting fear of loving.

Chapter Thirteen

In the graying dawn, with dew stippling on the grass and the peaceful babbling of the brook over which Will reckoned he was walking for the last time, he felt unsettled, like a man leaving a reward he had not earned. Doc had been good to him, and Will had come to believe their relationship was genuine. He worked hard, Doc paid him fairly. Doc taught him from his heart, a gift of love he called it. Will listened and learned well, testimony that what is given from the heart is received in like fashion. But one apologetic scream for a nightmarish dream had compromised that, despite Doc's efforts to make it seem inconsequential. Then hearing that the intertwining of their lives had been a trial, an experiment to hopefully say yes, blending a slave into Doc's world could be done. Except that Will's leaving wrecked the test.

Had the Dingees really been sincere? The doubt brewing inside him affected the gratification he needed to feel so that he could nurture his shattered self. He had learned to follow his feelings, believe in his own mind. Nothing would shatter that.

He left the carpet bag Mrs. Dingee had given him and departed with his earthly belongings in a shirt tied around a stick slung over his shoulder before she came downstairs. When Doc asked him where he would go, Will simply smiled and looked at the ground. No, he was not afraid. Yes, he was stronger and wiser for the experience of living there.

Yet, though he had walked dusty, winding Baltimore Pike many times those few years, often alone amid hostile stares and threatening gestures, that particular day the road seemed to unfold as if daring him to walk it, as if daring him declare a right even to be there. Then he thought about Charles and didn't give a damn about the road or anyone on it.

Will had recently begun grooming his hair like Frederick Douglass', growing it longer and parting it on the left side over his eye. Six foot, two inches tall, in denim shirt, bib overalls, hobnail brogans, a red work handkerchief around his neck, he reckoned that to many observers passing by he was the caricature of a young black man in a hostile land. He felt no more at home than the ugliest, meanest, biggest monster he could imagine walking the Pike for the first time. Would the stench of ugliness that permeated his being ever end, the wrestling with heartache, the softening in his penis, the fear of marriage, of raising children? Not without a fight. Why couldn't he, a young colored man, float about even moon-sick sometimes, like young white men? Will really had no choice. He felt more prepared for danger, relying on that razor-edge defensive instinct rather than on a white protector.

Fortunately for him, though abolitionists were a minority, most were an impressive lot—merchants, doctors, lawyers, and owners of vast farms, dairies, grist mills, lumber and coal yards—substantial propertied men who required more hired hands than were available. Their impression did make a difference in the general populace's attitude toward slavery, though it was more of an undercurrent, rather than any open warfare against the daily outpouring of hostilities. At least, it offered brave, stout-hearted black folks some degree of security in the community where they lived and worked. The more nimble at heart didn't venture far from what little safety a home within sight of a white family's protective eye provided, which was some small degree better than none at all. A young unmarried woman's brightest hope in her immediate future was a live-in maid's job. Black children were seldom seen, and then never alone.

A vague notion impelled Will towards Christiana where he might work for Joseph Scarlett if he could find him. But his mind was not on himself. His vow to save any person within hearing distance would lead him. For lonely, scared people, the direction of their voices would be the road he'd follow. Their crying would be his battle. No surrendering. Death, not capture, would be the price for losing.

Will surmised from the penetrating sun on his bare head and the dry taste in his mouth that he had walked a far piece since eating lunch at high noon.

"Hey-oh there, road agent." A hired hand, with a chocolate smiling face and dancing brown eyes, hailed him. He was harvesting wheat with several white men in black hats and wearing long black beards in a field turned amber by the rippened stalks of grain. "Ain't you heard or is it you just plain too walked out to pay attention?"

"What cause you to say that?" Will said, stopping in the middle of the road.

Will could see the rigors of farming, of toiling in the rich brownish-black dirt, had seasoned the husky man. He gathered the bundles of stems laden with balls of soft grain and piled them on an already loaded mule-drawn two wheel wagon. A team of four men three or four wagon lengths ahead of him continued their back-bending tasks; two with grain harvesting tools cutting the stalks a few inches from the ground, two gathering and binding them into bundles.

"Soul snatchers down in the valley, headin' this way."

"Where might this way be, stranger?" Will said, crossing a shallow ditch that separated the roadway from the field.

"Depends on where you headed. Peckerwoods from over in Smyrna say they going to whitewash whole Sadsbury Township. That means black speckled dogs too. Brown egg-laying hens better hide under the chicken coop." He waited but Will didn't laugh. "Yonder way is gettin' on up Penningtonville and Christiana way."

"Ain't no promise I'll get there either, is it, friend?" Will said.

"Cain't say that it is."

"Could I trouble you for a dipper full?" Will said. "I'm bound to rest."

An unhappy expression spread over the man's face. "Well," he said, tweaking his nose, "if you don't mind drinkin' after one of your own kind."

After Will nodded, the farm hand poured a swallow of water in a dented tin cup, sloshed it around, and poured it out. He refilled the tin and gave it to Will who drank, taking deep gulps, sounding like he was grinding cinders. The farm hand chuckled at Will's dancing adam's apple.

"Much obliged to you." Will gave him the cup and wiped his mouth on the handkerchief around his neck. He turned his head slightly, skeeted spit between his teeth, and ground it into the dirt with his shoe. "I'm looking for some stout hearted men, men ready to stand pat and fight for our God given right to protect ourselves." He stared with his fierce, hooded eyes.

The intensity of the questioning gaze overwhelmed the farm hand. He looked askance and sighed. "Ain't like I don't know what you talkin' 'bout, but you askin' for a heap. What rights a colored man got?"

"A right to be treated like a man, a right to act like one without being all the time scared of soul snatchers."

The farm hand hastily scooped up bundles of wheat and stacked them on the wagon. "Ain't sure I can appreciate that kind a talk from a stranger. Too many yellow dogs around in black skin." He hastily grabbed another bundle.

"Will Parker's my name." Will walked along beside him.

"Parker, hunh." He took a long, hard look at Will, then said, "Gibson, Merle Gibson. You free?"

"Damn tootin', I am." My God! What had Will said? What flew from his mouth without as much as giving it second thought? When had he become so courageously bold? The feeling astounded him.

"Since when?" Gibson said.

"Hunh?" Will said.

"How long you been a free man, Parker?"

"Since this morning. Been a fugitive three, four years."

"Heat done got to you, maybe?" Gibson said.

"Hell no. Ain't nobody's fugitive no more," Will said. "I'm free. You hear me? Ain't bought, weren't sold, nobody give me papers. Free dammit, because I say so."

Gibson tipped his hat, wiped sweat from his brow on his shirt sleeve. "Came here a fugitive seven years ago myself," he said, looking off into the distance. "I don't 'spect you a family man. I got me one to worry about."

"You worry because you can't think yourself a free man," Will said. "Go home after work and find nothing to see of them except blood splattered everywhere, would you stop worrying then? Naw."

"Know what I'm thinking right now?" Merle said. "You one ole piece a' raggedy mouth, trouble-making, road agent nigger and I got work to do."

"Didn't go to scare you none," Will said.

"I think you'd try make me believe I could peek up a pig's ass and see the price of lard stamped on his chitt'lin."

Will knew he should back away, laugh off the predicament he'd put Merle in, but he couldn't. "I ain't selling lard, ain't selling chitt'lins, and I know your mind is all clogged because you scared."

Merle bristled. "Ain't scared 'a nothing, dammit. Leastwise the likes of you."

"I know, I know," Will said, backing out of arm distance from Merle. "Nothing except soul snatchers. They make us worse off than we were down yonder slaving for ole massa."

Merle rubbed his lips and fingers like a boy who'd suspected his mother had seen sugar on them from her freshly baked cookies. "What 'n hell can you do that decent, kind, white folks ain't already doing?"

"Claim my manhood, make snatchers feel the hurt. God A'mighty Merle, fight back!"

Merle measured Will—height, thickness, and heart—while they stood facing each other in awkward silence.

"Well," Will said, "thanks for your time, ole blood. I'll be moving on. Snatchers roaming again and I ain't ready for'em yet."

"Wait," Merle said.

Right on schedule, one of the wheat cutters cupped his hand across his eyes and checked the sun's location in the western sky. He gathered his cutting tools and began walking across the harvested section of the field. The other three followed.

"It's a bad time for a black man traveling by hisself. I got myself a little spread down the road a piece. 'Spect you could stand a bite right along now, and maybe we could chew the rag a bit after supper. My missus and chillun be glad to have you. Soon's I take these bundles to the curing pile, and take care of the mule, we can hurry on."

Hunger in Will growled its agreement. "Mind if I help?" he said.

Merle laughed.

Merle's homestead, a log cabin style bungalow in the middle of a vegetable garden, captivated Will. Scarecrows, fake hoot owls, and other little funny things moved in some fashion with the breeze to scare rabbits, squirrels and deer away from the crop. It was in what Merle called hallowing distance of the man for whom he worked. Bright colored curtains with simple designs of homemade stitch adorned every window. Homespun odors of food frying in garlic and herbs flowing through the screen doors, and the lingering aroma of Merle's pipe lured Will into its sanctuary.

Inside, a tall slender woman commanded Will's attention. She set his soul yearning; the wrestling with heartache, the stench of ugliness about himself, the softening in his penis.

145

Dark brown expressive eyes darted nervously back and forth from Will to an oak table, bleached by daily scouring, on which she arranged supper. Lois, Merle called her, smoothed her apron and brushed back strands of hair, the tone and fragrance of ginger, into a bun. Her low, soft voice actually sang, yet was scolding when she reprimanded Merle for waiting so late to announce a supper guest.

Two little children, Brother and Sister, Merle called them, greeted Will and observed him with the intensity of timid rabbits. Their faces were scrubbed and shining like the earthenware dishes and ashen chairs on which they sat.

"You got family, Mr. Parker?" Lois said.

"Nobody but myself, ma'am."

"A fine, young strapping man like you not married?"

He laughed. "I thought on that myself this morning for a long time."

"And," she said.

"I don't aim to rush it none."

"Will's mind ain't on marrying, Lois," Merle said.

"He didn't say that," she said. "What do you see that he's not telling?"

"He's got a calling, Lois. Don't be bashful Will. Chicken and dumplings don't stay around here too long."

Will laughed. Sister and Brother snickered.

"Oh, how nice," Lois said, "a young preacher man. My, my."

"It ain't that," Merle said. "He's looking for a way to stop soul snatching."

She balled her hands, one into the other, and began rubbing them. Will noticed beads of sweat forming on her keen nose.

"Merle, the children. Please! I've asked you not..."

"Well." Merle rubbed his head. His jaw sagged. "He's all about banding together, making a stand, Lois."

"God called you to stand up against white folks, Mr. Parker?" she asked. The sternness, the implied doubt in her voice unsettled Will. "Well, hadn't thought on it much thataway, ma'am, but..."

"You really ought to see yourself when you talking on it, Will," Merle said, offering Will an encouraging smile.

"It will cause trouble," she said. "Worse than what we have now."

"Can't be much worse, ma'am."

"It certainly can." She nodded her head up and down nervously. "At least now we got decent white folks on our side."

Will saw veins rising on her neck. "Decent white folks, they be like a walking stick, ma'am. Seems we can't take one step without that crutch."

Merle noticed Brother and Sister watching their mother with fear in their eyes, as the trepidation in her mounted. He stood, faked a stretch. "Mighty fine dinner, Lois. Brother, Sister, give me a hand."

146

"Sit down, Merle, and entertain your guest," Lois said. She stood abruptly. "Don't fool yourself, Mr. Parker." She called her children and began clearing the table.

Merle lighted his pipe and beckoned Will outside. They walked around the house, then out back behind the tar papered little cubicle with the quarter moon door that smelled of a strong concentration of lime. New fire wood was stacked on both sides.

"Got yourself a right nice place here, Merle," Will said.

"Three acres from the road around the house," Merle said, "enough trees for many winters of fire wood and room to raise my own food. That little spot over there, closest to the house, is Lois'. Always plenty lettuce, peppers, onions—you know, herbs and stuff like that for the table.

"I used to see myself at times with a few apple and cherry trees, a grapevine, a rose bush or two. But I can't see them kind of things no more," Will said with a forlorn gaze at the oncoming night.

"I shouldn'a brought it up," Merle said, "about what you aim to do." He smacked his forearm. "Dammit!" A black wet speck with tiny wings lay flattened in the palm of his hand. "Skeeters bad as hell this year."

"All these rich cow pies making everything grow good," Will said, "whatta' you expect? Aah," he frowned and slapped his neck a good lick. "Puff the hell outta that pipe, Merle. Smoke drives 'em away."

"Darkness makes them worse," Merle said. "Let's go inside."

"Won't argue one bit," Will said. "Lots of mean skeeters a bad sign."

"Parker, I 'spect you may be one big skeeter. You full'a more of it than my fields. Where you ever hear of such?" They both laughed.

Mrs. Gibson and the children had retired to another room. Will could hear them singing. Merle said she generally sewed while entertaining the little ones.

Merle placed two chairs near the window in the dinning area. Each sat quietly, listening to the night, an innate habit of finely tuning the ear for warnings, the disturbances that weren't made by nocturnal animals or an occasional timber wolf.

"Sleep don't come easy," Merle said, crossing his legs and sucking on his corncob. "Night's a terrible time for the chillun."

Loud rapping on the door startled them. Merle uncrossed his legs and with terror filled eyes, looked at Will. Will, leaning forward and tensed as if watching a rattlesnake uncoil, pointed his finger at the door and nodded to Merle.

"Who's there?" Merle said.

"Who the hell do you think? Open up!"

"Open up for who?" Will said. "Whatta you want?"

"You, gawdammit. I'll break it down!"

"Wait," Merle pleaded, "I'll open it."

147

As soon as he removed a long, thick security plank that bound the door to its frame and the wall, it flew open. A gangling man dressed in black barged in. His shoulders were rounded. He wore a gun belt. Long, iron-gray fluffy hair hung from under a wide brim hat that ringed his weather-beaten face. Two big and gruff, barrel chested, no-neck men followed him.

"I want my niggers."

"Whatta we got to do with your niggers?" Will said.

"You talk too gawddamned much," he said.

Merle stood.

"Sit down, nigger."

Merle promptly obeyed. Will stepped between the obvious slaver and Merle.

"He ain't your nigger, I ain't neither. This is his home, I'm his friend. We answered you, now go." Will pointed his thumb and nodded toward the door. His eyes were centered on the slaver. By watching him, he could see every move of the bullies who flanked him.

"Do what! Nigger, I'll teach you," he said, gawking at Will. But seeing angry determination etched in Will's face and his long, muscular arms swaying loosely by his side, he switched to Merle. "You don't live by yourself. Where's the wench?"

"In a bedroom with nobody but my two chillun," Merle said.

"I'll look for myself." He motioned to his henchmen and moved in a manner of attacking Will.

Will sidestepped him, shifted his weight to the right side, and swiftly hit the strong arm man closest to him dead center on his nose. The man backtracked out the door, trying desperately to keep his feet moving with the momentum of his body. He disappeared in darkness. The horses grunted, shifting and neighing at the disturbance around their hoofs.

"Gaw-wawd-damn!" the other strong arm exclaimed, looking timidly at his boss.

The slaver drew his pistol. Before he could aim, Will snatched a pair of heavy tongs leaning on the fireplace and swung. The slaver's shoulder caught the blow. It knocked his hat off, driving him against the fireplace with such force that he slammed his head against the bricks and fell.

The other strong arm gestured no contest at Will. "Hell no, fella. He pay me to do a job, not to get all busted up." He bent for the gun.

"That's mine, now," Will said, picking it off the floor. "Take him and git."

"Yeah," Merle said, "Git the hell outta my house."

He and Will followed them outside, closing the door behind them. Inside, the house was suddenly engulfed in darkness. Will and Merle listened to the three men, quite astonished and seething, mounting with difficulty and setting their horses to cantering.

148

"Paw." The soft quavering voice of his son called out.

"They gone," Merle barked. "G'won back to bed." He couldn't stifle the hatred burning in him, smoldering anguish that he generally banked with hard work and viciously chewing the stem of his pipe that glowed cherry red with strong tobacco.

"They make you mad, Papa?"

The hysteria in his daughter's voice made Merle self conscious of his seemingly cowardliness. Had she heard him obey that slaver? Did she know that Will, not he, had run them off?

"I'm gonna git my gun," he said to Will, "sit on that oak stump, and pray that Jesus sends them back."

Mrs. Gibson opened the door. "Come inside, Merle and Mr. Parker."

"I'll bunk outside," Will said, "here in the wagon."

"Can't let you do that," Merle said.

"That'd be better than you, settin' there half-asleep in the open."

"I wouldn't think of it," Mrs. Gibson said. "Anyhow, it feels like rain."

"That hunk of tar paper around back or something like that to cover me just in case is all I need."

"That won't keep you warm," Mrs. Gibson said.

"Ma'am, I aim to stay out here. Blankets and a pillow will do fine. Let's make haste."

Merle fetched the tarpaulin. Mrs. Gibson gathered the bedding. While she leaned against the wagon, making a pallet for Will, the strong odor of anguish mixed with her unmistakable femaleness invaded his nostrils. He suddenly stepped away, self consciously embarrassed as if she could actually read his thoughts, even though the feeling wasn't for her except that she was woman, a woman so extraordinarily winsome that inhaling her made him feel the heartache, the aching in his loins. That stench of ugliness invaded his mind again, except that now, he had a gun.

Rain, sprinkling at first then getting heavier and pitting on the tarpaulin, sounded like pouring gravel. The pungency of water pounding dry dirt and saturating the manured fields made him think of Baltimore. He turned on his side and felt the gun lying under him. He tried to ignore a dream in a half-awakened state of seeing Tawney eaten alive in the retching water among marsh grass and cattails. He lay awake for a spell, fingering the gun, trying to make the power of it in his hands rid him of the ugliness of himself, the feeling of having a wild animal deep within threatening to devour him from the inside out. With that gun he should no longer be afraid, now that he could admit it to himself that he had been. Guns the slavers and soul snatchers wore terrified fugitives and free black folks. Charles and so many others had surrendered to it. Will nestled it beside him and slept.

149

Morning seemed to come as soon as he had drifted off into slumber. Funny, he didn't remember going to sleep, but he felt darn good. His muscles, especially in the legs, ached some, but that couldn't diminish the powerful feeling, an acute awareness of Will Parker, strangely new to him.

"Hey-oh in there, Parkuuh," Merle called. "Coffee's hot, skeeters sleeping, peckerwoods gone to roost, and breakfast's 'bout ready. Thank God for all that."

"They knew we'd give'em a fighting good time," Will said, kicking the tarpaulin off and climbing from the wagon with his shoes, stockings, and shirt in his hand. He reached back in and brought out the gun.

"If you don't mind," Merle said, "guns upset Lois somethin' terrible."

"Don't mind one bit," Will said. "I'm a carry it in my sack, but for now I'll just hide it here in my britches."

He followed Merle out back to the pump. There on a wooden stand built around it, Mrs. Gibson had placed wash cloths, soap and a wash pan.

"Hot water on the stove if you need it, "Merle said. "Don't seen to me you need a shave every day, but..."

Will waved his hand. "Cold water's good enough. Need a little salt to knock ole man sleep out my mouth, he tastes so bad." He stuck his head under the pump spout.

"What I'd do to have guts like you," Merle said, pumping the water and watching the supple muscles in Will's shoulders, neck and biceps flex.

Will lathered his head, face, neck and arm pits, then stuck his head under the spout again.

"A wife, chillun, nice home, you rooted in the land, Merle. That takes heart, lots of what I don't have."

"You just ain't seen the right one yet," Merle said.

"That ain't it," Will said, drying himself. "I ain't looked none too hard." He stared at the ground.

"Yeah," Merle said. "Me and Lois talked on that last night. Lots of nice ones around. I could speak to Mr. Bond, he always need an extra hand."

"Ain't ready for that, and I got enough money to tide myself for a spell. I'm looking for six, seven men to come in with me. Ain't no law should be written that gives one man the right to bust in another man's home and take what he wants."

"But it's already in the book."

"If a white man got the right to bust down my door then I take the right to bust down his."

"Will, they'd think you was taking a fit and shoot you down like they'd do a mad dog."

"Naw, Merle, they think more of dead possums that buzzards won't eat, than you and me and all colored men for letting them get away with it."

"Well, I suppose so, but if it wasn't for nice white men like Mr. Bond, I 'spect every colored man and woman would die a slave. Ain't too much we can do about it."

"Supposing Mr. Bond died today. Supposing a scared, hungry runaway broke in his hen house and stole enough chickens to make him change his mind about slaves. That'd be the end for your family, now wouldn't it?"

"You sure do paint nice pictures, there, Will Parker."

"Can't be a man and slave too. They don't mix. Black man stands tall among men like Mr. Bond, Merle. Slave stand behind them. This is our fight, not theirs."

"Let's go in," Merle said. "Lois'll be cranky if the food gets cold."

Brother held the screen door open. He and Sister greeted Will with bright eyes and smiling faces, as if he was a relative they were anxious to see. Will guessed Brother was ten, a year or two older than Sister.

They sat down to a table with a piping hot Chester County country breakfast. Eggs and scrapple, maple syrup with hoecake, bacon, fresh milk and coffee didn't offer them much of a chance for conversation.

"God," Will said, "it's a wonder you ain't big as a house, Merle."

"Breakfast not like this every day, Mr. Parker," Lois said. "Eat real good, hear? We all thankful that you happened by yestiddy."

"Ma'am, I may be the reason you all had trouble last night," Will said, shoveling more into his packed mouth. "Being a stranger in this neck a' the woods. Spies and just plain ornery mean folks everywhere."

"Uncle Will," Sister said curtly, "you shouldn't talk with your mouth full of food, right Mommy?"

"Oh, honey," Mrs. Gibson said, "Mr. Parker's got so much on his mind, his thoughts could outrun a spooked horse. He chews his food that way."

Everyone except Will laughed heartily. "Uncle Will, hmm, that sounds mighty nice," he lied. "I was about to think you couldn't talk."

"I spoke when you came in yesterday," Sister said.

"You did? Do tell. Guess you'll have to excuse me then."

"And little miss busy-body excuses herself too, Mr. Parker. Where will you go from here?" Mrs. Gibson asked.

"Look!" Brother yelled, pointing to the window, "coming up the lane."

A two-wheel carriage drawn by a trotting chestnut approached the house. A woman wearing a sunbonnet and two children were in it.

"Why, it's Mrs. Bond," Lois said, rushing to greet them.

Mrs. Bond pulled tightly on reins, forcing the horse to an abrupt stop. "Lois," she sobbed, "I came as soon as I could. The children, is everyone all right?"

"Yes, why of course, Gertrude." Mrs. Gibson began talking rapidly as if cued by her visitor. "What is the concern?"

"The whole village is talking about it. Seems that Doctor Lemmon refused to patch up a slaver last night. He complained to the squire about it, said he had been out this way hunting runaways and someone jumped him."

"Then what?" Lois inquired.

"Well, from what I gathered from Mason, squire told him to find a doctor down South, said he probably deserved whatever had happened to him."

"Some men did come here, but my husband and Mr. Parker ran them off."

"Mr. Parker? Were they looking for him?"

"No. He's not a fugitive, no more than any of the rest of us. He's a young bachelor, on his way to somewhere but not to find a wife."

"Strange, strange indeed, but I shan't meddle. Mason thought the children and I should spend the day with you while Merle is away with the gang. But if I'm intruding..."

"Intruding, you? Of course not and we're mighty thankful for your kindness."

"Very well. I brought my sewing along."

"And you're in time for breakfast," Lois said. "Hi, Clarence and Dotty."

"A spot of tea, perhaps," Gertrude said. "We've already eaten."

Brother and Sister stopped eating, their friends were more important.

Will listened diligently to Mrs. Gibson's response to her friend's inquiry about him. Perhaps he was asking too much, particularly of a family man. He observed the friendly gestures between the black and white children and understood how Merle and Lois could feel reasonably secure under the protective wing of his boss—exactly as he had felt until tragedy struck.

Then it was too late, just as it would probably be too late for this family one of these days.

"I guess I'd better be moving on," he said. "How far's Christiana, Merle?"

"Oh, I'd say the better part of a day's walk. Half a day if you'd be passing through in a hurry from Georgia on your way to Canada."

"Don't aim to move that fast," Will said, with a smile. Without the gun he would have not thought it funny.

"Fella named Orville Rhodes got a place out the road aways. Mostly colored hired hands batch there. Go on through town and take the left fork at the Y. Take the right, you'll end up in Gap Hill and that's big trouble. Gang of thugs—a lowdown ornery bunch—hang out there. Fella' named Clemson's the leader. Him and Bill Baer, they's the ones slavers hire to hunt down fugitives. Better that none of the rowdies see you."

"I'll be all right," Will said. "Ain't worried one bit."

" 'Tis possible our paths may cross again, Mr, Parker, we attend church there," Mrs. Gibson said. "Reverend Clarkson is our pastor, a fine man."

"Don't know no preachers, ma'am."

"These are trying times, Mr. Parker, especially for us colored folks. You will be looking for a church home soon, won't you?"

"Can't say that I will, but if I do, I'll look him up. Goodbye, ma'am and goodbye to you too, Miss." He nodded to Mrs. Bond before shaking hands with Merle and concealing the gun in his knapsack.

On the road, Will heeded Merle's warning to avoid Gap Tavern, though a foolish urge to maybe stop in for a mug of ale fought with a conviction derived from seeking a respite from mental turmoil that Doc Dingee had explained so vividly to him: seek not what you know in your heart are foolish encounters.

He hadn't wrestled with the decision very long when a brawny man rushed from the dense woods. His hair, straight and black, flowed to his shoulders from under a Stetson hat. He muttered aloud and strode headlong like a person rushing to save a burning barn. A scythe was poised in his hands as if any minute he would begin cutting down the world.

Will, trying to conceal his apprehension of the Black Indian seemingly gone mad, moved from the center of the roadway, giving him plenty of room. When he passed, neither as much as grunted. In a swift exchange of glances though, Will read unsettled night in his dark eyes and sensed communication with him, certainly not hostility.

"Christiana get bad like down South," he said. "Nobody safe no more. Paleface buckra walk right in nice white man house, snatch what he want, his property or no." His voice, deep and leathery, befitted his weather beaten face.

"Where?" Will quickened his pace, in cadence with the angry man. He dared not say anything that would be in the least way irritating, though he knew that whatever gnawed the man's nerves had to do with soul snatchers. Will wanted to befriend him.

"Moses Whitson, Quaker man place. Black woman work for him they come for her."

"Where is Christiana from here?" Will asked.

"Past Penningtonville and over Zion Hill, but I go this way."

Chapter Fourteen

Will stood in the road watching his hopping-mad friend turn onto a lane and hurry towards a white frame, colonial-style house. It sat atop a knoll amid a rectangle of oak, maple, and poplar trees. Shades of green fields, tender wheat, of young corn and garden vegetables, fodder, and blossoming cushions of flowers around the house bespoke an energetic, happy homestead. But an eerie silence enveloped everything. Nothing moved, not a stir from anything except a windmill weathervane barely spinning on top of a white barn. Then a little man burst from a side door that opened to the barnyard. From a distance he reminded Will of Silent Charles the butler—short, clad in black trousers with black suspenders, white shirt and black bow tie.

"Zeke," the man cried, running toward the black Native American. "They snatched Libit come daybreak. She was in the kitchen making breakfast."

"Pull trick," Zeke said. "Somebody tell them she here and they pull trick. Where Mr. Whitson?"

"He and the missus propped up in his study like two dead folks, just sitting and thinking to themselves."

"How many knew snatchers come for Libit, Ben?" Zeke said.

"Hmm." Ben rubbed his chin and rolled his expressive brown eyes away from Zeke to Will coming towards them. "Far's I know, just us few. Harvey Scott, John Roberts, Slim Carroll, you and ma'self, ones we thought'd make a stand for her when word come that slaver done sworn out the arrest. Slim is the only one who wouldn't come."

"Slim's guts made out of slime," Zeke said.

"Standing up to slavers like facing a mad dog," Will said, eager to get involved. "Let him know you scared, you ain't got a chance."

"Don't 'spect I've seen you in these parts before," Ben said.

"Nope. Hail from Dingee Nursery over London Grove way. Will Parker is my name."

Will noticed that Ben's light brown hands were not calloused by pickhandles and digging in dirt. Unlike Silent Charles, he didn't wear white gloves.

"Why you stand there listening?" Zeke said, facing Will with his scythe menacing. "You stick your ugly nose in. Why? Maybe the rat come back for more corn."

"Ain't nobody's rat," Will said, "and I don't like the stink of flippy lip cheese. If you can listen, I'm trying to tell you, we run snatchers off Gibson's place last night. Could be the same bunch."

"Merle Gibson from over Sadsbury way?" Ben frowned. "Lordy mercy."

Will doubted from the expression on Ben's jolly round face that he believed him. "His family is safe as a black man's family can be."

"Saved by you, hunh, Will Parker? Merle and Lois are good, churchgoing folks," Ben said. "Rev'm Clarkson say it every Sunday, 'prayer best weapon we colored folks got.' You ain't dressed right for an angel, mister."

"How prayer save Libit? Tell me." Zeke lay the shining blade of his tool on the ground, and pounded his heart with his index finger. "Tell me!" His scournful eyes raked over Ben.

"Her name Libit?" Will asked with an amused frown on his face.

"Elizabeth," Ben said. "Ain't much bigger'n a minute with a heart that's big as Mr. Whitson's barn. Everybody crazy about her, especially Chief Zeke here."

"We take search party," Zeke said.

"I see two good romping horses in the pasture there," Will said. "Where's the wagon?"

"Lordy mercy, listen to you, talking like a fool," Ben said. "They were six of the strongest, burliest mugs with guns, whips, and chains that I've ever seen."

Will wouldn't be intimidated by a scared little rascal like Ben. "We got a gun, we got a scythe and look there, two more coming, one totin' a rifle."

Ben began yelling before the two men were within hearing distance. "Too late John, Scott, Libit..."

"Not enough time for so much crying, Ben." Zeke grabbed him by the scruff of his neck. "Hitch horses to wagon."

Ben cringed. "Let go 'a me, Zeke," he said. "Better check your nasty habits too." He rubbed his neck where Zeke had bruised the skin. "You ain't taking them horses without Mr. Whitson's say-so."

"Go tell him we bring back Libit," Zeke said, walking towards the barn. "I hitch team."

"I done told you, he don't want no bother."

"Go tell him now," Zeke roared, while going about his business of hitching the horses to a Conestoga wagon he found behind the barn.

"Father in heaven," Ben cried, stomping off to the house.

Will watched Zeke take three maddox handles from the tool shed and stick the long handle of his scythe in a post hole on the wagon. The shining, curved blade glistened in the sun as he turned it to his satisfaction, displaying their mission as a warring party. Zeke summoned him and the other two men for a quick parley.

"I drive team. You got rifle," he said to Harvey Scott, a short, light complexioned, chunky man with kinky sandy hair and angry gray eyes.

"Plenty big man like you only need pick handle," Zeke said to John Roberts, a robust man with big black eyes, huge hands, a shiny bald top with a ring of thinning hair.

"Pick handle for you too, Will Parker, since you big tough guy."

"Keep it for yourself," Will said, "or give it to Ben."

"Ben too much like squirrel. We leave him here," Zeke said, climbing into the driver's seat and motioning for them to get in.

"We need Ben," Will said. "Five of us look stronger'n four. He saw 'em and knows which way they went."

"I know before Ben," Zeke said. "Three ride horses, one guide and two bounty hunters. Three ride in buckboard."

"They chained Libit to the wagon," Ben said, closing the kitchen door behind him, "and left when night started lifting."

"If snatchers come before breakfast then," Will said, "they'd stop some place close by to eat."

"Quaker man say okay, we take wagon?" Zeke asked.

"Said he wished ya'll wouldn't do nothing," Ben said. "The men at Meeting will ask Squire Lemmon who took her and they'll send a lawyer to fetch her back."

"We leave now, Ben," Zeke said.

"Naw," Ben said, shaking his head slowly and looking at the ground. "Mr. Whitson's a good man, and a wise one. Why cross him?"

"Because it ain't his fight," Will said, jumping from the wagon. He paced back and forth beside it. "Your boss man is good people like the rest who take chance on losing everything helping us. But we got to stop shifting from one of them to the other. Ain't but so much they going to do. Nothing will change unless we make it happen."

"You mighty right about that," John said. "What you reckon we oughta' do?"

"We make a stand, no matter what it cost." Will looked squarely in the eyes of each one, surprised that Ben didn't turn away from his stern gaze.

"First time you say anything worth hearing," Zeke said. "But we'll soon know if you good warrior like Ezekiel Thompson." He pointed his thumb at himself. "Ben, point way but stay out fight."

"Don't tell me what to do, Zeke," Ben yelled. "I'll go to hell for Libit so just shut up."

"But you not like fight," Zeke said. "Probably get hurt..."

"Let's get on about our business," Will said, climbing into the wagon.

Zeke whistled and startled the horses to a lively gallop. Will grabbed Scott's pudgy hand to keep from tumbling out of the rear end.

"Where would a slavecrat eat breakfast with a colored woman chained to 'em that wouldn't kick up a racket?" Will asked him.

"Heap 'a places," Scott said. "McKenzie's Tavern be a likely place as any, down county towards the Mason-Dixon. If she is there, inn-keeper most likely lock up and won't let us in."

"We'll shoot the lock off and break in," Will said, reaching in his knapsack and retrieving the gun.

Scott and Roberts looked at each other, astonished at this stranger's fortitude and the blue-steel, long barreled, expensive piece he rubbed and turned over and over in his hands.

"Slavecrat tried to use it on me last night, that's how I come by it."

They sat quietly and stared, the blue steel had shocked them to the cold reality that the likelihood of death rode with them. Five black men racing at break-neck speed in an old wagon pulled by two sleek horses, one white and one chestnut brown did unsettle passersby of the Lancaster County countryside. Especially with the scythe, its long crooked handle and elongated blade serving as an emblem of harsh justice, the visible indication of their mission.

McKenzie's Tavern was hidden in the mountainous wilderness that separated Pennsylvania's freedom from Maryland's slavery. The rescuers were moving slowly now, up a meandering wagon trail on the northern slope of a steep hill. Tall pine trees whistled in the wind as if warning the five rescuers they would find trouble so close to the lion's mouth. At the peak, they turned sharp-left and began descending the rocky southern trail. At a dark spot in the woods where Satan would wait to waylay unsuspecting souls, John cautioned them.

"Hold up," he said, "over there." He pointed to a windowless log cabin fifty yards or so down slope and off the trail, to the right. "I do believe that's it." The tavern sat at the base of a hill rising behind it that leaned in a southwest direction.

Zeke guided the horses off trail, into a cluster of trees. "Good place to watch," he said, jumping to the ground. "Any sign of horses and wagons down there, Ben?"

"My eyes kinda jumpy," Ben said. "I don't see nothing but some smoke coming out the chimney."

"Me and you go down for close look," Zeke said.

Ben looked timidly at Zeke and then at Will.

"G'won," Will said, taking the gun from his knapsack and sticking it under his belt. "You the only one who saw them." He toyed with the butt of his pistol, setting it high in his waist."

Zeke began moving across the forest floor as if stalking a cougar. "If they come out with Libit," he said, "shoot and come running with the wagon."

Scott loaded his rifle. "This is a fur piece for a true bead with a hand me down bird gun," he said. "Hand kinda shakey too."

"If they walk out with her," Will said, "shoot the sky and hang on."

"Riding in a buggy with spooked horses ain't the worst that can happen," John said, "now that I'm here looking this situation dead in the mouth. I must be crazy. What can a pick handle do upside a gun?"

"We come for Libit," Will said. "We ain't leaving without her."

"With or without a scrap?"

157

"We didn't come to parlay," Will said. "If you scared lay down, stay hid. When we get to fighting, jump in the wagon with Libit and drive off. Take a handle with you, just in case."

"Just in case what?" John said.

"In case you need a little help," Will said laughingly.

"I don't rightly see nothing funny," John said.

"It ain't, but I can't promise anything," Will said. "Zeke apt to go plum crazy with that weed chopper and slice up everything he can unless somebody shoots him. My plan is for you and me, Scott, to draw'em into a fight. John, you get Libit, no matter what and look out for Ben, You go'n have to do it any way you can."

"Wonder what's taking Zeke and Ben so long," Scott said.

Just then, a twig snapped. Will, John and Scott whirled. Ben stood behind them grinning. "If I was a snatcher," he said, "I'd have me three trapped niggers in chains."

They stared at him with dour expressions on their faces.

"They inside," Ben said, feeling self consciously foolish. "Zeke went in, but the inn keeper pulled a gun and run him out. He didn't see Libit."

"Where is Zeke now?" Will said.

"In the woods waiting for us. He say we should leave Mister Whitson's horses here and come down there with him. He said for you, Will, to bring along his bush whacker."

"That could be a big mistake," Will said, jumping from the wagon with the scythe.

Ben led them to Zeke, sitting on a hidden boulder where the lane from the travelers' respite intersected the wagon trail. As quietly as Will thought they approached him, Zeke heard the rustling and assumed command of the planned ambush without looking away from the cabin twenty-five or thirty yards in a straight line ahead of them.

"They come out soon. Scott, stay here," he said, "aim at one riding horse. I take other one. Will, you and John, go other side, hide behind tree. When I yell, jump in wagon fast. Put gun up slavecrat's nose. Pull trigger. If anybody else want fight, John smash'em with pick handle."

"My God Almighty, Zeke," Ben said, shaking, suddenly chilled.

"Take Libit and go hide, Ben. I find you."

Will gave Zeke his scythe. "How many inside?" he said.

"Two saddled horses in corral beside wagon," Zeke said. "Other rider Ben saw probably guide. Him go on home, or back to Gap Tavern. Why?"

Will didn't answer. He studied the terrain then pointed to a tree with jutting thick branches where Zeke had told him to hide. "Five of'em," he said. "Hmm. Scott, can you climb that tree?"

"Better'n a spry coon."

"Why he climb tree?" Zeke said, with a ring of anger in his voice.

"Five guns against two," Will said. "I didn't come to get shot. A gun is faster'n your blade or John's axe handle."

"You ain't never seen me use it," Zeke boasted.

"Look!" Ben pointed a shaking finger. "There's Libit, and look they got another woman."

"Christamighty, Ben," Zeke said, "why yell. Run over tell'em we here."

"Gawddam'em!" Will nostrils flared, his temples pounded. "C'mon Scott," he said crossing the trail. "Put one foot on that big branch and..."

"Don't tell me how to climb. just hold this a minute," Scott said, giving Will his rifle and muscling himself up and over the branches.

"Shoot the first somebody that pulls a gun," Will said, extending the rifle up to him.

Two men on horseback, dressed like rough riders and wearing guns, led the wagon from behind the inn. In it, a ruddy complexioned man in Southern gentlemen's clothing tilted a Stetson hat back on his forehead. He placed a booted foot on the rim of the buggy, belched and rubbed his belly. Beside him, a man in the driver's seat coaxed two horses pulling the buckboard into a slow gait. A third man turned around facing two forlorn women, and began whistling a Dixie melody to the cadence of the shodden horses' clopping and the wooden spoked wheels rhythmic creaking.

Now they were close enough for Will to see the women shackled at their wrists and chained together. A length of the chain was wrapped around a post beside the slavecrat. His whip lay on floor boards that were covered with a sprinkling of yellow dirt. Will guessed the one with a round chubby face was Libit. Her hair was tied in a scarf. She wore a dirt smeared apron over a knee-length calico dress. No stockings or socks on her feet, just a pair of runover working shoes that he'd bet she would never let anyone see her in, not even the Whitson household. Her face was as barren of expression as the closed petal of a morning glory. The other one was a girl who seemed to Will not yet twenty-one, slim, short and seductive like a black pearl, even though her face was vivid with dread and knowing. Will's sight fully absorbed her almond shaped eyes, uptilted breasts, the contour of a nubile body beneath a clinging dress. He felt the immediate hungering in his stomach, then woeful denial, that softening in his penis.

Zeke's blood curdling war cry shattered the tense quietness. He hurled himself through the air with the scythe, pressing the sharp blade against a rough rider's neck when he touched down. Will dashed from his hiding place and leaped on the other one, pulling him to the ground. They tussled and traded vicious blows, but Will's anger and experience in brawling quickly overpowered him. John, watching the slaver pull a derringer from his boots, sneaked up close and laid a hard blow across his hand. The slaver cried out, gripping his paralyzed fingers with the other hand, seeing John with the pick handle cocked, ready to deliver again. Scott, with a bead on the driver, watched him ease his hand over the butt of a gun in his holster. He whistled. Will turned, whipped out his pistol, and delivered a savage blow across the driver's chest.

"Git the hell down out of there," Will said to the hurting man, half dragging him from the seat. "Whydn't you shoot'em, Scott?"

"Didn't wanna spook the horses. They headed down big-foot country way."

Scott's whistle had so startled the rear sentry that he sat stock still, acting as if he didn't see Ben removing the pins from the tail gate, and coaxing the shackled women from the wagon.

"Wait, Ben," Will said. "Unlock the shackles," he said to the slaver.

"You drunked up, black sons of bitches," the slaver said. "Let this crazy half breed talk you into this, you'll swing along side him."

"Take off your gun belts," Will said to the driver and the bounty hunters. "All of ya', back up against the buggy."

Not one minute did the driver and hunters waste in complying. The slaver though, now standing and bent over with the puffed-up hand against his chest, seemed as if locked in a state of shock.

"No more beg," Zeke yelled. He put his scythe under the tail of the slaver's coat and ripped it off his back. A ring of keys fell on the floor boards. "Neck come off next."

"Zeke," Libit yelled. Hysteria ringed her face.

Her unexpected voice—a bewildering plea to Zeke—begged of Will an act of compassion against his will to save the snatchers from Zeke's deadly vengeance.

"Your heart beat like chicken now," Zeke said, placing the blade of his scythe against the slaver's neck. "What you say about swinging?"

"We got what we come for," Will said, throwing the keys to Ben. "Nobody shot. Nobody hurt real bad, Zeke."

He saw more intense hardening in Zeke's eyes, more swelling in his arms and shoulders, a tensing firmness in his grip on the scythe handle.

"He make good nigger," Zeke said, scowling at the slaver. He hawked loudly and sloshed a mouthful of mucous-filled disgust in the dirt at Will's feet.

Will heard silent screams of intensifying anguish goading him to the point where anger at Zeke and hatred for the slavers would become one overwhelming madness. Yet he said, "Leave him be, Zeke."

"He trusty slave," Zeke said to the slaver, and nodding at Will. "Beg for you like woman." In a wild dazzling move, he swung the blade from the slaver's neck and pressed it against the trembling driver's gullet.

"Wait," the driver said, his tearful eyes begging for mercy.

"G'won git in your wagon," Will said. "Ben, throw 'way his keys."

"No," Zeke said. "I mount his head on stick, they take his body. Let white man carry his justice back home."

"Leave him be, Zeke," Will heard himself say. He caught himself stalking Zeke, felt Zeke stalking him.

"Who you are, telling Zeke what to do? You sound like fool, like somebody runaway slave."

Silence, tension packed challenging silence, and querying eyes demanded Will reveal his true self. It demanded he tell how he happened into these folks lives.

"I'm a free man, I'll die for it," Will said. "Kill too, if it'd come to that. But ain't one grunt of fight left in the whole parsel of 'em, Zeke."

"A freedom fighter, oooh-wee." The younger woman whispered loudly enough for everyone to hear. "Look at'em. He ain't afraid of nothing. My my."

Swiftly, faster than an ambushing wasp could strike, Zeke swung his blade, slicing it into a wagon wheel up to its metal ring. A chip flew off into the woods. Will turned to the snatchers. He saw mounting terror on their faces.

"Tie your horses to the back and git in the wagon. You too," he said to the driver.

The driver moved away from Zeke as if his knees had locked, and climbed into the driver's seat while rubbing the indented mark the blade had made in the skin on his neck.

"Git on down the road," Will said, "that way."

"You're one goddamned mean sonofabitch," the slaver said. "We need a doctor." He held up his aching hand. It had swelled to the size of a pork loin. "And look at him!" He pointed to one of his exhausted gunman.

Will's nostrils flared. Again, he held on, checking that goading urge to obliterate, to pulverize to the last fiber, every vestige of the slaver. He smacked one of their horses on the rump, startling it to prancing. "Don't look back," he said. "Go to a doctor down south."

"Let's find our buckboard," he said, motioning to Ben leading the way with the women, "and git the hell outta here."

Snatched from the lion's opened jaws, Libit and Eliza, as Ben introduced them, had reasons, five of them for being ecstatic with adoration. Will listened to playful, almost shouting reiterations of the rescue, those little personal renderings of what actually happened to satisfy certain fantasies of imagining.

Libit, sitting on the driver's seat with Zeke, tugged at his long curly hair then tipped the hat that practically sat on his ears to one side. "Four apple pies," she said, counting on her fingers. She turned around and pointed to Scott and John. "For you and you. And especially you, Will Parker." Her voice dipped to a slow, obvious depth of admiration.

"Will Parker?" Zeke said. "Hell, Libit, he ain't but a scrappy rooster without a hen house making noise. Ben spread word about snatchers coming for you."

"Zeke," Libit whispered, snuggling closer to him, "he kept us out of trouble with the sheriff." She turned around again. "Ben eats more pie than both the Whitson's and its their kitchen, so he won't get one."

"I'll make Mr. Parker's," Eliza said. "Lordy, how you can fight." She sat very straight, a perfectly arched back and jutting breasts that a clinging thin dress left little for him to imagine. She breathed deeply, while staring, as if in an effort to absorb every inch of Will.

Will couldn't avoid her gazing eyes that made every fiber in his body tingle. Lilacs, honeysuckle, red velvet roses invaded his nostrils. Then he felt that recurring ache in his stomach and the woeful denial. In an attempt to counter that craziness overtaking him, he unintentionally yelled at Zeke.

"Join up with me, Chief. We stick together and grow strong, freedom fighters protecting our own."

"Parker, you too scared to spill a little blood," Zeke said.

"Scott, John, what do you say?" Will acted as if he hadn't heard Zeke.

Scott fidgeted. "We need to, that's the God's truth. But we couldn't do much without bringing the whole United States of America down on us."

"You mean with guns, Will, and training like the army?" John said.

"No," Will said, "like a secret, we only strike when kidnappers and slavers come around. Course now, if you scared," he said, looking at all of them, "just say so."

"Hot dammit, Parker, you been a briar scratching my ass since I laid eyes on you. Zeke afraid of nobody but Zeke fights his own battles." He cut Will a dreadful stare.

"Awright, Zeke," Libit yelled. "You forget I'm here with a young lady? Tell us you didn't go to say that."

"Tell Will Parker Zeke say go to hell."

Ben slapped his thighs and bent himself as if an excruciating pain had doubled his short body. John howled. Scott sat there with his mouth closed, and laughing through his nose while tears streamed from his eyes. Will laughed too, though it was more of an attempt to melt the hostility between him and Zeke. He looked off to a distant pasture where men were harvesting grain. In his vision, he saw a village of fugitives and freed folks doing for themselves. Men full of fire and anxious like Zeke, men quiet and deadly like Scott, farmers like Merle, storekeepers like Ben, himself a freedom fighter, protector, constable. Constable? For a moment he felt elated with his vision, but that awful feeling washing over him again made him feel so self conscious. He turned quickly and seeing Eliza staring at him, tried to smile.

She had indeed been studying him, the contour of his lean, expressive face changing as thoughts came, occupying his consciousness. Moonbeams danced in her head. "What kinda' pie would you like, mister freedom fighter?" Eliza moved to the edge of her seat, indicating that she wanted him to sit in the narrow space beside her.

Will, making awkward gestures, spoke gruffly in an effort to resist her magnetism. "Who will they snatch next, tonight or tomorrow?"

"I can see the pain," she said.

"Haw, you ain't much more'n a kid." Will tried to laugh, but felt uncomfortably certain by the way she looked at him with her mystical liquid eyes that she could peer deep into his consciousness, see the Will he didn't want revealed. He felt clammy squeezed against her. The warmth and firmness in her thigh was soft to the touch against his.

"How old must I be?" Eliza asked, with a smile she hoped would release the tension between them.

Will struggled for something to say. "How did that soul snatcher come by you?"

Eliza looked at the floorboards. "I don't belong to him," she said.

"How'd he know where to find you? How'd he know where to look? How'd he even know you were in this world, unless somebody told'em?"

"Somebody had to," Scott said, chiming in. He and John had been chuckling and winking at each other, watching Will trying to maintain a safe distance from Eliza.

"Most likely same somebody who told on Libit," John said. "I bet that watermelon man got something to do with it."

"Who?" Will said.

"Ole white man comes around most nigh all the time, selling rags, watermelons, clothes, anything a somebody'd be crazy enough to buy from him," Scott said.

"He comes by Marsh Chamberlain's place," Eliza said, "always wanting to sharpen his knives, and buy rags."

"The same man?" Will asked.

"If he's got a billy goat pulling a two-wheel buggy that leans to one side, it is."

"That's him. I-God, that's him," John said, shaking his head angrily.

"And he spends too much time over at Slim Carroll's place," Ben said.

"Who's he?" Will said.

"Slim's free born. He lives by hisself in a shack beside the railroad line in Christiana. Always coming around, asking about things that ain't none of his business. Hates white folks and can't stand nobody black except me. I tell him to run to the out-house with that lie and sit a spell. He mostly gets mad then and leaves. A week or so later, he's back."

"Is that right?" John said. "Sounds like we got a nigger amongst us."

"Yeah," Scott said, "Ben knows every black somebody in these parts."

"Ben knows Mr. Whitson's glad to see us back with Libit and his horses," Ben said.

Across the greening fields, where hired farm hands weeded wheat, corn and vegetables, a thin woman standing in the barnyard with three men began waving at first sight of them.

"Wave back, Libit. See Mrs. Whitson there?" Ben said. "Stand up and wave, will'ya, girl?"

"Oh Ben, stop making so much fuss," Libit said. She smoothed her dress and stroked her hair at the temples.

Now they were closer and could see Mrs. Whitson in a white bonnet and long starched skirts at the top of a knoll. The men wore black suits and black hats. Zeke coaxed the horses to trotting.

"They had meeting," Ben said, "Mr. Whitson don't look none too happy."

"He ought'a be," Will said. "We brung back Libit."

"Libit ain't the point I know he go'n make by the way he standing there," Ben said. "That's him, in the middle."

Zeke turned into the Whitsons' lane. Workers in the fields within sight of Mrs. Whitson's elation, began clapping and calling Libit. She waved and smiled with tear-stained eyes. The two men with Mr. Whitson walked toward the kitchen door and stood in the shade of an oak tree.

"Yep," Ben said, "there's Squire Lemmon. The other man, Mr. Mendenhall is rich enough to buy Mr. Whitson and the squire."

Mr. Whitson, a tall, lean man with austereness etched in his small, keen face, strode toward them. Ben jumped from the wagon. Mr. Whitson's cold blue eyes bore down on him. Ben stepped back a pace and returned the stare.

"Bravery will always find its place in the hearts of God-fearing men," Mr. Whitson said, "nonetheless, thee violated the seal of trust that molded an inseparable bond between thee and I. Can you explain thy reason for interfering with our plan to buy Libit's freedom?"

"Twern't me so much as Zeke and Will Parker," Ben said, pointing to Will. "They came up making a lot of big talk I couldn't believe at first, and wouldn't pay no mind."

"Whoa," Zeke said, pulling rein on the horses. "Scott, John, and you, Will Parker, we unhitch horses and put wagon back."

"No matter for whatever reason," Mr. Whitson said, "or at whoever's insistence..."

"Mr. Whitson," Will called out, jumping from the wagon. "What you do for us colored folks is good, but you got to stop treating us men like boys."

Astonishment glittered on Mr. Whitson's flushed face. A thin wrinkle spread across his forehead. Squire Lemmon and Mr. Mendenhall looked at each other, quite amazed.

"My word." Mr. Whitson rubbed his chin thoughtfully. "I don't understand how thee could misjudge my compassion so erroneously." He adjusted his hat nervously. "Thee may have ruined Elizabeth's chance of ever being free."

Will raised his hands before him and motioned in a calming manner. "She's back, and so is the girl, Eliza. Nobody knew she'd been snatched. We black men got to grip our problem in our own hands, no matter how much the trouble. Our women folk and children, they look on us respecting 'n such as they can, but you always there, big man, ready to give us whatever you think we need—protection, jobs, food, even land—always at the price of our manhood."

The love-for-tender-weary souls expression Mr. Whitson generally held for Libit and Ben changed to the one of stern, eye level equanimity with which he viewed his peers in the Quaker meeting.

"Mister, er."

"Parker, sir, Will Parker."

"Thee are a strange one, so young and seemingly loose," Mr. Whitson said, "like I'd imagine a swarthy buckaroo, to speak with such seasoned authority."

"A swarthy somebody, hunh? I can tell you ain't poking fun, it ain't your nature to talk dirty. Let's just say I been treated some by a big man," Will said, looking everyone in the face, forcing a smile from them. Scott looked at him and winked.

"Ah, Miz Whitson," Libit said, hugging and patting her on the back.

"I'm all right," Mrs. Whitson said. "Speck of dirt in my eye, really makes it smart." She blew her nose in a tiny laced handkerchief. "Come, lemonade for everyone, my treat."

"No, missy, but thanks," Eliza said. "They be worried sick, my sister, Marsh Chamberlain 'n them, wondering what happened to me."

Will surprised even himself with responding haste. "You got no business running off by yourself."

"That's mighty nice, Will Parker, but if one of you'all would point me in the direction of Mr. Marsh's, I hafta do just that, run along."

"The Chamberlain place is a mile or two north of Christiana," Mr. Whitson said. "Christiana is a stone's throw or so from here so I'd say one and a half hours. Two if you walk slowly would put thee right there, but not by thyself."

"G'won with her, Will," Libit said, teasingly. "Little cute thing like her got no business on that lonely road by herself."

"Will Parker can run on about his own business," Eliza said. "Don't make a big fuss over me. I'm obliged to you, Libit, for teaching me to pray for myself, instead of crying my fool head off."

"See what it brought us," Libit said. "Coming to church Sunday?"

"Come Sunday," Eliza said, "if I can find my way."

"How long you lived in these parts?" Ben asked.

Eliza didn't answer. She swallowed hard as if to contain a quick, disturbing answer. Of course, they all knew. She turned and hastened down the lane.

"She go your way, Will Parker," Zeke said. "Why you just stand there like cornered jack rabbit?"

The urge to hit Zeke was stronger in Will than it had been since he crossed Will's path early that morning. Just one lick to shut his goading mouth. Will bit his lip instead, and put his hands in his pockets. He turned and watched Eliza's nubile body—left hip, then right, gracefully, sensuously—suddenly jealous for they too were watching her. Even though the aching knot around his navel felt larger and the pain in his loins made him more irritable, he began taking giant strides with the knapsack over his shoulder, and quickly overtook her. They walked for a spell as if unaware of each other.

Then she said, "You don't like Quaker folks."

"Who said that?" he barked.

"Me, I guess I'm kinda asking. They treat us so nice."

"They can't give us everything we need. But Whitson don't believe that. Doc don't believe it. That family you work for don't believe it either."

"You don't even know Marsh Chamberlain 'n them, so just hush."

"Hush!" Will said, frowning so hard that his hooded eyes crossed. "Why'd I even bother talking men stuff to you?"

"Well anyhow, my sister must be worried sick," she said, trying to match his stride, every so often skipping or running.

They were soon a distance from the folks at the Whitson homestead, becoming smaller like two birds in a backdrop of sky, then like one flyspeck in a portraiture of sloping hills meeting the horizon. Fortune had blessed Will and Eliza to tread upon the sun-kissed though bitter earth in the same interlude of time.

Chapter Fifteen

Three weeks later, Will was eating supper in Orville Rhodes' boarding house when that big, devilish, roly-poly fellow boarder across the dinner table finally spoke. He'd been eyeing Will with a question etched in his face for days.

"Merle Gibson say hello."

Will didn't pause in gobbling down his supper of crispy fried chicken, ham-hock flavored mustard greens, and buttermilk cornbread. So much small talk going on among the six tired, irritable black men sitting there, Will acted as if he hadn't heard him.

The man chuckled, watching him swallow such huge chunks of food. "Merle said he ain't forgot ya."

Will burped and looked up from his plate. The man's big brown eyes danced in his sweaty cocoa face. Will suspected he wanted to trick him into a joshing contest, like he often did with some of the other bachelors. Maybe he wanted to ridicule.

"Who's saying he ain't forgot me?" Will said, making a disgusting slurping sound while sipping coffee.

"Me, Sam Hopkins," the man said contemptuously. "That's who."

"Hopkins, aye." Will looked away from Sam at a broken candelabrum suspended from the high ceiling over the table. "Did Merle forget that any day he might come home to a empty house?"

The image of Lois became vivid in Will's imagination. "Pity that pretty woman. Pity his poor children." He waved his hands in a dismissing gesture then pushed back his chair and rose to leave.

"Well-ah," Hopkins said, slowly rising from his chair. "I promised Id keep it quiet and I would too, if I thought it wouldn't be all right to chew on amongst us colored fellas here."

"Chew on what? What the hell you talking about?"

"Why you gettin' wind in ya' jaw?" Hopkins said, challenging Will's attitude. "Merle offered you a job, said he did. But seems like you bent more on get'n yourself a right nice reputation. Raising a whole bunch of hell with them white folks, ain'tcha? The way Merle talked, I'd expect somebody bigger'n a snortin' black bull."

"About your size, hunh?" Will said, noticing that Sam was taller than he, and looked as if he could miss a week of suppers without going hungry.

"You wanna get personal, hunh?" Sam said. "Okay, I'll give it to you straight. We colored men works hard here, and we gets treated like men, at least by the home folks."

"Home folks?"

"You heard me right. Quakers, Pennsylvania Dutch, the Mennonites..."

Will interrupted him. "I walk across Christiana every day," he said, talking rapidly. "I hear men talking, I see meanness in their faces. I don't stop and ask them if they home folks."

"They didn't bother you," Sam retorted. "We don't have to tip-toe around town after nightfall like haints in the dark. We go anywhere we please."

"Until a soul snatcher lassos you," Will said.

He and Sam stared across the table deep into each other. Will hoped Sam would stop agitating him. Little patience did he have for arguing, especially with fools. Some of the boarders were watching them, Will noticed in turning away and going to an open window in the dinning room. Looking out across the porch toward the village center, he recalled that day's trek across Christiana and the rolling hill countryside.

Will had circled Rhodies, an old manor home, just as he had done every morning to convince himself the ten-room house was as secure as it had been the last time he had checked. Rhodies set close by the wagon trail two miles from the village center. The heavy doors and closed shutters over windows of the first floor were still intact. He hadn't detected any fresh horse or wagon tracks on the bare, neglected landscape. No cattle grazed there, no greening produce covered its fertile soil. A worn path led from the kitchen door past the out-house through some low brush to the woods. Will wondered where the path would lead.

Three mismatched chairs, a tobacco stained spittoon, and a rocker set on a porch that extended across the front. In warm evenings, boarders often talked through the two opened front windows of the dining room to menfolk sitting on the porch or its railing, chewing, smoking, and spiting, Some mornings, especially on rainy days when she couldn't sit out back, Miz Erelene, the cooking lady, sat by herself in the rocker shelling peas and such. The spacious dining room, and the big rectangular oak table reminded Will of the great house at Roedown. The living room was Miz Erelene's private quarters. Only one other woman ever stopped by. Dixie, Miz Erelene's close friend, frequently came after breakfast for a biscuit, tea and to chat.

Will strode into town with the gray dawn, just as hustling—bustling Christiana beckoned the rising sun. Over the din of the echoing clatter of hammers, he heard carpenters yelling to black laborers for more lumber before it could be unloaded from horse-drawn wagons. Will walked by, shaking his head in disgust. Not one black carpenter did he see. He wondered how many of those laborers had driven nails and pegs into wood that had made plantations before some of the carpenters knew the difference between a peg and a hole.

He passed by Alcorn's Feed store, the fourth time in a week, projecting that swarthy attitude, fueling angry debates among the group of farmers gathered there. Who the hell did he think he was, acting like a white man? Too many coloreds, especially fugitives, were taking jobs from decent, God fearing white men. Too many damned, disgusting abolitionists wouldn't hire a white man these days, even if one would work beside a colored.

Beyond the feed store, Will came upon Irish and German immigrants laying a section of shiny-new curved track that would bring the huffing locomotive right up to the entrance of Fred Zercher's Hotel and Tavern. Will walked on, listening to the strangers speaking in their peculiar tongues. He didn't greet a soul.

Will hadn't seen anyone with whom he would have felt comfortable to inquire about Joseph Scarlett and reveal that he didn't have a job. He did need one, his money being a bit lean since he had paid a month in advance for meals and a room at Rhodies.

Will needed more than just a job. He needed more than a link with some white man, however kind, to protect and sustain him with the frugal needs of a young black man in a hostile place. Only Scarlett had indicated a semblance of knowing—saying the things he did at Charles' trial, befriending Will in his fit of desperation to find his brother. Of all the white men he had encountered, even more so than Doc, Will felt that Scarlett came closest to understanding that thing deep within and disturbing, propelling him to an eventful destiny. Merle, Scott, John, and Ben certainly felt some of what Will felt inside—they were simply too scared to act. Not Zeke, but his rage was so fiery that wherever it peaked, he was apt to behead anyone who'd dare cross him.

That afternoon, Will walked out to Marsh Chamberlain's place. Within sight of the homestead, that clawing in his groin wouldn't let him go any further so he tarried a spell, watching lumberjacks fell virgin trees and denude branches. Then he turned around. During the lonely trek back to town, he tried to erase Eliza from his thoughts, ease that awful churning in his stomach. He walked up a low grade hill past the tinker's shop with the huge porcelain night chamber in its window. He strode by the candle-stick maker, inhaling the fragrance of bayberry and jasmine. Again, he noticed the dark interior of the apothecary, the flowing gown and bolts of fabric in the millinery shop, the Jocko statuette grinning in front of the general store and post office. A sign in the store window read: no slave labor goods sold here. The merchant inside waved to Will. He only nodded.

As usual, Will arrived at the manor home in time for supper, in time to hear the six bachelors, sometimes an extra one or two, gathered around the table relive their harrowing tales of escapes and captures, of families and friends disappearing in the night, of an increasing number of bold daytime soul snatchings. How much outrageously, merciless and inhumane treatment would black men endure before they would damn the fear and come together for self protection?

A sudden, loud clatter of hard shoes scraping and banging the porch floor startled him. Two fugitives, their scared eyes bulging, ragged and smelling like the swamp, barged into the dinning room.

"They runnin', gawddamned hard too. Look at'em," Will heard a boarder say and watched him scoot out the door, cross the porch and vault the railing. He disappeared in the encroaching darkness of night.

Boarders dashing from the table, breaking dishes and strewing silverware across the floor, jammed the doorway.

"Oooh hell," another one said, climbing out the window, "boogey man can't be far behind." He vanished.

Will, rushing to cover the spent fugitives, was jostled and kicked by the stampede at the door.

Miz Erelene rushed from the kitchen wild-eyed and yelling. "All right! You-all forget I'm here? Oh! Lordy, lordy, how they get..."

"Piece bread, please suh," one of the fugitives said, his raspy voice hardly audible. The other one, soaked in sweat and breathing as if fighting for air, sunk to the floor on hands and knees pitted and knotted like potatoes. He slumped over on his side, too exhausted to raise his head, too tired to care.

"Can you give'em a morsel or two?" Will called, turning to Miz Erelene and noticing Sam Hopkins standing at the base of the stairs. "Settle down," Will said to the fugitive prancing around him, "you amongst friends."

"Lord a mercy, no!" Miz Erlene yelled. "Take'em to Jocko. Sam," she turned to Hopkins. "Help that new youngster get'em outta here. Rhodie'll have a mad dog fit."

Will knelt to the man on the floor and tried feeding him water from a cup left on the table. It bubbled out and ran down his bare chest.

"Not even a piece a bread, a cup a water, a safe place to rest with his own kind?" Will asked.

"You got your people's mixed," Miz Erelene said, leaning her head slightly to one side and placing her hands on her hips. "Ain't never been no runaway. My freedom's been bought and paid for, I'll thank you. And the food ain't mine to give away."

She smirked at Will. But then, reading the nastiness in his eyes and the snarl on his lips, she cowered. "I suppose a mouthful and a little coffee to clean the gullet won't hurt none." She bristled. "But not in my dinning room."

"We'll take'em to Jocko," Hopkins said.

"I'll take'em to my room," Will said.

"And Rhodie'll kick all of you out," Hopkins said. "But see'in how I ain't the innkeeper, do what you want."

170

Will watched the fugitive prancing about and listening to them in painful bewilderment. "You wanna use the toilet?" Will yelled at him.

"Just a bite 'a bread, a dipperful 'a water, suh."

"Take'em out back, beyond the pantry," Miz Erlene said. "Soon's I give'em a bite." She pointed a scornful finger at Will. "You and Sam haul'em down to Jocko."

"It's mighty damned sad," Will said, pulling the prone man by his hands to a sitting position then hoisting him over his shoulders. "We depend more on the grinning clay face of a somebody who ain't real than we depend on ourselves."

"Ain't no more we can do," Hopkins said, "without laying ourselves open to big trouble. Slave runners can't hurt Jocko."

"Aww bull-shit." Will muttered, following Miz Erlene.

"Be-e-ware! Snatchers coming!" The high pitched urgency in the town crier's alarm alerted them to the nearness of danger. He ran back and forth across the street, calling out, knocking on doors and windows. "Boogey man down in the valley heading this way!"

"I knew it," Sam said. "I felt it in ma' bones when I first layed eyes on them. Now what you go'n do, Will Parker?".

"Can't put'em out, now," Miz Erelene said. "Sweet Jesus, don't let Rhodie come in and see'em at the kitchen table."

"Going to my room," Will said. "Be back d'rectly." He rose up from propping the sick fugitive into a sitting position on the floor against the wall.

Hopkins grabbed his shoulder. "Naw, boy," he said, "that trick is old."

Will spun and thrust his hands under Hopkins' arm pits, pinning him to the wall. "Merle didn't tell you the whole story. If you got a need to know me, better stop by ole man Whitson's place and ask Ben."

"Unlatch'em, boy," Miz Erelene yelled. She stood behind Will with a broom poised over his head. "Don't, I'ma give you a corn-broom fit. I mean it!" She faked a lunge at him.

Slowly, Will released Hopkins, but stood so close their noses almost touched. "Don't cross me a second time, Sammy."

"Name's Sam Hopkins, like I said. You ain't go'n run off and leave now that you done stuck your nose in the underground's business. One other thing, youngster," Hopkins said, tucking his ruffled shirt back inside his pants. "If you ever snatch me again, I'ma put something on you them hoodoo ladies can't get off."

"Prayer wouldn't hurt neither one of y'all," Miz Erlene said, suspecting the anger in Will would reach an explosive point. In quiet desperation, she watched the fugitive who had been prancing, cramming food in his mouth with dirt caked hands. He swallowed the food in chunks.

171

"Miz Erlene," Will said, "wydn't you go'n to bed? By morning slaves'll be caught and whipped. This one will probably be dead." He pointed to the fugitive on the floor with his chin slumped on his chest.

He was tall, about Will's height, but unnaturally thin. Dark shadows under his closed eyes sunk into a gaunt face. His blistered feet were hard and calloused. Dark scaly rings around his ankles and wrists indicated he had been shackled. Will suspected he had escaped from a chained trail of captured slaves hiking to the cotton fields.

"Rhodies be like nothing ever happened," Will said. "Hopkins'll be setting out there waiting for breakfast, ready to eat his fat rump closer on into hell."

"Parker," Hopkins said, with a tremor in his voice and anger blazing in his eyes. "Whydn't you git the hell away from here? Nobody knows a blessed thing about you. Struttin' around town like you own the damned place, these white folks go'n hang your black ass."

"Put some mess on me the hoodoo lady can't get off, first," Will said. "C'mon Hoppy, give it ya' best shot."

"I done tole you once," Miz Erelene said, grabbing the broom.

Will hurried from the kitchen muttering, "Damned signifying 'n praying colored folks worse'n fatback burning up in hot grease."

When Will returned with the pistol jammed in his waist, Hopkins had his ear against the outside wall. He glanced frightfully at Will then gazed at the wall as if he could see through it. Miz Erlene knelt on the floor, trying to feed the sick man.

"Kind 'a worried about him," she said, looking at the gun. "Son, don't git yourself in no trouble."

"I'm taking them to Jocko. C'mon," Will said to the fugitive drinking coffee. "Help me carry him."

The man acted as though he hadn't heard Will.

Will watched him for a moment, noticing that he was slight of build, not much taller than Ben. His arms were disproportionally long and well developed. The back of his neck, dark and parched like old tan-hide leather, sloped down to wide, curved shoulders.

"Heh," Will said, grabbing the fugitive's shoulder. "Git off ya' butt."

In belligerent slowness, the fugitive wiped coffee from his lips and wiry beard. With a deep, down yonder Southern drawl that sounded like a bee droning, he answered. "I die befo' I run one other step."

He mumbled something that Will should have asked him to repeat, even though Will suspected from the hostility ablaze in his reddened eyes it was an expression of anger that fate had dumped him there, an expression that would probably singe Will's ears. The mistrust that Will understood so well, compelled him to try digging beneath the runaway's mask of belligerence, force a friendship. Will's patience though, had been worn thin, and the constant aching in his loins that kept him wound as tight as a ball of soaked leather would not let him express the kind of compassion he knew he should reveal.

"What's your name?" Will barked.

The fugitive cleared his throat. "Hog," he droned.

"Now ain't that a dandy for a runaway. Hog Slop, Hog Pen, Hog Jigaboo? N' I suppose his name's Dirt, hunh?" Will pointed to the prone man onto whose face and neck Miz Erlene applied cold wet rags.

"Ask him," Hog said.

"Don't play with me, nigger," Will volleyed back to him.

Hog looked at Will's pistol then scowled. Will read him correctly: Hog hated that word as much as he did, hated what it meant, hated that Will implied he had acted like one.

"My name is Pink," Hog said. "Now fuck with that."

Miz Erelene retorted with a rush of words. "Shut up your mouth, fool. Mr. Pink raw Hog, whoever the devil you are, I know you got some manners. Don't, you be dead long before now. And you eating food I cooked, off Rhodies' table."

"Yes'm, that is low-bred talk that wasn't meant for your ears." He nodded at Will. "I said it to make him look back to where he's been, so he'll know for sure that Alexander Pinckney ain't letting no man ride rough shod over him no more."

Will glared at Hopkins, daring him to laugh while actually trying to conceal his embarrassment and elation. In Pinckney he believed he had found a comrade.

"I ran across him in the hills," Pink said, pointing to the sick man.

"Better hurry him to somewhere," Miz Erelene said. "Fever's takin' him on down."

Will knelt in front of the sweating, limp fugitive. "Help me get him across my shoulder, Pink."

"How do we know you taking them to Jocko?" Hopkins said, watching Pink balance the unconscious man over Will's shoulder. "You ain't said one word or did one thing to tell us who you are. Was your travel a dark night?"

Will searched himself for the answer, realizing the question was part of the underground railroad secret code. Then he remembered Joe Diamond and Caleb. "The North Star was damned bright a long time ago. But I don't trust you," he said, wrapping his right arm around the legs of the limp figure which hung over his shoulder and standing upright.

"Don't trust Sam?" Miz Erelene said. "Folks around here depends on him getting fugitives through. He pokes a little fun around the supper table. To ease the pain I suppose, or maybe to find out about you being a stranger. But he ain't low down."

Will didn't believe her. His eyes expressed it.

Hopkins knew he had no other reason to question Will's sincerity. Will had carefully chosen words that rhymed in his answer to Hopkins' question about the underground. Yet, Will had embarrassed him in front of his friend, Miz Erelene and Pink.

"He probably can't act no other way but nasty, Miz Erelene. But I'm obliged to help him. The streets ain't safe, Parker, and even if you get past the snatchers, you can't just walk up to Jocko and expect him to do magic."

Will really didn't have a choice. He nodded at the thick oak door.

Miz Erelene blew out the candle and eased it open. She watched them moving stealthily single file down the narrow path—Hopkins, Pink, Will with his load. They disappeared in darkness. She bolted the door, and sat at the table with her hands folded. But she was afraid to pray from fear that what she wanted might not be in God's plans, considering the way Will had presented himself. After several minutes though, her dominant thought persisted. Lord, he is mean as fire, but in your merciful, unexplainable way I believe you sent us a miracle. Not one to be so selfish, please let it be him."

When the four of them reached a clearing near the railroad workers' camp, they heard the Irish brogue and music of that strange dance called the jig. Hopkins shuddered while crossing the railroad track, at the thought of being caught down there alone by those foreigners. Then he was suddenly overwhelmed with admiration for Will. A strange feeling it was, like Will bringing along someone stronger than any of the four of them.

"Parker," he said, picking up a small dried-out stick.

"Hunh," Will replied.

"How old you claim to be?" Hopkins said, for need of something to say, because of the urge to utter Will's name.

"Twenty gawddamned two," Will said.

Hopkins sighed in desperation. Why had he bothered to ask? Yet, he'd bet that Will would carry the runaway to the edge of earth if the man's life depended on Will doing it.

Will hadn't given one thought to Hopkins' reason for asking his age. His mind raced on. The gun hot in his hand and blazing. He had earned the right to kill. The half dead fugitive on his back brought a message from Charles, from Grandmom Rosey, from Tawney, from Aunt Aida and Levi. Indeed, his load had become quite unbearable, but bear it he would or shoot Hopkins and Pink before he'd let them see him stumble one step. He followed Hopkins leading them through some thick brush and across a plowed field.

They stopped at a white picket fence that enclosed a garden of corn and other vegetables indiscernible in the dark. In the center, bundles of old corn stalkes leaned against what appeared to be a four-foot high mound of compost.

Beyond the garden, past several big trees, lanterns shone in the rear windows of a two story brick house.

Will wondered, but didn't question why Hopkins dragged his stick over each pale of the fence, making a rattle in perfect timing with his steps. Hopkins turned the corner and continued his rhythmic message while leading them toward the house. At an opening in the fence close to the mound, they stopped again. Wild flowers and budding vines growing from the top spilled over the sides. An eye-watering stench of decayed corn, potatoes, apples, and only God knew what else reeking from the pile, laded the night air. Hopkins cursed and spit at a raw cut where a chunk of the organic rot had been sliced from the bottom.

Will waited with the numbing load on his shoulder, while Hopkins looked all around then went to the mound. He stuck his hand through the vines, and knocked—two heavy raps—on wood. His lips moved, as he counted to himself.

Then he tapped seven times in rapid succession. From the inside they heard a scratching sound like metal rubbing metal. Hopkins, hunching down and almost covered by the vines, repeated his light tapping. A door opened under the mound. Hopkins motioned for them to hurry, then he stooped and disappeared.

Pink went in and disappeared. Will stooped and almost fell, then regained his balance and entered into total darkness. The odor of salted pork invaded his nostrils.

Someone gently grabbed his arm.

"Bend thy head more. That's fine," a voice said. "Now step down."

"Easy," Hopkins whispered, guiding him by the other arm.

After they guided him down five steps, Will heard the door close.

"Daresn't move or stand up straight," the voice commanded, "until I light a candle."

It was a voice Will had recently heard when passing by the general store. Then, in the yellow glow of light, he saw the proprietor standing with his back bent low and his head tucked. He was lean and taller than most tall men, with a face that could have been carved from stone, except for a full auburn beard on his chin and neck.

"Goodness," he said to Will. "We must relieve thy burden."

They were in an underground stone room hardly six feet high that had been a smoke house. The gentleman Friend motioned Will to one of three cots lined on both sides of the room.

"Carefully, ever so gently with him," he said, helping Hopkins and Pink lay the sick man on a straw tick.

"Him and Pink here run in on us a while ago, Mr. Lewis," Hopkins said. "They done ate, at least Pink did."

"Friend, please. Elijah is sufficient, Elijah is proper. Let us make haste, but quietly. We need hot water, soap, a scrub brush. Very hard to distinguish God of man in a mistreated, dirty body. A bath and a change of decent clothing lends much to a positive attitude."

"This'n needs a doc real bad," Will said in a hushed voice.

Elijah shook his head slowly. "Even were I to try Doctor Henderson, he wouldn't come."

Will's nostrils flared. He stood without thinking and bumped his head a resounding thump. But instead of cringing, he gawked at Elijah.

"He is afraid that slavecrat sympathizers will report him," Elijah said, "for aiding and abetting runaways. Spies are everywhere."

Elijah bent over the unconscious man and peeled back his eyelids. He put his ear to the man's heart. "Sam, fetch me the blankets over there in the corner. He's near physical collapse. I charge thee, friend uh..." He looked squarely at Will and waited.

"Parker, Will Parker."

"All right, friend Will. He's thy responsibility. Thee daresn't let him chill."

"Well uh, but he's sweat'n."

"Yet his body is cold. Use the power in thy hands that comes from the one source. Thee must make sure he doesn't slip any further, until I get back with Doc Williamson."

"That old horse doctor?" Hopkins said.

"Aah," Elijah said, shaking his head. "But a good one. We can't be choosy. Come." he motioned to Sam. "And," he said, "it is Pink, I believe. Follow me."

He led them down a set of steps. "We'll have to crawl. It's only a short ways," he said, bending to his knees. Pink and Sam followed, creeping along a bricked-in chute, with boards across the top, only inches beneath the earth's surface. They exited by crawling through a chimney into the basement of the house.

"That wasn't so bad," he whispered. "Build a fire under the kettle of water over there on the stove. Use the wood tub inside that lean-to. Soap, a scrub brush and towels are beside it. Go back to the room as soon as possible. Thee will be safe here, Pink, so shed thy slave self and become whole. I'll return shortly."

After Pink's bath, he and Sam lingered a moment at the steps after crawling through the chute, listening to Will fuss with the unconscious man.

"Damned if you go'n die on me, boy," Will said, wrapping another blanket around the escaped slave and wondering what else he could do. He remembered Grandmom Rosey and Miz Sady the root lady rubbing the feet of old and fever-ridden slaves in their final hour, hoping to keep the spark of life aglow.

Will uncovered the slave's feet. They were so blistered massaging was impossible. He could only press his hands against them.

Sam, seeing grim determination in Will's face—the stubborn set of his chin—realized that he too had sprung himself free of the lion's jaws. Without saying a word, Sam took one ugly foot in his hands.

When Elijah returned with the veterinarian, Will and Sam were quietly kneeling at the sick fugitive's cot, each with a foot under his shirt against his bare chest. Pink was sprawled on a cot, making an ungodly noise in his sleep.

Will nor Sam stirred until Doc. Henderson checked the slave's vital signs and mumbled without looking up. "Uncover him."

Will removed the blankets.

"Turn him over, quickly now, on his stomach."

Will rolled the fugitive over. Doc ripped the filthy, ragged shirt off his back, gingerly touching ripples of whip-lash scars. He kneaded the fugitive's middle back with a strong liniment and covered it with a piece of heavy cloth.

"On his back once more," Doc said.

Will turned the runaway over again. Doc wrapped him in the blanket, exposing only his chest, and began rubbing his diaphragm with the liniment, making small rapid circles. The slave's eyelids fluttered. Doc covered his chest with cloth and pulled the blanket around him. He passed the liniment under the slave's nose.

"I'll be damned," Will said quietly in Sam's ear, watching the slave's chest heave slightly.

The slave's eyes opened and rolled back into his head.

"Old worn-out mule carried on just like that," Will said, "when the vet brought him back for his last day's work before they shot him."

Sam didn't laugh. He watched stone-face Doc treating the slave and noted to himself, that was the first time Will had said anything pleasant to him, if he should call that pleasant.

"Sit him up," Doc Williamson ordered. "Put a blanket around his shoulders. A drop of hot broth on his tongue, Elijah. Touch his lips with the spoon, he'll open his mouth. Good, another spoonful or so, if he'll take it."

The slave responded to the Quaker's meticulous feeding as if it were an unconscious gesture of trusting thanks.

"That's enough," Doc said. "He's dehydrated and in a severe state of shock. Lay him down."

The slave's head immediately slumped to the side. Will and Sam stretched him out on the cot.

"Stay beside him at least two days. Whenever he stirs, give him water first, and as much broth as he will take, He should pass through all right. In a week or two, he'll be ready for..." Doc shrugged his shoulder. "Whatever is to come. I'll be on my way, Elijah."

Sam Hopkins left with the vet. The hour was late, well past his bedtime, 4:15 a.m. would come too soon.

Will stayed with the sick fugitive and Pink. The next evening Sam brought Will supper, an ample supply of warm, tasty food from Miz Erelene. Actually it was enough for Pink and the sick man he had nicknamed Stuff after he began slowly responding to their care.

Chapter Sixteen

Not far from where Will held steadfast to his vigil with the sick fugitive, an excited courier riding in the dawn reined his horse. He whipped his leg over the white Mustang's back and slid down, having arrived at the Whitson homestead in time for breakfast. He tarried only long enough to warn Ben of the impending crisis, having time neither for coffee, nor water for his horse. Libit tucked a couple slices of bacon in a hot biscuit for him. The courier was soon off again, driving the horse as if he could actually feel Satan's hot tongue licking his heels.

Ben hitched the buckboard. On his way to Rev. Isaiah Clarkson, curiosity forced him by the Atkinsons' little homestead. Broken furniture, an open door hanging loose met him. Father, mother, and three children gone, five grim reminders of the terror that abolitionists with their political ties and sympathetic gestures could not alleviate. No amount of refined words or money could remedy this worsening situation. Ben, choking back tears, spurred on by anger and fear, sped straight away to the Reverend.

Something urgent, Rev. Clarkson agreed, must be done. Certainly, everybody, not just part of the congregation on bended knees praying earnestly to a God of vengeance, could unleash a power that would part the sky like it had opened the Red Sea for Moses. Surely God would see the beacon and answer their prayer.

Rhetoric seemed like mostly empty rhetoric considering how despair had so twisted their way of interpreting, the Reverend admitted to himself, watching Ben ride away. Not a lie, he simply couldn't reveal what he knew to bolster his unswerving belief that slavery would be crushed. A movement deeply imbedded in spirituality had begun in Philadelphia. Though young like an infant with strong lungs, it held promise. Rev. Clarkson sincerely believed the movement would grow. On the wings of it would ride the hopes and aspirations of millions—slaves and freed persons. For now though, how else could he implore them to hold steady their faith in a God of vengeance when all about them, except for the little hope rising from that young chap he hadn't met, the night of despair was getting darker? More slaves were escaping, more were being caught. Pure logic, but he'd never argue the point.

Ben, fired by the inspiration in the reverend's plan, spread word of a sunset gathering far and wide, beseeching everyone he knew to come, urging them to warn others. Eliza saw a speeding dust ball rising in the distance grow bigger. She recognized Ben hurrying towards her and ran to meet him in the lane. After he explained, she assured him she would be there and begged him to notify Will. No, she hadn't seen him since that eventful day, but she knew, don't ask her how, he'd be at Orvil Rhodes' boarding house,

179

Will wasn't there, Ben soon learned. Miz Erelene hadn't seen Will in a goodly little spell, but she had a vague idea where he had gone. Somehow, she'd see to it that Will would get the word. Ben hoped she would and departed, off to rally more support.

Rev. Isaiah Clarkson, a free man, had earned a special kind of respect from white folks. It was an appreciation from the Christian-Quaker community, he reasoned, for maintaining the precarious balance between chaos and black people's tempered walking-the tight-rope existence. Blacker than midnight he was, with a head full of black curls, big, fluffy and silky locks that shook whenever his head moved. A husky man, he had huge black and white eyes. Whites in Christiana and thereabout called Rev. Clarkson the preaching farmer. White folks to Rev. Clarkson were decent, God-fearing people whose love for all humankind embraced the Golden Rule. It was a caring so all encompassing that despite life's hardships, nothing in it could be worthy of undermining their divine principle of treating the Reverend exactly as they would want him to treat them.

That respect for Rev. Clarkson held other whites, who certainly were not folks, at bay. Dirt-dumb and shiftless, they were a free black man's burden, pawns for slavers, in league with bounty hunters. No question about the harsh reality of that. Only one thing boggled the Reverend's mind, one grin factor in the unfolding American trauma completely befuddled him, even more than having been run out of New Orleans after helping defend the city against the British invaders. How could Scots-Irish and German foreigners so early in their beginnings in this new country hate him with such seemingly artificial vehemence? They were so narrow-minded and hollow, especially for such downtrodden, earthy kind themselves. The only apparent justification could be that hating him was essential to them for establishing an American identity. Yet, they fumed and fussed with each other in their old country tongues for choice picks of vegetables and fruit the Reverend sold twice a week in Christiana Village. The peppers, beets, beans, corn, September grapes, and October potatoes he and his wife, Miz Lucille, raised were the best.

Rev. Clarkson's customers, kind and sympathetic men like grist mill owner-operator Castner Hanway, and Squire George Pownall in the village asked him about the young stranger. He was anxious to meet him too, the Reverend told them. He was as concerned as they about the tales and half-truths flying about like so many black birds being rousted from their perching thicket. "Did'ja hear? Atkinson folks third family to disappear in that many days. Did'ja hear? Young fella, name's Will something or other, with a handful'a men, chased a bunch of snatchers clean over into Maryland. They shot it out with pretty-near a whole town of scalawags and brought back a wagonload of snatched folks. He go'n git hisself an army, put an end to snatchin'. They claim he's tough enough to do it too. But seem like for everyone he save, two more up and vanish. Hope he comes to the meeting, I wanna see what he looks like."

Half of the Reverend's barn, though not a big one as barns generally were in that area, had been converted into a sanctuary in 1813 by the men of the congregation. It mysteriously caught fire on a cold night in 1822 after slave runners, hell-bent on capturing runaways, shot the door full of holes. Years earlier, Bishop Richard Allen preached there at Mt. Zion, conferring its acceptance in the African Methodist Episcopal Church conference. Rev. Clarkson relished God's blessing from Rev. Allen to rename the church Mt. Zion AME, linking it with Mother Bethel AME of Philadelphia. The Zion Hill community wasted little time in building a new church across the road from the charred remains of the original on ground purchased by the church and endorsed by the AME conference. Several rows of crude, rough-hewn pews surrounded a pot bellied stove squatting in the center like a fat matron warming her brood. When fired, it sent a vespertine column of gray smoke from the crest of Zion Hill, a gesture of hope to the Reverend's weary flock.

Within an hour of the urgent meeting, Rev. Clarkson sat quietly in the pulpit, studying shadows of budding branches cast on the darkening cast wall by a springtime sun shining on trees and throwing reflections through the west windows. He reasoned the evening gathering would probably be the most difficult he'd ever encounter. Miz Lucille lit the wicks of lanterns mounted under each window and adjusted them to a rosy glow, while he sat quietly in the pulpit, praying the ambiance would help calm the multitude's ragged nerves.

Merle Gibson and his family arrived first, then Libit and Zeke, Ben, Eliza and her sister Hannah. John Roberts and his missus, Harvey Scott, Miz Erelene and Thomas Bentlow followed. Men, women and children soon filled the little sanctuary to overflowing. The numbers attending warned Rev. Clarkson they were an anxious, scared lot who hadn't come to worship. He was their rock and for him to hold steady from that vantage point, he'd better speak the truth, though it might be as harsh as old massa's lash. He'd better speak sternly, be quick in countering any attempts to change the course of their journey thus far across the arid desert of slavery.

The Reverend began the discourse by getting right to the point. "Any kind of organized resistance with or without guns, bricks, branches, hatchets, or corn cutters is unlawful." He admitted the countryside was getting meaner, more white neighbors were switching over to support slavery, while more fugitives settled in. "Vengeance is mine, sayeth the Lord," he reminded them. "Black folks, free or fugitive, taking up arms is begging suicide."

"But Reverend, more foreigners moving in than us black folks," Harvey Scott said.

"Yes, they were invited by the United States government. We weren't."

"Praying to God don't seem like it's doing much good, Reverend."

"It is not prayer, Brother Ben, that is deceiving us. Every black man and every black woman appealing to God for the same thing, all praying in earnest, will work. Somebody is doing dirt and prayer is flushing it out. That's vengeance working. Who among us isn't sincere? We'll soon know."

They searched each other's faces. Ben's hot gaze found the man whom he and Zeke suspected. Ben watched him staring straight ahead at no one.

Despite its grumbling, the bewildered and unsettled congregation was orderly. With the Reverend elevated above them, firing calculated answers fast and furious as their questions bombarded him, his stinging repartee held them in check.

Then Libit stepped into the aisle, looking this way and that, waiting until every pair of eyes were on her. "I prayed for my men folks to save me..."

"Don't mistake meekness for weakness, Sister Elizabeth," the Reverend hastily responded. "Weak men hide. Meek men are sustained in courage. If it were not for meek black men, free black folks would vanish, fugitives wouldn't have a chance..."

"You should'a seen them." Libit maintained her quiet, clear voice amid the disquieted souls, winning their appeal.

"I prayed too," Miz Erlene said, interrupting Libit and waving her arm in the air so the Reverend could identify her. "I prayed to my savior for strength to fight back. I do believe he sent us Will Parker."

"Will Parker, hunh? Where is the swarthy one?" Rev, Clarkson said. "That's what the white folks call him."

"Ain't seen or heard from him close now to two weeks," Ben said. "But Miz Erlene said she'd see to it that he got word."

"I heard about his talk of gun against gun," Rev. Clarkson said. "That means fool against fool trading death for death."

"I hope he shows," Miz Erelene said.

"Careful, Sister," the Reverend retorted, extending his hand towards her. "Armed resistance is suicide. It cannot replace a community praying to a merciful God of vengeance."

They suddenly stopped listening. Rev. Clarkson watched their heads turning towards the door. He heard them murmuring the name of a youngster entering his church wearing that defiant demeanor, that be-damned attitude with the butt of a pistol visible under his shirt. Sam Hopkins flanked him.

Rev. Clarkson seethed. Yet, he too, though he would never admit it, right from first glance had to admire Will. A fine cut of young man, Will reminded the Reverend of himself decades ago fighting in the War of 1812. But his church needn't know that.

"Well now," Rev. Clarkson said, "mister armed rebellion in the flesh."

Right from the beginning, Will disliked the Reverend. Something too beguiling about him. Neither did Will like being scrutinized by a sea of querying faces, nor hearing his name uttered in so many eddies of whispered small talk. If Sam had not been there anchoring him, he would have left. Sam, meanwhile, basked in Will's attention.

Rev. Clarkson sensed Will coming apart. If he could hold Will right there, sweating in that overwhelming tide of confusion long enough, he'd regain command and send Will spinning like a whirlwind that had only made a big scare out of sight, out of mind.

Will looked and looked for a soft face to say yes, I'm glad you came. But in the darkening room with flickering lamps and everyone staring at him, he could discern no one, even though he stood close enough to Eliza for her to grab him by the pants leg. She, like so many others, waited anxiously for him to acknowledge his name, to redeem his pledge.

"Seems like church's the wrong place," Will said, "for black men to talk about protecting they women folks and chillun." He turned to leave but Sam grabbed his sleeve. Will whirled, scaring Sam. But he held fast. Will gingerly pried Sam's fingers loose without looking at him.

"Mr. Parker, please stay. You're really why we're here," Mrs. Gibson said, having stood. "Tell him so, Merle," she said, realizing she had denied her husband the opportunity to speak first.

Will fixed his eyes on her, so tall and strikingly beautiful.

For a few anxious seconds Merle observed Will drinking in his wife. Then he stood beside her.

Eliza, though starry eyed and eager, couldn't bring herself to stand. She jabbed her elbow into Hannah, pushed her, then pinched her on the buttocks, forcing Hannah to spring up from the bench. Will saw Hannah and caught sight of Eliza. His gaze met hers. Both were strong and compelling, though for only a brief moment. Even with the annoyance confronting him, it rushed on him again; that aching knot around his navel, the pain in his loins. Time to retreat.

Ben stopped him. "I hid the guns we took from the snatchers, Will."

Will shook his head briskly from side to side, trying to step around Ben without pushing him.

"My boss wants to see you, Will."

But Will wanted nothing more than to leave. Then Harvey Scott, John Roberts, Miz Erelene, Libit and others, all of then ignoring the Reverend's warning, stood and applauded, giving Will resounding support. A sudden urge came on Rev. Clarkson to scorn Will, to rip him apart with rhetoric against which Will could not defend himself.

Holding his flock sheep-like in its passive image that had for years won the silent approval of decent, establishment white folks was the Reverend's obligation—his alone. Establishment power, its silent influence held the vicious, poor white-trash wolves in check, kept them from eating black folks alive. "Young Parker," he said, "Just what are you after?"

Will didn't know what to say. He held his hands in front of him, palms up with a blank look on his face. "Church don't seem like the right place for colored men to talk about fighting back."

A hush settled over the church.

Then Ben spoke. "Tomorrow," he said, "we come together, brotherhood for protection, in Mr. Whitson's barn. Now say something, Will, to make us believe we doing right by joining up with you."

"Travel together, lock your doors," Will blurted. "At the first sign of trouble, stand by the fireplace and commence to beating on pots or pans and yelling. Kick up a big enough racket to wake up the whole countryside. Keep your guns loaded. Shoot everything that moves if it ain't suppose to move."

A unexpected grunt jumped from Rev. Clarkson's throat. "Young fool," he said, shaking a trembling finger at Will, "lead them to water, not to hell!"

"What water?" Will said, "and I ain't none of your fools, man."

"Well," the Reverend said rather sheepishly, "it's clear to us, you don't know water is the bath of redemption."

"Nope," Will said, "and don't much give a hoot. I ain't up to any of that stuff you talking about." He wished he could be rude to the old man, give him a good old down in the country cussing-out. But he was in the man's church.

"I want a minute or two with you...alone," Rev. Clarkson said, pointing his finger at Will, "as soon as this meeting is over."

"For what?" Will said, hunching his shoulders and turning to leave.

Rev. Clarkson hurried from the pulpit and stood, blocking Will's path. "I'm holding you responsible for any harm that comes to any of my people for this, this brotherhood protecting thing of yours."

"A tub's got to sit on its own bottom, Preach. Any man who wants protection for his family, let'em join. I need me five, six good ones, that's all," Will said.

Sam Hopkins cleared his throat and rolled his eyes out of focus at Will for making the demeaning slur. "I'll go over and check in on Pink and Abe," he said, milling with the crowd. He doubted that Will heard him.

Except for Miz Erelene and a few persons lingering to try eavesdropping on their conversation, Will and the Reverend were alone.

"There's a lot more to responsibility and black manhood you better understand, strutting around here acting like half a man."

"Rev'm." Will pointed a tense finger right under the Reverend's nose. In his mind's eye, Will's fist had already exploded the Reverend's jaw, sending him sprawling on his back. "Don't mess with my manhood," he said. "I didn't wanna come here in the first place."

Rev. Clarkson was not intimidated. "It's way too late for that now, son," he said, though easing his blistering challenge. Perhaps it'd be more to his advantage to ask questions the youngster couldn't answer, make Will see himself in comparison to the Reverend, a man inspired and wrapped in the bosom of God. "Do you really know why you happened by this place, Christiana? Do you know anything about yourself, anything other than what you can see or feel? If you don't, how can you be anything but half of what Will Parker really should be?"

Will placed his hands on his hips, cocked his head to one side. "Mister, I didn't even let my old master make light of me. Man, I done told you."

Rev. Clarkson knew he had baited Will. He knew that Will, though quite angry, would listen. Smart young men, particularly the head-strong, couldn't resist curiosity. Will had at least that much working for him, he wasn't a dumb nigger. "Let me ask you another way. How do you behold your savior? Do you think about him like a slave thinks, or do you think about him like a slavecrat?"

"Well, well," Will said, stepping back. He rubbed his chin. "You want the truth, hunh? Okay, I never gave more'n a thought to old Mack's bill goat parson, or that slave jack-leg preacher either."

Will's naive response tickled the old man, though he kept that stone face, knowing he had penetrated Will's facade of toughness. "Forget them, son. Your savior is the I in you, your very soul, knowing exactly what Will needs to understand his manhood. I is buried in your heart. Go deep, search yourself until you find him. Then you will know exactly what Will's nature is to be and to have."

"My nature to be and have what?"

The Reverend chuckled. "Them who don't runaway," he said, "blame everything on ole massa, even the heavy rain on days they harvest cotton."

"Ain't many who can get away," Will said.

"Ain't many," Rev. Clarkson said, "who don't blame ole massa."

"Ain't nobody else," Will said, "unless they blame themselves and that ain't..."

"Easy now," the Reverend said, "think on that a good while before you answer." Rev. Clarkson believed he had fastened a grip on young Will's mind strong enough to turn him wrong side out, but more importantly make him need the Reverend.

"A slavecrat wouldn't give one hoot to the kind of Jesus slaves and fugitives beg. He relies on what he knows is God's grace to give him exactly what is his nature to have. Slaves and fugitives, even many free black men spend way too much time, like the rest of their lives, thanking the savior and begging his help to get through one more daily trial after the next. And Jesus does just that, brings them through just one more day."

"I don't beg Jesus."

"Naw sir, you sure don't," Rev. Clarkson said. "You don't know much about sin and redemption either. Do nothing, get nothing, do dirt get dirt ain't hard to understand, but..."

"I do know about the inner light," Will said, in sudden rejection of the Reverend's obvious ridiculing.

"Oh," Rev. Clarkson said, realizing he had taken too much for granted. "Slavecrats don't believe slaves can understand how God's light shines from the souls of all men, making them brothers. What you think about yourself deep in your soul, they believe, decides just how much of God's grace will bless you. We, except for a handful who got white daddies, are soul-less and stupid. Without souls, we can't ever be their equals. When you understand their way of thinking, you be fitting to lead somebody."

"How you go'n tell me what I'm fitting to do?" Will said, with crisp belligerence. "You don't know me."

"What I may or may not know isn't important. Looking beyond what you actually see of yourself to what the eyes can't behold is not easy, son. That's how you freed yourself from slavery, but you don't know that either."

The Reverend was strutting inside himself. He had cornered Will but hadn't burned him. Singed him a little maybe, but that had come about in the course of infusing the mystery in Will's rambunctious mind. Deep in the heart of him, he admired Will, even though he would never admit it. He knew, at least he hoped, whenever the time came for the mystery to begin unraveling, Will would return.

Will left with his head hurting, and mumbling not so quietly to himself. He knew the Reverend had purposely confused him, though he didn't know why. How in the world could a black man bring himself to believe a slave should blame himself, unless he had never been a slave? Will wondered why he hadn't thought to ask the Reverend that. Will really didn't dislike the Reverend, but that he'd have a hard time explaining.

Will hadn't walked far when he happened upon Eliza sitting on a tree stump that had been carved into a bench beside a bed of flowers. Her sudden movement jolted him from the deep concentration of himself. Inundated with Clarkson's burdensome challenge, he was hardly eager for a playful interlude.

"What in hell?"

She stood in front of him, legs slightly parted, hands on hips. "Don't spoil it," she said.

"Out here by yourself, bouncing 'round like you want buckra to catch you. Whydn't you gone home with that other girl?"

"Listen to you, all balled up inside yourself, and acting like a hornet to keep me from knowing."

"From knowing what?" He spit the words at her, feeling that gnawing again in his navel.

But she wouldn't be deterred. "From knowing that you scared."

"Will Parker ain't afraid of nobody, little bits. Move outta my way."

"Except me, a woman reaching out to touch you." She mimicked him, repeating his name, "Wi-ill Pah-kuh. A fugitive slave woman, seventeen years old, going on twenty-eight. But it ain't worth bleeding about. There's more to both of us than being so tough."

"Made that way, good thing for a whole lot of folks that I am."

She shook her head from side to side. He watched her curving, slender body sway with the movements.

"Just like a man. Tell him he's tough, he growls louder and thinks about nothing but his fists or his behind. Do you ever think with your heart?" She touched him.

He tensed, anxious to leave, threatening to bowl right over her. "Get away from me with that gooey stuff."

"I know what you really feel, Wi-ill. Her voice suddenly took on another quality as if floating flute-like in its soft African dialect. "It shows."

"You know nothing," he said, wheeling on her with his mouth wide and snarling, the redness of anger scarring the olive-black and ivory-white African sheen in his eyes that were hooded like a crow's. "How could you know how it feels when a bastard slaver yanks the covers off a black man's bed and snatches his woman? You know what it's like having a slavecrat track you across miles and years, then watch him strap your kin in chains?" His sharp tongue continued lashing. "Can you feel like a little boy in bed with his cold mama, knowing she took death before she'd whip him for her master?"

"Stop it!" Eliza raised a balled fist, as if to hit him.

Will caught her fist in mid-air. He clamped his iron hand over it and squeezed, feeling her whimper, reading the terror in her face, yet keenly aware that she had not cowered. He loosened the tight clasp. For a moment they stood still, hanging in awkward silence. He heard a roaring in his ears like the sound of the sea lapping the wave-eaten shore. In his head he felt the pounding of waves against the breakwall in his brain, holding back from gushing through his long body the tide of nature's stimulation that makes sour apples sweet.

"Wi-ill, you think my head is filled up with pretty things like pink lace and petticoats?" she said. "I live nightmares too. Don't be mean, don't run from me." She came closer, impelled by her passion, sensing his desire for her intensifying. Her breathing, deep and sensuous, drew him with his hot, jumpy breath to her.

"I weren't bent on hurting you, little bits," Will said, "it's just that I, uh..." He slid down her body to his knees, pressing her hands to his face, craving her, yet rejecting the urgent need in him to squeeze tenderly until the last drop of honey had been extracted from the flower.

She pressed her smooth stomach to his hot, sweaty face and put her arms around his neck. His arms enwrapped her midriff. The breakwall in Will's brain let go. She tasted of char-broiled barbecue laced with honey. His kiss, urgent and exploring, felt punishing and angry, though it sang in her veins.

"No-oh, Wi-ill, not here. Rev'm or Mrs. Clarkson might be peeping."

Somewhere close by, in the star-studded night they quickly entwined, taking love madly as if there would be no tomorrow. She bit her tongue to stifle her outcry. He breathed in deep soul-drenching gasps. Moonbeams cascaded in the meadow where they lay and then swooped them up high and higher in the sky until the moonbeams were spent. Will and Eliza tumbled down to earth, pleasingly exhausted. A deep feeling of peace came over her, while lying there hearing him succumb to the numbing sleep of a contented lover. They slept until a meadow lark awakened them.

The dormant sexuality of the young fugitive slave woman, bound and submerged by fear of capture and rape, had been awakened in Eliza. There would have to be more than Will's first touch. She and he planned an early rendezvous the next day. Unfortunately for them, the freedom fighters were scheduled to organize later that evening. On his way to Marsh Chamberlain's farm, erotic feelings pressing Will were more potent than fear that Eliza might be snatched away from him. Yet, while reliving the night before with her, the Reverend's harsh condemnation kept interfering, forcing him to think again of the dreaded fear that knotted his stomach. The entire matter annoyed him so, he wanted to think only of Eliza.

She was bustling about the Chamberlain household as if her maid's chores were a new-found joy. Having finished early, Eliza began preparing a basket dinner, hoping to surprise Will with succulent delights a bachelor seldom had the opportunity to savor. After cooking her delicacies to tasting satisfaction, she packed them in a picnic basket. Exhaling a long sigh of contentment, she peeped from behind the curtains. A sudden, extremely warm glow spread over her. She watched Will approaching, telling herself repeatedly, a lady must wait until he knocked. Her heart though, beating faster and faster with each of his giant strides, wouldn't listen. With basket in hand and a dazzling smile that set Will's pulses racing, she greeted him at the gate under a hemlock tree.

His face split into a wide, mischievous grin at the sight of her. Eliza's hair, dark, thick and long, was parted down the middle. Two thick braids were wrapped around her head, just above her ears. Will inhaled long and slowly, letting his eyes feast on her slender, lithe body. Prominent cheek bones accentuated a thin, tapered face. How beautiful she appeared to him, like a wild rose tempting him from deep within the bosom of its thorny bush.

Eliza, feeling the magnetism in his bold, seductive gaze sliding downward over her body, cleared her throat, thus breaking his trance. She handed Will the basket and chanced holding his hand, He didn't resist, though she thought the grip rather limp. They strolled along the periphery of Marsh Chamberlain's farm, her leading him through fields recently cleared and empty meadows full of scrub grass and clumps of dark green clover in mounds of old, dried cow dung. She was searching for a secluded spot, a safe haven where they could be alone together, the ideal place to implant in him a definite need for her. Brushing her body against his and squeezing his hand a time or two, she sensed Will becoming pensive and said, hoping to humor him, that Rev. Clarkson's brick-chimney body had tensed and leaned one-sided like he was having a stroke when Miz Erlene testified that she believed God sent Will to them. Eliza expected Will might laugh and say something that would make her proud, but he didn't. He simply said most of the men at Mt. Zion Church wanted to unite, but only a few would. Church folks had argued, Eliza said, with the Reverend in Will's favor.

But Will wasn't listening. He was plying his mind for a plan that would bring the brotherhood together without the church. He looked in the woods, at the ground, everywhere except at Eliza for a sign that would spring an idea to mind. She could've just drifted off, Eliza mused, in another direction. He wouldn't have even noticed.

Will asked her if she had brought some apples. Strange, strange man, she thought, pulling him gently by the hand under a weeping willow tree and taking the basket from him. He surprised her, sitting on the ground, leaning against the tree, just as she asked him. For that she gave him a juicy rust-colored apple. He took a bite and sat straight up. A look of bemused wonder spread across his face. He bit and chewed furiously, watching Eliza spread the table cloth, inhaling the fragrance of sweet potato custard, baby okra and tomatoes, deviled eggs topped with mustard sauce, chicken fried in egg and cornmeal batter. Will ate heartily then sat there tossing the apple core into the air and catching it. Eliza tried talking about herself first and then about the two of them. But Will didn't say much. When he did offer anything more than a thought or two, he complicated it with something or other about the freedom fighters. She was glad he ate heartily, even though he sat there afterwards tossing the apple core into the air and catching it. She sat close, touching him, feeling her heart hammering against her ribs, and noticing the sun, a huge orange ball, sliding half-way into the horizon. Time had come for them to leave.

Ben, Sam Hopkins, John Roberts, and Scott had become quite restless waiting in Whitson's stifling hot barn. Not wanting to attract attention, Ben had closed the door. They sat in a circle, inhaling barn odors and waiting for Will; Ben and Sam on wood crates, Scott on the floor leaning against an animal stall. Roberts was stretched out with his hands folded behind his head catnapping in a wheelbarrow. Small talk, mostly about Will, began shifting from praise to bickering doubt. Then Will strode in with a plump apple and the core of another one dangling between his thumb and forefinger.

"Evening," he said, matter-of-factly.

Sam cleared his throat. "Been evening a long time," he said. "And you go'n have to do better than a winesap and a limp apple core to explain why you so gawd-dang late."

"Took a little time hashing out a way to explain us so it'd be best understood," Will said, placing the apples on wood crates Ben had stacked in the middle of their circle.

"Apples?" Roberts said. "A chicken head with blood dripping through your fingers would be more like dead serious."

"Sounds to me like that apple he ate," Scott said, chuckling with a dry cynical sound, "been soaking in jack a mite too long."

Will's left eyebrow rose a fraction of an inch. His right eye lid closed halfway. He steadied that fixed gaze on Scott. "Anybody who's guts ain't tough enough to hold ashes that'll get hotter'n the coals in a blacksmith's bed," he said, "better g'won home."

Scott fidgeted in the loose hay strewn on the floor and sat up. "I was kinda ribbing you, I guess. I been sitting here so long."

"If you can't trust yourself, leave whilst you still free to back out ass first."

"Git on with the idea," Roberts said. "Sounds like you just may be on to a little something worth hearing."

"Okay, then," Will said, "staying means all of us swear to die before whispering, not even to the air, one somebody's name. We got nobody to look after the handful of us except each other." He held up the brown-stained core. "This is us now, the brotherhood. Ain't much, but nobody knows how weak or how strong we really is except the handful of us." He threw the core into a dark corner of the barn. "Colored folks know we their only real hope for safety from snatchers." He held the juicy apple in his big fist and squeezed while the veins swelled in his arm. "Folks depending on us is the apple, we the core. They hide us, we protect them. Everybody stop living in fear day by day."

Sam's eyes twinkled devilishly. "Ain't you got that a little backwards? Ought'n we be the apple?"

"Nope. Lemme finish, Sam."

"Sounds like something I heard a preacher yapping," Roberts said, rubbing his forehead, trying to recall the memory. "Blackberries and sweet bushes, something like that."

Sam chuckled. "Most likely, he said blacker the berry, sweeter the juice. But that's old."

"Berries outta season and berry seeds too small," Will said. "Forget the damned preacher."

"Uh-oh," Sam said, "Rev'm must'a got to you right funny like."

"Seeds, Will?" Ben asked.

"I don't wanna talk about it, Hoppy," Will said.

Sam bristled. "I thought we settled that Hoppy crap sometime ago."

"Every time you signify, Sam, it just comes up. I don't think on it."

"Will," Ben said. "You go'n tell us about the seeds or jab at Sam?"

"Jabbin' is part of 'em, Ben, like white gloves and serving old man Whitson's tea is part'a you. Ain't pokin' fun, it's just the order of things."

"Each one of us," Will said, ignoring Sam, "is a seed in the apple core. Any man we let in becomes another brother-seed."

"And one rotten seed," Scott said, anxious to be involved, hoping he could add some constructive thought, "can spoil the apple."

"Men," Will said, looking gravely at each one. "Seeds don't rot, no seed ever spoiled the apple. Can't happen." He waited for some response, a rebuttal, an argument.

"I ain't one to drag things out," Ben said, shaking his head dejectedly, "but what in the world is apples and brother-seeds got to do with us colored folks in Christiana?"

Will rubbed his hands together and sighed. He saw Sam's lips trembling while his mischievous comrade wrestled an almost overwhelming urge to let go a whooping roar of laughter. "We the seeds, our colored community is the apple. The apple can be squashed, ate-up, or worms can rot it. It needs us protecting it as long as there be slave runners and no laws to protect us."

"But that stuff about seeds," Ben questioned, "You just saying that to make us think we somebody like Samson?"

"No, no," Will said, "No, no. It's like, say, ah... Yea, Adam and Eve, you know about them eating the apple?"

"Of course," Ben said, rather indignantly. "Probably better than you."

"Okay, okay, Ben. Did you know they couldn't stomach the seeds?"

Ben stood and began talking loudly, pointing his finger. "Just how in, excuse me Lord, how in the hell would Will Parker know that?"

"Its a fact, Ben, however many they may had swallowed came out the same as they went in. Empty a handful in your gullet, look for yourself."

"By Jesus, Parker," Roberts said, "it sounded right dumb at first, but damned if you didn't break it down, just like big money folks do it. I'm with you."

"Will," Ben said, smiling, "I already made myself clear at the church."

"Sam?"

Sam Hopkins smiled, while nodding his head yes. "You a mess. Damndest story I ever heard."

"Scott, we need a sharp eye and your bird-gun."

"Count on it, Will."

"Okay, brother-seeds," Will said, smiling. "Nobody signs nothing."

"Wait, just a minute," Sam said, "I wanna make sure somebody other than me noticed Will Parker laughing. Why, it's a blessed miracle."

"First time for me too," Roberts said, "but damned if he ain't."

191

Ben and Scott snickered.

Will waved his hands at them. "Keep it all up here," he said pointing to his head, "hid from everybody except you and God." God? He hadn't thought to say that, but he dared not reject it.

Before the inductions Will explained how yelling, screaming, and beating on pots, though it seemed awfully dumb, would work. At least one comrade would surely be somewhere close by. He could summon everybody within hearing distance to arms and lead the rescue.

Will swore each man in the presence of only himself to a commitment as demanding and powerful as he believed the individual could stand. The oath sealed a bond between Will and the man, a bond amendable only by death. Nothing was written that night, but little would slip from any comrade's memory. They departed late, proud to be associated, determined to live by the code of solidarity that mandated each one his brother's keeper.

Will beamed with the pride. Eliza, watching him from the kitchen window, could tell by the way he swaggered and whistled back to a bird in the hemlock along-side the picket fence. He whistled a greeting to Eliza, sounding like a crazy warbler. A broad smile bespoke her approval. Soon they were strolling again, continuing their week-long romance, getting to know one another. After the seventh night, nuptial bliss was their only yearning.

Will flat-out rejected Eliza's desire for Rev. Clarkson to marry them. The more he thought about the Reverend, the more determined he was to circumvent him. Calling Will half a man, blaming the slave for his own predicament, Rev. Clarkson had aroused in Will something unacceptably mind boggling. He appealed to Elijah Lewis to name a sincere official who might unite them in a holy matrimony recognizable by state law. Their children must be free citizens of Pennsylvania.

Elijah Lewis, having come to respect Will after watching him lure the sick fugitive, Abe Johnson, from death's door, recommended Squire Pownall in Christiana. Eliza's sister, Hannah, was maid of honor, Pinckney was best man. The roomful of folks watched man and wife sign the wedding certificate, Will nervously scribbling some impossible jibberish, embarrassed Eliza making an X beside her name, which the squire had written with his quill.

"I'll be able to write it next time," she said.

"Next time?" Will responded, amid hearty laughter.

"I do it for the foreigners too, Mrs. Parker," Squire Pownall said.

Mrs. Parker. My my! A pride welled inside Eliza's heart, making her feel as if she could reach out and hug all the space she could see between earth and sky. But she wouldn't let Will see her cry.

Eliza continued working and living at Marsh Chamberlain's. Will went about the task of finding a home for his bride, and more importantly, finding work. Elijah offered Will the job of making his early crop, since the bustling village demanded more of his time in the post office and general store. He hired Pinckney instead, on Will's recommendation. Without a job, the fugitive only several weeks out of the lion's mouth was not safely grounded in anyone's protective custody. Asking Elijah for such a favor disturbed Will, but Pinckney's security was more important than his pride. Will accepted Mr. Whitson's offer to run his threshing machine, but declined an offer to live on the spreading farm. He needed his own living quarters with absolutely no ties to his boss.

Chapter Seventeen

Seemed like most everybody Will met while searching for a home was a member of the Pownall clan. Certainly enough of them for Will to quickly understand that Squire Pownall speaking well of him would guarantee acceptance by all his Quaker kinfolks. One Pownall sent Will to another who sent him to another until he came upon farmer Levi Pownall.

Levi's spread, a few miles west of Rhodies Boarding House, was a vast and fertile undulating quilt of hay fields, pastures, and cornfields seemingly split and zippered down the middle by a rutted lane. Long Lane they called the dirt trail, intersected Upper Valley Road—the northern east-west artery from Christiana—and Noble Road—the southern east-west artery from the village center. Valley Run, a shallow stream meandering across the farm some distance then along the near side towards Chester Valley, created a natural boundary and watering hole for dairy and beef cattle. At the far side, where the terrain sloped gently upwards, dense brush leaned over a sagging fence that separated the self-sustaining farm from thick woods. On three acres at the north end of Pownall's place, between an orchard and Upper Valley Road, the newlyweds Will and Eliza, lived in a two-story brick house. A rustic fence and the peach, apple, and pear orchard isolated Will from his landlord's homestead.

Will and Eliza's home was connected to Long Lane by a short rutted track. Its name, Short Lane, was nailed to a fence post where it intersected Long Lane. Beside Long Lane a field of new corn, its tassels turning deep green on stalks taller than Will, extended the length of the farm, from Valley to Noble Roads. The couple's view from their front porch was corn—nothing but corn and more corn. In Valley Run, half an acre or so behind the house Will stacked rocks he gathered from the creek bed, creating a pond Eliza would use for washing clothes. He spent a great deal of time back there, staring at the woods and pondering. For certain, bounty hunters were in there, watching and waiting.

Pink and Abe moved in with the Parkers, their house being much too big for only two people. Abe's being there allayed Will's fear of leaving Eliza alone at least for a while, even though Abe, still drawn within himself, spent most of his time in his sparsely furnished room. He ventured past the back door only to draw water from the well.

One evening, returning home after work, strolling Long Lane in a wheel's rut, Will stared disbelieving. Abe was by the creek chopping wood with Quaker Pownall. After supper, sitting around chewing the rag, Will asked Abe about his day's work. He listened and while explaining to Abe why working for the landlord was not good for the defenders, realized he had struck a tender nerve. Abe, knowing he hadn't regained his strength, still feared for his life. Yet he demanded the right to pay his way as best he could and express thanks in some small way for the merciful care from the Quakers. Will couldn't argue the point without revealing his obsession with fear that Eliza would be captured. The next day Will brought a bugle home. He, Eliza, Pink and Abe quickly learned to deliver a loud summoning blast.

Pink fared well working for Elijah Lewis and began calling on Eliza's sister Hannah. During the cold winter he often worked in Quaker Lewis' store.

On most Sunday afternoons after Eliza returned from church, their rear yard soon resembled an old fashioned camp meeting, rapidly filling with a multitude of black people. Free folks and fugitives sewn together by the common thread of fear, having fun. Family men, most of them idling around the barbeque pits under the poplar tree, cursed, chewed tobacco and smoked like concerned fathers often did when meshing old stories of the times with bleak forecasts of the future. Black miners recently losing jobs in the coal pits, lumberjacks forced on the run from the forest, railroad laborers fired, all had been driven from their jobs by gangs of Irish and German laborers fresh from the old country. These angry men disagreed only in their reasons why the immigrants were so prone to riot as fiercely as they had done in Columbia, in Harrisburg, in Philadelphia, and in Pittsburgh. During the heated discourse, while cooking the pork and sampling the sauce, the group of freedmen and fugitives often burned choice sides of meat. Or they made the hot liquid so pungent it actually repelled menacing horse flies and mosquitoes. They drank cider as fast as it could be squeezed from the apple to quench their fiery thirsts.

Six of the men guffawing and milling about were the inner core—Will, Ben, Hopkins, Roberts, Scott, and Pink having recently joined. Zeke and Abe had not pledged to the oath of allegiance. Still, their presence with the others reaffirmed their commitments to protect fugitives and free colored folks from slave runners. Among themselves they made small talk of late night sneak captures that were bungled by beating on pots and pans, blowing whistles and horns. Sometimes gunshots aroused the dogs, that awakened their masters, that sent someone running to Will or another of the guard, who chased the boogey men away or apprehended them with whatever force necessary.

Curious white men in the increasingly concerned community frequently stopped by. That is how Will met a neighbor, Casner Hanway, owner and operator of the grist mill. After an explanation of reasons so many colored visited most every Sunday and assurances from Will regarding the aim of his band of protectors, the men would express admiration at least in word, for his conviction. If they hung around long enough to sample the barbequed pig, apple cobbler and mulled cider, their mixed admiration generally changed to praise for Will's forthrightness. Among them was an inquisitive Quaker farmer, Joseph Scarlett, the man whom Will had come to Christiana hoping to find.

First Sunday in July, the ground still wet after a week-long rain that had finally let up the past evening, Scarlett came upon Will leaning against the fence along Noble Road. Will, immediately recognizing him astride the white mustang, smiled a greeting. But Scarlett identified himself as if they were strangers with an attitude that unnerved Will. The only white person on whom Will was certain he could rely to really understand him was not warm and talkative as he had been on that day at the trial, speaking out for Charles and lending Will his fast horse. Will was surprised to hear he lived so close, several miles west on Noble Road.

Scarlett's reason for being there, he didn't waste time explaining without even dismounting, was that in attracting so much attention, Will was creating a consequential challenge to the ever-present forces of evil that would sooner or later destroy the quietude that fostered peace. Like the beautiful Tigris-Euphrates Valley in the Holy Bible, Christiana was a village cut from the wilderness by Quakers and honed by their idealism of the ever presence of God in man. No colored folks lived in the village, but not because they were not welcome. Why not? They worked and shopped there. But God forbid, if they would be snatched off the streets, setting the village in turmoil.

No colored people were welcome to live in Christiana is what Scarlett really meant. What happened to change Scarlett's attitude so radically, Will reasoned. Why was he scared for Quakers who were not afraid?

Perhaps Scarlett saw the question on Will's face. Constantly disagreeing and talking rapidly, he acted as if he could read every contradicting thought surfacing in Will's mind. Scarlett carried the guilt of his deceased grandfather, he admitted. Most often, it was he on a white horse racing across the countryside, warning the colored to hide from slave runners prowling the area.

Scarlett's grandfather had owned slaves until John Wolman, the Quaker minister from Mt. Holly in West Jersey, convinced him to free them, lest God unleash a wrath of hailstones that would pulverize the entire valley. Granddad Scarlett then hired every slave he had owned. Some freedmen, grandchildren of the slaves, still lived on the farm. Others moved on, mostly settling in their own conclave on Zion Hill, just across the line in Chester County overlooking Christiana village. Zion Hill was land endowed to former slaves by an unknown repented slave-master.

In parting, Scarlett told Will to seek him if ever in a jam, especially to avoid blood-shed. He then asked Will if he had received any word about Charles. Will simply thanked Scarlett for defending his brother, and turning away from him Will wondered, were Quakers really afraid of hailstones.

Down by the creek bank Will walked upon a bed of wild flowers and clover. Funny, he mused, he hadn't noticed them before. Shiny yellow petals attached to white buttons looked like bright eyes smiling at him from the fertile, black soil. Thin, blue wings seemingly floated on green clover like resting butterflies. Deep red blossoms with black centers resembled bumblebees after nectar. Really seeing the untrammeled flowers and listening to women doing their family wash in the creek, laughing about serious things that for the moment seemed silly, Will affirmed to himself that by God or whatever force Quakers and slavecrats knew the good life, he would also know it. He smiled at children splashing and romping, making as much noise as they pleased without care of the attention they drew from the wilderness. In there were bounty hunters and road agents watching the picnicking folks from a safe distance across Willows Creek, Will was certain of that.

He pointed out different imagined animals to the women and children, spicing it with tidbits of memories from Grandmom Rosey's and One-Ear Tom's sagas. He mingled briefly with single men dressed in their Sunday best like Slim Carroll wandering by, hoping an attractive, lonely miss might be sitting there bored with all the hullabaloo and nothing to do.

Though Will could not fathom the depth slavers' influence had imbued the southeastern Pennsylvania atmosphere, he knew he had come a long way in his quest for freedom. When news of his daring band spread across the county, the state, and southward, blatant daylight yankings from homes and byways did abate considerably. Even though the nightmare of soul snatchings and capture still held Sunday's folks bound in fear, a warm how-dee-do, sometimes a covered dish, and a smile were the only requirements for acceptance among the gathering of friends.

Occasionally, wayfarers would stop by Short Lane and gawk—hucksters, Indian traders and such—without making much of a stir, except for that grizzly, unshaven trapper dressed in coonskin cap and buckskins. One cool, crisp Sunday in early October, when the air was laden with the scent of apples and cinnamon cooking, he slid off a mangy mule and walked right up to Ben as if he knew him.

"Say there, boy," he snickered, his voice deep and hollow. "I need Alexander Pinckney and Abraham Johnson to help me butcher some venison."

He stared down at Ben with eyes cold and unpredictable, yet with an intensity strong enough to boil ice water. Ben, though small in stature, yielded not one inch. He returned the hostile smirk and called Will.

Hearing the alarm in Ben's voice over the frolicking din of women making apple butter, Will strapped on his gun and interrupted a gathering of men making plans for escorting their children to the new Quakers' school for colored children.

"Firearms out sight but not out of reach," he said, signaling the guard to their strategic positions and walking swiftly upon the trapper as if he would step right through him.

"The road that brought you by here keeps on going." Will stretched his long, sinewy arms, pointing into the distance.

"Jesus, neegras wearing guns. What's Pennsylvania comin' to?" the trapper said, his head bobbing up and down. "Be careful, boy, that thing don't go off and blast your foot all to hell and Africa. Ain't nowhere in all'a God's creation for a one-leg neegra."

"Hear me, ole rascal, if it goes off, woe be it unto you and your boogey man buddies in the woods over yonder."

"Oh hell, boy. I'm just an ole mountain man needing couple pair steady slicing hands. But everybody clean to Harrisburg knows what you doin' here."

"What could you know about that?" Will said.

The mountain man shook his head in disgust. "Tell me this parcel of neegras getting all liquored up didn't come for training to kill all us decent white folks. Gawddamn boy, you do think I'm dumb."

"You do look dumb, but just acting so. Better stop though, so you hear what I'm a telling you. The road leads thataway. Go, don't look back."

"Is this the way a neegra s'spose to treat a white man?"

"Git the hell outta here while you can walk away."

The trapper spit a wad of foul-smelling tobacco. "I scent a little pork sizzling on the grill. Hard to tell amidst them damned boiling apples. Mind if I go over there and..." He tried to look past Will at the crowd gathering behind him.

Will knew the trapper was testing his courage. "Step past me, ole man, I'll set your soul free from your raggedy behind. Better read me right."

With deliberate slowness the mountain man acquiesced. He climbed on the mule and just sat there. Not until Will began walking toward him did he nudged the animal and dawdle away. Will's guests began clapping, but he watched the trapper until man and mule disappeared over the knoll west on Noble Road.

The applause appeared to unsettled Will. He turned around. A deep scowl rippled across his forehead, turning his heavy eyebrows into arrows pointing to the gathering storm in his eyes. A sudden chill came over him.

For a brief moment, Will knew if he had told his friends to kill the trapper, they would have done it. If he told them to settle in Christiana despite resistance by Quakers like Scarlett, they would do it. If he told them to never be taken alive by slave runners, they would drown themselves or make the bastards shoot them.

A surge of pride welled up inside him. He actually heard a little voice inside him say, *you did good, Will.* An instant later, the exalted feeling had escaped him. Will couldn't believe he had felt so noble. Though he didn't know how to search deeply within himself, in his manner of reasoning, he believed he then understood the Reverend's probing question: *what is your nature to be?* Though he couldn't answer it, the unexpected discovery of a greater Will Parker had surfaced without conscious effort after the tough war of nerves with the trapper in front of everyone. He wished there were a way he could've harnessed that ennobled perception of himself.

Rev. Clarkson probably could help him, but Will vetoed that notion just as he had rejected the minister's condescending quip: "There's a lot more to responsibility and black manhood you'd better understand."

Thinking about it angered him, so rather than consult the Reverend, Will blamed his inability to grasp that magnified attitude on the heavy yoke of responsibility draped over his shoulders. Twenty-two years of age with Eliza pregnant, having to fight constantly for basic God granted rights—eating, sleeping, loving his woman without intrusions by lowly bastard slave runners. A community of free black folks and fugitive slaves did not feel secure without his presence. He, who dared wrest their fate from cruel men who sought to keep them in bondage. He, whom Lancaster County white citizens had come to admire and respect or fear and hate.

"I want a mug'a cider and a mess of meaty, charcoal ribs," he said, with a heavy sigh to Eliza, retreating to a shady spot on the ground under a tree.

The gathering had gone back to their frolicking, leaving Will with his perplexing thoughts and Ben out front with a dish of apple cobbler. So engrossed was Ben with the juicy helping of pie he didn't see a tall, handsome, black fellow duck into the cornfield and take a healthy swig of corn liquor from a pocket flask. The slender young man's hawking from deep within his throat drew Ben's attention. Ben watched him spit a wad of phlegm, stretch his eyes wide, and curse. He stepped from the cornfield and swaggered towards Ben grinning. His kinky hair, slicked straight back, glistened in the sun.

"Hi-dee tha'r, Mr. Benn-nee," he sang the greeting.

Ben nodded without looking up, then turned and watched the rascal moving about, just as he had done two or three Sundays before, paying no particular attention to anyone, but familiarizing himself with every face at the picnic. His clothes were finer than any other man's there.

Ben found Will stretched out on the ground leaning against an elm, wearing an inhospitable frown. Several boys were standing close by, staring at his gun and watching his big white teeth tearing a chunk of barbeque from an almost clean bone. "Say Will, struck me kind'a funny," Ben said, standing between his comrade and the little boys, "but I ain't laughing. No sooner'n you run off that old buzzard, a young one pops out of the cornfield,"

Will didn't stop chewing. "Oh yeah?" he said. "Who?"

"Bastard curdled ma' cobbler," Ben said. "He got no darned business here."

"Who the hell is he, Ben?" Will said, flinging the bone away, setting his face in a angry expression.

With a prudish air, Ben cocked his head to one side. "Excuse me?"

In one fluid motion, Will stretched up from his comfortable spot and stared menacingly at Ben. "All right, sir Benjamin, the bastard that curdled ya' cobbler."

"Over there, with his hair loaded with axle grease, eye-ballin' them young gals. Tom Bentlow. Got some moonshine on his hip too. I know all about him."

"You saw him drinking?" Will said, rubbing his forehead and shielding the afternoon sun from his eyes.

"Yep. Lives by himself. There he go," Ben said, scanning the crowd, pointing and watching Bentlow move about. "Don't go to socials. Ain't never held one at his house. He don't go to church regular on Sunday. Ain't got one good reason for being here."

"A bunch of us here don't go to church. I promised we'd help everybody," Will said, "even them you don't like. I don't go to church either, Ben."

"If you did, you'd be a better judge of people. Why you fighting his battle?"

"Because you want me to run a man you don't like away from my place. Christomighty, Ben!" Never had Will fought a stronger urge to rail at Ben for his outspoken, quick condemnation of character. "You know so much about his habits. Tell him, pour out your lightning, Bentlow, or leave."

"Tell him your confounded self." Ben's cryptic voice dripped with mockery. "Don't baby me if you ain't got the stomach to run off a skunk. All of us—well, most of us know. Bentlow hangs with them trashy kind of white folks that creates so much trouble for us colored."

"You know for a fact, he runs with the Gap Gang? Somebody's seen him?"

"Words spread, the mess follows the man. He's here fingering somebody."

"Will?" Eliza, overhearing him and Ben, had excused herself from a group of women. "You and Ben getting a lot of attention. And you li'l boys go somewhere else and play," she said, rubbing one of the little fellows idolizing Will on his head, smacking another on his behind.

"All right, Eliza, I heard you. Where is Bentlow now, Ben?"

"Over there with his sockets glued on Ceelie. He was a minute..."

"Wait Ben," Will said. "He may be part of a bigger mess that's brewing, better leave him be." Running Bentlow off, Will reasoned, would be the same as warning him he'd better run away before they caught him.

"I know he is, but it don't matter now," Ben said. "He's sneaked off."

"We'll ah..." Ben and his quick-tempered judgement, it so infuriated Will that he lost his trend of thought. "Listen," he said, waving his hands as if shooing Ben away from him. "Fetch the apple-seeds to my cellar," Will said, quoting the code which meant tell the fellows, drop everything and hurry. He told Abe to stay outside, in sight of the others. He would explain later.

Standing at the bottom of the cellar steps, Will greeted each one entering the semi-dark and dank basement with a solemn nod, as if he hadn't seen them earlier. He hastily explained the argument between him and Ben, then reminded the alliance that whatever the agreed action, it would bind each one equally responsible. He told them he expected slave runners would attack and snatch anyone they could grab. The trapper was after Pink and Abe.

Pink twitched. "That bag of fleas don't know me." His voice was heavy and wavering.

"Let me finish, Pink," Will said. "He may be in cahoots with Bentlow."

"Will," Ben said, rolling his eyes in a gesture of agitation. "You keep acting like you don't want to believe me. Tell him Sam, Scott, John. Black folks shy away from Bentlow for good reason; he's a lowdown skunk, ugly black and dirty white all over."

Sam Hopkins, John Roberts and Harvey Scott nodded their heads, mumbling agreement with Ben.

"Okay Ben, we'll do it your way," Will said. He'd heard enough of Ben's questionable conviction. "You all say Bentlow's a nigger, we'll lynch him in a way that will look like the Gap Gang did it. That would be justice due him for looking like he's black, but is for sure, poor white trash. Now, who'll fit the rope around his neck, you Ben?"

Ben stared at Will quite pitifully. His eyes blinked. "So you making me the lying Judas, hunh? he said, raking his foot in the dirt floor.

"Well?" Will said, with a scornful twitch of his eyes.

"Hell no!" Hopkins roared, coming to the front beside Will. "Tar and feathering Bentlow, and roping him to a rail car'll be just as good as a killing."

"Nope," Will said. "Death to squealers, that's the rule. I say we team up and watch Bentlow. If he is a snitch, we do him in. If he ain't, we tar and feather him then sit him astride a blind mule."

"What the hell you trying to say, Parker?" Roberts asked.

"Either Bentlow is a nigger or he ain't. We got no business messing with him just because nigh every colored somebody thinks he snitches, or because he don't go to Mt. Zion."

"Well, er a," Roberts cleared his throat. "Now that you put it that way, it does make a heap more sense, at least to me."

The men began talking among themselves.

"Got to hand it to you, Will," Scott said, coming forth and shaking his leader's hand. "You come through shining again."

"Will," Pink said, "We ain't go'n do Bentlow up like them white boys do us if we was to catch him wrong?"

"They got nothing to do with us," Will said, urging them to cut the small talk.

With Will's insistence, they agreed to a nightly vigil of Bentlow's house, hoping to convince themselves he, though probably a tricky rascal, wouldn't stoop to the level of vermin that thrives only at the bottom of dung piles.

"Meeting's over," Will said abruptly. "Picnic too. Sun's going down. It'll be dark d'rectly." He walked in the yard, among the disgruntled folks, hastening and reminding each one to be ever alert. After Eliza went inside, and he, Pink and Abe were tidying up the yard, Will told Abe the mountain man asked specifically for him and Pink.

Fear glittered in Abe's eyes. "That's the damndest lie he could ever tell, and lying is the buzzard's game. I show up here one day more like a ghost than a man, and then I hear somebody call me Abe Johnson. That's how I come by my name. The old one I left on the plantation when I run away."

Will handed Abe a gun and gave him a reassuring squeeze around his shoulders.

"Be careful, Pink, walking home at night from Marsh Chamberlain's," he said, giving him a gun. "The devil and his mates probably know every step you take from here to there and back."

"Think they know about Hannah, too?"

Will sighed. "We best off thinking they do, than trying to believe they don't. Whyn't you get married? She can move here, be close by Eliza."

We plan on working awhile," Pink said. "She over there, me on the farm and in the store. We want to buy a little spread some day. 'Course with Eliza'a baby coming on... We'll talk on it some more."

"I'm going in," Abe said. Inside his room he sealed the shutters over both windows, even though he slept upstairs like the others.

Will went to bed full of remorse. Who could ever be so lowdown to turn slave runners loose on his own kind? The painful thought would not let him sleep. How could any man exposed to the harsh reality of slavery stoop so low? Worse, if their suspicions did ring true, and they killed Bentlow, the law would intervene, thus exposing other fugitives. The pangs of uncertainty, the perplexity of his reasoning, the inability to unequivocally rely on the strength of his conviction actually made him dizzy. No one to ask except himself, but he didn't know how to reach that little voice inside him that he'd heard earlier that day. He longed for the reassuring whisper, *you did good, Will.*

For days, Eliza braved the winds of Will's fretfulness, the short temper, the gruffness of speech without reason. Perhaps it was the coming child, she thought. Her stomach had swollen so and was hideously unshapely. He probably needed time to adjust; she wouldn't pressure him. By Wednesday evening at supper though, Will had become so unbearable that Eliza told him whatever was weighing so heavily on his mind made him look as if he would rip out her throat, He simply put on the face that she had come to know meant he wouldn't discuss it.

"Come to prayer meeting with me this evening, Will," she blurted out. "You too, Pink." She doubted Abe would go except for the reason that he wouldn't stay home alone. He still needed plenty milk, beans, cornbread, ham, greens, and sleep.

Pink rubbed his nose. "I ain't quite ready," he said, excusing himself.

"Nope," Will said. "Maybe some day, could be soon. But not this evening."

"Oh, I done heard all your reasons," Eliza said, while preparing to leave. "You got so much threshing to do for old man Whitson. So much farming to do here, so much to do over there..."

A knock on the door interrupted her. Hannah called out, telling Eliza that Libit, Ben, and guess who, Zeke with his brother were in the wagon waiting. They were going to prayer meeting at Mt. Zion AME.

"If I ain't here when you come back," Will said, "go on home with Hannah 'n them. Don't stay here by yourself. "I'll come get you."

Eliza hesitated, wanting to ask why Abe wouldn't be there. But Lordy, Will's deepening scowl. She raised her hands as if exasperated and left.

Will stood in the doorway watching until they were out of ear-shot. "Abe," he yelled up the stairs. "Get dressed and come down. Hurry-up."

"Pink!"

"Yeah. Out back here, Will, having a smoke."

"We got to talk."

When Abe finally took his seat at the table, Will told them Sam Hopkins and Roberts had seen five white men leaving Bentlow's place the other night. Strange, or maybe not so strange, Will said, one of them was Bill Baer from the Gap Tavern. Baer was a definite indication that Bentlow was involved in stealing free persons and fingering fugitives. Through all this, Abe sat there half-asleep.

"Wake up Abe, it could be a long night. If you got a mind to sleep, better know, you could wake up back down yonder in the lion's jaws."

"Abe ain't trifling," Pink said. "Man who sleeps a lot, Will, is plain worn down or done give up. Either way, trifling don't fit him."

Will saw the immediate look of concern in Abe's face he hoped to arouse. "I know he still can't get around too good, Pink, but danger is amongst us. I'm beside him, but Abe's got to stand for hisself. I can't talk anymore about it unless you, Abe, swear to keep your mouth shut, and run with us tonight."

"I'm ready to go," Abe said.

"Pink, step outside for a minute," Will said. He swore Abe to the oath of allegiance, emphasizing the declaration of death for divulging any matter of consequence to the welfare of black people of Christiana, who had only those seven determined men for their security, their only semblance of equal justice.

"Tonight, we visit Tom Bentlow," Will said, calling Pink back to the table. "He likes his friends to come calling after dark."

Will, Abe, and Pink talked on, chewing the fat, Will called it, while waiting for certain members of his guard. Zeke's strange way of explaining himself made it especially hard for Will to describe why Zeke wouldn't humiliate himself by swearing to be faithful. No question about what he would do to a weasel with that scythe, but his unpredictable temper made him less liable to reason before acting. Loyal comrade that Ben was, and though he hated Bentlow, Will doubted he could stomach the brutality involved in meting out justified dues to a traitor.

When the others arrived—Hopkins, Scott, Roberts—and had gathered around the kitchen table, Will reminded them, the secret alliance was dedicated to protection by any means, hanging included. Will listened carefully to Hopkins' concern. Quite possibly the Gap Gang knew or accused Bentlow of being a fugitive, and the only way he could keep himself out of the cotton country was to squeal or maybe even lie. Smuggle him to Canada. Will agreed, lynching was tough, but necessary to discourage betrayal. Anyone they knew or didn't know who stooped so low to reveal or identify any black person, fugitive or free, to anybody, even under the threat of intimidation, deserved death. So, under the cloak of night six fugitives, not one legally a free man, set out for a hanging, though it seemed they forgot the executioner's tool. None of them had the rope.

A harvest moon, its full, pale face partially obscured by clouds, looked down at them moving in a double column through the woods on Zion Hill, behind the church. The wailing intonation of an old man praying for God's mercy, the chanting of the others' response to his pleading, seemed to lift and move in the night air like a warm, humid breeze foretelling a storm. The guard slackened its pace, despite Will's trying to hasten them beyond earshot of the emotional lamenting.

"Whooee," Pink said, with a quaking voice, "damned if he ain't puking his guts. Jesus, he gives me the creeps."

"Probably got nothing to live for," Hopkins said.

"He's just tired. Plain tired," Roberts said, "and aching from the misery." He laughed but none of the others did.

"He's too old to fight back, got nobody to protect him," Will said, hoping he would entice them to reject the old man's emotional grip, though he felt it too, dragging him into the morass of the old man's helpless state of mind.

A cloud crossing over the moon colored it ox-blood. All of them stared. Anxiety swept over Will. Was it a warning of doom; a precursor to what lay waiting for them sent by the old man begging to whoever was responsible for the lowly dreg of himself?

"Think he's about to roll a seven?" Scott said.

"He's too old to work," Will said, "ain't no more white man to look after him. He's got nobody except us."

At that very moment the cloud faded, revealing a brilliant orange moon.

"Let him go on home to glory, Will," Hopkins said.

"Damned right." The mumbled chant passed from man to man.

"He wants us to raise our guns if we must and make good our aims," Will said, "to protect our elders, our women and children. Control our community, weed out the unfit, silence bloodsuckers like Bentlow, if for sure he is one. If we must die, make his cause ours, and when the old man flies away to glory, he can look down at us from the moon and smile. He wants us to get on about our business."

"Take me to the nigger," Abe said, as if Will had suddenly unlocked his conscience.

"Let's find out first," Will said, "if he is one."

Their laughter at Abe drowned Will's words. First a snicker, then it spread until Will cautioned them again about the secrecy of their mission.

Chapter Eighteen

From afar in the eerie moonlight, Bentlow's home, a dirty, gray squat frame house with a high pitched roof extending down over tightly shuttered windows, resembled a gremlin's castle. It looked as if he had left in a hurry some tine ago, and the empty abode was sinking in high weeds. Will's eyes swept the wooded terrain of night shadows and settled on an oak that resembled trees in old graveyards. Its bent trunk and odd shaped branches looked as if folks interred over the course of years had entwined around its roots, drawn to it for life everlasting, thus guiding its branches in the direction they lay rotting into creation. But this wasn't a cemetery. Driven by an unrelenting curiosity, he and Abe went to explore while the others waited in the shadows.

Will circled the ground under the oak, stepping on what he soon realized were wood planks recessed in the ground and concealed by thick, tall grass. "Abe," he said in a hushed tone, "I got something." Will knelt and began prying with his fingers. The lid moved fairly easily. Close inspection revealed a hole big enough for a man his size to fit through.

"Abe, run'n tell Hopkins to bang his fist against the door when I whistle. I'll wait 'til you come back."

When Abe returned, Will fixed his fingers against his puckered lips and teeth, then let go a shrill, high-pitched tone. Hopkins sudden, hard jar against the door shook the house. Someone inside screamed. It sounded like the cracking voice of a young boy passing into manhood. Hopkins put his big foot to the door. It didn't budge. Then he, Roberts and Pink, at least six hundred pounds of agitated masculinity surged against and bounced off the door until the wood splintered and let go. Light from a lantern spread across the yard, Will saw Scott with his trusty bird gun trained on the entrance.

"A boy's in here, all bound up," Hopkins yelled.

"Abe," Will whispered, "run! Tell'em I'll be there d'rectly."

The planks moved. Bentlow, crawling and huffing and cussing, rushed from his escape chute into Will's arms.

"That's you all right, a lanky, ugly one," Will said, hugging him like a wet sheet wrapping around a clothes-line pole on a blustery day.

Bentlow went limp, his dilated pupils fixated in shock. "Wait, Will Parker, I got some money. Don't hurt me none. Lemme git it out ma' pocket."

Will hit him. A crushing blow to the face lifted Bentlow off his feet, hurling him sideways to the earth. A murky river rushed upon him, its swirl carrying him down to its dark bottom, but Will wouldn't let him sink. He snatched Bentlow to his feet, slapping him repeatedly until his unfocused eyes opened. Bentlow's head rolled about as if his neck had broken.

"I wish you was a cat so I could break ya' neck nine damned times," Will said. "But you ain't and we didn't bring a rope, so we go'n pull you apart like you is a hundred feathers in a chicken's behind. Get along."

Will pressed the barrel of his pistol to Bentlow's head and shoved him in the direction of the house. The others, hearing the commotion, came stampeding with the boy in tow.

Bentlow stepped back into Will. "They made me do it, Mr. Parker."

Pink, growling like a bear, walloped Bentlow. The lick drove him backwards into the kitchen across a table, caving it in. He lay sprawled on the floor. Hell bent on killing, Pink, Scott, and Roberts jumped him.

"Back off!" Will commanded, wedging himself between bloodied Bentlow and the assailants. "He's got some talking to do. Give it to me straight," Will yelled. "Who paid you to steal that boy?"

"They made me do it, Bill Baer'n them from Gap Tavern."

Pink, Scott and Roberts were on Bentlow again.

"Mr. Parker, please!"

Will acted as if he didn't hear Bentlow, though the pitiful pleading in his raspy, stuttering voice so vexed Will that he considered shooting him.

"They ought'n do him in so bad," Hopkins said. "Ganging up is bad luck."

Hopkins' and Abe's staring scornfully at Will made him feel worse. He snatched a coal-oil lantern from a window sill and threw it against the wall. Splattering kerosene ignited. It burst into a roaring fire of blue, red and yellow flames, engulfing the kitchen. The defenders retreated beyond the periphery of the lighted night, leaving screaming Bentlow to fend for himself in the blazing inferno that licked the trees and burned with a ferociousness fanned by winds from hell.

"I don't feel good about this," Hopkins said, "man-handling a weakling."

"No need for you feel thataway," Will said. "Ain't no man, even one soaked with guilt, crippled or crazy, without sense enough to run from fire. How'd that boy get here?"

"You mean that's all you go'n do or say about Bentlow?"

"What else, Sam? No need'a watching for him at his cubby-hole. If he ain't out by now, God have mercy on'em. How'd that boy get here?"

Will and Hopkins simply stared at each other until Hopkins said, "I don't really know. He told me he's fifteen but I think he's lying some. Bit his lip and went to scratching his foot in the dirt when I asked him how he come by Bentlow's place."

Will eyed the lad pensively. He was about five-foot nine, sinewy, with a face full of pimples. He'd be worth a healthy dollar on the slave market. Swiftly, like a cougar snatching an unsuspecting rabbit, Will clamped his hands around the lad's neck, yanking him off his feet. He put the trembling boy's face so close to his their noses rubbed. Will scowled.

"You smell worse 'n a dead coon in a rotten corn crib. You been drinking liquor?"

The boy couldn't speak. Will felt him trying to shake his head yes.

"What did Bentlow promise you?" Will put the boy down, and relaxed the hold on his neck.

"He, he say we'd get drunk and a, he say we'd lay with some era ah."

"Some what? Don't lie to me, boy!"

"He say some whoahs."

"And you, dunce," Will said, "come'a running?"

"A ah..."

"Hurry-up, don't be thinking up a story!"

"Yessuh, I did."

Roberts put his fat hand across his mouth and snickered, He hunched Scott, who looked away from Roberts, rolling his eyes at the sky. Will stared, musing on a private memory with Tawney, wondering whether to hit the boy for being so gullible or wrap his protective arms around the lad.

"Damn, Will," Pink said. "S'pect I woulda' too. Human is human."

"Ain't it the truth," Abe said.

"We oughta' take him home, Will," Hopkins said. "Where you from, boy?"

"Home can't hold him," Will said. "His sap's rising. Slave runners done baited him. Best we can do is drop him by Rev'm Clarkson. Maybe he can knot up the fool's nature long enough to teach him some common sense. If you don't mind, Hopkins, I'll ask you to do that."

The ensuing days were tumultuous for Will. He worked like a mad man during the day. At night he hardly slept; Eliza peeved with him, worrying about the boy, fighting images of the fire too vivid to cast aside as dreams. Bentlow's screams echoing in the quiet night haunted him. In the turmoil of his imagination, Will was the mountain man with Groit the slave runner, and Bob Wallace the black slave foreman from Roedown in the blazing hell rescuing Bentlow. The four of them were inside a pig's bladder, rising with fire and smoke, gliding over the Pennsylvania hills to Maryland. Hot sparks from exploding pine cones pierced the bladder. They tumbled toward the snarling, cavernous mouth of the lion, just short of entry Will snapped out of the nightmare. Had God sent him a warning? In whom could he confide wise enough to interpret it? Doc Dingee had warned Will of the grave danger in killing, but he was as distant as last winter's snowstorm. Rev. Clarkson? Hell no.

He would work harder at forgetting. Most black folks suspected Bentlow was a traitor and had fallen prey to his own vicious business. Most white folks didn't give the incident much thought one way or the other. Yet, the sleepless nights continued. Will became so unbearable that Eliza threatened to leave. She would live with her mother, thus revealing a secret she had sworn to keep about the old woman walking from Eastern shore Maryland to Lancaster County in search of her daughters.

Too worn to work, too old to bear profit for her master, he threw her off the plantation. She walked until she found Eliza and Hannah in Christiana. How she found them, nobody knows. Only Eliza and Hannah knew she lived in an earthen hut that no one could find unless they had been taken there.

Will's wife though, living in the ground? Never.

The following Sunday, Eliza came home moved by the holy spirit to ecstatic heights. She found Will in the back yard and began telling him about Rev. Clarkson's sermon. Will, half listening, continued preparing for the afternoon social until she said the Reverend asked if her husband would attend his child's baptism—the cleansing of its soul, the establishment of an identity with God.

"Clarkson talks too damned much."

"Will!"

"Will what!"

Eliza's scathing eyes filled with tears.

"All right," he said, looking at the ground. "I feel bad about yelling, but why do our baby need its soul cleaned? It can't be dirty."

"I didn't understand him to mean its soul would be dirty," Eliza said.

"Is that dipperful of creek water supposed to rub the skin off our baby so it won't be black and carry the mark of a slave?"

"Aw naw, honey. It's more to it than that. If something was to happen it'd be saved."

"Saved from hell, hunh? When it come's here kicking and squealing, pouring water on its head won't save it from a soul snatcher. God'a mighty, woman, ain't no worser hell than that."

"I don't think he meant much by saying it. He ain't seen you in such a long time and everybody's talking so about how they ain't so scared now."

Now that Eliza was so enraptured by the Reverend's spiritual guidance, how could he tell her Rev. Clarkson had shackled him with a formidable challenge? Him with his overpowering words, making Will feel so small, so unworthy of his manhood, while good men, black and white, praised him for his courageous leadership. Yet, repulsive as Rev. Clarkson seemed to Will, he wouldn't deny Eliza the benefit of spiritual support that would neutralize the brain washing of self-uselessness the old slave master's preacher had infused. But wait, was the Reverend indeed doing that? Or was he undermining Will, forcing Eliza to view her husband with the same incriminating eye as the Reverend's? Supposing Will just grabbed his knapsack and left town, he and Eliza. Everyone would be left helplessly alone, fending for themselves. How safe would he and his family be? Where could he go with Eliza in her condition?

Will went to bed full of remorse and suffered another rugged, sleepless night. At daybreak, Eliza was sitting up in bed, staring at him. He needed a drink of water, cool fresh water from the deep well. In his haste to avoid any discussion that involved the Reverend, he slipped on his bib overalls, pulling one strap over a shoulder and absent-mindedly grabbed a mason jar instead of his regular metal cup. He went downstairs and outside to the pump. God, the water felt good in his mouth. He spit out a mouthful, then drank heartily. His stomach gurgled satisfaction. For really no reason, he shook the half-filled jar, watching tiny, fascinating bubbles form. When the water settled and the bubbles disappeared, he saw himself in the jar sitting on a pile of charred fire-wood worrying, that deepening furrow etched across his forehead.

What would happen when his guard was forced to turn back an army of slavers with Gap Tavern rogues and bounty hunters? What would happen if he or if both he and Eliza were killed? Who could he trust to wrap his protective arm around their baby, find a good home for it? Would that person make the child understand that it must avenge its parents' deaths, that it must die before yielding to slavery, that it must wear its citizenship proudly for being born in a free state, that it must raise Will's grandchildren in a manner beneficial to future generations?

Eliza, sitting on a back doorstep, broke his trance. "If you going to the field this morning, better make haste instead of all the time day dreaming. You do that so much nowadays."

"I'm going see Rev'm Clarkson."

"What did you say?"

"You heard me right."

"What come chasing you last night?" She waved her hand. "But God will be pleased. Need to slick down your hair a little though, and put on some fresh clothes."

"Ain't going over there to be nice, Eliza."

"Will? Please? C'mon and get dressed while I fix a little breakfast. It'll smooth out that rough edge in your voice, Sugar."

"Sugar? All of a sudden I'm sugar," he said coming into the kitchen, "because I'm going...?"

"That's what I feel all the time inside, Will. I pray Rev'm Clarkson can help rid you of what's eating us up."

Deep in the heart of himself, Will too hoped the Reverend could help relieve him of the burden and guilt strapping him: burden of being something less than a leader of his people, burden of wondering if he was capable of giving his child eternal love, burden of guilt for whatever happened to Bentlow. After dressing and eating breakfast, he attempted to brush past Eliza standing in the doorway.

"Will," she said, placing his hands on her swollen stomach. "Better hurry back."

"Be back d'rectly." He left, holding his hands together as if retaining the feel of the baby's kick in his palm.

Nearing the top of Zion Hill, from a distance he saw the Reverend and Mrs. Clarkson working a flower garden. Getting closer, he could hear them—her voice a warbling contralto, his a soft baritone—harmonizing a song about a deep river, a peaceful song he vaguely remembered from some incident a long time ago. But he was in no mood to think on it.

Mrs. Clarkson smiled and sang a polite, "Good morning." Then she went to the house.

Rev. Clarkson came to meet Will. "Warming sun and early morning air of flowers better for my bones than snake oils and voodoo folks all batched together," he said with a wide smile that he quickly wiped off his face. "Your load is heavy, son," the Reverend said.

Rancor so contorted Will's face, he actually looked wild. "Your dickty words and crazy ideas about baptizing got Eliza all upset," Will blurted. "That's my load, all because of you."

"Saving your child from eternal damnation is but one way of loving it, Will." The Reverend stopped abruptly. He felt so sad. The moment Eliza delivered her baby, love would assert itself in her. Providence wouldn't be that kind to Will. Enwrapped in defensive bitterness, Will needed strong, subtle persuasion to make him capable of sustaining love to Eliza and the baby. Somehow the Reverend must impress it upon Will without further mystifying and antagonizing him.

"Well," Will demanded. "I'm listening."

"Why work these people up into an uprising? This is a free state."

"FREE!"

"I'm standing right beside you. Ain't a thing wrong with my hearing."

"You can't really believe that stuff you trying to sell Eliza?"

"It could be worse," the Reverend said. "We don't know bloodshed, blood turning the ground ugly red like when it's spilled on the battlefield."

"If blood is spilled it'll be from them who won't leave us be. If I'm killed, one of the guard will step in my place. We can't lose."

Though Rev. Clarkson knew Will couldn't envision the magnitude of the challenge that was bound to confront him, for certain the Reverend had underestimated Will. He was tough, dangerous and more charismatic than the Reverend; quite valuable if he could be tamed enough to envision himself a leader. Stop arguing with him, the Reverend decided. Tell Will a story, an intriguing tale that would immediately grab his imagination.

"I've been a witness to killing, Brother Parker, black against black, black against white, white against white. Sit a spell, if you've a mind to."

"Long enough," Will said, "for you to tell me what a story's got to do with baptizing Eliza's baby. I got me a day's work to do."

Rev. Clarkson gritted his teeth and rubbed his fist across his lips. The mean rascal certainly gave him no quarter. "Years before you were born," he said, leading Will to the back porch, "I fought the British in the Battle of New Orleans with General Andrew Jackson. December 18, 1812, I remember it all too well. *'To the free colored inhabitants of Louisiana.'* Gen. Jackson rode into town reading us black men a proclamation. It was an invitation no sensible free black man in a slave state would refuse.

"We were some proud men that day. *'As sons of freedom,'* the general said, *'you are called upon to defend your most estimable blessings. Your country looks with confidence to her adapted children. As fathers, husbands, brothers, you are summoned to rally around the standard of the Eagle.'*

"I joined up, hoping to get as much distance between me and slaves as possible. We fought Louisiana slaves who joined the British army on promises of freedom they never got. After the surrender, as many as could escaped with a black captain on a ship following the British running to Nova Scotia. The rest of them..." The reverend held his hands in front of himself in an act of exasperation.

Will watched him with somber curiosity.

"We were paid the same as the white soldiers, wore the same uniforms, ate the same food. But after the British scooted and the town settled down, the nasty crackers we had saved from destruction run us free black soldiers out of town. So I grabbed my money and headed North."

"Why'd you stop here?"

"One day in the war, my path ran across a black comrade singing a spiritual. His was a rough baritone voice that I knew wasn't southern. Funny, he kept singing the same lines over and over again. It moved me like I'd never been moved before in my life. I asked him how he come to know that strange music so well. That's how I come about the spirituals. He explained what it meant about black solidarity, how unity is transmitted from one to another through song."

Will listened on, his mind drifting over incidents in his life and settling again on the night his master went to the Baltimore waterfront and locked him in the slave compound. "So that's what the old lady was telling me," he said.

"Old lady?" the Reverend said, noticing an uncanny awareness in Will's eyes.

"Broken down slave woman serving food in jail, kept humming that song I heard you singing just now with your wife. But she sounded like a night owl hoot'n in a dark cellar. Just kept on droning until I paid her some attention."

"The life each one of us face in our day by day struggle," Rev. Clarkson said, "is expressed in the way we sing our best-loved spiritual. Deep River is one we like best. Probably, that woman's too. She was..."

212

"She kept me from acting like a hemmed-in bird, probably saved my life," Will said. "I don't know that I listened much. I must have some, I guess. But I don't sing them."

"What you mean is, you don't pay attention to them."

"Paying attention, singing, whatever, Rev'm. But that ain't why I come over here."

"I'm getting to that, Brother Parker." Rev. Clarkson leaned sideways, putting his face close to Will's and speaking in a whisper. "You only have to listen." He sat back in his chair.

"Most of the reading and writing I learned in my parish school came from studying the Bible. I was free, raised Catholic, and thought I would never be subjected to slavery, but I saw the truth. Real quick, I made fast my way to Philadelphia. Came by boat, looking for Rev'm Richard Allen and his church. The day I wandered into Mother Bethel, some rich freedman were there at a rally trying to entice Rev'm Allen to join their back to Africa movement. You should've heard them argue so eloquently, especially Paul Cuffee from somewhere near Boston. Even I was ready to sail. Then Rev'm Allen spoke. Actually, he was a bishop. His message was clear to everybody packed in the church. *We will never turn away from our enslaved brethren. Wherever fugitive slaves fellowship with us free men, we must change their despair to hope.* Before the rally ended, he organized the Free African Society. Bishop Allen taught me to preach. His dying will entrusted me with that commitment. Mine and every minister in the AME conference."

"Whyn'd you talk like this before, instead of using them great-big words to tell me things you knew I didn't understand, like saying slaves got to blame theyselves for being slaves?"

Rev. Clarkson smiled, his eyes sparkling with approval even though Will still glared down on him. Finally, he'd gotten through to Will. The Reverend looked about, pondering his thoughts. "I don't recollect saying just that, but if that is what you heard, all right. Blaming yourself is taking responsibility for yourself away from any man who claims he owns you."

"Aww c'mon, Rev'm," Will said disgustedly. "Here we go again,"

"As long as a slave's got somebody, his master or the overseer to blame, he's got an excuse, a reason to fight that little fellow in his gut driving him to run, be damned what could happen."

"He stays because he's scared, Rev'm."

"Amen, Brother Parker, that is precisely why. But, for whatever reason that sent you high-tailing away from that plantation, leaving wrenched responsibility from your master and placed obligation for your life, good or bad, squarely on Will Parker's shoulders."

"But it can't happen like that."

"Like what?"

"Like waking up one morning and saying to hell with this shit'n scoot'n... Oops, s'cuse me, Rev'm."

Rev. Clarkson chuckled. He noticed Will trembling slightly. Beads of sweat formed on his nose. "Brother Parker, I questioned your insight on Jesus when you were here before, but left it hanging. I didn't want to make you any more angrier. But now you must know, the main thing that separates a slave from his master is the way each believes in Jesus."

Will drew his heavy brows together in a resentful expression.

"No, Brother Parker, don't treat me thataway."

"G'won," Will said, "let's hear it."

"A slave believes Jesus came to save the world from sin," Rev. Clarkson said. "Slavecrat knows Jesus came so he may have life and have it more abundantly. The first belief is despair, the second one is hope. The freedmen I heard at Mother Bethel believe as I do, hope and responsibility together is our way of life. Join the church, Brother Parker. Help me keep our folks in it, spread solidarity, bring me the fugitives. As a husband, father, leader, you must shoulder the obligation of all three."

Will began shaking his head and looking at the ground. He raised and lowered his hands rapidly, as if chopping wood with the edges. "Rev'm, I done told you before..."

"I'm sorry," Rev. Clarkson said, anticipating that Will might snarl and bare his fangs. "You've grown, I can tell. Last time we talked, I said that... Well, really I see no need to talk about it."

"I remember," Will said, slumping in the chair. "But a safe place, free from slavers where we can live together, laugh a little, work a lot, make our children grow up smart seems so far away."

"That is your sense of direction, Will?" the Reverend said, trying not to appear astonished. "Not what you call protection? Not fighting, though it may be necessary at times? Good, decent white folks can understand that. They do it all the time. Sing the spirituals with your mother, Brother Parker."

"Don't remember her singing them, she died so long ago."

"Father, grandfather, grandmother?"

"Grandmom Rosey's dead too."

"Doesn't matter, Will. When all is quiet tonight, hum along with her. The spirituals will make you listen to yourself thinking. They'll make you believe what you sing, sing what you feel."

A shallow smile spread across Will's face. Though he tried not to reveal it, the Reverend's years of reading body language assured him that Will had touched a place deep within himself.

"Well," Rev. Clarkson said, "now that your lamp is lit. Mt. Zion needs a good class leader. By the way, the boy Brother Hopkins brung by here is safely wrapped in the bosom of Mother Bethel."

"Uh-oh." Will stood quickly facing the direction of his home like a Labrador Retriever hearing something in the wind beckoning him. "Best I can say right now is I'll give it plenty thought, after I find out what it is." He shook the Reverend's hand, excusing himself rather abruptly, blaming Eliza's condition for his hasty departure. He ran through the woods, remembering his promise to hurry back. Running downhill due west, bypassing Christiana Village, he made good time. From Long Lane, he saw Abe at the fence waving frantically and sliding his hands down from his stomach as if dropping it. Will leaped the fence, and taking quick strides past his laughing comrade, he bound up the stairs to Eliza, surrounded by two women, one of then holding a squalling baby girl.

"Will, you were gone so long," she said.

"Aww," Will said, looking about nervously. "We talked so on this'n that, about a whole bunch'a things. He made me a class leader but I don't a bit more know what he's talking about than she do." He pointed to his daughter.

Eliza clasped his hands. The smile he hadn't seen for a spell caressed her face.

Will became class leader. Every member of his band for self protection and Zeke joined Mt. Zion AME. Most fugitives settling in the area hastily affiliated themselves with the church. Will and daughter Mariah, born in 1846, were baptized together. While time passed, Sunday's crowds continued gathering in their yard. He and his men became more daring in the act of protecting their loved ones, and defying local marauding gangs and slavers who challenged them. Will's name followed his deeds the length and breadth of Lancaster and Chester Counties to Philadelphia and beyond. Yet, the capture of fugitives and stealing of free black persons continued. Slavers, becoming more angry with Will Parker and his ilk, pressed the U.S. Congress for more stringent legislation. Local justices of the peace and magistrates became more irritated with the entire matter of slavery. Then Congress passed the revised Fugitive Slave Law of September, 1850.

Chapter Nineteen

Edward Gorsuch, wealthy planter from Harford County, Maryland, stepped from the Philadelphia-Wilmington-Baltimore train at the Market Street Station in Quaker City and froze his gaze on a sparkling carriage drawn by two groomed, lively horses. He tipped a black Mississippi gambler's hat back on his round, keen head and read the bold-face advertisement, **MINTON CATERERS**, spread in a half-circle on both sides of the carriage. A caption, *Henry Minton, Prop.* was painted in small print on the lower right side.

"Morning, Mr. Minton," Lum Applebee called across the cobblestone intersection of Market Street at Eleventh to a copper-tone man loading produce from a rail car into his carriage. Lum, a wiry black chimney sweep in a top hat and frock coat, waved with an assortment of long and short handle brushes in his hands.

"A fine morning it is indeed," Minton said, his voice a rich baritone. "Wouldn't you agree, Mr. Applebee?"

Gorsuch shook his head in disgust. He, a tall fine-boned grandson of one of the original Baltimore founding families, hated Quaker City. It, like Boston and Cambridge, was an insult to America's fine, aristocratic heritage—harboring fugitive niggers and treating free Negroes like white men. How could these Pennsylvania Quakers, claiming to be his Christian brothers, and those self-righteous, pious Yankee Puritans justify such flagrant obstructions of justice? If his grandparents had not willed that he attend the venerable school, never would he have undertaken his studies at Harvard.

He scanned the train depot yard for fugitive slaves among the cluster of Irish, German, Black and Chinese railroad laborers, testing his claim that in one eye-sweep he could distinguish a fugitive from a free laborer. Some Black men stared back in response to his condescending gaze. A few looked away or at the ground. They were fugitives, of that he would swear. In eye contact truth was revealed, though none of them belonged to him.

For certain, his runaways—four ungrateful, foolish boys whom he promised to emancipate in a few years—were in Lancaster County, where the increasing threat emerging from contraband renegades had worn thin the fabric of a genteel and chivalrous southern society. White men were known and respected by their acts—imaginative men ruled, owned land, paid taxes. Unimaginative men were ruled, owned nothing, paid with their labor for the right to tramp upon this good earth. White men were created equal. Why did some act like blooming idiots when all white men's privileges were sanctioned by God and government? That confirmation willed them inestimable rights.

Idiots like Pennsylvania Governor William F. Johnson. Imagine him, a Whig too, having the grit to demand the gentleman governor of Maryland extradite a slave master convicted in a free state court of stealing a free Negro. A generous tax-payer like him, owning a huge parcel of acreage in Pennsylvania's Lancaster County, deserved an apology from Johnson for his witless conduct. Johnson's ungodly behavior further poisoned the minds of renegade niggers.

Gorsuch made his steadfast way into the rush of big city activity around the station; the clop-clop of horses' shoes resounding against the cobblestones, the gaiety of travelers in an omnibus a prancing team pulled from the station. Mercantile stores and manufacturing outlets in block long rows of single room three story brick and wood buildings lined both sides of Market Street—McAllister Hardware, Coulter-Importer of Fancy Baskets, Joseph Feinour's tin copper brass & iron House, the Stove Store. Sidewalks were cluttered with people stopping abruptly in front of Gorsuch, fingering the merchandise, bartering with the proprietors. Overburdened bay horses, their heads bent low and bobbing up then down with their loping gaits, pulled two-wheel drays laden with barrels of molasses, pitch, nails and who knows what. A big Irish cop standing at Market and Tenth Streets, twiddling a night stick in his hands entwined behind his back, observed the throng. In old English accented by country brogue, he gave Gorsuch directions to Slave Commissioner Edward D. Ingraham's office.

Lum the chimney sweep, hustled past Gorsuch, singing a merry solo about the fine art of chasing soot. Despite the irritation of being jostled along on a street crowded with foreigners, the Harford County planter did manage to chuckle at Lum's nonsense. Before boarding a Watson's Gazelle livery coach, Gorsuch bought two bite-size lemon pies from a noisy hawker to sweeten his breath and cool the burning in his throat. Black, grimy coal smoke had poured from the train's boiler.

Lum knew the tell-tale signs. His heart, pumping blood faster and faster, warned him. This well-dressed man with a granite, arrogant face, would pay for fugitives or buy stolen black folks. He meandered along some distance behind Gorsuch, then hurried back and climbed into Mr. Minton's coach. They followed Gorsuch down Market Street, seemingly oblivious to everything around him.

One dominant, irritating thought commanded Gorsuch's attention. He took a letter from his coat pocket and read it again, line by line.

Lancaster County, Aug. 1851

Respected friend, I have the required information of four men that are within two miles of each other. Now, the best way is for you to come as a hunter, disguised about two days ahead of your son and let him come by way of Philadelphia and get the marshal John Nagle, I think is his name. Tell him the situation and he can get force of the right kind. It will take about 12 so that they can divide and take them all within half an hour. Now if you can come on the 2nd or 3rd of September come on and I will meet you at the gap. When you get there inquire for Benjamin Clay's tavern. Let yourn son and the marshal get out Kinyer's hotel. Now if you cannot come at the time spoken of, write very soon and let me know when you can come. I wish you to cone as soon as you possibly can.

Very respectfully thy friend,
Wm. M. Padgett

Gorsuch was grateful for friends like Padgett, whom he didn't know. Though it seemed Padgett wrote without the benefit of a gentlemen's education, Gorsuch respected him for his bravery and would adequately compensate him.

The livery coach stopped at Head House Square, Second and Spruce Streets. A mahogany shingle with the title, U.S. Fugitive Slave Commissioner burned in it hung suspended from a clapboard front, swaying in a humid, late summer breeze coming off the nearby Delaware River. **We enforce the United States Government's Laws.** Gorsuch read the sign in a colonial window. This would be Commissioner Ingraham's office.

Ingraham, a big Englishman with green sleepy eyes, fat cheeks and a prominent forehead, sat in a high-back cushioned chair behind a huge oak desk. He wore his thick, auburn hair long and parted on the left side. Behind a pot bellied stove in a far corner, a sterling silver tea set waited on a small corner table. He's the manner of man I'm seeking, Gorsuch thought, standing in the open doorway.

Ingraham gave Gorsuch a moment to ponder. "Yes sir," he said, "you're in the right place." From Gorsuch's tight-lipped pomposity and dress, Ingraham presumed him a southern gentleman, an angry slave master. "Chair's comfortable, coffee's hot or we'll make tea if you prefer," he said to Gorsuch, closing the door behind him.

After Gorsuch had gone into Ingraham's office, Lum alighted from Minton's carriage some distance behind and hurried across the street to Leroy Henry.

"Ice man, ice man," Leroy hollered. Short, dark and muscular, Leroy drove his ice tongs into a square of ice that had been cut from the Delaware River during the past winter and kept in a thick, wooden ice house beneath the ground. Leroy threw a cool wet burlap sack over the square and hoisted it to his shoulder.

"What sayee, Lum?" Leroy said, tarrying a minute, but not looking at his friend.

"I believe a slave runner's in the commissioner's office," Lum said.

Leroy hustled on, nodding his head, the ice dripping cold water between his shirt collar and neck.

Since Ingraham had been appointed to the special commission for rigid enforcement of the revitalized fugitive slave law, catching fugitives had become one of the Quaker City's thriving enterprises. Having authority to deputize U.S. marshals provided him a vested interest few others had in the business. Gorsuch changed his mind about liking Ingraham. He had difficulty confiding in a man who talked too fast, particularly out of a crook in his mouth. Ingraham's head even tilted in the direction of the curled, upturned lips of his high-sided mouth. Yet, his reputation for apprehending fugitives, known from Wilmington to the Rio Grandé of Texas, from Baltimore to Baton Rouge stood unchallenged.

"Just arrive," Ingraham asked, "or did you spend the night in our fair city?"

"Your city is a haven for indigents, for fugitives from work. And it's a mockery to all great men truly dedicated to molding this mighty nation of ours into the greatest the world will ever know. I certainly did not spend the night here."

"Oh," Ingraham said, faking concern. "Then Philadelphia is not a city of brotherly love?" Listening to slave masters' angry complaints had become second nature to him, a matter of routine-sympathizing, agreeing, assigning a marshal, deputizing a posse. It supplemented his law practice, helped pay for his recently acquired home beside the Schuylkill where he and his wife relished their evenings with the sun's reflection on the still water, day-dreaming of the estate across the river they would eventually own in the wooded countryside. If it meant arresting every fugitive hiding in Quaker City, he'd do just that.

After he poured Gorsuch some coffee and invited him to a comfortable chair, Ingraham sat at his desk and placed several forms in front of him. He dipped his quill in ink then placed his writing hand on a form and looked at Gorsuch in a patronizing manner that further angered him.

"Ice man, ice man," Leroy called out, opening the rear door of Ingraham's office.

Ingraham didn't acknowledge Leroy. "I take it you're hunting runaways, Mister ah, whoever?"

"Edward Gorsuch. Yes, five of them."

The ice Leroy was fitting into the ice box almost slipped from his hands. Quickly though, he regained his balance, making enough noise to satisfy Ingraham that he wasn't listening. That Leroy was a fugitive was a well-kept and old secret even his Philadelphia born wife didn't know.

"My word," Ingraham said, "that could be bloody expensive. I do understand your resentment, Mr. Gorsuch."

"I know four of them are in Lancaster County," Gorsuch said. "But I'm forced by your sleazy state law to get warrants, then pay a marshal for serving them."

"Unfortunately, this is not a slave state. If you take matters into your own hands you might get hurt. I suggest at least two marshals just in case one or two of your nigras might need a little whittling."

"I doubt my boys would ever get that uppiddy."

"Ah, Mr. Ingraham," Leroy called out. "I 'spect you be needing another twenty-five pounds tomorra' too. These hot September afternoons, most of yestiddy's done melted."

"Excuse me, Mr. Gorsuch," Ingraham said, turning his head towards the rear. "God, boy," he snarled. "Do what needs be and be quiet."

"Yes sir, yes sir, soon's I drag the pan from under the ice box and dump the old water."

Ingraham blew a lungful of air from his large chest. "Mr. Gorsuch, if you think I'm gouging you, any commissioner can issue warrants."

Gorsuch crossed his legs and gritted his teeth. "Quite frankly, I'd rather rely on Ebenezer Scrooge but he isn't licensed. Most of you commissioner fellows, your backbones aren't thick as a gnat's. I'll apologize to you, but that's how I generally feel."

The ends of Ingraham's lips turned downwards, nearly to the end of his jawbone. "Now see here, sir." He stood and blew his garlicky breath in Gorsuch's face.

"I need a strict man of honor," Gorsuch said, frowning and turning away from Ingraham. "A man of high ideals to handle a gentleman's business." He banged his fist on Ingraham's desk. "It's revolting enough that I must hire a bunch of foreigners to enforce what our government demands of these Pennsylvania abolitionist hypocrites. I'm from somewhat humble Quaker beginnings too, like some of them, but..."

Leroy closed the door firmly behind him, interrupting Gorsuch.

"Mister," Ingraham said. "Are you implying in your God high attitude that we are afraid of a bunch of armed niggers and half breed Indians?"

Gorsuch's eyes blazed then glowed. He sat on the edge of the chair, leaning forward, resting his arm on the desk. "Neegras and Indians armed? Insurrection right under your nose! You've not contacted the federal authorities? God, man, have you not heard of Nat Turner?"

"Nobody's complained except you." Ingraham caught himself yelling. "Pardon me, sir, for my seeming impatience at your presumptuous assertions. Biggest thing they've done is scare off a rustler or two caught stealing or beating nigras. The leader though, big strapping nigger named Will Parker, is pretty damned bold, I'm told."

"Ingraham, by God," Gorsuch said, springing from the chair. "No devil dealing, rum-soused nigger or the likes of one, a hundred, or a thousand will intimidate me." He began pacing the floor. "I'll go by myself, hand deliver my boys to a local magistrate over there."

Ingraham rubbed his hand across his fat chin. "That could be a costly mistake. I've got one of the best slave catchers around. Henry Kline, good man, afraid of nobody. I'll deputize Agan and Tully too."

"Certainly, send an army. Fine ole Englishman that you are wouldn't dare charge me by the pound. Isn't that right, dear Mr. Ingraham?"

Ingraham forced himself to laugh. "I must say, Mr. Gorsuch, even in your obvious anger, you do have an even tempered sense of humor. But I beg of you, don't try snatching what you presume is originally yours."

"I know exactly where my boys are, I know who they work for. A guide who's waiting..."

"You confuse me, sir," Ingraham said. "You've hired a guide so why doesn't he bring along a posse?"

"Because someone would warn every nigger in the area. What guarantee do I have that your boys can deliver?"

"Give me names, I'll issue warrants. Pay half now, the other half when we deliver. Kline will be on the first train out tomorrow morning. Where did you say they are?"

"I didn't, but they are in Christiana, thereabouts."

"All right, Mr. Kline will track them and stay over in the Penningtonville Tavern. I'll send Tully and Agan with you. Thursday morning Kline will rendezvous with you three."

"I'll ask you again. What guarantee do I have he can deliver?"

"Shackle the fugitives and bring them here. I'll hold court. You pay the remainder and take them home to Maryland. Their names?" Ingraham said, while rolling his impatient eyes at Gorsuch and twiddling the quill between his thumb and forefinger.

Gorsuch sighed and sat in the chair. "John Beard alias Nelson Ford, Alexander Scott, Jim Kite, Samuel Thompson."

"Thank you, sir. Consider the matter in capable hands."

Later that morning, while Sam Williams, innkeeper of the Bolivar House, poured ale and chewed the rag, as black men were prone to call commonplace matters, a hushed murmur suddenly spread throughout the tavern. The topic of their usual banter, big and full bearded, Henry H. Kline walked in. His thin mouth was set in a cynical twist. Under his coat Kline wore a gun. Though in a shoulder holster, it was a big pistol obvious at first glance to anyone looking. Several men at the bar and sitting at tables gulped their beverages and hastened on.

221

Kline bristled then swaggered with a slight limp across the room toward Williams. "Mornin' Sam," he said.

"Constable Kline," Williams replied. "What brings you over Sixth and Chestnut way?"

"Marshal Kline to you, Sam. United States marshal, permanent commission last week. I'm headed over Lancaster way. Gang of horse rustlers raising hell. Right now though, I'm looking for a couple colored boys who skipped out owing back rent. I got bench warrants and I aim to deliver."

Williams, wiry, rather tall, toffee complexioned and always wearing a starched shirt and bow tie, began wiping the bar with wide, circular energetic motions. "Do you see them here?" he said.

"Didn't grab anybody, did I?" Kline said, looking around the room. "A mug of ale, Sam." He took a long swig and wiped foam on the back of his hand. "It's bloody insulting. Every time I come in here, the damned place pretty near empties the hell out. Why? I ain't after them."

"United States marshal, aye," Williams said, running his hand over the few strands of long black hair hanging from his smooth head. "Is that got anything to do with the new fugitive slave law?"

"I can track'em anywhere in continental United States."

"There's your answer."

"Good, hard working free colored people got no cause to fear none."

"Fear?" Williams said. "Pull your chest in, Marshal. The sight of you sets them in a rage. Your face or your name alone, makes them mad enough to go outside and kick the shit out of the lamp post, if I must be so crude. They're family men, Kline. Need I say more?"

"Careful, Sam. You've got an insulting streak about you too. Okay?"

"Every time I pass that empty lot at Fourth and Pine," Williams said, "I still see flames licking the sky. I hear little kids and old women screaming and choking, and begging anyone listening to save them. I see timbers falling. I hear something like fire-crackers shooting off in all directions. I stood there that night listening until the last plea of God's mercy had quieted. All the while I'm watching the immigrants, most of them fresh off the boat, not one word of English among'em, standing back shaking hands, nodding their heads for a job well done. Why? Because the man who owned the California House had a white mother or father and took himself a white wife. Be careful? The unfortunate part of it is that none of the killers are worth going to the gallows. Do you hear me, Marshal?"

"C'mon Sam, any black man brave enough to run an inn smack dab in the middle of us establishment white folks and name it after a South American revolutionist, ain't afraid of taking on a few foreigners. Hell, Sam, you're next door to Dr. Jaynes' Arcade. That Bathhouse is the busiest place on all of Chestnut Street."

"You haven't heard a gawddamned word I've said, Marshal."

"I will enforce the law," Kline said, turning and limping away. "Be careful and don't forget it."

"I know the slave commissioner gave you a free ticket to do whatever you think is necessary," Williams said, to Kline's back.

As soon as Kline left, Williams ran the index finger and thumb of his hand across his forehead as if wiping sweat, and snapped them in the air as if slinging off perspiration. Lum got up from the table in a darkened corner and eased himself out the door. North on Water Street along the Delaware River waterfront, Lum with his brushes hustled along past the New Jersey Steamship Ferry Line and a maze of ships setting sail or anchoring, where slave runners caught fugitives or ambushed careless, unsuspecting black folks. On Dock Street he passed black men laboring with imports and exports, running errands, or lingering in concealed places, all casting their eyes about, ready to befriend solitary fugitives. North on Second, past the pickle houses and meat process plants and warehouses, then turning west at Popular Street, Lum crossed the tracks of Philadelphia's massive railroad network that surrounded and crisscrossed the Quaker City. Lawyers smoking and chatting idly with bounty hunters lingered there. Perchance some naive down-country railroad tramp unaware of the lucrative sporting game of tracking fugitives might jump from a slow moving freight train.

William Grant Still, president of the Vigilante Committee and clerk of the Pennsylvania Anti-Slavery Society, happened by the window when Lum crossed the street in front of the combination office at 31 North Fifth. Still waited until Lum knocked and announced his sweeping services before unlatching the door. Though Still was busy printing the latest edition of his semimonthly publication, he acknowledged the message that Sam Williams would be there within the hour. He urged Lum to summon grocer, William Whipper, then he shut down the press and sent a courier to notify James Forten and Robert Purvis. While waiting for the men to gather, Still prepared himself a cup of tea and sat for a moment of quiet reflection.

His parents, both former slaves, earned their freedom from moral disrespect by paving their way into the hearts of God fearing men. Still's father, Black Jim of the Pines, white folks in the New Jersey Pine Barrens called him, had been a root doctor. From as far back as Still could remember, his father had healed all sorts of ailments by prescribing sunshine and herbs mixed with mineral-rich Pine Barren water, water purified in a sand aquifer with rare plants that grew wild in the Medford, New Jersey woods. Black Jim's merciful deeds appealed to men who measured a man's worth by the light that shone forth from his soul. What stories Still could tell about his father restoring sight to the blind and removing lesions from patients doctors had abandoned!

223

Still was documenting his adult life in Philadelphia from the myriad tales that crossed his desk: black people disenfranchised by a revised state constitution, the State legislature retracting black men's right to vote, lucrative rewards and stiff penalties of the new fugitive slave law turning white men into bloodhounds, the vigilante committee he organized to fight Irish-Catholic dense hatred of black folk, the state legislature refusing to educate black children beyond elementary grades.

The patience and virtue that had guided Still's parents through a fairly decent life—farming, raising his brothers and sisters, and healing—would hardly suffice. He removed his apron and put away the cup. The vigilante committee would arrive soon.

William Whipper, a Sixth Street grocer, was busy tallying charges in his credit book for food a woman had ordered when Lum barged in. Lum, understanding the bitter disposition of the formerly prosperous lumber and coal dealer, got himself a bottle of sarsaparilla from the cooler and drank while waiting.

Whipper had fled Columbia several years ago, he told the young woman standing there listening patiently, after his entire enterprise along with his home on the banks of the Susquehanna River was torched and burned to ashes. Now the thickset, aging man suffering bouts of a lingering illness, lived in the New Market Ward, under the umbrella of Mother Bethel's community around Sixth and Pine Streets. Lum listened, just as he knew he must after the woman left, to Whipper blaming his misfortune on the multitudes of fugitives that wouldn't go to Canada. Yet, he still surrendered every moment he could spare to the Underground Railroad, the Vigilante Committee and the Anti-Slavery Society.

Whipper arrived at the society's headquarters before Still expected him. He quickly sat, staring at the wall, breathing heavily.

Sam Williams, a thrifty, sharp-tongued man with a towering sense of civic responsibility and community progress, came shortly after Whipper. His voice often trembled when speaking of the trend he foresaw in the rapid erosion of the limited guarantee of protection by state laws.

Still called the emergency conclave to order with five of the seven committee men present, including Minton the caterer, and Robert Purvis, wealthy entrepreneur and president of the Pennsylvania Anti-Slavery Society. They were the executive arm of a secret order of black men—artisians, teachers, ministers, brick layers, caterers, stevedores and hod carriers—working to unite men of color and link a protective shield around black enclaves from riotous Irish-Catholics.

"Sam," Still said, "you sent the courier."

"Yes," Williams said, clearing his throat. "I'll get right to the point. Our kind, gracious, rent-collecting constable is now a federal marshal. He came in the Bolivar Tavern awhile ago boasting that he had warrants for some fugitives. Then he threatened me." Williams pointed his index finger at his chest. "I, a law abiding inn-keeper, have a legal responsibility to help him catch them. Can you imagine that?"

"He expects you," Still said, "to rat on any suspected traveler who happens by your tavern?"

"The lying idiot," Williams said. "He can go to hell."

Purvis, medium built, soft-spoken and pale complexioned, interrupted Sam. "Satan's not through with him yet," he said. "We need a quick strategy, Sam. He is treacherous. I'm sure you know why, so tell us."

"If I don't sneak messages to him, he could exercise his power to arrest me."

"He's the federal government," Minton said, talking rapidly, "enforcing slavery in a free state. That's what it amounts to."

"Gentlemen," Purvis said, standing and straightening his vest. "We know Kline is a braggart. Sam called him a liar and an idiot. For what specific reasons?"

"He wasn't making sense, said he was going to Lancaster to track horse thieves."

"And you're suspicious?" Minton said.

"Please let Sam talk," Purvis chided, quite agitated.

"Horse rustling is not a black man's crime," Williams said. "Stealing a loaf of bread, a ring of sausage, a chicken maybe. But we sure as hell can't eat a horse on the run."

"Seems reasonable then to believe Kline expects he'll find certain fugitives," Purvis said, looking directly at each person. "Do we agree?" He idly tapped his finger on the *Lancaster Examiner And Herald* newspaper, lying on the table around which they were assembled.

"Lum followed a wealthy man," Still said, "from the Eleventh Street Station to the slave commissioner's office. Leroy on his ice route saw Kline go into Ingraham's office while the man was still there."

"He is planning a raid," Williams said. "Let's presume that is accurate."

They, except Whipper, glanced at each other. He was reading the newspaper.

"I'll wager this is the answer, front page," he said, dropping the paper on the table and placing his fat index finger on a headline:

Dateline Gap Hill—BLACK VIGILANTES RESCUE SUSPECTED FUGITIVE FROM SLAVE CATCHERS.

In a daring shoot-out, an armed band of colored men freed a suspect fugitive slave woman from her abductors Tuesday last. Two of the abductors were severely wounded. A third member did not receive medical attention, but was quite shaken by the attack.

An eye witness said the armed negro band, which calls itself an organization for mutual protection, took the woman and warned her abductors, next time they may not be so lucky.

Terror is sweeping Lancaster County like a wind-driven prairie fire over the rising number of incidents surrounding the rescues, attempted rescues, and threats made to tavern owners by this gang led by a young colored farm hand from Christiana named Will Parker.

Whipper began shaking. "Twelve years ago, I befriended him and his brother. Got them safe passage to New York. Begged them to go. My lumber yard, my home burned to the ground. Soon there'll be open war."

Williams stood, looking down at the table, rubbing his hand nervously across his bald head. "Parker hasn't taken anyone, Bill. He saved that woman's life. He's fighting back in the only way he knows how."

"But he's a fugitive." Whipper's voice rose to a high-pitched whine, a frustrated man given in to exasperation. "He's got no right doing that."

"Colored man got no right period, except what little he takes," Still said. "With that being wrong, there is no right for us. We are all fugitives in a sense."

"Twelve years ago, Mr. Whipper?" Minton said. "You don't know that he is still a fugitive."

"But street fighting? Carrying on like hoodlums? That's exactly what the slavers tell those sorry scamps they hire for a cheap shilling to hunt us," Whipper said.

"They'd do it for less," Minton said. "They hunt us, all of us, anytime, slave or free. I'll tip my hat to young Parker."

Purvis stood again, smoothing his vest. "Gentlemen, judging from the majority comments, we must decide if we will help them in any way we can and then choose a course of action."

"Entice every fugitive who comes to us with money," Whipper said, "all that it will take to keep them running."

"How much is enough?" Williams asked him, "beyond the $150 per man, per woman, or per child it takes to get them hopefully into Canada. Sometimes Bill, I think you've become too bitter, well quite frankly, to reason clearly..."

"So many innocent folks losing everything after we've worked so hard..."

"Bill, we are not the underground railroad," Purvis said. "Running will not abolish slavery. It is necessary in many instances, and everyone knows it is a lucrative business for railroads, steamship lines, stage coaches, and only God knows what else raking money out the pot. But any person willing to fight we will help. Seems demoralizing perhaps, given you were born free. Well, slavery is demoralizing. If you feel humiliated, consider how humiliated I was in '34 when Daniel O'Connell, the Irish patriot wouldn't shake my hand until I assured him I was not only an abolitionist but an American Negro in England raising money to bury slavery. We didn't discuss the underground railroad. I support the underground, my finance records speaks, like yours. Much of the money we spend comes from benevolent philanthropists on our proven record that we spend it wisely."

"It's settled," Williams said. "I'll catch the early morning train for Lancaster and warn the folks thereabouts."

"I have names of the four men Kline will be hunting," Still said. "We believe they live in Christiana. If that is correct, you should get off the train at Penningtonville."

"Excellent," Williams said. "If you could print a warning and run off a batch of copies with the fugitives' names, I'll send a courier over this evening."

"So much burning, screaming in the night, suicide. When will it end?" Whipper sighed. "Oh God."

They watched Whipper talking at the ceiling, acting as if his mind was somewhere else.

"When slavery ends," Minton said.

"We hope," Purvis said.

"I doubt it," Still said. "Freedom has never been handed to anyone. It's got to be won."

Chapter Twenty

Wednesday, September 10, 1851—Edward Gorsuch, pacing the platform of the Philadelphia-Columbia train station early that morning of another very hot day, suddenly caught sight of a free black man watching him. An arrogant Negro, no doubt, standing bareheaded in the shadow of a wood pillar, Gorsuch surmised, a pernicious fool in a suit of fine cloth, much too fashionable for a butler's dress. He would do well with a few years on Gorsuch's Retreat Farm to learn and respect his limitations. Gorsuch popped open the lid of a timepiece he took from his vest, and studied the dial. He frowned at the gray streaks of dawn etching across a hazy, cloudless sky, then returned the watch and entwined his fingers behind his back. Slowly, his head bowed, he began pacing again at the 274 Market Street station.

Two men, a boisterous pair approached Gorsuch, interrupting his anxious thoughts. They flashed deputy U.S. marshal badges and wore gun belts slouched under their bellies from which hung pistols slapping against their thighs. Thompson Tully and John Egan, no doubt, stout men with big heads, dressed like twins going to the wilderness for a day of shooting up the woods for coons and ground hogs. Each had a long duck-shooting iron.

"You're late!" Gorsuch confronted them.

"Weeelll." Tully smiled, scratching his unkempt beard. "We kinda loped along," he said, belching in Gorsuch's face.

Gorsuch screwed his face into a nauseating frown, and turning his head, he spit. The uncouth rascal's breath smelled like garlic in stale beer and coffee grounds. "No one lopes on my time," he said, wiping his lips on the back of his hand.

"Hell, capt'n," Tully said, "won't cost you a plug nickel more. You can't leave no-how 'til the train comes."

"I really shouldn't pay you. I believe my slaves are armed; therefore, I have legal authority to demand your help without reward, mind you. So don't take advantage of my good nature."

"Your nature ain't that damned good, mister. You ain't paid us."

"The name is Edward Gorsuch. I paid..."

"Mr. Gorsuch," Egan said. "If we're going where I think we are, we'll be tangling with a wild bunch of renegade niggers and half breed nigger Indians. We want our money up front."

"Absolutely not," Gorsuch said. "I paid Commissioner Ingraham yesterday. He hired you, not I."

"Now just you hold on a minute, Eddie," Tully said. "Egan's trying to explain something to you in a respectable way but you're taking advantage of his, like you said, good nature. Those ain't our niggers. We can't own 'em. I have a good family, a right nice life I ain't planning to lose. Your niggers that's raising hell over in Lancaster don't much give a hot damn about life or death. Hell, man, can you imagine the damnation that'd come from a renegade nigger killing me?"

"He's telling you, Eddie, if he was to be ambushed," Tully said, "Ingraham wouldn't give his wife as much as a wilted rose, not even a damned loose petal."

Gorsuch knew the two were working a con game, but they had him strapped. How nasty was the situation in Christiana? They had described quite a frightening scene. But he was a shrewd man, too astute for a couple dumb hustlers to cheat him. "Away with your coward's talk. I'll not pay dastardly men."

"Pay," Tully said, "or we go home. One hot minute to make up your mind. Hear the train whistle?"

The color of Gorsuch's flushed face deepened to crimson. Indeed, the train was approaching. "Bloody shysters! Only a retainer, mind you, and you damned well better earn it or I'll see you hanging for treason."

"Tsh tsh," Tully said, forcing himself into the line of passengers purchasing tickets. "Take it, Egan. I'll take care of our fare."

Quaker City, Gorsuch mumbled under his breath while retrieving his wallet. Every sonofabitch is a crook or a nigger lover.

The station platform came alive with Irish railway workers talking and laughing in their brogue, white and black farm hands, general travelers, and as only seasoned eyes like Sam Williams' could distinguish, bounty hunters and soul snatchers. They squeezed into two gondola cars with low roofs. After the conductor had collected fares and the chugging locomotive began inching away, Tully grinning and looking about, hunched Egan in his side.

"Well, I'll be go to hell," he said. "Look who's here."

Egan followed Tully's eyes to Williams. Williams looked up casually, then buried his head in a book, as if deeply concentrating on reading. But how could anyone possibly read? Hot, black smoke and cinders billowing from the stack of an over-fired boiler and fanned by gusts of dry wind, settled on crowded, uncomfortable passengers. Rail cars jerked and dipped dangerously from side to side.

Williams discreetly scrutinized Gorsuch. Lum's description of the slave-crat was as accurate as the hands on his shining gold piece. In Gorsuch, Williams read disdain, the ugliest scorn possible that only a man treated like God by acquiescing men, and thinking himself thus, could muster. Williams noticed the pearl handle of a revolver extending from a holster. Probably was a long one, Williams presumed, from the length of the black holster tied to his thigh.

He chuckled at the quick hustle the deputies had pulled on Gorsuch, feeling more of pity than contempt for men like them. Blind allegiance to a system of hatred had warped their mentalities so badly they couldn't understand, those black men in Christiana were fighting for life. Death was not a matter of choice for them, as it was for the deputies. They could simply go back home. For the black men, death was the penalty for losing.

Williams sighed, thinking about Bolivar, the South American creole revolutionary, and compared his struggle with what he fantasized would happen in Christiana. Under the book on the life of Bolivar in his lap, he carried a stack of leaflets to distribute throughout the Christiana countryside.

Tully and Egan departed at Penningtonville. Williams rode on past Christiana and Gap, departing at Kinzer Station, fifteen miles east of Lancaster City. He rented a surrey with a top from the livery stable across the street. After wandering about, making sure no one, particularly Gorsuch, was following him, Williams headed east along Lancaster Pike then turned South toward Christiana. To every black person he passed, Williams gave a leaflet. If the person stared at him, Williams read the message and asked him to spread the warning—*slave hunters are planning a sweep of the countryside*. Most of the day he traveled, though he did not cross Will Parker's path. The few times he asked about Will, grateful expressions suddenly changed to apprehension. After arriving at Zion Hill later in the day, he accepted an invitation to rest and eat.

By late afternoon, hysteria was racing like a ravaging twister through the area, touching down even in remote byways like Jackson's Hollow of southeastern Lancaster County and neighboring Sadsbury Township in Chester County. Josephus Washington and John Clark, two farmhands hurrying home from the day's work, met Dr. Augustus Cain in Noble Road chatting with a young Quaker gentleman, Henry Young. Washington carried a rifle in one hand and a wrinkled paper with his shot pouch in the other. Instead of the greeting common among gentlemen of the area, Washington abruptly shoved the paper in Dr. Cain's hand. "Can you read this for us?" he said.

Dr. Cain studied it, then looking at Clark with anxiety clouding his eyes, read aloud the names of men Gorsuch claimed were his slaves. "It says, *slavers and bounty men coming with U.S. Marshal. Notify all people*. Are you prepared to meet them?" Dr. Cain asked, giving the paper to Washington.

Washington glared, holding the rifle aloft, squeezing it until every vein and tendon stood out firmly in his arm. The two black men walked on. When they were beyond earshot, Dr. Cain told his friend he didn't know the other man, but he knew Washington was a caring father and he would indeed use the rifle to protect his family.

Will Parker's day had been long and hot, sweaty and tiring since leaving home at daybreak. Threshing hay and wheat kept him steadily in a hurry from sunup to sundown, especially during those dry, sun-drenched harvest days when short-tempered farmers fussed with anybody who'd listen to them decrying the sins of permitting ripened produce to wither in the fields, orchards and vineyards. Will didn't have time for plucking grapes or gathering apples or picking beans and corn, not even from his own garden. Good that Eliza cared for their acre patch. For supper she'd fix him a fine meal of fresh leaf lettuce, tomatoes, scallions with ham-hock-flavored greens and a big jar of lemonade.

A commotion inside his home startled him. From Long Lane he recognized Pink and Hannah and Abe. But there were other grown-up voices and little Catherine, his year-old daughter, was crying so hard, he wondered if she might burst her small lungs. Where was Eliza, where were the other children—Mariah and John T? Nothing Will could imagine except capture or abduction would cause that much turmoil. He walked faster, afraid of the worst, and began running.

Abe saw him leap over the fence. Knowing Will entrusted him to take charge and knowing he would be impatient and irritable as usual at day's end in harvest season, Abe met Will in the yard. Abe thrust the pamphlet at Will, and stuttering hastily, said a big-shot colored man brought it all the way from Philadelphia. Will looked at Abe with eyes that screamed far more loudly than a simple what-the-hell-is-it. Abe tried reading the warning, but he read so terribly slowly and erratically that Will, knowing Abe was actually reciting from memory, snatched the paper and followed the aroma of ham-hocks simmering in onions and collard greens, laced with freshly ground black pepper.

Excited and disjointed conversation among the scared kitchenful subsided. Will, looking around for his seven year-old daughter and three year-old son, saw them standing beside Pink, his arms around their shoulders. In their wide, tear-ringed eyes he saw panic, and knew they expected him to allay their fear. He nodded thanks to Pink. Hannah sat at the table, nursing her babe in arms.

Eliza, dreading the moment Will would appear and gaze at a table not set with piping hot food, stood by the stove, rocking Catherine in one arm, stirring greens with the other. "Oh," she said, "you already know."

"I know my supper ain't ready," Will said, "and you'all acting like something Lucifer run outta hell done broke loose in here."

Nobody laughed, not that Will's funny wasn't worth it. They knew, joking in that manner had become Will's way of relieving temper, grappling with situations that angered him. Yet, try as hard as he might, Will could only be so amusing on an empty stomach.

"Jim and Tommy, your shiny behinds ain't busting through no raggedy threadbare pair of old Massa's slave duds. So don't try making me believe you just leaped out the lion's mouth. What's yapping at your heels, who's got you so worked up?" Will said, as if it wasn't obvious, seeing Jim Kite and Sam (Tommy) Thompson standing there terror stricken.

231

"Slaver master coming for'em," Eliza said, pleadingly. "Says so on that paper." She nodded at the pamphlet in his hand.

"Don't believe it," Will said, going to the stove and removing the lid from the greens. "This ain't the first time somebody's come a' running, uprooting the whole countryside, keeping us holed up all night waiting for nothing." A pillow of steam laden with the succulent odor of cooked lean pork gushing over his head overwhelmed his hunger pangs. He saw the pan of warm bread Eliza had removed from the oven.

Eliza heard the heavy tint of belligerence in his voice and resisted insisting he wash his hands. "Jim and Tommy asked us to help them," she said. "Take a minute, read the paper."

Inhaling deeply, Will lifted out a ham-hock and put it on top of a thick hunk of bread he tore from the loaf. "Ain't meaning to sound mad, gents, but I'm go'n eat a mouthful or two before I can listen to anybody or read anything."

"They after two other men," Pink said, "living not far from us. We don't know exactly when they coming, but the Philadelphia man say it's a big posse, United States marshal, slaver, deputies, one helluva slew."

Juice popped out on Will's lip and soaked into the bread, making it cling limply to the hock. He inserted a fresh cut of hot pepper lying on the counter between the bread and pork, and bit again. They watched him—Eliza, Abe, Jim, Tommy, Pink and Hannah, his children Mariah and John T—chewing ferociously, burping, digesting the full import of the warning.

"Abe," Will said, "we'll try'n be back before dark. Taking the chillun for a visit. Don't let nobody in. Nobody. Eliza?" There wasn't any need for him to explain; plans had already been made for a crisis. She knew what they must do.

"But Daddy," Mariah said, "school's tomorrow."

"No," Will said, watching her pouting lip protrude like Eliza's. But cold determination had already shaded him. He wouldn't smile; indeed Eliza knew he wouldn't say anything without unleashing angry wrath.

"Come, chile," Eliza said, "help me gather some things for baby sister."

"How's it look out back, Abe?" Will said, sticking the pistol in his waist.

Abe smiled and held up his thumb. "If you run," he said to Jim and Tommy, "you be on your own. Stand pat, we all die fighting together."

"Let us be gone," Will said, already in Short Lane, taking giant strides, then reminding himself that Eliza with their little girls and John T were stumbling along trying to keep up. He waited until they were beside him, then taking Catherine in one arm, and rubbing John T's head, he pulled the boy alongside him. Mariah walked beside her mother.

Pink and Hannah with their baby were behind Will's family. At the end of Long Lane they went in the opposite direction, taking their baby to an ancient lady living alone. The two families had agreed, when a crisis struck only the parents themselves would take their children to safe keeping. No one else need know, for reasons that no amount of torture could extract a child's whereabouts from its mother or father. Will and Eliza took their youngsters to a Quaker family.

As soon as Will and Eliza returned, everyone began fortifying the home. Pallets were made on the floor away from windows. Everyone would sleep upstairs fully clothed. Chairs, a table and food for several days were taken upstairs. Downstairs window shutters were boarded, doors barricaded, firearms loaded.

When they were almost finished, Eliza began singing:

"I'm a soldier, a lonely soldier

Traveling though, this barren land."

Abe, busy boarding shutters on a front room window, moved about tapping his feet and humming.

"My load is heavy, but I'll not falter

Beside the Jordan, I'll make my stand."

"Sounds good," Pink said. "You lead Eliza, I'll join in."

Eliza obliged him. Before long the entire house was enveloped in song and hand clapping,

Just before darkness really settled, Eliza heard a tapping on the front door.

"Quiet," she said. "Will, somebody's knocking."

Slowly, Will stuck his head out a bedroom window. "Yeah?"

"It is only I, Sarah..."

"Mrs. Pownall?" Will called out.

"Yes, Mr. Parker, I'd like a word with thee if I may."

"Well, er a, yes, I'll be right down." Strange, he thought, his landlord's wife calling, especially at that hour. "Yes'm," he said, opening the door, waving his hand for the tall, willowy woman to enter.

She wore a thin veil shawl. Her hair, a mix of blond and white like faded lilacs in the soft lantern light, was pulled into a bun.

"Please excuse the look of things," Will said, "we expecting visitors who ain't welcome."

"I've heard the bad news. That's why I've come, to beg of thee, do not lead our colored friends in resisting the fugitive slave law. Escape to Canada, the hunted will follow thee."

Will stared into her small, tight face, slim pointed nose and thin lips. "You shouldn't come here, talking with me about this. I..."

"I'm sorry," she said, "if I cause thee pain."

"The only pain," Will said, "is holding back what I really feel."

Narrow bluish-green eyes studied his face. "Mr. Parker, thee will not treat me like a wimp. Talk to me, a strong Quaker woman, like thee talks to thy wife, a strong Negro woman."

Will looked askance, biting his bottom lip, not wanting to speak so bluntly. "You know, the laws that protect white people don't protect us. We have no choice but to fight. If slaver runners come and we do battle, please tell decent white folks, stay away. It's not your fight."

"There's more at stake for decent white folks, Mr. Parker, than simply obedience to a law. All of you seem so jovial, so content with yourselves singing and making a fortress to kill or be killed, laying our farm to ruin."

Clearly then, Will understood. The fear gripping her was not the uncertainty of him being killed, his family and friends captured or abducted. Yet, even with anger rising in him, he wouldn't attack her self-centered reasoning.

"We ain't happy, Mrs. Pownall. We getting ready. White men make laws that we must break to protect ourselves. If I run away so we don't break the law, they'll jump somebody else. Jumping me won't be so easy," Will said, watching her complexion turn scarlet. "It could be dangerous out in the dark tonight. I'll walk you home."

"No, I'm not afraid," Mrs. Pownall said, bidding them good night. She had tried, despite her husband's strong rejection of the idea. Yet somehow she must find a way to force Will to realize the tragedy in store for her family, ever mindful of her husband's gentleman agreement with Will not to interfere.

Some hours after the warm September night had spread its star-filled ceiling, Sam Williams stopped by the Penningtonville Inn. Afraid that exhaustion would overtake him before he could return the surrey to Kinzer Station, and aware that he was not immune from abduction by highway men, he reserved a night's lodging. Quietly assessing the innkeeper's attitude towards a black man, Williams ordered a drink of plum wine. He politely declined the innkeeper's friendly invitation to shoot the breeze after talking briefly with him, even though he was the only patron in the dim lantern-lit tavern. Reclining in a comfortable chair at a corner table and alone with his thoughts, Williams gazed into the purple liquid.

After the day's events, Williams didn't want to think about tomorrow. He could still see the inquisitive frowns on black people's faces changing to fear. A black stranger come all the long way from Philadelphia warning then of danger? From what he'd heard about Parker, he must be one giant of a man. Williams wondered, after Ben had invited him to Will's apple butter party come Sunday, would there be a Sunday? Certainly the day would come, but would Sunday find them alive and still in Christiana? He sighed and stretched. Glancing around, he noticed the innkeeper nodding in a chaise lounge on old cushions long since shaped by the contour of his heavy body.

No sooner than he had chance to get really comfortable, the pounding hoofs of a running horse and squeaking wheels of a fast approaching wagon disturbed the quiet, lonely sound of nothing except chirping crickets. The

heavy oak door flung open. Marshal Kline hobbled in, huffing and cursing at himself.

"Kindly close the door, sir, the hour is quite late," the irritated innkeeper said.

"Well, yeah, yes of course." Kline stood slouching in the middle of the room, looking about. "United States Marshal looking for a posse that may have come by here looking for horse thieves?"

The innkeeper looked at him inquisitively. "Oh hell, man, what is the big noise about tracking horse rustlers? Two rowdy sports, said they were from Philadelphia, slouched around here until about sundown. One of them, bending his elbow a little too much, called a few of my regulars horse thieves. Woulda' got his jaw broken if I hadn't booted them out."

"Did you see which way they went?" Kline asked.

"Naw," the innkeeper said. "A tall, severe looking man, a planter from Baltimore with five mannerly and well dressed men came shortly after that and stayed past dark."

Kline frowned. "Gimme an ale," he said, speaking gruffly. "What in the dickens is severe looking?"

"He had a stern, you could say a mean, pious attitude about him. Ate supper, but drank nothing except water. I heard him quoting scripture to one of the others who suggested he might relax with a little brandy. He asked me about horse thieves and said they were waiting for you."

"Yeah, yeah. I know," Kline said.

"I tell'ya, it's been a strange night. Little while ago, that colored man over there came in for a night's lodging. Said he heard about rustlers too, and figured he'd be safer bedded down than on the highway by himself. But like I told him, we don't have much of a problem in these parts with horse thieves."

Kline, favoring his right leg, hobbled over close enough to recognize Williams. "Sam, what'n hell you doing here?"

"Waiting for the morning train, Kline. Seems like your horse thieves up and left."

"Gawd-dammit! I'll run you in for interfering with the law. I know why you're here."

"Run me in for visiting friends?"

"You're a liar, Sam," Kline said, throwing one of the crumpled warnings on the table. "This is your doing."

"Hmm," Williams said, reading the paper and faking surprise. "You're not after rustlers. Why did you tell me...? Oh, I get it, you fed me that yarn, thinking I wouldn't believe it and if my fugitive friends were here, you'd only have to track me to find them. Nice try."

"Get the hell on back to Philadelphia, Sam, before you get arrested!" Kline turned to the tavern keeper. "If they return, tell them we will rendezvous here at 5 a.m. No, better tell them to wait for me. Now, if you don't mind, sir. I'm bound to rest for a spell. This gawddamned leg..." He rubbed his left thigh and knee cap.

"Certainly," the innkeeper responded.

"I'm warning you, Sam," Kline said, ascending the stairs slowly, being careful not to bend his left knee.

"Marshal," Williams said, "I really do believe you enjoy making me sick."

"That's a promise, Sam. Mark my word."

Williams retired shortly after the marshal. Knowing he was in the nerve center of the capture or abduction planned for daybreak, he couldn't sleep. He contemplated leaving immediately. If the slavecrat's party with God knows how many deputized men came there before he could clear out, he'd be in the worst of grave situations. If he left at that very minute, Kline would follow him. Williams shuddered at the thought of Kline or the slavecrat and his posse finding him alone on the highway.

It seemed like only minutes later that Williams heard someone coaxing a horse to running. No doubt about that gruff voice being Marshal Kline's. Williams checked his watch. Four in the morning, he hadn't slept a good half-hour. But jumping out of bed, he hurriedly made his toilet and put on the wrinkled shirt he'd worn the day before, leaving it open at the collar. He inquired of the innkeeper a shorter route to Kinzer Station where he could return the surrey and catch the early train to Philadelphia. The innkeeper directed him to Christiana then west on Noble Road, rather than following the main route through Gap. A tough ride through hilly back country, but it would save a few miles. Williams thanked him and departed.

At the top of the Zion Hill past Mt. Zion AME Church, Williams set the horse to a fast trot descending into Christiana. Heading west he wasn't aware of passing close by Will Parker's home, which in a matter of hours would be the stage for a fugitive slave rebellion. The armed resistance would shock the nation, pierce the heart of Dixie, draw out Northern support for the South from fence-straddling advocates of human bondage, and herald the rallying fervor of abolitionists in their unswerving demands for slavery's demise.

Parkesburg, Penningtonville, Christiana, and Gap, north westward stops along the main-line railroad in that order, were only a few miles apart. Marshal Kline, suspecting Tully and Egan followed the local train tracks eastward on foot towards Philadelphia, backtracked from the Penningtonville Inn to the Parkesburg station. He found them asleep in a bar room, waiting for the first train bound for Philadelphia.

Plenty of Negroes lived in the area, but they had not seen one, Egan told the marshal. That was a terrible omen, for if Will Parker was half as mean as reputed, he and his boys, about fifty strong, would ambush then on his first chance. Kline called Egan a lying bastard and ordered him and Tully to surrender their badges. They were an unnecessary expense.

Kline had spent Tuesday, his first night in the area, at Gap Tavern with men begging him to deputize them. Few slavers came there anymore looking for guides and strong-arm support, they told Kline, since Will Parker began terrorizing the countryside. The next day Kline scouted the area, spending considerable time watching Negroes run in and out of Will Parker's home. Then he found a copy of the warning.

Desperately needing deputies, but already too late for the five o'clock Thursday rendezvous with Gorsuch at the Penningtonville Inn, Kline headed for the Gap Tavern. Hurrying along the rutted wagon trails in early morning darkness, Kline prayed he wouldn't cross Gorsuch's path before he had deputized a posse. At five-twenty he passed the inn at the Penningtonville train station. No indication of Gorsuch there or at Zercher's Hotel at the Christiana train station at five-fifty. Kline began worrying. Maybe Gorsuch had already left. Kline probably could overtake him but not without deputies who'd probably know a shorter way than his.

Quite relieved, but embarrassed, Kline found the slave master outside the Gap Tavern with a slave hunting party; his son Dickinson, a nephew Dr. Thomas Pearce, his cousin Joshua, and two neighbors, Nathan Nelson and Nicholas Hutchings. Nelson and Hutchings believed they owned slaves who had fled to Christiana.

"Kline, it's damned near six-thirty! What kind of a fool do you think I am?" Gorsuch said. "Over three hours late, and your deputies, where the hell are they?"

"Now, now," the marshal said, "I understand your resentment, I can appreciate your anger, but my obligation also includes your safety."

"Oh, hogwash, Kline. I've suspected all along, you are a lazy, incompetent scoundrel. You should stick to collecting rent and evicting little old black aunties from their tumble-down shanties."

"That wasn't very nice," Kline said, "for a fine educated, Christian man you go around claiming to be so..."

"Uncle," Dr. Pearce said, "your blood pressure. You've been under strain for too long over this."

"To hell with your jibes," Gorsuch said, ignoring his nephew. "He's been gone since Tuesday," Gorsuch said, looking at his son, Dickinson. "We left Lancaster yesterday, looking for him. He has the warrants, only he has authority. Only he can arrest my boys. They belong to me, but I can't take them without his permission."

"That is correct, sir," Kline said, taking advantage of the opportunity to demand respect. "A Negro from Philadelphia followed me. I know he is a spy.

I lost him, but this wagon ain't worth a shit. It broke down. Held me up damned near half a day."

"A likely story," Gorsuch said. "One that can't be contested. Where are your deputies?"

"I sent them home. They won't gun-battle with niggers."

"Why? I paid those spineless skunks."

"Poor judgement," Kline said, pointing his finger at Gorsuch. "The commissioner doesn't know that. I do because they work for me. Of course, I'll make them give back your money."

"After we get our slaves, we're going home, straight home, not to Philadelphia," Gorsuch said quietly to his son. "I'll not be humiliated by the company of this, this poorest of white trash any longer." He spit his disgust in the dirt. "Lead us to Christiana."

"I suggest we deputize some local boys here," Kline said, "and wait until the wee dark hours tomorrow morning."

"No and hell no," Gorsuch said, climbing into the wagon with his son. "An old whiskered fart, Bill Baer, calls himself a recruiter, offered his service. But he's too cut-throat for a gentleman's work. The lot of them are a bunch of dreg rowdies who'd kill my boys just for the sport of it. We're off, Kline. Lead the way, or get lost."

"Understand me clearly," Kline said, getting into his rented surrey, "I make the arrests. If not, I'll deputize every man inside and arrest the lot of you for attempting seizure without warrants. Don't underestimate me."

Gorsuch's face reddened. He gritted his teeth. Beads of sweat popped out on his nose.

"Please," Dr. Pearce said, frowning spitefully at Kline, "must you continue this stupid bickering?"

"You bloody cockroach," Gorsuch said, "get the hell moving."

Marshal Kline chuckled. That will cost you an extra fifty, he mumbled and began assessing the slave catchers. Dickinson, Gorsuch's son, perfect image of his father twenty-six years ago. An aristocratic air about him, and he, like his cousin Dr. Pearce, was too majestic to fear fugitives. Obviously the two were related, though Pearce was an inch taller and looked more illustrious in riding breeches and a highcrown Stetson hat. Gorsuch's nephew Joshua, several inches shorter, didn't favor the clan. His keen nose didn't ride high on his face. He didn't stare as if an icy wind was chaffing his face. Though he glanced with a casual smirk when Kline turned and looked at him, Joshua's personality wasn't so readily perceivable. The neighbors resembled two lean, roughshod cowpokes.

Dr. Pearce, Joshua, and the neighbors rode horseback two abreast behind Gorsuch and Dickinson in the wagon. Gorsuch, certain that Kline didn't know the best direction for them to make a surprise attack, looked about for the informer, though doubtful he would intercept them. Padgett had specifically recommended they strike before dawn.

Chapter Twenty-One

Thursday, September 11, 1851, 7 a.m.—Edward Gorsuch's slave hunting party took guns from the wagons and corralled their horses in a dense cluster of trees near the railroad line. Silently, with Marshal Kline leading, they walked the train tracks between Gap and Christiana. Something rustled in the woods. The posse froze. Kline gripped his pistol.

"Edward Gorsuch?" A white man coming from the forest, spoke in a hushed voice.

"It's our guide," Gorsuch said, rather jubilantly. He recognized the wide brim straw hat crammed on the informer's head and a white rag tied around it, details mentioned in the letter to him. "I apologize," Gorsuch said, "for being late, but the timing in this matter is one of darn few in my life over which I did not have control, Mr. Pad..."

"Don't call my name," Padgett said. "Here's the reply you sent me. But gosh, mister. You're taking an awful chance. If those bastards see us coming in broad daylight, sure as hell was created for the colored, they'll dig in and fight."

"Mr. whatever your name," Dr. Pearce said. "It has been my experience that slaves, fugitive or otherwise, lack the courage to defy law and the white man's power."

"He means, my good fellow," Dickinson said, "they will never, ever be so courageously foolish to instigate the brutal winter of a white man's wrath. Now what is your die-hard concern that we are a few hours late in tracking our slaves?"

Padgett didn't particularly like Dr. Pearce or Dickinson and his God-high attitude. Actually, Padgett hated him. "You don't believe they'll shoot white people? You think their guns are made out of wood pulp and they shoot paper pellets?"

"I suppose," Dickinson said, cryptically, fanning his hand, "incidents beyond the norm do occur. So what?"

Padgett smirked, "So stick to writing verse, mister. You don't know belligerent neegras."

"Time is wasting, fella," Kline said. "Obviously you've been hired to guide, not to teach the basics of handling neegras."

"Suit yourself," Padgett said. "We leave the tracks here, take a short cut through the woods to the ridge. From there, we'll see the whole valley. I'll show you where they're holed up."

After a trek in the forest to the high ground, Padgett pointed to a new house an acre or so away on a descending slope. "Nelson Ford lives there. He is your John Beard slave."

"John will come without any trouble," Gorsuch said. "His wife is still at my place. Marshal, I'll take the guide and four men. You..."

"Don't be so hasty," Padgett said. "Ain't no chance of surprising 'em at this hour of the morning. He may be gone to work."

"What do you suggest?" Gorsuch said.

"Will Parker's house ain't far," Padgett said. "He's the leader. Once we cross Chester Valley here and get up yonder ridge to the high road we'll take a damned good look. Kite and Thompson are with him."

"That seems agreeable," Kline said. "We'll grind Parker and his bunch into mush, grab Beard on the way back." Kline really wished he had stuck to his demand that Gorsuch wait until just before dawn of the next morning. From what he had been told by a reliable source, only a surprise attack would avoid a shoot-out. If they encountered resistance and anyone was hurt, including Gorsuch's fugitives, the adverse publicity would tarnish the commissioner's reputation. More so, Gorsuch would blame him for the bungled captures and demand that Commissioner Ingraham return his money. Commissioner Ingraham would lift the badge, demoting Kline to constable, back to collecting delinquent rents. Kline hoped that Will Parker character wasn't stupid enough to make a scene.

From Upper Valley Road, overlooking the sloping valley, Padgett pointed out Will's home and his landlord's spreading homestead. "Lookit," he said, "ain't a blessed thing stirring down there. Not a sign of life on the busiest farm in these parts. Farmer Pownall ain't nowhere in sight. Ain't that fair warning?" He spat the question at Gorsuch.

"My word," Dr. Pearce said. "Uncle Edward hired you to lead, not foretell our doom. Get on with your task."

"Follow me then, gents," Padgett said, with a sarcastic grin.

They descended the hillside onto Pownall's farm, leaving the cover of woods behind them. Sarah Pownall's keen eyes, scanning the landscape, recognized them in the distance, trespassing single file on land endowed and made precious generations ago by her family's labor of love.

In tilling the soil the Quakers worshiped God, and year after year reaped a bountiful harvest. Disheartened that Will would not leave, and mindful of her husband's agreement not to interfere in Will's affairs, she believed if blood were spilled the land would become sallow acre after acre. Future generations would grow weaker and eventually perish.

In the still dark morning, Sarah had eased out of bed while Levi slept fitfully. She went to the window and sat in Meeting, beseeching God for a miracle. When day broke, she instructed her daughters to manage breakfast. After reminding Levi of his and their two sons' promise to work only in the barn and tack shop, she hurried to the upstairs window, and sat there meditating and praying, meditating and praying while staring across acres of a golden harvest to the tree line. The slavers came from the woods, moving stealthily. Without conscious effort, a verse from the Bible formed on her lips. "If you love me," she whispered, "and keep my commandments, I will give you... She immediately thought of Elijah Lewis. Thanking God, she got out of the chair, tied on her bonnet, and hastened straightaway to consult him. On the way she prayed that Elijah, a white man whom Will really admired, could appeal to him, could penetrate the nearsighted protective shield to Will's soul, to the God of all men within him.

Mrs. Lewis, Sarah's close friend in the Quaker sisterhood saw her approaching. Fearing the worst, she ran from the kitchen and met Sarah in the barnyard. After they had hugged, Sarah relayed her terrifying heartache to Mrs. Lewis. Together they pleaded with Elijah.

Through the meadow, Padgett led the slave catchers alongside Valley Run into the long, wide field of tall corn. In the field Padgett felt a bit more secure. Dr. Pearce removed his hat and, kneeling on a big flat rock, he put his face in the shallow, cool water.

"We rest for a minute," Kline said, "Fix your ammunition."

"Good place for us to square up," Padgett said to Gorsuch.

Hutchings and Nelson loaded their rifles. Gorsuch took an envelope from an inside coat pocket and gave it to the guide. Padgett nodded thanks, and slowly continued through the cornfield, stepping gingerly amid the stalks to avoid tramping any. At the field's edge, he knelt beside a narrow log-bridge where Valley Run trickled under Long Lane, and motioned for them to gather around.

"Stay low," Padgett said. "Look'a yonder, the two-story stone house. Ain't that a dandy for a nigger, beside a orchard no less, that's loaded with apples, and pears and peaches? Parker lives there. His gawddamned Quaker landlord, Levi Pownall, lives on the other side of the orchard there, beyond the vineyard."

Shutters on both downstairs front windows on either side of the door of Will's house were open. The two front windows upstairs were open. "Looks like we just might surprise 'em. But then again," Padgett said, "it could be full of niggers just wait'n. It's a big house, walls a foot thick, three rooms up and three down, windows around back too."

"Where in hell is Noble Road?" Marshal Kline asked. He had observed the activity at Will's house the day before while hiding in the cornfield near Noble Road.

"Over there," Padgett said, pointed to his left. "This wagon trail will take you to Noble Road."

"Goodness, I do declare," Gorsuch exclaimed, "what have we here?"

Jim Kite, whistling a happy tune on his way to work, late but glad the slavers hadn't struck the previous night, cut a little jig on Short Lane and spun as he turned onto Long Lane. While the slave catchers watched Kite, Padgett

eased backward into the corn, disappearing quickly and silently as he had appeared.

Hearing a slight rustling in the cornfield just ahead of him, Kite froze. Gorsuch sprung from his hiding place in the corn stalks onto Long Lane. Kite's mouth opened, but the scream jammed in his throat. He spun around and raced back to the house, hearing the all-too-familiar ring in his master's voice commanding him.

"Kite, hey you up there, boy. Jim-mee," Gorsuch said, following in hot pursuit.

Kline ran and leaped the orchard fence in an effort to overtake Kite on a diagonal, but didn't clear the top. He landed on his side and rolled onto his back, cursing and grimacing. Gorsuch's crew hurried by without as much as a questionable look at him sprawled there on squashed apples.

Kite jumped the few steps to the small porch, crossed it and heaved against the door, leaving it open. "Will!" He ran upstairs screaming. "Soul snatcher! Lord of demons hisself down, down!" He stood there trembling and pointing.

"Jim-mee, come on home boy without any trouble mind you," Gorsuch said, coming up fast in the front yard, "and I'll overlook your reckless mischief."

Kline jumped up and began hobbling with a limp, dragging his left leg. Jesus God, did it hurt! Brushing past the slave catchers gathering in the yard, he followed Gorsuch through the doorway, scanning the bare room, the hardwood floor, a set of stairs against the opposite wall, leading to an upstairs landing. Through an archway he noticed a huge, cold stove in an empty kitchen. He could see part of a fireplace and was about to go check the back area when Will Parker appeared at the top of the stairs.

"Who in the hell? What you mean, barging in my house 'thout knocking?"

Kline and Gorsuch heard the hustle and bustle of people moving about, grabbing guns. Dr. Pearce and Dickinson joined them in the room. Nelson, Hutchings, and Joshua stood on the porch with guns drawn, guarding against intruders.

"My slaves know why I'm here."

"I am a United States marshal.'

"I don't give a dam about you," Will yelled, "or the United States."

"You're talking to an officer of the federal government." Kline moved towards the stairs, trying not to reveal the limp.

"Take another step, I will break your neck."

Kline stopped and chuckled. "You sure got some long arms, boy, along with a rapscallion nature," he yelled. "But I'm taking you in."

"Do it," Will bellowed, "and for sure, your name will make history for this day's work."

"Mr. Kline, wait," Gorsuch said, passing the marshal and slowly walking up one, two, three steps and stopping. "I'm already tired of him. Follow me."

"C'mon up," Will said. "But you won't walk back down."

Gorsuch took another step, stopped and gasped. A five-pronged fish hook flew past him. With eyes wide and fixed, he watched Abe wind-up and hurl a hatchet. He ducked. "Sweet Jesus," he lamented.

The hatchet's cutting edge splintered a chunk of wood from the wall. Dr. Pearce drew his gun. Dickinson rushed to his trembling father, easing him down the steps.

"Mr. Gorsuch, let me remind you, I'm in command. I'll serve the warrants," Kline said, reading the list of four men named fugitive slaves from Edward Gorsuch's Retreat Farm. "All of you have been officially notified. As for you," he said to Will. "You will pay dearly for interfering."

"Not a one of us will you take alive. Believe that," Will said.

"Nigger," Gorsuch screamed, getting up off the floor. "You're not my property."

"Wait, father," Dickinson said, gingerly restraining his father.

"No niggers here and men are not property," Will yelled back. "See if the bed, or the bureau, or the chairs down there are your niggers."

Gorsuch looked pitifully at his son. "The black idiot must be sick," he said, "but I'm long past tired of waiting."

"Milk the cow in the barn, see if any nigger's in its milk. Peep up one of the hogs' behind. See if any nigger blood is in its pork."

"How dare you make mockery of me!"

"Uncle Edward, please," Dr. Pearce said, "your pressure."

"Transgressing black Satan," Gorsuch shouted, as if he hadn't heard his son and nephew. "I'll see you hanged from the gallows and gibbeted for meddling in a white man's business!"

"Father, wait," Dickinson pleaded again, having listened carefully to Will. Judging by his stinging articulation and apparent courage, he would not be intimidated. Perhaps Will was a mulatto, his father a white man. Dickinson hadn't gotten close enough for a good look at him. "We'll hire reinforcements," he said. "Marshal, go to Lancaster and bring back fifty, a hundred men, however many you think it will take to force a surrender."

"An army won't be necessary. Fetch some straw from the barn," Kline said, cupping his hands around his mouth. "We'll burn them out."

"Yeah," Will said, "a coward would do just that. But even roasting in hell on a barbecue stick, we ain't giving up."

Suddenly, a trumpeting horn sounded from a garret window.

"Who's doing that?" Kline yelled, rushing outside. "Knock whoever's blowing that trumpet the hell out of there," he hollered to Gorsuch's cousin Joshua and his neighbors Nelson and Hutchings.

They hastily positioned themselves in an apple tree and began firing. Dr. Pearce ran outside and climbing a tree in the orchard, joined them. Gorsuch and Dickinson retreated to the front yard. Eliza, kneeling beneath the window, blew again and again as if announcing judgement day. Shot poured in thick and fast through the attic window. Pink and Hannah were crouching in a corner of their bedroom, wrapped around each other, affirming their mounting fear. Kite and Thompson withdrew into corners of a room, their guns trained on the door. Brandishing a rifle, Abe stood at the landing behind Will.

Hearing the trumpet some distance away, Elijah Lewis, tall, wiry, full-bearded Quaker postmaster and storekeeper, quickened his pace. He hadn't slept well the past night. Then an hour or so ago Mrs. Pownall had thrust the burden of defending the Quakers' unalienable right to a peaceful existence in Christiana squarely on his shoulders. On his way to Will's place he stopped by and summoned the miller, Castner Hanway.

Hanway, tall, lean and thirty-one, two years older than Will, also heard the trumpeting. Though he had suspected trouble brewing, it hadn't curbed his appetite for the king-size breakfast his new bride had prepared. Will could handle the situation. Yet, hearing fear in Lewis' voice, though Hanway had an abundance of customers' grain and corn to grind, how could he not accompany his dear friend? Lewis refused the offer for breakfast but insisted Hanway finish eating. He would go on ahead, hoping Hanway would overtake him before reaching Will's place.

Will ran to a bedroom window. A shot from the yard splintered the pane directly over his head. He ducked back inside, shaking fragments of glass from his head and shoulders. From a lower corner of the window, he carefully aimed at Gorsuch and fired just as Pink grabbed his arm. The shot went wild.

"Don't kill him, Will," Pink pleaded, "We'll all hang, Eliza and Hannah too."

Will turned on Pink, aiming the gun at him.

"No," Hannah yelled, scrambling from the corner and grappling with Will, forcing him and herself into full view of the slave catchers in the yard. "Eliza, don't let him kill my Pink. He's all me and his baby daughter's got."

Marshal Kline eased his pistol from the holster and quickly fired at Will. But Abe, seeing Kline, snatched Will and Hannah from view. The shot embedded itself in the ceiling.

"Y'all standing there together like three fat turkeys," Abe said, carefully aiming at Kline, "waiting for some hot lead. If anyone a' ya', marshal, old man or that boy who looks like you so much as quiver, I'll open 'ya up."

Kline, his gun hanging limp in his hand, Dickinson with his arm around his father's shoulder, and Gorsuch stood stock still.

"If you don't shoot," Kline said nervously, seeing Abe's rifle extending from the edge of the window. "I will stop my men, give you fifteen minutes to surrender. Hold your fire over there in the trees."

Shooting from the orchard ceased. Eliza, sitting quite winded with her back against a thick stone wall and covered with lime dust, climbed down from the attic. Pieces of brick and mortar were stuck in her hair.

"Go'n the hell back to your corner, Pink."

"Naw, Will. I'm giving up. What's the use'a fight'n?"

"Please, Eliza," Hannah said. "Make Will let me and Pink go."

Eliza grabbed a corn cutter. "I'll chop off both ya heads and watch 'em roll down the steps. Don't tempt me." She glared with eyes like a panther's at her brother-in-law and Hannah.

"You up there, Jim-mee and Tommy," Gorsuch said. "I've come a long way, boys. My patience is damned well spent, and I'm hungry. But I'm taking you home or I'll eat my breakfast in hell."

"Old man," Will said, standing behind the window frame with his head turned toward the opening. "I see the sword coming. If you stay here your blood will be spilled by your own hand."

"Don't ask them anymore, father," Dickinson said. "Marshal, we will hire a hundred men and make them surrender."

"Then we'd better hurry. Look-a-yonder. Joshua," Kline called to Gorsuch's nephew, "you gotta do it. Hurry to the Gap. Spread the word. Bring back as many fighting men as your money will buy."

Joshua scrambled from the tree. "I'll find my way, guarantee it," he said, running across Long Lane. He ran alongside the cornfield towards the creek, but the sight his eyes beheld compelled him to enter it at that very moment.

Dr. Pearce, Nelson and Hutchings scaled down from the trees as if they had awakened a hibernating lynx. Beyond the orchard Elijah Lewis, wearing a straw hat and walking fast, came in front of Hanway astride a bald-face sorrel horse. From the fields beyond the creek, and through the orchard black men armed with guns, pitchforks and corn cutters were hastening toward Will's house. Sam Hopkins, John Roberts, Daniel Caulsberry, Lou Cooper and many others responding to the trumpet sound, the warning from Philadelphia, and word of mouth, positioned themselves behind trees in the orchard. Some crouched beside the fence a distance from Will's yard, but within rifle range. Inside the house Kite and Tommy hugged each other and wept. Kline looked at Gorsuch beseechingly. Eliza and Abe cheered.

Hanway stopped, and looking in all directions, frantically waved his arms. "I'm appealing to your conscience, men," he said, calling each freedom fighter by name. "Do not shoot!"

"For God's sake, marshal," Hanway said, running his hand nervously through his thick black hair. "Can't you see the danger in trying to arrest them? Leave!"

"No," the old slave owner said. "I will not leave without my property."

"You men," Marshal Kline said to Lewis and Hanway, "are required by law to assist us. We will hold our fire if you convince them to surrender. You can control them."

"What would you have us do that we haven't already done?" Lewis said. "They have a right to defend themselves."

"They do not!" Gorsuch yelled. Kline nodded his agreement.

"You can see," Hanway said, his blue eyes dancing in their sockets, "they're prepared to die. Are you?"

Kline didn't answer. "I'm holding both of you personally responsible for the safety of my men," he said.

"You have full authority, Marshal," Lewis said. "I and Mr. Hanway can serve no useful purpose here." He began walking away. Hanway nudged his horse to a slow gait beside Lewis.

"Go ahead," Kline yelled, "leave. But I'm holding you liable for the value of his slaves too. If they are butchered up, or even scratched in any way you will pay, and dearly."

Dickinson whispered to Gorsuch, "Look who's coming, Father."

Frowning, squinting, momentarily disbelieving what his eyes actually beheld, Gorsuch exclaimed, "Noah Buley!" He pointing to a copper-complexioned man dismounting a handsome gray horse near Hanway. "He sneaked off ages ago and is living here like high society white folks, less than a day's travel on a blind mule from my plantation. By thunder, this hell-hole is crawling with fugitives. Your sin will eat you alive, and that's prophesy," he said to Lewis and Hanway.

Lewis and Hanway stopped and looked back. Bulcy fastened his horse to a tree. Hurrying to Will's house with his rifle, he positioned himself behind a side entrance to the cellar.

"The more I'm exposed to this abomination, the more I'm inclined to swallow the bitter truth," Dickinson said to Quaker Lewis and Hanway. "You people are an alliance of blackguards in the guise of Friends. Believe me, our supporters in the state legislature, those owning considerable tracts of land in your state, shall hear about this."

Will appeared downstairs in the doorway.

"You can't come out here," Gorsuch yelled. "Marshal, they'll all get away."

"I pay the rent for this place," Will said. "I want you the hell outta here."

"That's damned jolly of you," Gorsuch said. "But if you step beyond that threshold, I'll empty the contents of these in you." He pointed two pearl-handled revolvers at Will.

Will stopped.

"Parker, withdraw your men," Kline said. "Mine have withdrawn."

"No sir!" Gorsuch stomped his booted foot on the ground. "I'll not leave without my property, including you too, Buley."

Buley steadied himself in the crouched position and trained his rifle on the slave master. Then, Marshal Kline saw Zeke, formidable and bigger than big itself, making giant strides in Long Lane with his scythe poised, wide shoulders stretched, head slightly bowed, blood in his eyes.

"Look'a there, Edward," he said. "It's gonna get bloody nasty in a matter of minutes."

Gorsuch looked away from Will. "Shoot him, Marshal, before he comes any closer."

"Only a fool, which I'm not, would attempt that, Ed. A gun's trained on us from behind pretty near every damned tree in that orchard, from the windows and him over there," Kline said, pointing to Buley. "They're armed with rifles and corn cutters, and that colored giant of an Indian with that scythe. Holy-Christ, retreat! That's an order, mister." Kline stepped backwards toward Short Lane. "Call off your men I say, Parker."

Hutchings and Nelson hurdled the orchard fence and, crossing Long Lane, plunged headlong among the corn stalks. Zeke went after them, cutting stalks in his path faster than three average men could slice a winding causeway through gangling reeds in a swamp.

"Too late," Will said, crossing the yard, stopping ten paces in front of Gorsuch with a pistol crammed in his waist. "If we don't settle today," he said to Gorsuch, glaring at him and Dickinson, "you'll come back tomorrow. Old man, if your gut's big as your mouth, c'mon take me."

"Black Satan," Gorsuch screamed.

"Don't fire, Uncle," Dr. Pearce yelled. "Can't you understand? We are in a very grave predicament."

"I've heard tell of your kind of neegra, you black rascal," Gorsuch said, shaking a revolver at Will, "but you'll not curse me!"

"Father, this...foolhardy nigger," Dickinson cried, spitting the word at Will and drawing his revolver, "shall not disrespect you."

"Nigger?" Will asked, clipping Dickinson on his jaw with a swift right fist at the same time a shot from Buley's rifle rang out, A shot from Dickinson's pistol quickly followed, skimming Will's forehead, cutting a swath through his hair.

"Never again in life," Will said, "yours or anybody else's."

Will's lick dislodged the gun from Dickinson's hand, sending him sprawling in the dirt.

Gorsuch grunted. His body stiffened as if jolted by lightning. He shot wildly in the direction of the orchard. Buley ran up behind the old man and hammered him across the head with the rifle. Gorsuch's knees sagged.

"Come back, Marshal," Dr. Pearce cried, backing deeper into the orchard, watching Kline limp away into the cornfield.

Will took to the cornfield after Marshal Kline.

Buley stared with his mouth hanging open, knowing he had shot Gorsuch but amazed at the old man's fortitude in shaking off the blow, making an effort to steady the revolver, determined to shoot Buley.

Tommy, seizing the chance to free himself, ran from the house and snatching Buley's rifle, clubbed Gorsuch. The slaver sank to his knees. Tommy looked at the gun bent out of shape on Gorsuch's head, amazed at the slave owner struggling to stay on his feet. Kite, running from the house, began pounding Gorsuch with his fists until the old man fell and in a weakening voice, cried out, "For ye there shall be no day of atonement."

Dickinson got up, staggering and zigzagging aimlessly toward the orchard. Pinckney, anxious to vindicate himself with Will, took a bead from a window and fired. Dickinson fell. That set off a round of firing from behind the trees.

"They'll kill all of us," Dr. Pearce cried, rushing to his cousin. "Oh God," he gasped, "they shot me!"

"For thy own sake, neighbors," Hanway yelled, "do not shoot anymore!" He turned, finding himself in the line of fire between Abe on one knee aiming at the doctor. "They are whipped, Abe. Pink, you in the orchard, let them flee." The seething stares and knowledge that guns he could not see were trained on him, made Hanway extremely afraid for himself. "Nothing more I can do," he said, galloping off.

Lunging, Dr. Pearce grabbed Hanway's leg, and held on while the horse dragged him. At the bridge crossing over Valley Run, Dr. Pearce let go. He crawled into the cornfield. Edward Gorsuch lay still in a pool of blood. Flies began buzzing around his battered body.

Chapter Twenty-Two

A quiet, not peaceful silence, but a goose-pimple stillness pervading the aftermath of battle, and the stench of gunpowder augmented a pall of gloom settling around Edward Gorsuch's death. Will emerged from trampling the cornfield after Marshal Kline to find Levi Pownall, his landlord, standing in the yard over Gorsuch's body. Quaker Pownall, tall and rawboned, looked about, jerking his head in every direction like a hare in a field of scattering tumbleweeds. Will's freedom fighters, having congregated inside his house, stared at the body apprehensively, mumbling among themselves, not really conscious of what they were saying.

"Will, the heat will cook the corpse if the flies don't eat it first," Pownall said, his dark and earnest eyes seeking Will's. "Give me a sheet, would thee to cover it?"

Will returned Pownall's gaze then looked down in the dead man's quiet face and turned away. Gorsuch's closed eyelids reminded him of drawn windows shades of sad houses suddenly emptied by raiding soul snatchers. Gorsuch's cheeks that had been fiery red with anger were white as buttermilk. His angry threats still rang in Will's ear, yet it was difficult for Will to visualize that body as the shell of man made wicked by his belief that being rich and white gave him the right to buy, sell, and rob persons of their lives, lives really not unlike his own. Will thought of Doc Dingee: "beneath the slaver's facade of greed is a human being just like you." Thickening red blood oozing on the ground turning black, and fingers of both hands still gripped two pearl handled pistols. "I'll see if Eliza can spare a cover," he said harshly.

"Here," Hannah said, throwing a sheet from an upstairs window. "Eliza's busy tending to herself."

The urge flamed inside Will to swear at Hannah, but instead he caught the sheet and waited, expecting she would, though she didn't tell him what ailed Eliza.

"The remains of this slavecrat represent an empire," Pownall said, taking the sheet from Will, "and thee has sliced thy way to the very heart of it." He tucked it under Gorsuch's feet, pulling it over his entire body. "I'm giving back the balance of thy rent for September," he said, reaching into his pocket.

"You throwing me out?" Will searched Pownall's eyes with his full of surprise.

Pownall nodded his head slowly. "Thee must flee," he replied with cold frankness.

"Hemming and hawing don't sound like you, Levi," Will said, his voice taut with anger. "If you running me off your place, least you can do is say why."

"Need I say 'tis not a safe place? Harm will come to thee, thy wife, thy children, thy friends."

"You want me off your place, ain't much I can do about that," Will said. "The battle is over."

"Killing is a result of it. Angry, vicious men will come seeking revenge," Pownall said, rubbing his hands together.

"We will fight," Will growled. "Better dead men than living niggers."

"Am I," Pownall said," my wife, my children not thy friends, Will? We didn't interfere when you unified to resist beatings and capture."

"I tried to be a decent man," Will said, his voice rancor sharp. "Me, my wife and kids will face the dogs wherever we are. I can't speak for my friends."

"You speak for me, Will," Pink said, climbing out a window and joining them around Gorsuch's body. "I never cared too much about what somebody else thought of me 'til Eliza questioned my manhood like it never been questioned before. She made me see myself going back to living worse'n a dog." Tears flowed freely down Pink's cheeks. "Gawd-dammit, she made me see a man!"

The pounding of a horse galloping up Long Lane drew Will's attention. It was a brown horse, all lathered, pulling a dearborn. Counting three men in it, Will recognized Joseph Scarlett. Fred Cooper, a neighbor farmer, tightened the reins and stopped in the yard.

"We better get the doctor, he's just about done for," Scarlett yelled to Pownall. He sat behind Cooper, holding wounded Dickinson Gorsuch's head and shielding the sun from his eyes. Dickinson's torn body slouched beside him.

"Take him to my place," Pownall said, shielding his eyes from a bright sun. "This house is full of angry men. I will do what I can to save his life."

"Some water, a drink please." Dickinson stirred. His murky eyes rolled and closed again. "I'd never believe our boys would treat us this way," he said.

"Your boys men now," Pink said.

Pownall turned to Dickinson. "I will go prepare for thee and send for Doc Patterson," he said, walking away through the orchard.

Scarlett put the back of his hand on Dickinson's head. He felt fever rising. Sweat beaded Dickinson's face and neck. "He really needs some water, Will."

"Not your men anymore," Pink said, "black men now. Think on that whilst I fetch you a drink from the well."

"Will," Scarlett said, "I believed thy cause a just one and I befriended thee in thy darkest hour."

"That you did," Will said, shaking his head.

"But now, thy cause is greater than thee. Send the men home, or consider thyself responsible for the death of everyone who surely will be killed. Just as Gorsuch represents slavery in its ruthlessness, thee represents the most obvious relentless opposition to it."

"We must fight. The constable, army, bandits, soul snatchers all join hands when it comes to crushing us."

"Wherever thee goes in these United States there will be killing. For thy own safety, Will, please go on to Canada."

"No Canada," Will said. "We fight to the finish."

"My path crossed Marshal Kline's a while ago," Scarlett said. "He's in Penningtonville mobilizing a right-sized army right now. I hear he's deputized that entire crew of Irish immigrants that ran the new curved railroad track behind Zercher's Hotel."

"Go help him," Will replied with all the rebuke his tone could carry. "With you, my landlord and a thousand more, maybe he can get up the nerve."

"Will," Scarlett said, his voice deep and trembling, "I do resent thy terrible nasty insults."

"We better get him to Levi's place," Cooper said, nodding at Dickinson. "The sun's well past ten o'clock high. Git along." He whistled at the horse.

Will sighed. One man dead, others sure to follow if Kline returned.

"I'd be hasty about it," Scarlett yelled over his shoulder to Will.

Will watched them turn onto Long Lane. Quakers, his friends for so many years. Well, what had he really expected? For certain, he knew every man had a limit to befriending another. But turning him out completely, after so much talk about brotherhood? Would Levi have been that mean to his brother the squire, or to Joseph Scarlett? Will doubted Levi would, but he had yet to learn, freedom was more than winning one hard-fought battle.

He and Pink went inside. Pink joined the restless men downstairs. Upstairs, Will found Eliza at the dry sink letting Hannah wash her bruises and dirt-smeared skin, He placed a chair at the window and stared for a while down at Gorsuch's covered body. Will began pacing the floor, biting his bottom lip, looking out at the Pennsylvania rolling hill countryside.

"I wish I could've got my hands on him," he said. "I shouldn't a never let him get away."

"You talking about the marshal?" Eliza said.

"Yea," he said, taking the cloth from Hannah and gingerly dabbing at the cuts with a finesse Eliza didn't know he possessed. "That old man didn't have to die. He brought it on himself."

Eliza looked at him, pleasantly surprised. As clearly as Will saw the sparkle in her eyes, he saw Tawney. He hadn't thought of her, God Almighty, when was the last time? He remembered how she had tended him when he'd come home black and blue after fighting for Master Mack. Then he'd soothe her whiplashed, scarred, and aching body the way she had taught him. Eliza certainly didn't resemble Tawney in any manner. Not that he didn't care for his wife, but marrying her simply seemed the natural thing to do at the time.

Though she had encouraged him in her own little ways to give love a chance, he really hadn't given the tender touch of caring much of a thought until then.

"Ouch, Will. That smarts a plenty."

"I won't let Kline bring his army down on you and our friends."

"You not go'n tell me what's ailing you?"

"Pownall gave the rent back for the rest of September."

"Why! We ain't even gathered the crop. Did'ja remind him that it is ours? Did'ja remind him that canning time's just beginning? Did'ja remind him our hog be ready for slaughter soon? Did'ja ask him what we go'n feed our chillun come winter?"

Will didn't answer. A buggy stopping in the yard drew his attention. Joseph Scarlett and Fred Cooper hurriedly placed Gorsuch's body in the rig and left.

"Well! Did'ja?"

"Get some things together right now," he said, giving her the money and the towel. "Go to the secret place by yourself, and stay there until I come. If you don't hear from me by tomorrow, go straight to the kids, nowhere else. The missus there will know. I'll get word to her husband. I'm sending our men home. Hannah's got to go with Pink. I'll leave after them. Abe will stay and watch the house 'til I get back. If Kline and his dogs already out there watching, they'll come chasing after us. Then you leave. Don't tarry."

Will turned away abruptly. Downstairs, he explained the impending danger, why his comrades must return home, flee to Canada, or find a well-concealed hiding place. With downcast eyes, he shook hands and watched them leave single file as if marching to the drum roll of a funeral procession. Then he hurried through the orchard, talking to himself. He jumped the fence and walked Long Lane for a spell, noticing how severely the tall stalks, laden with ears of corn, their tassels brown and ready for harvest, had been broken and tramped. He disappeared in the woods bypassing Christiana, on his way to Rev. Clarkson's.

If good news traveled one-half as fast as bad, the deeds of virtuous men would far out-distance evil acts. By late morning passersby on the road to Penningtonville knew of Marshal Kline; they were aware of his wrecking the community, Despite his demands that melted to pleadings, no one offered sympathy or assistance. Some listened but they rebuked him, for he had lost the fight and they were afraid. Carrying, dragging, and helping Joshua Gorsuch maintain his equilibrium while descending Zion Hill into Penningtonville, Kline couldn't even buy a ride.

He had found Joshua wandering up and down Long Lane in circles, talking nonsense and bleeding from his mouth. Kline suspected that Joshua had crossed paths with the mad Indian. Why he hadn't been butchered by the scythe-wielding savage was a mystery. Joshua's moaning attracted Kline in a far corner of the cornfield where he had himself retreated from most definite disaster.

In Penningtonville he left Joshua in the care of a doctor and finally coaxed several men under threat of arrest to help him find the wounded old man, his son and nephew, and bring them to Penningtonville. Three men agreed only if he stayed there in the inn, treated himself to a hearty meal, and rested until they returned. They would not risk their lives traveling with him.

By noontime the searchers were back, informing Kline that Gorsuch had died. They didn't know the whereabouts of his body. A doctor was tending Dickinson in Levi Pownall's home. They hadn't heard anything about Dr. Pearce.

Marshal Kline's hostility grew. He threatened to arrest the whole damned town for their too friendly attitude toward men and women of color living among them, for not demanding to know whether they were free or fugitive. Soon he was aware of himself threatening no one except the inn-keeper, who really wasn't listening.

Commissioner Ingraham, empowered to execute the fugitive slave law to its fullest extent, would ruin him. He, a God-high Englishman hated King George IV only because he himself wasn't the monarch. Everybody whose stature was less than the king Ingraham loathed vehemently, including himself. Day by day he sunk deeper into indignant despair, making everybody's life around him more miserable. If Gorsuch hadn't been so damned head-strong!

From hearing it preached to him every time Ingraham ordered him to investigate or execute an arrest, Kline had memorized the federal statute describing his responsibilities as a U. S. marshal policing slavery.

Any marshal who fails to properly execute the fugitive slave law will be fined $1,000. He is liable for full payment of any fugitive who escapes his custody. The penalty for knowingly obstructing a fugitive's arrest, for assisting a fugitive's escape or for harboring or concealing a fugitive slave, shall be a fine of no more than $1,000 for each escaped slave and imprisonment no longer than six months.

Unless Marshal Kline arrested every black man and woman in Will's gang and every white man who urged them to resist the slave posse, he'd be indentured to Ingraham the rest of his life. He'd be the commissioner's servant, no better off than a slave. He went to the livery stable and rented a dearborn with a spirited horse. He needed names and strong arm men, real patriots anxious to rid Christiana of its colored problem. Hurrying to Gap Tavern where he would mobilize deputies, Kline passed by Mt. Zion AME Church, where Will was seeking the Reverend's help in making his decision.

Will, having come to trust his pastor the way he trusted Abe, found Rev. Clarkson behind his mule plowing. "What might you be turning the ground over for this time'a year," Will asked.

"Turning it under, son, the harvest we have sown," Rev. Clarkson said. "At least that's what it seems like I'm doing."

Again, he completely befuddled Will. Knowing that, he said, "Getting ready for the inevitable, son. Thought you'd be gone long before now."

Will walked beside him in the furrows. "That's what I come to talk about, Rev'm. Ain't no way I can leave my wife and little chillun."

"Got more'n them to worry about now. Whole country of black folks soon be watching you, now that you carry the torch."

"Can't help it. Only Eliza and my three kids I care about. My friends, of course, but..." Looking at the ground, Will scratched the palm of his hand.

"Years ago," the Reverend said, "I remember sitting out back with you the day you found yourself. I saw the lamp light up in your eyes. Now it's a flame."

"You tryin' to make me think I'm a giant. I ain't big at all, Rev'm. If I was, no question about it, I'd stay and battle to the end."

"You'll be a hero only as long as you stay alive. Most stories of black champions of justice are soon trampled into the dirt. Scared folks soon forget, never tell their children."

"But I'm just one man, one simple ole farmin' country man."

"Aye," the Reverend said, pointing his finger skyward, "a thousand tongues will sing your name, Will Parker, but you won't hear them. You'll be in Canada, son. Every slave in America will soon know you went because the slavers coming for you. They going to turn over every rock, barrel, stump and hen house, but won't find you. All the while, so many be following you from the plantations and cotton fields that it'll soon look like that great getting-up-morning. So many going to escape until nothing will be left for the slavecrats to do except free everybody or fight."

"But why me? Takes me near-bout half a day to read a sheet of newspaper. Ain't never had no learning to mount..."

"They go'n kill you if you stay, and black folks go'n be slaves to nigh eternity."

"And what about you, Rev'm, and Miz Emily when they come here looking for me?"

"They'll come, crushing the flowers, making our place ugly. But persecution without a cause is worse'n damnation in hell without a sin. Now that you stood mighty against the sword, that's the price we pay to keep you alive. The crats go'n bury your story, all right, but it won't stay down. Truth crushed to earth shall what?" He looked Will squarely in the eye, his face shaking vigorously—a man reaffirming his determination to stand mightily against his foe, whatever the cost.

"Shall rise again?" Will asked.

"Let it be, son. Great God a'mighty. They'll be here soon, I'll be busy plowing." Rev. Clarkson gripped the ploughshare. "Git on up there, Hobo," he said to the mule.

Will wanted to grip his hand, hug him, stay right there feeling warm and protected by the strength in his words. Rev. Clarkson went on about his business.

Will tramped through the woods, feeling small, indeed scared, unable to comprehend the sudden magnitude of Will Parker, making himself more homesick. Eliza and Mariah and John T and Catherine left to fend for themselves, at the mercy of the meanest, lowest bastards in the land.

A head popped up from the thicket. Will recognized Abe waving his arms frantically, urging him to get off the worn path.

"Will, your house is surrounded. Must be at least fifty, could be a hunnert, armed, some got chains and balls, them ole long buckboards. But not me, no sir. We run or I die. One or t'other."

Pink came crashing through the brush from his post at first lookout.

"How long you been hiding?" Will said.

"Ain't been long. Man, we heard the noise, hallowing like they about gone mad," Pink said.

"Eliza!" Terror, stark and vivid, glittered in Will's eyes.

"She hiding," Abe said, "her and Hannah."

"She's what! I told her, stay to herself!"

"She'd die of fright, Will," Pink said. "Hannah's her sister."

"Her sister almost talked you into giving up this morning?"

"I wish you could forget about that, Will," Pink said.

"I wish I could too, but doubt's lay'n right here." Will pointed to his chest. "You, me, Abe we got us a big job, but you scare too easy."

"I ain't no more. Tell 'em, Abe."

"That's a big order," Abe said, "but the years done sewed us together like brothers, and I owe you one from way back. Christ my witness though, Pink. You break up on me or Will, I'll throw you a seven, without showin' ma' hand like Eliza did."

"You on trial, Pink," Will said, "that's the best I can give ya'."

"Will, c'mon." Abe said, grabbing Pink's arm. "Let's us get fit to battle."

"We can't fight," Will said.

"Huhn!" Abe threw his gun on the ground. "Just what the hell we go'n do, lay down and die? I ain't going back. We fight to the end, that's the way its gotta be, that's what we sweared to do."

"I can't die," Will said.

"Well now, just what the hell? You been resurrected? Pink and me can die, but you go'n just float on up,"

"You do sound a little strange, Will," Pink said.

"I carry the torch." Will said.

"Pink," Abe said, "I understand what's going on inside his head. You got a missus and a young'un too. I only got me, so I'm go'n fight to the end, take many as I kin with me."

"We got to keep it alive, Abe," Will said. "It's on me and you got to help me."

"So we carry the torch, and that's you, hunh?" Abe said.

"Yep."

"Which way we go, Will?" Pink said, seizing the opportunity to reestablish his comrade's trust.

"We wait until dark then head out. Now I gotta' see Eliza, tell her how brave she is 'n all."

"Will, you ain't making much sense but too late now, anyway," Pink said. "Hear that racket? They coming this way!"

"Which way we go, Will?" Abe said. "Tell me before I commence 'a shootin'."

Will stood there, shaking his head in short jerks from side to side. Abe picked up his gun and began loading it.

"Shit, man, do somethin'," he said, looking for a vantage point behind a tree.

Pink began running. "If I die it'll be with my wife."

"Jesus God," Will muttered to himself. "Wait, Pink. We need food, but we can't go home. N' without the Underground Railroad we won't get outta the county. C'mon, maybe we can hide at a friend's place close to the Chester County line til night."

At the three o'clock hour of that very hot and humid afternoon, shortly before Marshal Kline arrived in Christiana, an inquest had been convened in Squire Joseph D. Pownall's office. Kline learned of it after asking a passerby leaving the general store on Bridge Street for directions to a justice of the peace. The stranger directed him to the squire's office around the corner on Gay Street, next door to the apothecary. Tipping his hat, Kline walked rapidly, the limp quite noticeable in his long strides.

The door was open. Kline barged in, making a most disturbing racket. Squire Pownall, glancing at him and studying his badge, pointed to a vacant seat beside a member of the jury in the last row of a little crowded room. A hot, disturbed breeze foretelling a long overdue rain, floated through the door and open side windows. The squire sat at his desk, leaning against the wall behind him, facing Kline and four men of the jury. Constable William Proudfoot, sitting at the squire's right beside a window with his back to the wall, began drumming his fingers lightly on a table reserved for him. A wood file cabinet had been installed in the corner beside Proudfoot. Directly across the room facing the constable sat a chair reserved for sworn testimony.

Dr. Ashmore, a soft-spoken blond man, didn't stop reading a deposition he and Dr. Patterson had prepared for the jury:

> "Dickinson Gorsuch critically wounded, eighty squirrel shots in his arm and side.
>
> Dr. Pearce, a huge black eye swollen shut, squirrel shot in his wrist and shoulder blade, a scalp wound, his clothes shot full of holes, at least thirty of them.
>
> Joshua Gorsuch, knocked senseless, couldn't fare for himself.
>
> Two of Parker's fighters shot, one in his thigh, the other in his arm."

When the doctor finished, Lewis Cooper the jury foreman, read a statement accounting for the other men in Gorsuch's party.

"No sign of Gorsuch's two neighbors; they retreated with United States Marshal Henry H. Kline before the battle raged."

Kline huffed and puffed while listening to the jurists' contradictory statements until they were ready to render a verdict.

"Just hold on a minute," he said. "Squire, you haven't examined one witness. I demand that my word be read into the record."

"Mr. Lewis," Squire Pownall said, "what did thy investigating yield about the marshal?"

"We have the sworn testimony of several persons that he didn't witness the actual killing," Cooper said. "How can his word be part of the record?"

"I heard a statement here that is worse than wrong, it is downright damaging..."

"Truth is," Cooper said, interrupting Kline, "you have already told a different story of the incident, which I repeat, you didn't see. The jury voted to discredit your testimony." He waved his hand, indicating the other three jury men, Issac Rogers, Miller Knott and Henry Burt. "It would have been a waste of time, let the record show that."

"All right, gentlemen," Squire Pownall said, writing in his journal. "Read the summary."

Cooper began:

> "The neighborhood was thrown into an excitement by Edward Gorsuch, the above-named deceased and some five or six persons with him, making an attack on a family of colored persons for the purpose of arresting some fugitive slaves as they alleged. Many of the colored people of the neighborhood collected, and there was considerable firing of guns by both parties. The deceased came to his death by gunshot wounds by some person or persons to us unknown.

After the riot subsided, neighbors found the deceased lying
on his back or right side, dead."

"Excuse me please, Squire," Kline said. "Would you think it ungentle-
manly of me, a measly old federal marshal, to ask where the body of Mr.
Edward Gorsuch might be? Believe it or not, I have authority to investigate the
entire matter, including the body and the record of this inquest..."

"Yes sir, thee does, but not the right to interrupt. Nevertheless, hold it a
minute, Mr. Cooper. At Fred Zercher's Hotel, Marshal. Continue, Mr. Cooper."

Marshal Kline stamped out muttering to himself. If the newspapers
released that report before he arrested everyone who took arms against
Gorsuch, it would ruin him. He felt as if Commissioner Ingraham was walking beside him along Gay Street to Fred Zercher's Hotel, yelling threats in his
ear. Outside the tavern entrance to Zercher's place, he sat on a bench slouching forward with elbows on knees wiping sweat from his neck and brow with
a big red handkerchief.

Actually, Zercher's was the Christiana train station, the town tavern and
hotel. After the new curved tracks of the Philadelphia-Columbia Railroad
brought passengers right up to the front entrance, Zercher's became a community meeting place, the most popular spot between Penningtonville and Gap.

After deciding the most advantageous way out of his predicament,
Marshal Kline went inside to a room where he found the undertaker, E. D.
Calhoun, preparing Gorsuch's body for his kin to claim.

"Might you tell me, sir," Kline said, without introducing himself, "where
I can find a justice of the peace who will issue arrest warrants in due haste,
who will not wait until his friends have been warned that the marshal is coming? This fine gentleman's death must be avenged."

Calhoun, tall as Kline, but scrawny with long wisps of white hair extending from under his stovepipe hat, straightened up from leaning over the body,
removing his white gloves. "What say?" he asked, his voice loud and vibrant.
He cupped his ear and leaned towards Kline.

"Where'n the hell is the squire's office?"

"Shh, for decency's sake. The man is sleeping in peace."

"The hell you say," Kline roared.

"My word, Marshal, you are most obnoxious, and you've made yourself a
host of enemies. All of us are not neegra sympathizers, we simply don't like
your manners. Mistreat another person here like you did two days ago seeking
the whereabouts of that wild band of cut-throats..."

"I have mistreated no one, at least not yet."

"See there, good fellow, that is precisely my point. Your manner is, is so
coarse. You anger so easily. You demand, never asking that our kind citizens
tell you about certain neegras. We are saturated with this nastiness from out-
siders every day, the slavers, the bounty hunters. Then this morning, sending

259

that party of whiskey heads for Mr. Gorsuch, telling them a most questionable story about the shooting...

"You people treat Negroes like white people, and expect me to like you?"

"We treat them like human beings because they're in our midst."

"Well, we could argue the truth in that, but I came to see if anyone has requested the body."

"No."

"Then prepare it for shipping by train to Baltimore."

"Do not order me, Marshal," Calhoun retorted, throwing Kline a sideways glance. "Ask me, if you know the difference."

"All right, all right. I'll see that his family here is notified and that you are paid, after I find a fair, impartial squire if there be such a thing in these parts."

"Go down Gay Street to Squire Pownall, Joseph Pownall."

"Christ, man, he heads the list of nigger lovers!"

"Not Joseph," Calhoun said. "Mayhap his brother Levi leans in that direction. Talk with Joseph, you'll see."

Kline really didn't mean to do it. Nonetheless, he slammed the door behind him and didn't look back. Already it had been too long a day. Perhaps a coffee would stem his dull headache. He ordered a cup in a little eatery, but after sloshing down a hot mouthful or two, he was back on Gay Street again, wearing a hostile scowl, wiping sweat and burping. Passersby gave him a wide berth. At the squire's door, he laid a hand on his stomach and released one final burp, tasting the breakfast he had eaten many hours ago in Penningtonville. "Jesus," he muttered.

Squire Pownall and Constable Proudfoot were finalizing the inquest report when the marshal entered. Kline wasted few words, abruptly explaining that he wanted seventeen affidavits for the arrest of two white and fifteen black men. Listening to Kline's hurried and angry accusations and writing depositions was an impossible task. Insisting he relax didn't help, so Squire Pownall asked Proudfoot to note the names and specific charges while he made entries and signed warrants. How Kline knew the names of so many black men he had seen only that morning was a mystery to the squire, even though he charged each one for aiding and abetting in the murder of Edward Gorsuch.

Kline asked for the warrants to arrest Castner Hanway and Elijah Lewis, but the squire told him Constable Proudfoot would notify them. He pointed to a noisy crowd gathering outside and, noticing several scoundrels, told the marshal that justice, not mob rule would prevail. About the men of color, unfortunately, he wouldn't interfere with federal law, and since they had taken arms—it was a matter of fact—terror snapped like a rabid cougar at the throats of all white people. God help us, he thought, while completing the legal work, and giving Marshal Kline warrants to arrest the colored people. God help them too.

Nine o'clock in the dark moonless night, three hungry black men easing themselves from cramped, secret quarters between the kitchen wall and pantry, went outside and crept along the rear of an abolitionist's house. One after the other, they ran across the yard behind the barn and disappeared. They emerged from the woods on the slope beyond Valley Run between Will's and his landlord's homes.

Candles burned brightly inside Levi Pownall's place. In the sitting room, Levi's wife Sarah tended to Dickinson Gorsuch's wounds. In the kitchen two grown daughters, Ellen and Elizabeth, washed a mound of dirty dishes accumulated by a number of the Gorsuch family's friends from Maryland, and by local residents there to protect the Pownalls and Dickinson from whom they had begun calling the insurrectionists. Will, Abe, and Pink crossed the creek and pasture to the barnyard. Abe hid behind the barn watching. Will with Pink beside him, crossed the yard and rapped on the kitchen door. Ellen opened it and, though startled, seeing them standing there in the candlelight, quickly extinguished the candles and sent her teenage brother George for their mother. After excusing herself and leaving Dickinson, Mrs. Pownall, dumbfounded, stood perfectly still in the doorway a minute or so. Then she summoned Will, Pink, and her two daughters to the darkened pantry.

"Ellen," she said, "Get a clean pillowcase. Thee and Elizabeth fill it with bread and meat."

"But mother," Elizabeth protested, "we've a house full of people to feed and barely enough bread for breakfast."

"Mix more bread." The whispered command was terse and final. "Mr. Parker, Mr. Pinckney, do not move until I give thee consent. George, run place this food at the foot of the golden apple tree. Hurry back."

When George returned she sent him for her eldest son, who with his father was entertaining their guests in after-dinner conversation, that being the custom among Quaker gentlemen.

"Levi," she said to her son, "I need two beaver hats and two long overcoats."

"Mother," Levi protested, "that's gentlemen caller clothing I need for myself."

She read the obvious scorn expressed on his face, but said quite simply, "Would thee run to Penningtonville in the hat and coat with a quart of buttermilk spilling over thee to save a man's life?"

"Of course, mother. Does thee doubt that I would?"

"Then bring them and do hasten, Levi," she said, lighting a candle and placing it in the pantry.

Will and Pink stepped out of the pantry wearing the beavers jammed down to their ear lobes, the high coat collars turned up as if they were ready to bear a winter storm. Quite irregular dress for a humid September night, except that gentlemen callers sometimes behaved in inexplicable ways. Arm in arm—Ellen with Will, Elizabeth with Pink—they walked the dark front pathway past the sentries to the garden gate that swung open to Long Lane.

"Godspeed on thy long journey, Lawrence," Ellen said.

"Yes," Elizabeth said, "do write, Edwin. Let me know thee arrived safely."

Will and Pink bowed, touching their hat brims, then turned and disappeared into darkness. At the tree they found Abe with the sack of food over his shoulder, ready to travel. "I wanna bust out laughing," he said, "but I 'spect how you come about wrapped in them duds ain't funny."

"Whew, I na, need a minute," Pink said going off into the woods. "The outhouse, my nerves, feel like I'm a blow up."

"Make haste," Will said, caustically. "We daresn't tarry. I'm sweat'n to beat the band. But we can't leave these things here."

They arrived in West Marlborough, West Chester County, with the breaking dawn. Will saw Jocko beckoning him in the yard of Edwin Coates' big white frame house. He rapped a secret code with the door knocker, while Pink and Abe watched him from behind a thick evergreen bush. A young white woman immediately responded without expressing surprise, ushered him inside, then waved for Pink and Abe to hurry. Water to wash and quench their thirst, hot tea with sugar, an opportunity to shed the heavy clothing, but no time for idle chatter between strangers dedicated to the Christian proposition—I am my brothers' keeper. After packing Will, Abe, and Pink in his dearborn, Coates transported them to James H. Taylor's haze in West Marlborough. Taylor transferred them to his dearborn and hurried to Issac and Dinah Mendenhall in Kennett Square. When Taylor returned home, detectives flanked by armed hunters were warning his wife and daughters about the impending danger of harboring colored people fleeing Christiana.

Many sympathetic Quakers befriended Will, Abe, and Pink those days after Gorsuch's death, none of whom they could name or describe even under brutal torture. Historians intrigued by the Underground Railroad network in Lancaster, West Chester, and Montgomery counties unveiled their names years later in tracking the legacy of Will Parker.

Yet, each milestone compounded the impending danger. Whisperings livened the air—did you know Will Parker, leader of the Christiana Insurrection, passed through last night? Travel by day was impossible, by night dreadfully treacherous.

At the Mendenhalls', Will, Pink, and Abe picked corn with other farm laborers several days and slept in the woods at night. Then Dr. Bartholomew Fussell appeared with a stern warning.

"Issac," he said to Mendenhall, "thee has been detected and the Governor is offering a thousand dollar reward for the capture of Will Parker. Need I say more?"

"The other two," Mendenhall said, "what of them?"

"No others were mentioned," Dr. Fussell said, "but they've arrested fifteen men of color and two white men. One is a friend. They have been charged with inciting the colored to riot."

"Our good Governor Johnson," Mendenhall said, "yielded to pressure, I suppose."

"I'll not speak so kindly of him, Issac. He's trying to do two conflicting things at the same time."

"Ah yes," Mendenhall said, "intelligent, sensitive man that he is, should know thee cannot serve two masters."

" 'Tis pressure, Issac," Dr. Fussell said. "Edward Gorsuch and some other slave owners had formed a consortium. They own lots of Pennsylvania land. The governor's response to the killing is explainable, even though I suspect his motive is political and that is wicked."

" 'Tis strange though, Bart," Mendenhall said, "why the white men, not Will, have been charged with inciting the people of color to resist. Yet, the reward is on him."

"So the North," Dr. Fussell said, "so we abolitionists, so men of goodwill toward all men shall not exhault his name."

"Perhaps Bart, but I wouldn't dare think 'tis that simple. We should ask Will."

"Danger will not permit it, Isaac. Thee best send him and his comrades away with me. Take them a short distance and I'll overtake thee so thee can hurry back."

"Where can thee take them, Bart?"

"I shall not say," Dr. Fussell answered. "For certain, thee will not know. Hurry!"

Those days Will often thought of Timber, the big fugitive roaming the peak of South Mountain like a mountain lion, thinking it was Canada and being just as deadly protecting it from intruders as if it were a lion's lair. Was Timber's life worth his mountain? Was Will's life worth passage to Canada, a run to another country from where he would be some kind of make believe torch burning? Timber was better off, and at that moment in time, Will wished he had stayed up there in the desolate hills with the alpine man. A thought worth considering with Abe and Pink, but they didn't talk while bedded under so much who-knows-what. With disillusion and loneliness coursing inside them too, maybe it was just as well.

Fear dominated Dr. Fussell's thoughts as he approached Kimberton. He had no place other than to a conductor of the Underground Railroad he suspected was surrounded by detectives or informers. Where, oh God, could he go, after he had driven so far from his home? Who would be least suspected? The answer came as suddenly as if it had floated down like a bird's feather from a tree top—a young white woman, his niece Graceanna Lewis. But drag her into this? Heavenly father, he had no choice.

They arrived at her place around midnight. The doctor left his cargo imbedded in the dearborn while he awakened Miss Lewis and beseeched her assistance though warning her of the consequences. When he begged her response, Graceanna told him she and her two sisters, Mariann and Elizabeth were known by William Still as quiet workers of the antislavery movement.

"A girl lives with us whom we cannot trust," she said, "so thee must take them directly to a room on the third floor. Tell them the door locks from the inside. They are not to unlock it except for this sound." She rubbed her hand across polished wood three times.

"Now make haste. My Friend neighbor will take them food."

Several cots, a table, and five or six chairs were in the huge room. A corner section was partitioned by a piece of heavy drapery. Behind it a night chamber set for toilet facilities. Will, Abe, and Pink spent the night and day quietly, each man primarily occupied with his own private thoughts or watching the roadway from the two windows. Then time had come to travel another fifteen miles to the next station.

Day by night by dawn by evening, hour by hour, Will, Abe and Pink traveled on, entombed in darkness, at the mercy of men and women guided by the light of God they saw shining from the fugitives' souls.

Will clenched his jaws, grated his teeth, balled his fists, squeezed his toes together to keep from kicking that mold-ridden, dirt clogged, tattered carpet off him. One second he felt as deadly as a rattlesnake, the next he felt as unwanted as galloping consumption. Then he would settle down and think of people and events that had profound effect on him. Grandmom Rosey would thank him, maybe rub his head for breaking the bond that had held her family captive lo those many years, for avenging the murder of Ofeutuey by old Major Brodgen, Master Mack's father. For certain, Will was not aware of the anger and paranoia sweeping America over the Christiana incident. Good that he couldn't imagine what had happened there.

Chapter Twenty-Three

Friday, September 12, 1851—The crowd gathering in front of Frederick Zercher's Hotel spilled across Gay Street, clogging the five-points intersection that surrounded a circular horse watering trough and blocking access to any trains at the Christiana station.

A lanky rabble-rouser standing on the train tracks yelling, "Here come the nigger lovers," enticed others to chant with him. James Ellis, a Philadelphia police lieutenant, cautioned his charge of fifty officers guarding twelve men of color Marshal Kline and his posse had arrested.

"Eyes straight ahead," Ellis said. "See everything, stare at nothing. Let the folks yell whatever they please, but don't let anyone break our circle around them," he said, nodding at the black men huddled in a corner of the porch.

Then an outburst of yells and boos punctuated the chanting, Marshal Kline, rushing from a temporary office of Squire J. Pownall in the hotel, collided with Lt. Ellis at the front entrance, knocking his hat off, and forcing a loud grunt from the slightly built officer. Ellis stumbled backwards against a porch column. Several policemen moved swiftly towards Kline. But Ellis, picking up his hat and staring angrily at Kline, motioned for them to back away.

Marshal Kline, towering at least a foot over Ellis, began swelling—his neck and jaws puffed, his chest bulged. Kline stood, legs apart and arms akimbo, glaring at Castner Hanway and Elijah Lewis walking Gay Street through the crowd and turning onto the hotel porch. They attempted to enter, but Kline with his thin lips turned downward in a menacing pout, blocked their way. He grabbed Lewis' shoulder.

"You white-livered scoundrels, surrendering before I had the chance to track you down, aye."

"Surrender to what?" Lewis said, pushing Kline's hand away. "I've come for the squire. I don't know if that's any of thy business."

"Leave him be, Kline," Lt. Ellis said, forcing himself between Lewis and the marshal. "Mister, you don't have to answer him."

"Who do you think you are," Kline said, "interfering with a federal marshal? Stick to keeping the peace and guarding suspects."

"Seems like he and the other man here,' the lieutenant said, nodding his head at Hanway, "came peacefully on their own."

Kline pointed his finger in Ellis' face. "I pleaded with these dogs for my life, begged them not to let the niggers fire at us. What did he do? Told them to shoot us."

"I did not," Lewis said, his eyes narrowed menacingly.

'You're a liar," Kline yelled.

A man drawling in the dialect of down Eastern Chesapeake shore joined in the affray. "Down Maryland way, we got a sure cure for nigger lovers."

Hanway, standing on the porch beside Lewis, looked at the swelling mob of strangers and people from the village jeering them.

Lancaster Alderman, J. Franklin Reigart, came from Pownall's office and placed his hand on Kline's shoulder. "I hope you aren't making a disturbance," he said, escorting Hanway and Lewis inside. "We will charge the suspects legally and orderly."

"Do your business as you well please," Kline said, "and I'll do mine. I've got sixty-five men and warrants for some more niggers and a few nigger lovers who support them in defying the law."

"Where are the murderers?" the Marylander yelled.

"Twelve of 'em over there," Kline said, pointing to the black men sitting there quietly.

"Which one's the Parker nigger?"

Reigart came out and whispered to Lt. Ellis. "We're holding the white men without bail. Get them out of sight. Third floor, lock them in the garret, This crowd is getting wild."

"Haven't found Parker yet, but for God and country, we will," Kline said, pushing past the lieutenant. "Out of my way, you."

Lt. Ellis grabbed Kline's coat sleeve, ripping it on the seam.

"You midget sonofabitch," Kline said, surveying the damage.

"That's two insults," Ellis said, bristling. "The third one won't be taken lightly."

"My, but that's a fine way for a lawman to act." A tall, broad blond man dressed in gentlemen's garb stepped onto the porch with seven burly deputies. All of them except he brandished shot-guns. "Marshal Kline, you must be," he said.

"Who's asking?" Kline said gruffly, fumbling with the torn coat.

"Lancaster County District Attorney John L. Thompson," he said. "Go on, Lieutenant, take the prisoners to the garret. Open the side windows and leave ten of your men to guard then with orders to forcibly detain anyone attempting to interfere."

Thompson's men spread out, positioning themselves across the narrow porch that extended the width of the three-story tavern and hotel.

"Law and order in Lancaster County is my business twenty-four hours a day, Kline. This is an anxious crowd," Thompson said. "How do you suggest we handle it?"

While Kline fished in his brain for an answer, the Philadelphia- Columbia-Harrisburg train pulled into the Christiana depot belching steam and spewing hot embers, forcing people off its tracks. United States Marines from the

Philadelphia Naval Base spilled from the cars. The cadence of their heavy boots on the porch and in the lobby, sounded like thunder rattling from the depths of earth. Dressed for battle, the marines encircled the hotel-tavern and train depot as if occupying it. Yells and jeering threats subsided. Colonel Hayes, the commanding officer, approached county DA Thompson.

"Our orders," he said, saluting the prosecutor, "from Governor William Johnson are to assist in the capture of suspects alleged to have participated in killing Mr. Edward Gorsuch."

"It seems, Colonel, "Thompson said, "you arrived in the nick of time. Would your detail include quieting mob violence?"

"Violence, sir? Against who? If you're asking if we will protect the coloreds from attack, I repeat, my orders are to arrest..."

"It is not a matter of choosing, Mr. Hayes. Mob aggression is a violation of state law, which was part of Governor Johnson's concern when he asked President Fillmore for federal troops. Pennsylvania's personal liberty laws protect all suspects from mob vigilante justice."

"I'll not argue, sir. We simply can't be here containing a crowd however unruly, and in the countryside rounding up insurrectionists."

"Well, Colonel," Thompson said, "your business here is quite clear. What are your specific orders, Lieutenant?" he asked Ellis.

"To arrest suspects, but I will assist you however I can " Ellis said, offering the county prosecutor a smile.

"Very well," Thompson said. "Everyone arrested will be officially charged here, and Slave Commissioner Edward Ingraham will begin the preliminary hearing Saturday in the hotel. Marshal, a word of caution. Lancaster County will not become another bleeding Kansas. If any innocent white people are hurt, you will be held responsible."

"Hurt like my dear friend, Mr. Gorsuch?" A little man dressed in a stylish aristocratic suit, pushed his way to the the porch. "Edgar R. Bedford, sir." He tipped his stove-pipe hat. "The Gorsuch family's personal attorney. You people aren't taking this matter seriously enough, Mr. Gorsuch," Bedford said, tweaking his nose and stroking a thick reddish-brown moustache, "impressed powerful men, right up to the White House front door. Be aware, Millard Fillmore himself is giving this, this blatant disregard for law and order his personal attention."

" 'Tis true," Kline said. "You have no idea, mister ah..."

"Edgar Bedford, Esquire."

"Yes sir," Kline said. "They have not made my task an easy one."

"I'll make no apologies simply for the sake of appeasing you, Mr. Bedford," Thompson said. "Justice will be served. What is largely responsible for the difference in your and my approach to upholding that moral principal is that Pennsylvania entertains certain rights for its people a slave state doesn't. Kline is not a lawyer, he wouldn't know about that."

"One need not be draped in legal finesse," Bedford said. "The guarantee of equitable punishment for a transgression is an inalienable right throughout this grand republic. An eye for an eye, Mr. County DA?"

The crowd cheered while Bedford sucked his teeth, making a most obnoxious slurping noise. Thompson, surveying the crowd and seeing many persons who had voted for him straining to hear his argument, realized that he stood all alone in supporting the commonwealth's personal liberty rights. That crowd wanted vigilante justice, to which he would not yield. But he'd fare better politically by letting Bedford and Kline rabble-rouse to their hearts' content.

Kline wouldn't let him back off that easily. "What are your plans for them, Mr. Prosecutor?" he said, pointing to the black men.

"They will be locked in the Lancaster County jail by me and held until Saturday. By the way, Marshal, tell me?"

"Tell you what?"

"How could you positively identify twelve black men you never saw until yesterday morning and in a state of hysteria?" Thompson said, laughing. "On second thought, never mind."

Kline bristled. "I identified them with witnesses," he said, "exactly as I will do the others I arrest."

"But you ain't got Parker." A scraggly bearded man with a pig's belly and smelling like ale, pushed his way unsteadily in front of Thompson. "All this jibber-jabber about rights and who's been arrested, and the leader still running free. I don't care if Maryland or the President hisself offers a five thousand dollar reward, you won't find 'em lessen I take you to 'em,"

"John Baer," Alderman Reigart said, shaking his head, "drunker than a maggot in a vat of rotten peaches."

"Mr. Gorsuch's estate is prepared to reward handsomely," Bedford said, "for the capture of any person actively involved, stranger."

"Me and ma' men know where the nigger's holed up," Baer said. "How much we talkin' about?"

"His men," Reigart said to Thompson, "are the Clemson gang, a bunch of drunks who constantly wobble out of the Gap Tavern."

"Upwards to a thousand for the ring leader," Bedford said, frowning and turning to Kline. "Marshal, a dozen of Mr. Gorsuch's friends came to help in the manhunt. Deputize them and lets get on with it."

"Step right up, boys," Kline said. "Must be deputized first, and remember, you can't go around terrorizing the countryside, like the niggers done."

"Naw. Uh-uh." Baer spit a mouthful of tobacco juice and wiped his mouth on the back of his hand. "Thousand gawddamned dollars can't split but so many ways. Me and ma' boys will take Parker alone."

"Damn the money," someone yelled. "Let's get the niggers."

"The hearing begins tomorrow and I've got to track down, let's see," Kline said, licking his finger and leafing through a handful of warrants. "Thirty-eight take away twelve, that's a..."

"Sounds like twenty-six," Bedford said, snickering and rubbing his hand across his lip as if stroking his moustache.

With a posse of marines, police, and deputized men one hundred fifty four strong, Marshal Kline set out to find twenty-nine men—twenty-six black and three white. The Clemson gang went its own way looking for Will Parker they said, but combing the countryside for fugitives. What they would do was best described several days later by David R. Forbes, editor of the nearby *Quarryville Sun* newspaper.

"There never went unhung a gang of more depraved wretches and desperate scoundrels than some of the men employed as officers of the law to ravage this country and ransack private homes in the manhunt which followed the affray."

The news media would alert America, making Christiana hamlet the liveliest spot in the United States and its territories. The Philadelphia-Columbia Railroad would increase its frequency of trips. From Parkesburg to Lancaster, along that main rail line every hotel and tavern would be filled to capacity with reporters, slave agents, government officials and lawyers attending the hearings.

En route to Worcester, Massachusetts, U.S. Abolitionist Congressman Joshua Giddings of Ohio, would read an editorial in the New York Tribune that would shrink further his tolerance for passive resistance.

"It was good counsel from Quaker friends to flee rather than fight and it is deplorable, the Negroes did not heed that advice," the piece would state. *"Horror is expressed because white men perished attempting to execute a law of the United States and we are deeply shocked, though we cannot hold the Negroes guilty of murder. They opposed civil law, it is true, but a divine law of Nature was on their side. They defended an inalienable right to their own persons. No act of Congress can make it right for one man to convert another into his personal property or make it wrong for that other to refuse. Slavery is a matter of violence and by violence resistance to slavery was authorized. But whatever be the absolute natural right, had they fled rather than fight, the blacks would have found aid and comfort on their journey. By their act, they have changed the case, now being regarded as aggressors instead of sufferers."*

In a speech before a packed house, Giddings would declare; "Reading the accounts of the terrible tragedy, I could not but rejoice that the despised and hunted fugitives stood up manfully in defense of their God given rights and shot down the miscreants. Time will come when the names of these men will be enrolled with those of the noblest warriors of the Revolution."

In the South, angry threats of secession from the Union were rekindled. A North Carolina newspaper would warn Northerners to obey the fugitive slave law, *"If not we leave you! If you fail in this simple act of justice, the bonds will be dissolved."*

A Florida newspaper editorial would ask the question: *"Are such assassinations to be repeated? If so, the sword of civil war is already unsheathed."*

When the hearing began, September, 13, 1851, an alerted nation was the only defense for the arrested black people. Officially, Thaddeus Stevens, anti-slavery Whig and Lancaster County Representative to the United States Congress, was the leading defense attorney. But despite his unchangeable hostility to slavery, he declared his intentions to uphold all compromises of the Constitution and carry them into faithful effect. The arrested black men did not know Stevens represented them. He had said nothing for or to them.

Lawyers, prosecutors, reporters, writers, and observers, many of whom were Gorsuch's family and hometown friends, overflowed the community room in Zercher's Hotel. The county prosecutor's armed guards, deputized volunteers, police, and marines kept the peace, protecting hysterical white people from bands of renegade slaves and free black men, even though the area had been raked clean of fugitives and many free persons who did not or could not flee.

Slave commissioner Edward D. Ingraham conducted a hearing that reflected his reputation. Black persons' testimonies that could not be substantiated by reputable white people were rejected. Some individuals caught in the sweep were released if it had been impossible to charge them with contributing to Gorsuch's death, or if they were not claimed by a slave owner. Others who had not fought in the battle were charged and incarcerated in Philadelphia's Moyamensing Prison to await trial.

Marshal Kline presented the government's evidence against the arrested men. His only witness, Harvey Scott one of Will's inner guard, had been intimidated by Kline after he had gone to Gap Tavern and bought information from Bill Padgett. Padgett, the poor white farmhand who had written to Gorsuch about his slaves, supplemented his meager existence bumming around as a clock-maker, gathering information on black people. Scott testified under oath that every shred of evidence Kline presented against each person was factual. Twenty-seven of thirty-six black men arrested were held for trial. The four men identified as Gorsuch's slaves fled after the fight.

The more that unholy band of avengers raked the land looking for Will, the more they resembled wild dogs. On Sunday morning they caught Joseph Scarlett, the Quaker who had sped throughout the community warning people of slave hunters. He was beaten, chained, dragged before Ingraham, and thrown in jail, all in one fell swoop. Eliza Parker and Hannah Pinckney were arrested, released by Ingraham and arrested again, the second time with their mother, Cassandra Warner, in her home.

Monday, September 15, 1851—Daybreak seemed late in coming that morning for Cassandra. The sun finally revealed its bright red face in an overcast sky then ducked behind a cloud as if it would rather hide than splash its warm rays on the ugliness of that day. Cassandra, locked in the third floor garret of Zercher's Hotel, awoke long before dawn and prepared herself as best an old, frail woman could with the worst of limited facilities.

When Marshal Kline thrust open the door, snorting like a bull, she was sitting at the window, watching the crowd out front, unmindful of her slow, sporadic droning of some spiritual. Kline waved his hand for her to come out. Cassandra, hardly bigger than the rifles carried by the two marines flanking her, walked out slowly in front of Kline.

Cassandra's soul, a rock bed of endurance deeply rooted in the subconsciousness of black slave womanhood, would again hold her steadfast in the determination to defy intimidation by that roomful of slave traders. Years before her daughters were born, she had stood on auction blocks, turned and stripped to the demented delight of slavers. It had happened since their births, again and again. Then, too old to breed, too old to sell, too old to keep, actually worked to the bone, her Godless master had put her out to pasture one morning. Cassandra set out walking from somewhere along the Virginia-Maryland border until she stumbled upon her daughters in Christiana. Since then she had lived the life of a recluse, shying away from most everything except her daughters, their children, and midnight.

White men crowded into the hearing chamber; others jamming themselves against the hotel entrance for a glimpse of her, were held at bay by the armed authorities. Cassandra hesitated to avoid stumbling at the first landing. Her knees were limp and weak like watery grits, but they'd never know it. She didn't reach for the banister.

"That's her, Mamie. Dad-gummit, I'd know her any place," a person in that sweltering sea of onlookers said. "Ran off three years ago, but ain't changed much."

"Mamie, my ass," another proclaimed. "That's my Cassy, makes the best sweet potato pie in all of Virginia. She wants to go home. I can tell."

"Friend," a third unidentified man responded, "you sound just like a sweet potato liar I used to know."

A roar of side-splitting, belly-bouncing laughter swept through the hotel.

"Gentlemen, gentlemen," Commissioner Ingraham yelled, standing and banging the desk with his gavel.

Cassandra, guided before Ingraham, looked up into his huge, puffed eyes through the set of pince-nez poised at the very tip of his nose.

"By jove," he said, "this jousting, this dastardly behavior, I'll but warn the lot of you once and only once today. Be gentlemen, we have a full day's work."

Ingraham cleared his throat and glanced at defense attorney Stevens and David Paul Brown, an abolitionist lawyer assisting him. They sat at a table near the wall at a ninety degree angle from the commissioner. Directly across from Stevens and Brown, U.S. District Attorney John W. Ashmead from Philadelphia, Alderman Reigart, and County Prosecutor Thompson sat crowded around a table. Kline seated himself in a chair beside Ingraham.

Rifling through some papers spread in front of him, Ingraham asked Cassandra if her name was indeed that. She simply stared at him.

"Are you a run-away slave?"

She continued staring.

"Who claims this negress?" he said, impatiently. "She goes by the name of Warner..."

"Cassy, that's right, sir. Cassy Warner, got the papers right here in my hand." A young man pushing and shoving his way to the bench, waved his papers in the air.

"Your name, sir?"

"Davis, Albert Davis, Anne Arundel County, Maryland, and she is my family's slave. Never been a bad negress, somebody must've forced her to run away, yes sir. Been gone nigh three years come November."

"There's no contesting status, Commissioner," Kline said. "She wants to go back."

"Oh," Ingraham said. "From what authorized source did you make that determination?"

"Her," Kline said. "She said it without me asking."

"How did you come by her, Marshal?"

"Some deputies were tracking her daughters in their search for Will Parker. The girls led them to the old woman's earthen hut. We're holding them too, Parker's wife, Hannah Pinckney and her baby."

"Lucky bastard, somebody is," Davis said. "Three for the price of two. A baby no less."

Ingraham beat the desk with his gavel. "By jove sir, mind your foul tongue. Don't make me slap you with a contempt of court." He tallied the bill for Cassandra on the papers Davis had shown him claiming ownership. "Sixty-five dollars," he said, sliding the warrant and the ink quill to the edge of his desk. "Sign and pay, please."

Davis grumbled, while pulling a fistful of wrinkled currency from his pocket. He signed his name, paid Ingraham, and fastening a shackle to Cassandra's wrist he said, "Me thinks you Northern boys running a little game on us from down yonder way, Commissioner. You can bet my governor will hear about this."

"Hmm," Attorney John Ashmead said, rubbing his chin thoughtfully and leaning back in his chair.

"We'll take a ten minutes recess. Marshal, fetch the next two suspects, Elijah Lewis and Castner Hanway."

Cassandra looked straight ahead, as if looking at herself through Ingraham, his chair, the wall behind him and space to a place far away where mortal men didn't dwell. Davis turned around and began pulling her away. She walked as if he had wound and released a spring inside her that set her legs moving. Only when her gaze swept past the caring tenderness in the eyes of a young Boston news reporter from William Lloyd Garrision's *Liberator* did she return to that dreadful place.

"Is that really true, you want to go back?" the reporter asked her.

"So many white men come, "she said. "Kicked down my door, said they would bring the light horse up from Philadelphia and cut all the niggers to pieces."

"A light horse," the reporter asked. "What's that?"

"Ain't never seen it. A white boogabear, I hear," Cassandra said. "My poor little grandchildren... I might as well go on back so they might have a little chance at living."

Cassandra was forgotten as soon as she disappeared, what with the throng surging for a clear view of Lewis and Hanway entering from a side door, flanked by marines. Kline mentioned to Ingraham that a line across Hanway's forehead had deepened. His long wiry body sagged, his head tilted sideways.

"Looks like we might get the truth today," Kline said. "Three days in the pokey probably did wonders to his memory."

Ingraham, looking through his pince-nez at Kline, whispered cryptically. "Weren't much Thaddeus Stevens could do for the nigras, except sit there like mold on a rotten log. But he'll carve you up like a Thanksgiving turkey for them. He's a Whig, a slavery hating United States Representative. These abolitionists are his people. Be ye damned most careful," Ingraham said, rapping the desk with his gavel. "This hearing is now in session. Castner Hanway, Elijah Lewis, come forth."

Hanway hesitated, listening to Stevens quietly talking to him. In a roaring authoritative voice laden with a deep nasal Vermont accent, Stevens stood and spoke.

"Mister Slave Commissioner, Attorney Brown and I," he said, nodding to his partner beside him, "are defending the accused. However, we will not offer testimony in either man's defense at this time unless of course, a dire need arises that will lend itself to the probability of an incriminating technicality."

"Very well, counsel," Ingraham said, indicating with his gavel for Hanway and Lewis to stand in front of his desk. "Mr. Hanway, you are charged with aiding and abetting in the murder of Edward Gorsuch. You are charged with refusing to assist in the capture of run-away slaves What say you, guilty or not guilty?"

"Not guilty."

Ingraham sighed. "Mr. Lewis," he said, repeating the charges and asking Lewis for his plea.

"Not guilty."

"Marshal Kline, what evidence do you have against these men?"

Kline swaggered to Hanway, with fang-like teeth bared. "You dare say you did not help those niggers resist us?"

"I did not,"

"You and your friend here, Mr. Lewis, didn't coax them into rioting and killing Mr. Gorsuch?"

"Riot, sir? What riot?"

"Of all the confounded nonsense... By jove, hold on there, Mr. Kline," Ingraham said. "Mr. Lewis, do you share Mr. Hanway's opinion of the word *riot*?"

"Yes."

"Do you mean the nigras' behavior was not infantile, not spontaneous, not join-in-the-frolic behavior?"

Stevens stood and extended his hand in Ingraham's direction, but on second thought, sat down and wrote *riot* on a pad.

"I mean they were organized and determined to protect themselves against aggression of any sort," Hanway said.

"I asked Mr. Lewis," Ingraham said. "Not you."

"Mr. Hanway is correct," Lewis said. Though he spoke to the wall behind the slave commissioner, his stern baritone voice resounded throughout.

"You're telling us," Ingraham said, "they conspired to kill Mr. Gorsuch?"

"Absolutely not. They knew nothing about him until he appeared in Mr. Parker's yard."

"Mr. Parker, aye," Ingraham said. "I take it he is your friend?"

"He is indeed."

"Your friend and his nigras indeed did conspire," Ingraham said, "if they were organized. What say you about that, Mr. Hanway?"

"My good man," Hanway said, "Quite a few slave owners, kidnappers and such have left here in a hurry empty handed. Unfortunately, he's the first to fight to the finish, rather than flee."

"You've known all along, the nigras would kill white people. Why didn't you tell the squire?"

"Their activity was no secret in these parts," Hanway said.

"Did you ever warn your nigra friend about the consequences of his irresponsible behavior? Did you ever tell him he was breaking the law?"

"I told all of them not to shoot Mr. Gorsuch."

"Well, jolly good for you. Mr. Lewis. Why didn't you notify the sheriff, the squire, the county prosecutor, for God's sake man, somebody about that?

"Organization for mutual protection," Lewis said.

Ingraham's eyes dilated. The pupils rolled around and out of focus. For a minute or so, he looked as if regurgitation was inevitable.

"Lewis, Hanway," he said, "I'm asking the United States Attorney, Mr. Ashmead over there, to recommend a full scale investigation by the Department of Justice. You and the other suspects will return to the county jail or Moyamensing Federal Penitentiary to await final outcome of this hearing. The charge is suspected treason."

Treason! Elijah Lewis began breathing as in sleeping, his mind racing from one fleeting image to another—his wife, children, the Moyamensing dungeon, a foggy daybreak, scaffold, hangman's noose. Yet, hearing Ingraham trying to punish him with insinuated guilt, neither he nor his family would shed tears, even though he might not be with them when the first snow came. Elijah's eyes burned into Ingraham, watching the evil buzzard working out his propensity for hate and greed.

Castner Hanway's wife rushed to his side, gasping incoherently. But he didn't feel her clinging to him. In a dream-like stance, he was staring down the sight of a rifle barrel at himself, holding his breath, feeling the commissioner's hand on top of his squeezing the trigger slowly and steadily. But his sharpening anger held Ingraham's hand in check, for Hanway knew he could not be that which he had been accused. Indeed, if he could have summoned scalding fury within himself, the entire band of slavers would be dead. There would be no need for lying.

Treason! The word echoed across the room from the mouths of heavy voiced men snapping at each other. Reporters scribbled on note pads. Some abolitionist friends of Joseph Scarlett, Lewis and Hanway bristled with resentment. Slavers and volunteers of the manhunt began congregating in circles. Ingraham's gavel, sounding as if it were knocking holes in the thick oak desk, accentuated the pandemonium.

"Order! Order! Remove the prisoners. We will recess until the authorities restore order!"

Two of the county prosecutor's men surrounded Hanway and Lewis. The others spilled into the crowd, pushing not so gently, demanding silence.

"Mistuh Commissionuh, suh." A tall, rotund man with long disheveled black hair sticking from under a floppy hat, and a full black beard shoved his way through the crowd. His suit strained to the last thread to contain him.

"Tis my unduhstanding the good marshal apprehended two runaway negresses."

"A few minutes, sir. You'll have to wait." Ingraham said. Sweat poured from his fat, pampered face. He dabbed his eyes on a cuffed sleeve. Banging the gavel, he yelled. "If you fine, cultured gentlemen see fit to act orderly, we will continue. If not, our business here today will conclude."

"Mistuh Davis," the stranger said, "spoke of them earlier when he repossessed Cassy."

'What, pray tell," Ingraham said with a heavy sigh, "are you talking about?"

"I suh, am Elduh B. Ledbettuh, from Richmond. Too far I've traveled to this blackbird's haven for you to treat me with such uttuh disregard."

"I'm tired, sir. Three days of shameful, unbelievable testimony has worn me to a frazzle. I don't want to ever see another nigra in my life."

"He'd have to earn a living then," Attorney Brown said to Stevens.

"He is one pitiful liar," Stevens said, chuckling.

"I'm evuh mindful of yo'wa disposition, suh. Now please be mindful of mine," Ledbetter said.

Ingraham leaned forward, his chin almost resting on the desk. "I'm duty bound to do that, Mr. Ledbetter. Ah yes, you were saying?"

"Mistuh Davis, the man who spoke earliuh? His father sold me two teenage nigresses some time ago, years befo'wah his Cassy run off."

"Of course, of course. Marshal Kline arrested two that we suspect are fugitives. Marshal, the nature of them?"

"Yes, Eliza Parker and Hannah Pinckney and her little pickaninny."

"Will Parker's woman?" someone yelled from the crowd, and rumbling began again.

"Order, order," Ingraham said. "Marshal, fetch the nigresses."

"My pleasure, Mr. Ledbetter. Commissioner, I'd better take three or four marines with me"

Ledbetter frowned at Marshal Kline and the marines ascending the hotel stairs to the third floor garret.

"Why fret, Mr. Ledbetter?" Ingraham said with a smile. "You came for two nigresses, maybe you'll get three."

Ledbetter grinned and in a sudden self-conscious gesture, attempted to run his fingers through his hair. "Oops, s'cuse my hat." He tipped it by the crown, but didn't remove it.

"This isn't the House of Parliament. Relax," Ingraham said,

Standing on one foot, leaning on Ingraham's desk, and mindful of all eyes on him, Ledbetter said, "It grieves my heart to see such goings on with nigras as is heah. I've been proud of my Quakuh heritage. Yes, I have a strain running in my veins from my daddy's people, and pride myself in believing that accounts for the gentleness I have that so many planters don't have. Never been mean to my nigras, even take the time explaining why I need them. Yielding a decent crop against such competition just isn't so without them, and if I had to pay wages, I'd be bankrupt tomorrah."

He stopped talking when he saw Eliza and Hannah coming down the stairs shackled together by right and left arms. "Commissionuh, you suspected right. They are mine. But you needn't chain them, Marshal."

"Mister," Kline said, "This one, Parker's woman, is real bad, crying and screaming so many foul names. 'Twas all I could do to keep the men from boogeying her up real bad."

"They didn't?" Ingraham asked.

"I told them, Commissioner. We don't take too kindly to damaged property."

"They weren't bad nigresses. Probably coaxed to run off and picked up some bad habits. Say, where's the little pickaninny?"

"In the charge of a free nigress, an old mammy," Kline said. "She was duly warned of the consequence of hiding fugitives."

Hannah looked at the floor, her hands laced across her stomach, grateful that she was shackled to her sister. Eliza, staring at nothing, was grim and cold as onyx stone. She shed no tears but wept softly, trying to close the vault between the free life she had come to know, and the old forgotten reality; making her inner sanctum inaccessible so that she could deal with the agonizing calamity of returning to slavery. Will, her son, and her daughters, though their pleas were faint in her heart, wouldn't let her. She couldn't bury the tender feelings in the deep place inside where her husband had finally touched and savored, as it enraptured him time after time in their intimacy. She couldn't block out the tears and excited screams of Mariah only last spring when she had passed from the first grade to the second.

Ingraham looked at her apprehensively, a slinking black feline with deadly poison in her eyes turning red and shining. He leaned back and pushed his chair away from the desk.

Ledbetter saw a little wiry slave, mean and ugly as homemade sin with a docile sister who'd follow her to the end of earth.

"I'll be needing my chains," Kline said.

"I told you, Marshal," Ledbetter said. "I don't need them."

Ingraham, held out his hand. "The chattel papers declaring ownership, hurry, sir." He scribbled on the papers while studying Eliza as if at any minute a panther might jump out of her and claw him to death.

"Looks like one hundred dollars, Mr. Ledbetter."

Ledbetter gawked at him. "That's too damned much, Commissionuh."

"My good man, you heard the marshal testify, they fought like men in the riot? Insignificant? Certainly not, but I'll not complicate matters for you. I'm dropping murder charges and giving you the pickaninny without papers." He folded his hands across his rotund belly, prepared to barter, but glanced at Eliza. "All right, eighty." He raised the gavel, waiting for Ledbetter's response.

"One of these days, soonuh than most of you all think," Ledbetter said, "we Southernuhs going to get tired of being treated like clowns. My receipt?"

"Signed accepted by you and signed paid by me. Now," Ingraham said, banging the gavel, "these hearings are adjourned until the United States Department of Justice completes its investigation and the nigra personage of Will Parker is delivered to this court dead or alive."

Chapter Twenty-Four

Twisting in a tarpaulin, feeling as if he were on the verge of smothering in the bosom of a grizzly, Will pressed his face against the floorboards with his nose in a crack, filling his hot lungs with cool night air. Over the wheels' squeaking and the rattling of the horses' harness, he could hear Jay P. West, the Underground Railroad conductor taking him, Abe, and Pink to Phoenixville, fussing with his brother. He couldn't distinguish their words, but he needn't. What else did white men argue about so more vehemently than about black men? Will brooded, becoming more irritated with each passing mile; a passive kind of slow burning anger making his senses so acute he could look a stranger between the eyes and instantly read his mind, or smell a slaver and his pack of human hounds a mile away in any direction.

Jay, a husky young farmer with close cropped blond hair, trembled in cold sweat. He placed a finger across his closed lips, cautioning his identical twin riding beside him on the buckboard seat to stop babbling.

Thomas smarted and began mumbling to himself. Why had Jay committed them to deliver three fugitive slaves without asking if they were involved with that bunch from Christiana wanted for murder? The startling truth was, they had killed a slave owner. No greater sin could be committed against God. Worse yet, it violated the United States Government's Fugitive Slave Law.

These brothers were entrusted, Will thought, to secret him out of the country, to avoid killing more white folks, to stop him from encouraging other fugitives to resist.

Finally the travelers arrived at what Jay perceived, according to his directions, the next underground station. It was a red brick colonial, dark, seemingly empty and foreboding; no Jocko waited in the front yard, no single candle burned in a window. Reluctantly, Jay guided his team of horses down the lane beside the house to the barnyard and stopped. He really didn't want to knock, especially at that hour of the night, without some indication of its being the right place. So he waited.

Will reached across the wagon and hit Abe. The sharp jab in Abe's side alerted him; at the slightest hint of provocation, he, Will and Pink would fling off their covers and rise up speaking the powerful language of do-or-die survival. Abe, bound up in the tarpaulin, couldn't reach Pink, so he kicked him. Abe's hard boot in Pink's ribcage made him wince. Jay and Thomas heard him.

"Jesus, my savior," Thomas moaned. He wished they'd keep quiet. A nagging doubt warned him, this farmhouse was no underground depot. They shouldn't reveal their cargo.

A barn door creaked, but neither Jay nor Thomas could see far into the still darkness. Will lay tense, hearing his heart beat, ready to spring. He heard a man easing up beside the wagon on Jay's side, The man breathed heavily. Jay's nerves almost catapulted him from the buggy seat.

"Da-d-dammit, a joker could get hurt real bad, da-doing that."

"You're late, doc," the man whispered in a chopped, barking manner. "I shot the mule; he kept getting worse."

"It sure to God is a dark night," Jay said, looking into the overcast sky, "hard to make haste without star-light,"

Slowly, as if moving hurt his neck, the mystery conductor, a big, bearded man with a gruff voice, tilted his face skyward and chuckled. "Ain't a star in the sky," he said, "north, south, east or west. Travel tonight is next to impossible."

"My cargo's gotta make the train," Jay said. "Time is running out."

"Mother Nature done spoke," the man said. "She heard the president sitting on his throne in the United States government speak and shut down the train. Even the Big and Little Dippers stayed in."

Will nudged Abe. Abe nudged Pink. They flung off the covers and leaped from the wagon, startling Jay, Thomas and the conductor.

"My God, fellows," the conductor said, jumping back and staring intensely at the three black men. "We daresn't make so much noise."

He resembled a stone mason; rough sandstone hands, a leathered face, muscular and about Will's height.

Will sensed his irritation. "I lost track of time," he said. "What's today?"

"Monday," Thomas said. "I'd guess we're near fifty miles from Christiana."

"Feels like I been riding since last winter," Abe said, rubbing his tenderized behind.

"Do you have provisions?" Jay asked.

The conductor sighed. "It's real bad. Aye God, I'm a telling you, it is. Come inside," he said, leading them to his barn. "Be careful where you step, I daresn't make light."

In the barn he unhooked a lantern from the wall and lit it. They gathered around an old, weather beaten desk and chair in a corner of the barn. Several calendars, faded bills for seed, livestock food, and machinery hung from nails. He adjusted the wick. A shadowy light spread across the desk and front page headlines of the past Saturday's *Lancaster Express*.

"CIVIL WAR—FIRST BLOW STRUCK," the conductor read, his snappy eyes flashing across the page.

Fear spread across Jay's and Thomas' faces. Jay bent over the paper and began reading. "Jesus," he said, "listen to what it says here."

"We have a premonition, this is not the end, only the beginning."

"Lemme the hell outta here," Thomas said, his eyes blazing with fury. "My wife and kids are alone. Let's go, Jay. I knew I should'a brung along my rifle."

"Wait'll I read the rest of it," Jay said. "Listen."

"A fever of indignation; not so much at the Negroes as at those who instigated them to the deed."

"Wait," Pink said, "I ain't much with fancy words, don't read so fast. Sounds like they blazing white folks for making us fight."

"A pack of lies," Will said, "to make the whole world think Elijah and Castner showed us how to protect ourselves."

"Gawdamn," Abe said, his booming voice waking the barn. "Did you expect the white folks writing that shit would tell the truth?" In a dark, far off stall a cow responded.

"Aye God, man. Dare not yell again," the conductor said. "You have no idea, the destruction that will rain down on my home were someone to find you here."

"Let's git, Jay," Thomas said, grabbing his brother's arm.

"We'll only trouble you for a drink of water," Will said, "if we may. Point us in direction of Philadelphia, we'll walk."

"Impossible. Armed patrols are spread in a circle, must be a hundred miles; from Columbia up the Susquehanna to Harrisburg, from there to the Schuylkill, along the river to the Delaware in Philadelphia, down the river to the Delaware state line. Your only chance, and by God a slim one, is Norristown. Help is there if you get through. It ain't far, just across the Schuylkill River. My missus packed a lunch—some fruit, chicken, boiled eggs, a jug of cider."

His generosity surprised Will. "I'll pay," he said, reaching for the money sack tied to the inside of his trousers."

"Don't insult me," the conductor said. "I'd deny no poor traveler a meal."

Abe threw three shillings on the table. "We ain't begging," he said.

"Absolutely not," the conductor said, glaring at Abe.

Abe stared right back. "Our money pays or we don't eat. Listen good to me, mister man. Try hard to understand why we can't beg. If I pass out for want of food," he said, "you best shoot me 'cause if I'm hungry and ain't got no money, I'll take before I beg for a single crumb. You say it's stealing, I figure it's owed to me. Either way, I'll never cry to a white man for a gawdamned thing again in my life." He whipped out a pistol.

The conductor squinted his eyes. Wrinkles creased his forehead. "My heart is pure," he said, backing away. "Please..."

"No need for you or them," Abe said, pointing the gun at Jay and Thomas, "to fear. This is for Will and Pink, if they ever get so weak in the head to beg a white man and I hear them."

"You'd shoot a man for begging," Thomas said, "but wouldn't harm him for stealing?"

"That ain't exactly what I heard him say," Pink chimed in.

"I know what I heard," Thomas said. "What if a man was begging for his life?"

"These days it's better for a black man to die," Will said. "Man who ain't never run out the lion's mouth wouldn't understand nohow."

"Ain't never run out the lion's mouth," the conductor said, repeating it several times, his gawking at Abe settling to a thoughtful gaze. "Well, sir," he said, the rough-iron edge in his voice fading. "Your black pride sure draws the worst out of a man. But aye God, I ain't one to be so mean that I must hide my feelings. So what if I get mad whenever a pitiful fugitive comes my way? For whoever's sake I help him, I hate myself for being such a damned fool. I'm breaking the law. Now you're asking in a round-about way had I ever considered that if I were in your shoes, and you in mine, would I let you pity me?"

"I know damned well you wouldn't," Abe said.

"You know no such thing. I never had time to think about the fleeing man's conscience. I never considered it. And of course I can see its strength. How else could you defy the president and death—run out of the lion's mouth—like my granddaddy did in the Revolutionary War, fighting for what he believe God granted him..."

"Your money's on the table," Abe said. "We'll be getting on up the road."

Thrusting his hands in his pocket, suddenly aware of his eyes glued on Abe, the conductor looked at the barn floor. "The woods back of me are safe, but when you come to the river, night patrols will be there."

"The cemetery. Upper Providence Friends Meeting Burial Grounds," Jay said, snapping his fingers. "Hide in there."

"They'll have to cross the river first," the conductor said. "But no government agents or anybody else will go near that graveyard. Through the woods back here to Phoenixville Ford, you'll see the boats there. Cross over to Springs Ford. Cross the canal, then follow your nose to a steep hill. Climb it."

"Yeah," Thomas said, "Them old bones in the cemetery cry out for the hurt beast."

"A what kinda beast?" Pink said.

"Hurt beast, keeps intruders out of the graveyard," Jay said. "For sure, if he don't run you the hell out ain't nobody coming in after you. Some folks in these parts claim they hear old bones crying out soon's dusk of evening come."

"Wait a minute," Abe said. "If the beast keeps folks outta there, why you sending us in?"

"Can't fool him," Jay said. "He'll know you need his protection."

"Listen closely, fellows," the conductor said. "With your back to the river, Norristown will be downstream, to your right. Find Dr. Jacob Paxson. He's a faith healer, lives on Airy Street. Claims he cures by laying on the hands. Wouldn't hurt if one of you are deathly sick, talking out of your head some, maybe foaming at the mouth like a mad dog or something rabid bit you. Someone is sure to put you at his doorstep."

"Or the sanitarium," Jay said.

"God be with you," the conductor said.

They parted, shaking hands.

On the road again, the challenge of penetrating the hilly woods that skirted Phoenixville, of fording the creek, but primarily of worrying about Eliza and his children was bearing down on Will. He moped along, actually dragging behind, nibbling an egg while Abe and Pink devoured the chicken. He wet his lips with the cider and spat. Abe and Pink drank heartily, whispering to each other. Then Abe stepped into the lead.

Through tall trees from a distance, a smokey-orange afterglow penetrating the black night outlined the forest. Getting closer, they could see fires, lots of them, atop the banks of a murky, still river. Voices, gradually becoming loud, stole the quietude of the September night. Abe stopped on a railroad track running beside the Schuylkill, rounding a bend upstream and disappearing in darkness. The banks on both sides, though not very high, were sheer drops into the river except for the landings. Boats—canoes and flat bottoms—were moored there. On the other side several men with guns stood around a crackling fire chatting away. Several times they yelled across the river at each other.

Beyond the river valley steep hills of Montgomery County silhouetted in the night sky, loomed high above the shadow forest. Up there, Abe thought, would be the cemetery. Downstream he saw a block of undisturbed darkness, the only place they might possibly swim across. But they would be taking an awful chance in the still water. Not a single wave rippled the surface. Throwing stones upstream to draw the manhunters' attention would only alert them. Then, several big hulks in the canal that ran beside the river on the other side began moving. Men with booming voices coaxed hee-hawing mules on the tow pathways pulling creaking and groaning barges overloaded with tons of anthracite coal shipped from the Reading area mines.

Abe summoned Pink and Will. "Time to git on up," he said, with a hint of humor. "The hurt beast sent them guys and mules to kicking up a fuss so we can cross over."

From a dark spot on the tracks where they lay, Abe studied the water. "Will, Pink, it's deep right up to the rock edge. Y'all with me?"

"Git on with it," Will said, gruffly.

"Yeah," Pink said.

Abe eased himself down into the water, glad that Will had accepted his leadership, even though grudgingly.

"Oooweee," Pink said, "this is cold. Ma, my teeth chattering."

"Shhh," Abe said. "Swim like a dog, nothing but your face outta the water."

Abe, reaching the opposite bank first, floated around, feeling for the best spot for Will, the tallest of them, to stand upright against the rocky bank. With Will in place and Pink bracing him, Abe climbed from Will's hands to his shoulder. He planted a foot on Will's head, and muscled himself over the top. From Will's shoulders, Pink supported by Abe, hoisted himself up and over. Pink and Abe, lying flat against the ledge, grasped Will's hands. With his feet inching upwards from one crevice and jutting edge to the next, and with them pulling him, Will scaled the river's granite-like wall.

They climbed the floating barge, moving along at the mules' pace, and sneaked over its bed of coal. Jumping off the other side, they had crossed the canal and were safely in darkness again. Abe didn't slacken his pace. He climbed the long, steep hill as if charging in battle to occupy the summit. At the iron gate of the Quaker cemetery, Abe hesitated, looking about. Though he wasn't afraid, he waited just to be sure they were indeed welcome. He took one short step inside. No bones rattled or cried, no wisps of hot hairy air or frigid breezes raked his face. No vines, growths of entombed arms and legs, wrapped around his ankles. Only lonely tombstones stared, and frightened nocturnal prowlers scurried from Abe, Will, and Pink walking softly in single file.

How foolish, the thought occurred to Abe, for him to fear any spook that buzzed in the heads of white men. All the haunts, hurt beasts, or whatever else might visit a graveyard in the night were playthings compared to the flesh and blood beasts eager to pounce on them, especially on Will. Of the three of them, Abe mused, Will would be the likely one needing the doctor. Getting him mad enough to act crazy would be easy, but making him behave as if a mad dog had bit him could be a real headache. "Rest a spell and stay put 'til I get back," Abe said. "I saw a few things down yonder we may need."

Will sat on the ground, leaning against a granite slab, looking into the moonless night full of stars, hearing the quiet symphony of graveyard darkness. "Hear that, Pink?"

"What?"

"Somebody with a ball and chain around a foot dragging it through dead leaves?"

"Your load is heavy," Pink whispered, standing beside him, "Mine too, but we can't cave in."

"Don't know how much more I can take," Will whispered, between chattering teeth.

"We go'n keep that torch alive, even if we have to swim the Jordan."

"I shouldn't never left my chillun, Pink. I hear them crying. Mariah is holding Catherine. John T is laying down, not really wanting to get well. But I don't see Eliza."

"Where is Hannah and my daughter? You making it awful hard, Will."

"Where'n hell is Eliza?" Will drew image upon image in the night sky, but nothing of where his wife might be.

After the preliminary hearings had concluded and Elder B. Ledbetter granted ownership of Eliza and Hannah, he made them sit on either side of him in the rented dearborn. "You gals mighty fortunate that I cain't seek revenge. I don't forget, but I'm obliged to swallow a bad taste or two because the Lord warns me of extreme damnation if I don't. But you will work hard and prove to me that you trustworthy. I don't believe you bad nigresses, just weak in the head. I've a mind to send you down the Mississippi River."

"Oh, please not that," Hannah said. "Ain't nobody to see after my baby, she just a little biddy thing. Please, Master Ledbutter."

"Ledbetter," Eliza said. "For God sake, Hannah, Ledbetter."

"Don't worry about my name," he said. "Tell me you sorry for running off. Both of ya' tell me right now."

"Hannah ain't got the nerve to skip across a creek," Eliza said. "I made her run. Would'a killed her if she hadn't." She stared at space, feeling Ledbetter's mounting disgust.

Ledbetter didn't loathe slaves, dared not deny they were human. His lot though, would be better off without her. "You got children, Eliza?"

"No," she said. "How you know where to find Hannah's child?"

"Well now, I was just going to ask about it," he said looking around at the wooded landscape.

"Over there," Hannah said, "that house past the woods in the field. Hard to see it if you don't know it's there."

"Ain't no wagon trail back there?"

"Way round the other side," Eliza said. "We'd have to go back near to Christiana and take another road out of town."

"So we all walk," Ledbetter said. "Let's go."

"My baby was born free," Hannah blurted, "like Eliza's chillun. Why she go'n be a slave?"

Eliza saw Ledbetter's jaw sag, saw his eyes reflect a nastiness, read in his face a terrible shortening of temper, watched him grab a set of chains under the seat.

"The breaking stockade for you," he said. "Hey, what the hell you doing?"

Quickly leaping from her seat, Eliza cleared the sides of the wagon, her legs churning before she touched down.

"By God, I'll shoot," he yelled, jumping down in pursuit.

Eliza turned around only long enough to bend behind a tree and yell to her sister. "Run, Hannah!"

And run Hannah did, down the lane a short way, darting into a thicket full of blackberry bushes and low limbed trees. Like a hound picking up Hannah's scent and running to intercept, Eliza passed her, turning in direction of the little shack. Hannah was hard on her heels.

"Y'all will pay dearly for this," Ledbetter yelled. Though angry and humiliated, he couldn't catch the two nimble, scared sisters. But he'd get them. The thought of probably having to pay out more money for their capture made him more furious.

Eliza and Hannah rushed into a one-room cabin crammed with every color thread and cloth material imaginable. Hannah seized her baby from a scared golden aged woman sitting and rocking in a chair overstuffed with cloth remnants.

"I won't hurt you," Eliza said, taking a butcher knife from a counter and pressing it against the woman's throat. "Just want you to be still whilst we bind you. Buckra gonna bust in here any minute, and if you ain't strapped to this chair, he's liable to hurt you real bad."

The frightened woman nodded her head.

"We thank you for keeping Hannah's child," Eliza said, binding her with strips of cloth, faded aprons, and string. "Let's go, Hannah. If he asks, tell him I said we going to Canada. Don't say you don't know. He won't believe you."

They fled, having no idea where they were, taking turns carrying the baby, resting for short durations while the child fed from Hannah's breasts. They ate apples and raw potatoes, whatever was in the fields. Hannah chewed apples into mush and put it in the baby's mouth. The three of them pushed on, passing many houses but afraid to stop. A night patrol would surely find them asleep in a field or a barn.

Eliza looked hard for a sign, any kind of sign that might indicate a dwelling fairly safe to seek help. It appeared—a brightly colored kerchief that black women wore, waving from a clothes line. She went around back and rapped on the white door of a tidy farmhouse. The sweet aroma of plump, purple grapes invading her senses carried her back home——the Pownall's vineyard, her own little arbor, the children's indigo lips and juice soiled clothing. A heavy sigh of helplessness, of loneliness escaped from deep within her bosom, though she didn't have time to dwell on the hurting.

"Dear God!" A fairly tall and slender young white woman yelled, shaking and stuttering as if a cloud of locusts were devouring the door. "Julia, come quickly." The nerves on either side of her thin lips twitched and twitched, contorting an obvious passionate and calm beauty. An abundance of brown hair with a reddish tint she had bound tightly behind in a knot. She wore a polka dot apron over a long flowing gingham dress.

"What ails you, Miss Maryanne?" Julia, an ebony girl of Maryanne's height in her late teens hurried to her. "Have mercy," she said, looking at the destitute women, "some mother's dear children." Julia's thick, black hair was tied in a bun. Her shoulders were broad. She was not fat, though ruggedly built with fair-sized forearms. She looked out from under deep, black, expressive eyes in which Eliza read a kinship.

"Can you..." Eliza cried out to her. "We plumb out of... So tired... The baby... Saw your scarf hanging on the line."

"Who are you?" Maryanne said.

Eliza looked pleadingly to Julia. "Go'n and tell her," Julia said, "Miz Maryanne is Mr. Joseph Fulton's daughter. They's good people."

"We sisters. I'm Eliza, Will Parker's wife. She's Hannah Pinckney."

"That man they hunting from over yonder in Christiana," Julia said, her voice escalating, "is your husband?" Fear for her own well-being engulfed her. "Lordy, Lord," she said. "We heard this morning, the government men done caught him."

An agonizing gloom spread over Eliza face. "Did'ja hear if they killed him?" she asked.

"Don't know," Julia said, "I was hiding myself, when a bunch'a white men came by this morning. I couldn't hear much."

"No," Maryanne said.

"They ain't caught him then," Eliza said. "Will won't give up."

In Eliza's eyes Maryanne saw a cavern of fear, but fear mixed with grim determination, determination like a warrior with her sword beheading the Hydra. She actually felt Eliza's soul stirring, felt it moving her to action. Hannah was slouched and leaning with the baby in her arms as if at any minute she would collapse.

"Hurry!" Maryanne ordered. Though searching parties hunting Will Parker had stopped there three times in as many days, the fleeing women's burden became hers.

"Julia, spread supper in the cellar. Get fresh clothes and a bonnet for each one. Then run out the carriage. I'll dig out Mother's old swaddling clothes for the baby and ask Brother to hitch a horse."

Brother Ted, in the winery pressing grapes, read fear, stark and vivid, in Maryanne's eyes, her voice and her running with one hand holding the apron and dress the other waving at him. Yet, he warned her that everything the family owned would be confiscated. "Send them on their way before the patrols return," he said, quite tersely, his keen face expressing a sternness as determined as hers.

"You run them off," Maryanne said. "You put that little four month old baby in the hands of a slaver, not I. Papa wouldn't neither."

"They aren't worth everything we own! God Almighty, Maryanne."

"A fast horse, a carriage and me, Ted. Surely that much."

"Take old half-blind Nance," he said exasperatedly, hoping that would dampen her spirit. "What'll I tell Papa?"

"The truth."

He stopped turning the handle on the press, and sadly asked her, "Where will you go?"

"As far as a worn-out horse will take us."

"Oh God, Maryanne! You're my only sister."

"If you care, give me a healthy horse and hurry. We're ready."

Riding away, waving goodbye, Ted's question—where will you go—began haunting her. She let the horse have its way in cantering. After a few miles, Maryanne reckoned her best chance, the only reasonably safe one, was the Caln Friends' Meetinghouse. But no one was there, and among that community of Friends fear ruled supreme over her pleading for a night's lodging, or a few days' work for a place to hide at least until the patrols lessened their relentless search. They rode on. Eliza noticed the panic etching wrinkles in Maryanne's face.

"What can we do?" Maryanne said, beseeching Eliza and Hannah for an answer, though fully cognizant of their dependence on her.

"If you can tell us which way is North," Eliza said, "We'll lift our burden off your shoulders."

Maryanne didn't answer. Darkness began settling in the trees and across the low lying hills. They were well off the traveled road, heading in a unknown direction. She stopped and looked all around. Why, she really didn't know.

"Up ahead," Hannah said, "look."

As if she had been placed there by the hand of divine providence, a tall, lean woman appeared in the wagon trail at the crest of a hill. On her head, tied in a red and black head kerchief with two points sticking up like rabbit ears, she perfectly balanced a basket of freshly done clothes. She walked toward them with the rhythmic grace of a gazelle.

"Giddap," Maryanne said, speeding to her.

All three, Maryanne, Eliza and, Hannah, began talking. The woman, whose pear-shaped face with its high cheek bones was as passive as a rabbit's, let them babble until she caught the drift of their dilemma.

"Down yonder hill there, you'll see my house. Go in and sit down. Don't fret no more. I'll be back d'rectly."

Eliza, Hannah and her baby's journey from that juncture remains one of the best kept secrets of the slave exodus to Canada. They did board the Underground Railroad, traveling west past Pittsburgh to central Ohio, then north. When news of the escape associated them with Will Parker and began circulating through free black communities, a steady flow of support for their fare came to the Pennsylvania Anti-Slavery Society in Philadelphia from a host of church and benevolent groups.

Government men, slave traffickers, and all others anxious for the prize and the opportunity to vent hatred upon black people, heightened their assault and surveillance in their manhunt for Will, Abe and Pink. Every road, bridge, and waterway patrolled day and night. Searching the grounds of every known sympathizer, threatening and guarding every known abolitionist yielded nothing but angry resentment. Though generally a day late, the patrols always seemed close enough to find a fresh trail. Yet, where in the United States could they have possibly disappeared?

Will Parker, the most despised, the most revered man in America and his companions were entombed in a pile of shavings under a carpenter shop on Church Street in Norristown. Four long, lonely days and nights lying in the mound of cuttings, separated from the others forced Will to judge himself in a critical light of thought. The noisy chain constantly rattling in his brain, the foot slowly dragging the ball through crisp leaves tempted him closer and closer to madness, whether dreaming at a deep-sea depth or thinking wide awake staring at sawdust. Teetering at the edge of a huge, black hole, Edward Gorsuch the dead slaver came up from the chasm, laughing at him.

"Just finished my breakfast," he said. "Now I've come for you."

"Ate it in hell hunh, just like you said," Will told him. "But I ain't on the menu."

"Simpleton, how dare you taunt and tease a white man. One hundred tortured and dying misled black souls will haunt you long before death frees you. Then mighty men will melt you down to a spot of tar."

Mister slave master, how long could any one of your mighty men endure your brand of brutality before surrendering his manhood? Really now, who is the mightiest man?"

"Brainless idiot. You will never live to spread that myth! Your neegra woman is now at the mercy of a white man. Your neegra children, your children's children will die slaves. You have poisoned their minds, for you they must pay, must pay, must pay." Gorsuch's voice echoed in Will's mind.

Will lunged and grabbed. His grip went right through Gorsuch's neck. He swung. His fist fanned the air of Gorsuch's mocking face.

"You were warned even before me, by your friends," Gorsuch said, disappearing with haunting laughter into the empty hole. "You didn't listen. Now it is too late, too late, too late."

Fighting to maintain his balance on the lip of the chasm, feeling himself tilting headfirst into the bottomless hole, Will cried out, "God help me."

A subtle vibrating numbness beginning in his chest, gradually enveloped him. His eyelids felt as if they were glued shut. The faint ringing of a distant church bell heralded the coalesced energy of blended voices caroling some spiritual. The energy grasped and levitated Will. On the wings of that timbre-rich chorus lifting the weights of darkness from his eyes, he revisited every crossroads and town through which he had passed, seeing every black person he had known, their faces tilted to him soaring overhead, their mouths stretched wide shaping those lyrics.

The bell tolling five, six times seemed closer. Sweating profusely, his heart pumping wildly, Will looked about at the shavings, still hearing that song of deliverance, still feeling that tingling sensation. Lying there a greater part of time in deep concentration, revelations slowly piling one on top of the other, Will had arrived at the point of knowing that freedom actually was a gift of the spirit, his spirit that had been awakened by grace enshrined by the spirituals. He understood with clear perception that freedom was more than one hard-fought thing, more than winning one or two or ten battles with slave-runners and kidnappers. Freedom was a gift from God. Any man who'd deny that or not fight for freedom was evil. He believed America was rife with an abundance of evil folk. The saving grace that quieted a driving impulse to a rampage of killing, stamping out the ugly, was that abolitionists were more powerful in word and deed than hate-mongers. Faith would hold him steadfast in believing his family was secure.

Will would be forever grateful to Abe, even though many a day would pass before he'd tell him. Had it not been for Abe's quick mind and bravery, chances are they would be dead. Abe had gone back down the hill and scavenging through a scrap pile at the canal, returned with a couple wood planks and several lengths of hemp and heavy twine. While hiking Ridge Pike they decided by vote, considering each one's state of mind, that Will needed the doctor to rid him of the demons muddling in his ears, making him see terrible things in the sky.

At the edge of Norristown, Abe and Pink had made a stretcher and strapped Will to it. Few lanterns burned in the houses they passed. They saw no one. Abe stopped at a fork in the road. Which one should they take, Airy to the left or Main to the right? Abe lifted the front end, and reaching under the stretcher, nicked Will with a sharp instrument, drawing blood. Will yelled and cursed and struggled against the binds, forcing Abe and Pink to gag him. A white man running from his house brandishing a shotgun in a nightshirt and sleeping cap, demanded to know why the nigger was making such a scandalous noise in his quiet neighborhood at that hour of the night. Abe tried explaining, even offered to show him if he would run ahead and tell the good Dr. Paxson their friend needed treatment for mad dog bites on his butt, But not until Abe gave him a coin did the man leveling the gun at Will with doubt in his eyes, point in the direction of Airy Street and hurry back into his house. Abe, doubting the man believed him, hastened on. Soon they were in the midst of small, odd-shaped homes on both sides of narrow and hilly streets, with food stores on every corner. Regretful that he couldn't think of another way to get attention at that hour of the night, Abe jabbed Will on the other cheek. Will, balling his fists, straining against the straps binding him, vowed he would make Abe understand the pain, even though Pink's suggestion that Will should slobber to make it look as if he was actually foaming at the mouth, forced him to realize how determined they were to protect him.

John Augusta, a colored agent of the Norristown Underground Railroad connection, hearing the commotion, had dashed into the street. Without asking one question, he hustled them around the corner to Dr. Paxson.

Augusta, a tall, dark man of sound church reputation and civic pride, had been Will's, Pink's and Abe's only contact with the world beyond their dry, dusty tomb. Twice each day had he passed them food from a window on an oven peal extended across the four-foot alley between his home and the cabinet maker's shop.

On the fourth day, after bathing, shaving and haircuts, Augusta took Will, Abe, and Pink to Jacob Paxson's office again. When they arrived, Dr. Paxson, thick-bodied and moon-eyed with a wild tassel of auburn hair, and Dr. Hiram Corson, lean, older and calm, were discussing the likelihood of capture in certain modes of travel. Rolling his eyes over each one of them and talking so fast his speech was often incoherent, Dr. Paxson said they would be more at risk under a wagon-load of baled hay. Dr. Corson, speaking with the eloquent confidence that demanded agreement from Paxson and Augusta, believed that sitting upright in an aristocratic coach masquerading as nobility, was too dangerous. Smart, experienced government men had flooded the area.

Will resented those wealthy abolitionists' haggling as if he, Abe, and Pink were deaf mutes, to determine their ability to act uppity. He snatched a Bible from a dark-wood bookshelf and holding it closed across his chest, he recited with fiery oration a few passages from the book of Revelations. Few men hearing him would doubt Will's competence for saving souls from the doomful days of Armageddon that he prophesied would surely be visited upon America's slave empire come November's first snowfall.

Ready for travel, dressed in new suits of fair cut cloth and string ties, they set out in a northern direction for Quakertown. With Augusta chauffeuring them in Dr. Corson's elegant black carriage replete with lanterns, a dark velvet cushioned interior, and two black horses, they were indeed the personification of three pious gentlemen of note. While traveling, Augusta explained that earlier that day, four wagons leaving the shop had been stopped and searched. Of course, they were decoys. Augusta talked on, joking in the manner black men often did in describing insurmountable odds. Fortunately, slavecrats and their friends didn't have the power to leap over barns in upstate Pennsylvania as they did down Lancaster way. They could though, still clear the ground pretty darn good in some places, so Will, Abe and Pink should sidestep inquiries about their destination or trick questions that would reveal their origin. Answer everybody like Will had quoted the Bible in Dr. Corson's office. Scripture had a way of adding depth and mystery to otherwise stupid answers. Sleeping with the Bible under your head, he told Will, was a sure-fire way of lifting God's word from the book to the brain. Resting on prophesy would keep wisdom fresh in the head.

Saturday, September, 27, 1851—Augusta gave each of them a ten dollar bank note and bid good-bye at Richard Moore's home in Quakertown. Moore's would be the last Underground Railroad Station in their northward trek over the mountain wilds of Pennsylvania and New York State to Rochester. After a supper befitting hungry wayfarers' appetites, and a lively chat contradicting newspaper accounts of the Christiana incident, Abe insisted they hit the road. Will, asking Moore's family to join him in saying good-bye, appealed to God for a blessing of divine protection that electrified then, and raised high his, Abe's and Pink's spirits. At ten o'clock on a rather cool evening, a relief from weeks of hot weather without rain, they departed.

Early next morning they happened by a crossroads inn. After hiking all night they certainly had walked up strong appetites for the breakfast they were served without incident. Pink bought a pack of smokes in the general store, and hired a livery carriage with a driver who took them to Windgap. Will and Abe slept while Pink, though he could hardly stay fully awake, smoked and dozed with one eye open. Between snatches of sleep, his hands resting on the Bible in his lap, the newly renowned Rev. Elder B. Swift drowsily contemplated scripture most of which Rev. Clarkson had hammered into his brain. Yet, still struggling with heartache, Will railed that a prophet with his clothes full of smoke was worse than a jackleg preacher with no teeth. Pink, suspecting Will was still smarting over the stretcher ride, politely threw the butt away. Abe chuckled quietly, then relieved Pink, leaving him to his despair in fitful slumber.

At supper in a wayside inn, Will revealed to his comrades the ordeal with Gorsuch under the wood shavings. He explained how the name Reverend Swift suddenly came to mind without significance, except that it sounded just about right for their cover. But not until he assured them he held no grudges, did Abe and Pink tell how they withstood those brutal hours in the lonely, unfrequented wilderness of immovable seclusion, drowned in the midnight of their lives. Abe never lost sight of Will's sojourn, a torch lighting the trail to Canada, even though he believed it was only a land promised by abolitionists driving him away, avoiding bloodshed. Pink would not stay in Canada without his wife and daughter. He would gather a band of fighters to rescue them if possible, or to avenge his loss. If war came he would return and fight, leaving his family in Canada.

From Tannersville by way of stage coach, Will, Pink and Abe disappeared in the unsettled mountain wilds of upstate Pennsylvania. When they reappeared several days later in northwestern New York, Will had become fairly well adept at linking inquiries for lodging, directions, stage coach and train departures to lyrics of the spirituals mixed with his rendition of biblical quotations. Pink and Abe didn't bother cautioning him. Hearing the songs at Mt. Zion AME, they knew a lot of what he said was pure fat-mouth, but it worked. It changed many a wary, suspecting eye in isolated villages to fascinated glitter. Nasty attitudes on some stage coaches warmed to casual humorous interest.

They resurfaced one bright, golden morning at a junction hamlet boarding the Auburn-Rochester commuter train. Will plumped down beside a smartly dressed man reading a newspaper. Abe and Pink sitting together behind him and stunned by his boldness, noticed the stranger, with a sharp and assessing though cheerful look, stealing glances at him. Will sat perfectly erect, the closed Bible in his hands.

"It definitely demands a line or two," Will's traveling companion said, writing on a pad and talking quietly to himself. "Hypocrites who have soothed their souls with prayer and silent rationalizations about kidnapping free Negroes and capturing fugitives, have found themselves a scapegoat. Now the press can arouse the consciousness of America, backhandedly censuring the inhumane treatment of slavery without prejudice toward the system."

Will, his eyes flat, his face unreadable as stone, heard him mumbling and watched him write.

"Oops, darned ill-mannered of me, thinking aloud. You are aware of the killing in Christiana?"

Pink cringed and sweat while fishing for his smokes. Abe coughed as if in a spasm, momentarily capturing everyone's attention.

"Yes, some," Will said, matter-of-factly, then turning around and rubbing the base of Abe's head, as Dr. Paxson had done him. "What might you be reading, friend?"

"An editorial in the Boston Transcript. Do you mind if I ask you a question?"

Will humped his shoulders.

"What do you, a colored man, make of this?" he said, reading the last lines of an editorial. "*Abolitionists thirsting for the blood of Southerners, urged their innocent dupes, the colored mob, to commit a most foul murder. But they, whose higher law doctrine is like a musket and ball in the hands of the innocent Negro, are the real murderers.*"

"O brethren, my way's cloudy," Will said, over the train's tolling bell and the clackety-clack of the wheels. "But seems like old Satan missed the soul he thought he had. Now he's mad. My way is cloudy, my way."

Several persons in the crowd of Rochester-bound commuters overhearing the reading and having their attention drawn to Will's baritone sing-song response, began exchanging opinions.

"Should they hang that fellow Parker? Our local paper said several white men instigated the killing."

"If found guilty in a fair, impartial trial," Will's traveling pal said. "But that's impossible. What do you make of that, friend?"

"Down in the valley," Will said, "on my knees, I couldn't hear nobody pray. It must have been the hand of the Lord."

"I'd like to get my hands on Parker. A two thousand dollar reward, wow," a young, robust man said, briskly rubbing his hands together,

"He's probably quite powerful. And you colored people," Will's new friend said, looking at him, "should make him a hero."

"Every voice will lift in song," Will said. "It will come to pass, though my way is cloudy, my way."

"You're pretty clever with parodies," the youngster said, his lips twisted in a devilish smile. "Are you really a crusader or are you spitting heresy to cover your tracks?" He winked an amusing eye at Will's friend.

"Methuselah lived nine hundred and sixty-nine years," Will said, as if he hadn't seen the gesture. "Seems like a mighty long time for any man to greet the sun every day, waiting for God to call him home. Old Folks had to be doing good so when God finally called him, he went to heaven. When the roll is called up yonder in the Lord's due time I'll be there."

Will continued the sporadic banter explosions for miles, agitating some riders, amusing others, while Pink and Abe sweated nervously. The train began braking for the downtown Rochester South Avenue station. "Come brethren," Will said, standing and motioning to his comrades. "The trumpet sounds within my soul."

Will, Pink and Abe rushed from the train with the passengers, and found a black man he had seen from the car. Will and he held eye-to-eye direct contact, not one blink, not one squint,

"Are you traveling light?" the man asked.

"The North star was very bright," Will said, "But my way is cloudy, my way."

The End

Epilogue

In Rochester, New York, the imagination and historic fact untwine. Fate, the effect of causes determined by Will's demands on life, dealt him a hand from which he with his comrades had no choice except to play, and play hard. Will disappeared in Canada, soon forgotten, but later enthroned in memory.

After welcoming Will, Abraham Johnson, and Henry Pinckney into his home, Frederick Douglass informed them word had been received by way of the underground network that Eliza and Hannah with her baby were somewhere in free America, en route to Canada. Black people from as far away as San Francisco, responding to the Philadelphia Vigilante Committee's financial appeal for the Christiana patriots, sent money to supplement the expense of the women's escape and the prisoners' defense in the trial at the United States Court House of Independence Hall.

That evening in Rochester, Will became William Parker, hero of the Christiana Resistance. Wealthy abolitionists and philanthropists invited to an impromptu gathering in Douglass' home, stood in awe, praising William with congratulatory sentiments, though for only a few short hours. While the celebrants basked in after-supper limelight, Douglass and Julia Griffiths, assistant editor of the *Douglass Paper*, planned their hasty departure to Canada. With them in his Democrat carriage, Douglass rushed to the Genesee River landing. At eight o'clock William, Abraham, and Henry departed America in early October aboard a steamer crossing Lake Ontario and landed in Kingston, Ontario the next morning.

Canada, the legendary land of freedom, didn't excite William or his comrades. They were at rock-bottom with only a handful of shillings among them. Work was the priority; work in order to buy food for energy to work, in order to become self-sustaining but more importantly, to avoid starvation. They hunted for work. Yet, for several days, jobs for them were practically non-existent. Through every hamlet and town William, Henry and Abraham passed, Canadian citizens and poor immigrant British subjects accused them of stealing Canadians' livelihoods, overburdening the government with slaves' problems.

Tramping about Toronto, William learned that Canadian immigration officials had been requested by Pennsylvania Governor Johnson to extradite him. Though Henry and Abraham were against it, William, surrendered. That was a major turning point in their lives.

Terms of the Webster-Ashburton Treaty of 1842 required Canada to extradite criminals, which regardless of Governor Johnson's argument, immigration officials determined William was not, and referred him to the Canadian Anti-

Slavery Society. Waiting in quiet desperation, William was dumbfounded at the congenial handshake and greeting by the interrogator already familiar with his name. Answering questions designed to expose his entire life from as far back as he could remember, William revealed that he was a fugitive from slavery.

The preliminary hearing in Lancaster, Pennsylvania, resumed September 23, 1851, in the County Court House with Alderman Reigart presiding. The prosecution was overweighted with attorneys from Lancaster County, the U.S. attorney from Philadelphia, Maryland's attorney general, and a former U.S. attorney representing friends of Edward Gorsuch. Reigart, a mere alderman appointed judge over the tonnage of white supremacy jurisprudence expertise, upheld the slave commissioner's original charge of treason, despite the defense attorney's hammering of inaccuracies in the prosecuting witnesses' testimony, and presenting evidence that many black men already incarcerated had not been at the battle. A few men were released, a few others arrested were taken with the pack to Moyamensing Prison. Lancaster County Prosecutor John L. Thompson presented the government's case.

Two months later a federal grand jury in Philadelphia, indicted five white men and thirty-six blacks, including William Parker, and Sam Williams, a member of Philadelphia's Vigilante Committee and proprietor of the Bolivar House Tavern. Henry Pinckney and Abraham Johnson were not mentioned.

In the trial that began November 24, in Independence Hall and finally ended January 14, 1852, an impressive lot of government officials and attorneys on both sides presented a display of courtroom drama and manipulation intriguing to any discerning student of American History. U.S. Marshal Henry Kline's witness, Harvey Scott, crushed the government's case by revealing under cross-examination that Kline had made him testify to the veracity of the marshal's every utterance. The jury acquitted Castner Hanway, after which the federal government dropped its charges of treason against all defendants. The white men were released. Most of the black men, already charged with several summary offenses including riot, were re-incarcerated in Lancaster County prison. Kline was jailed on charges of lying at the preliminary hearing. Some weeks later in Lancaster County Courthouse, Kline was exonerated in exchange for the black men's complete acquittals.

Harvey Scott's quality of life as a blacksmith apprentice, living with his Quaker employer's family, begs exposure of a bigoted court, a bigoted news media, and history writers' stereotyping of the black men involved that is continually perpetrated. In the court transcript and in all but a few pieces of text written about the incident since it happened, William and his freedom fighters were cast as wretched, miserable, and penniless—situations preposterously impossible.

Few black men of that era could have lived in any white town or hamlet without working. Gainfully employed, working every day except Sunday, they satisfied a dire need for laborers. Money earned fed their families and maintained homes. In return, white employers protected them, as well as practical, against kidnappers and road agents not gainfully employed. Many of those "wretched, penniless" men built Mt. Zion AME, and were charter members of the church that proclaimed inclusion in Rev. Bishop Richard Allen's well-known African Methodist Episcopal conference.

When the trial began, Eliza and Hannah with her baby had recently joined their husbands in Toronto. With aid of the Canadian Anti-Slavery Society and part time work, they survived their first harsh Canadian winter. William's children arrived with the spring. He and Abraham parted company with Henry Pinckney and headed west to Buxton, a black settlement founded by a Scotch-Irish missionary on the southwestern edge of Lake Erie, fifty miles from Detroit, Michigan.

The missionary, Rev. William King, a former Louisiana slaver, had emancipated his slaves in 1849 and moved to Canada with them after his wife died. He secured nine thousand acres in the wild with help from the Presbyterian Church that were divided into fifty-acre plots offered exclusively to black pioneers at two dollars fifty cents an acre. William bought three acres, Abraham bought two. Within three years, one hundred thirty black families living there had built a school, church and parsonage, store, hotel, pearl ash factory, and blacksmith shop. They were the carpenters, the stone masons, the brick layers, lumberjacks, the midwives, the homemakers with years of experience.

The omnipresence of William Parker, symbol of a lighted torch, dwindled in free states as well as slave, while the nation progressed toward Civil War. He and Eliza in Buxton, Ontario, raised their children, attended night school, built a home, and farmed. Later, Will wrote his memoirs.